DEATH'S COLLECTOR: SORCERERS DARK AND LIGHT

BILL MCCURRY

BOOKS BY BILL MCCURRY

DEATH-CURSED WIZARD SERIES

Novels

Death's Collector

Death's Baby Sister

Death's Collector: Sorcerers Dark and Light

Death's Collector: Void-Walker

Death's Collector: Sword Hand

Death's Collector: Dark Lands (forthcoming)

Novellas

Wee Piggies of Radiant Might

© 2020 Bill McCurry

Death's Collector: Sorcerers Dark and Light

Second edition, November 2021

Infinite Monkeys Publishing

Carrollton, TX

Bill-McCurry.com

Editing: Shayla Raquel, ShaylaRaquel.com

Cover Design: Books Covered

Interior Formatting: Vellum

Death's Collector: Sorcerers Dark and Light is under copyright protection. No part of this book may be used or reproduced in any manner whatsoever without written permission except in the case of brief quotations embodied in critical articles and reviews. Printed in the United States of America. All rights reserved.

This is a work of fiction. Names, characters, businesses, places, events, locales, and incidents are either the products of the author's imagination or used in a fictitious manner. Any resemblance to actual persons, living or dead, or actual events is purely coincidental.

ISBN-13 (Ebook): 979-8-9853000-4-8

ISBN-13 (Paperback): 979-8-9853000-0-0

❧ Created with Vellum

To Cyn.
"He who jumps into the void owes no explanation to those who stand and watch."
—— Jean-Luc Godard

ONE

Every girl has accused somebody of ruining her whole life, and my little girl said that to me too. Not every girl gets stabbed to death by her father, though, not the way I killed mine. Wise and good people told me she was too dangerous to let live. They said I had done the right thing, but I loved her and could never think it was right.

I killed Manon in the thickest part of winter, which then shuffled on like it didn't care. I rode west, away from the city of Bellmeet on the Great Empire Road. Five hundred miles ahead of me, the road was a heroic, paved thoroughfare, but at piddly Bellmeet, two farmers' carts could hardly squeeze past without a fist fight.

I rode for two months, flung my sword in the ditch twice along the way, and went back for it both times. When the Great Empire Road thawed to a thousand miles of mud, I stopped in Bindle township and fell into habits that I figured would attract vermin. After the first week, everybody in town knew where to find me at anytime. That's how four frilly dead men came to be standing in front of my sad, swayback cottage, muttering among themselves about killing and thievery.

They did not believe themselves to be dead, of course. Young men can't comprehend a world that might exist without them. They had followed me from the tavern with plenty of life left in them, trailing fifty paces back, hands on their expensive swords, speaking rash words and giggling like girls. When I paused to straighten my cloak, they stopped too and stood by the muddy lane as innocent as fence posts. One of them had told me a joke in the tavern yesterday, laughed until his tears ran, and bought everybody drinks. I would kill him in a few minutes.

The idea was pleasant. My purpose in Bindle was to kill foul sons of bitches, the kind who would try to murder an old man for gold. I lured men like that by showing the gold around, a lump the size of a toddler's fist. I would cut off a sliver to purchase my meal before thunking it down on the scarred table in the tavern. Then I'd let it lay there while I ate and ignored every avaricious eye in the room. My hair had gone gray early, and I could appear so feeble that a child might knock me over with a fart. All the foul sons of bitches knew where to find me, so they followed me home, or to the privy, or to the stables, and that's where I murdered them.

I waited just inside my door in the first bits of twilight. The four ambitious thieves whispered and shuffled in their soft leather boots. Their cloaks were cut for style, not warmth. They didn't even need the damn gold. The porch groaned when I stepped outside. The young men jerked and gaped as if their ma had caught them stealing pies.

Hell, I couldn't just walk over and kill them for making a bad decision. I yearned to, but they looked too stupid and pitiful. One had cheeks shaved so pink he looked like a baby. I swallowed hard and waved the back of my hand at them. "I just sanded my floor last week, and I don't intend to let you boys bleed to death on it. You go on back to the tavern and get drunk. It's healthy. Healthier than this."

I think they may have walked away with a few curses and a bad gesture or two if it hadn't been for the short, gawky one with a chicken neck. He poked his tall, homely friend on the shoulder, and the tall man forced a smile. "Toss over the gold, Papaw, and don't fuss. I could break you the way I'd do a stick."

I sighed and didn't gut the insolent tadpole. "I don't have that gold anymore. Lost it between here and the waterfalls. You're welcome to search for it."

The tall one sneered. "You horrible, old liar. It's right there in your pouch, bulging. Isn't it?"

I touched the faded green pouch on my belt and nodded. "Let nobody say you're too stupid to piss downward."

He snorted, but his eyes were wide and he shuffled his feet.

Rather than kill them, I shoved my sword hand behind my back and grabbed my belt. "Boys, my only treasure is wisdom, earned with bruises and broken hearts. Go home, marry rich wives, make a bunch of fat babies, and spoil the shit out of them." I nodded toward a couple of shabby houses across the lane. "Forget all this. You can tell people how you faced down death in the wild lands." Bindle was no wilder than a billy goat, but compared to a wealthy Empire borough, it was a battlefield.

The baby-faced one backed up a step, but the jovial one held his ground. The short one edged forward and glanced at his tall, mouthy friend. "If you've gone all shy about cutting his head off, Conor, let me have him."

Conor waved him back like he was a pushy little brother.

We had collected spectators. Three men wearing yellow sashes had appeared from around one of the dirty, plastered houses across the lane, almost as if they'd been waiting there. A big man and two boys trotted up the lane from the direction of the tavern, one boy pushing a wheelbarrow.

Conor shouted, "Stop slumping on your butt, old man! Give it over, or I'll carve you right now!" He shook his sword hand, wiped his palm against his trousers, and didn't touch the sword again. He didn't want to kill me any more than he wanted to eat glass. His pissant friends were pushing him into it.

I pulled a silver coin from another pouch and tossed it to Conor, who fumbled and dropped it in the mud.

"Go have a little fun," I said. "If you had all that gold, you'd debauch yourselves until your dicks fell off. I'm offering you a kindness."

None of them bent for the coin that would have fed a family for a month.

"Go on!" I bellowed.

Conor jumped and staggered back, and his friends flinched. I opened my mouth to yell some abuse at them and shame them into going home, but Conor's chicken-necked friend drew his sword. "Give us that gold, you old fart!" Then he stood there like he was waiting for inspiration.

I had grown to become a mature gentleman in part because I didn't allow people to point weapons at me more than once. I assumed that if they threatened my life once, they would be pleased to do it again sometime. I considered this rule to be inviolate, or I did in those days.

I charged the short one, and my blade was in his heart before the others had armed themselves. I withdrew, and he fell straight onto his face. The fellow to his left was drawing his own weapon. He was the happy young man who found himself so funny. I opened his throat with a compact slice, and he staggered sideways, blood spurting.

Conor and his baby-faced friend had drawn their swords by then. They both ran at me as if they were an avalanche that could plow me under. I cut Conor deep across the thigh, and he flopped down while I dodged his friend's blade. Then I cut the friend so viciously on the shoulder that his arm dropped limp and his sword fell. He staggered back until he hit the bare plum tree.

The young man resembled a scared, bloody boy leaning against the tree trunk. He stared at my face, maybe waiting for whatever I was about to say. He looked shocked when I stabbed him in the heart without saying anything. Maybe he thought I was going to invite him inside so we could reminisce about the time I almost killed him.

Conor was staggering away when I turned to him. He glanced back. "No! You don't have to! I'm sorry! I really am!" He tripped over a root sticking up by an oak stump, but he rolled faceup as quick as a fish. "No! No!" Conor screamed like a child, and he was still at it when I stabbed him through the right eye. He shuddered and went slack.

I gazed around at the bodies and beyond. Blood had sprayed on me, the daylight was draining away, and I would have murdered a dozen virgins for a drink. Well, I would have called them names until they cried. I scanned the area, past the spectators, in case these four sad thieves had any friends, and I hoped to hell I'd get to kill them too. However, they seemed to have been friendless.

It was unneighborly to leave dead men lying about in front of one's house, but I didn't need to worry about that. I sat down on the front step with my sleeve dripping blood onto the sprouting green grass. My hands started shaking so hard I dropped my sword, and I let it lie there. I wanted to damn Harik, God of Death, a being so foul and boring that when he walked past a songbird, it could never sing again. I wanted to, but this slaughter was as much my fault as his.

I sat for a minute with my head down. Manon's hands had shaken like mine were shaking now. That didn't mean anything. It just made me think of her.

The big man and his two boys had begun stripping the dead and piling everything valuable onto the wheelbarrow. I watched him cut loose Conor's purse, empty it into his hand, and chuckle. "You shouldn't have acted like pricks, fellows."

The scavenger's name was Whistler. He sat in the tavern almost every day, drinking ale, scowling at people's jokes, and mooning over the bar girl, who wouldn't look at him. She didn't find his big nose, small chin, and brown teeth beguiling. I had killed two thieves near the stables one day, and Whistler arrived to rob the bodies and carry them away. By the end of the week, he had acquired a helper, and the next week, he started bringing a wheelbarrow.

I rarely spoke to the man. I acknowledged he was doing me a service by tidying up after my murders. He acknowledged that he was the only one making money from this whole tragic business. During the third week, two rough men set themselves up to compete with Whistler, threatening to break his neck if he didn't give over the monopoly. That afternoon, I saw Whistler trundling their swords and boots along in his wheelbarrow.

Ours was not a morally defensible arrangement, but it worked for us.

The three sour-faced men with sashes had watched the little fight from across the lane. Now they crossed toward me, and one shouted, "Those snippy boys might have killed you, Bib. If they had, I'd have paid them in gold." He gazed up and down the lane as he raised his voice. "If anyone kills you, I'll pay him in gold, and he can keep the gold lump. You bar the door to your shitty little house tonight, Bib."

I raised my head and grabbed my knees so he couldn't see my hands shake. "How much are you paying, Paul? I might decide to kill myself, although I lack experience. Why don't you go first so you can give me some pointers?"

Paul was the town burgher, sort of a headman and peacekeeper, and he looked at me like I was a pile of turds on his clean floor. He thought I was a threat to peace and orderliness. I knew he thought that because he said it to my face at least once a day. He was right too. Paul was a young, fit, brown-haired man, so handsome he was almost as beautiful as a girl. The townswomen pined for him openly, and they passed vile gossip about his wife.

Paul's thugs each toted a bladed club. Tettler stood on the left, just a hair shorter than Paul, twice as old and five times uglier. On the right, Sam stood hunched, favoring a poorly healed leg. A man in his prime, he hid his bald head under a peaked, woolen cap. He stared at me with intelligent eyes full of disgust, and he spat on the grass near the lane's edge. "Burn and die, you rotten fish!"

Sam was my wife's brother.

Their faded yellow sashes showed they were important men. When they stepped off the lane, I picked up my sword, hands steady. They faltered thirty feet from me. Paul cleared his throat. "If you insist on remaining around here, you will suffer Bindle's judgment. You must swear you'll come to the town square tomorrow at midday! For judgment. Swear it!"

My face heated, and I almost jumped up to put my sword

through his neck. I clenched my teeth against such a pointless display of anger. "Sorry, Paul, I prefer to enjoy the noonday sun while relaxing at the top of the falls, naked."

Sam sneered and swore at me using three parts of my mother's body.

Paul put a hand on Sam's shoulder. "Bib, if you don't swear, we'll lock you in the temple cellar. Lock you." He glared at my eyes for a second before blinking and glaring at my shoulder instead.

"Where are the rest of your faithful retainers, Paul?" I knew he had ten men working for him.

"Can't find 'em," Tettler grunted.

Paul hissed at Tettler and then shrugged at me. "It would be convenient for you to know where they are, eh? They could be anywhere, couldn't they?" Paul shook his head, his long hair waving. "No, you have to swear to appear, otherwise you must come with us." Sweat ran down both sides of his face.

They didn't seem all that dangerous. That meant that I should have killed them without hesitating. I have learned to heap suspicion upon those who don't seem dangerous. Paul was a snobby twit, but brave. I didn't have to kill him today. Maybe another day. Maybe never, who could tell? "All right, I swear."

"What?" Paul said, his eyes wide.

I pointed my sword at the sky. "I swear by all the gods and their private regions that I will call upon you and the other decent citizens of Bindle tomorrow at midday. At the town square. Should I bring anything? I could purchase the whole damn bakery if I wanted to."

Paul breathed deep. "Good, then . . . no, don't, I mean don't with the bakery, but fine with the square, just be there. Fine." He led his men at a fast walk up the lane.

I turned and found that my blue front door had closed. I pushed against it, but it didn't budge or even make a sound. Leaning my shoulder against the door, I murmured, "It's getting dark, the night's colder than walrus whiskers, and I'm covered in blood. Can we wait until morning for his shit?"

The door eased itself open, as slow as cold grease. As I walked inside, it slammed shut on my left foot.

"Damn you to eat hot coals in hell!" I hobbled around the main room. "I'm going to smash all your doors to splinters and use this place to store horse turds!"

Carpenter's tools, lumber, paintbrushes, and two lanterns lay clumped where I had left them around the main room. I snatched up a short board and hurled it at the blue door, maybe the most ridiculous act I had ever undertaken. I turned away from the door to cover my embarrassment, which was the second most ridiculous.

Although the fire was well-banked, building it up sounded like more work than building the whole damn fireplace. The fire remained un-poked by me. I ignored the bucket of water and the clean clothes beside it. My lanterns were useless without fire, so I trudged into the bedroom mostly by feel.

The new bed had cost as much as a wagon filled with pigs, and the new glass window should come next week. I felt a flash of rage that I had to wait. It flashed and left behind nothing much at all, so I lay down on my pallet with my sticky sword and started to ask Manon if she was cold. Instead, I closed my eyes and hoped I'd fall asleep sometime before sunup.

TWO

Cold water pelted my neck and face, and I opened my eyes to see veiled daylight. I rolled right to my feet away from the rain blowing in through the window. I refused the notion that I wasn't a young man, but my joints popped like a dead tree in a gale.

I brought my sword into the main room and saw that the roof I had repaired was leaking in two dozen places. I nearly threw my sword across the room in disgust. Instead, I sat on the floor with some rags to clean it. Without thinking, I laid down one of the rags. When I reached for the nasty thing, it was all the way across the room.

I glared around at the walls. "At least wait until I've had my damn breakfast!" It was a feeble plea since I couldn't face breakfast these days.

When my sword was clean, I stripped off beside the bucket, washed, and donned some fresh garments. The rain had eased, and I poked my head out the window to assess the time of day. A slight smell of baking bread eased across the town. The smith's hammer was still clanking, so that blubbery old hulk wasn't eating his first lunch yet.

A fair amount of time remained before my midday event at the town square. I decided right that moment I'd do something to astound the townsfolk, and by "astound," I meant horrify them so they'd start turning white whenever I looked at them hard. Daily murders had not proven sufficiently intimidating.

I smiled as I pulled the big bedroom door off its hinges, laid it on two boxes, and began sanding off untold years of grime and mold. Maybe painting the door some repulsive color would annoy the ghost, not that I could really bear to make the place so ugly.

My wife had hated this house through all our years together, if you took her fierce complaints and chill silences as evidence. Well, Lin hadn't really given a damn about the house. She hated that I never improved it, although every couple of months I promised her I would soon. She didn't mind that I ran off to enforce the will of harsh men who were wealthy enough to hire sorcerers. She never complained about the days I spent helping ungrateful sick people and encouraging their crops to flourish. She fed and tended my rough companions, some of them as wild as baboons. She weathered all of that with kindness, or at least minimal aggravation.

But Lin chewed my ass about replacing the roof and replastering the walls and repairing the old chimney. She wouldn't have minded having a new floor. The front step was likely to collapse and kill somebody. Every goddamn door in the house creaked and stuck.

I promised to handle it all, but something else always claimed my time. I offered to hire it done, but you would have thought I had offered to pay somebody to lie with her at night. The house caused us more hard words and callous behavior than anything else in our life together. I once considered waiting until she and Bett were away sometime and then burning the damn thing down, but Lin would have known exactly what I'd done.

The house remained unimproved on the day Bett, my first daughter, nearly died, and I saved her by promising to murder people for the God of Death. A week later, the house still looked like hell when Bett tripped over a tree root and broke her neck. Lin stopped bothering me about the house then. She slept a lot and gave me hard looks when she thought I couldn't see her. I still hadn't repaired a single stick of that house a year later when she died behind the bedroom door I was now sanding.

I sure as sheep shanks hadn't come to Bindle intending to rebuild this house. I had planned to rest my horse a few days and spend some unenjoyable time in the tavern. Ever since I stopped drinking, evenings had become boring as hell, so the first night, I walked over to see the old house. I found it more run-down than ever and haunted to holy hell.

The ghost was a vexing and destructive entity, so I never believed it might be Lin or Bett. But I conceived the idea that this ghost, whoever it was, might entice their ghosts to come back here. I thought it possible. I had recently spent some time chatting with the deceased, so I figured it could be done. Maybe Lin would forgive me and come home.

That was the theory, admittedly weak, and I had no single clue what I'd do if it worked. I resolved to test it anyway. I had no specific business in the Empire, other than searching for men who deserved killing, which would prevent Harik, the back-assed, bile-soaked God of Death, from pestering me about loafing around.

I sanded the door smooth and the other bedroom door as well, leaving not much time before my midday summons at the town square. I peered into the yard through the front doorway and dreaded getting locked out for the rest of the day by that malicious haunt. I felt sweaty and gritty, and I could have bathed had I not sanded that second door. I knew a pretty spot upstream from the falls, even though the water was cold enough to cut like knives.

I reached for my cloak at the door, glanced back, and stopped with the cloak still hanging. The lumber pile was stacked as straight as glass. The tools and boxes lay lining two walls, running by size from the smallest nail at one corner to the big mallet across the way.

The urge to burn down the house seized me, but I slapped it away. "You did the same fool thing last week!" I stomped toward the front door. "If you've got to be a pain in my ass, you could at least show a little creativity!"

Outside, I halted with one foot on the front step. A tall, broad-shouldered woman younger than me stood thirty feet away, about where I had killed Conor. She appeared unarmed, dressed in tough traveling clothes. Her hair and skin were deep black, and her face would have been lovely if it didn't look like she'd eaten half a dozen fried rocks for breakfast. By her expression, I couldn't tell whether she liked me or wished I'd die of a disease of the bowels.

We stared at each other until I got annoyed, which wasn't long. "You go first."

The woman swallowed. "This is unlikely."

"Oh?" I hung my thumbs in my belt, one hand close to my sword.

"The last time I saw you, you stood on those same steps. You must be a very boring person."

I tried to match her displeased expression. "What do you want? Lin burned your spare cloak. It was full of bugs."

The woman hesitated. "I heard that a crazy man was killing the whole town of Bindle. I thought it must be you."

"I may let a few live. What do you want?"

She looked me up and down. "I don't like what I hear about you."

"You'll make me bawl. I haven't heard shit about you."

"That was . . . " She gave a tiny shrug.

With no warning, rage shattered my insides. I marched halfway to her, but she didn't flinch. "Do you remember the last thing you said before you disappeared for ten goddamn years with no explanation?"

She squinted up at the low gray clouds rushing along.

"No? Well, sure, I'll be happy to remind you since you asked nicely, you farting cow! You said, 'There's rust on your belt buckle.' Then you walked away. Hell, I thought maybe you were headed off to buy me a new belt buckle!"

Still gazing up, she said, "Were you too poor to buy your own?"

"Not the point! The point is I spent a month searching for you and whoever captured you! Then I spent two months searching for your dead body. Halla, I kept that up until I found the fellow who sold you some new boots on your way south. That is the point!"

She stared at me, blank-faced. "You were a good friend." She said it the way she might have said, "You have a nose."

I drew back a fist but didn't run up and punch her. "Krak pound it smaller than worm shit!" I roared at the sky.

"Bib, I'm sorry."

"You're sorry? Well, I can die a goddamn happy man then, can't I?" I bent over with my hands on my knees and realized I might be angrier than the situation merited. Besides, yelling at Halla wouldn't hurt her feelings any more than it would a fence rail's. I smiled at her. "I'm late for scaring the shit out of some people. It was nice to reminisce. Go away."

With no warning, hard rain slammed down on us. I trotted back to get my cloak, but the blue door slammed shut. I shoved it, but it held fast. I kicked it twice, which didn't help.

Halla had pulled up her hood. "Do you have a problem with your house?"

I rolled my eyes at her. "Oh, no, I trained the son of a bitch to do that!" I kicked the door five more times and shouted an oath about an improbable thing Harik had done with an otter.

"I doubt that Lin will accept that for very long," Halla said.

I snapped, "She died eight years ago. Almost nine."

I turned and saw Halla's face melt like it had been crusted with ice. "I'm very sorry, Bib." She squinted at me. "Bett too, then?"

"Yes . . . her too."

From out in the yard, she said, "Come here."

I kicked the door twice more before stalking over to stare up at her. She stood more than a head taller than me, the tallest woman I'd ever met.

Halla examined my face through the heavy rain. "Did you remarry?"

"No. I adopted a daughter, but . . ." I licked my lips. "She died too." I stomped back to the door and shoved it as hard as I could. The creaking sounded almost like laughter. "To hell with the cloak! I'm already as wet as a turtle's toes!"

"Bib, look at me."

I waved her away and stomped off the porch, making a point of not looking at her. "Don't bother. Trust me, I'm more beautiful than I was the last time you saw me."

"Bib, if Lin is dead, why are you in her house?"

"Look at it. It's a damn palace." I strode past her up the lane but didn't rush. If Paul and the others didn't want to wait on me, they could go on with their normal day, cheating their neighbors and sleeping with each other's husbands and wives.

Halla called after me, "Why are you here? Lin is not here."

I yelled over my shoulder, "Hell, I know that for sure! I might have been the worst husband in creation, but she never slammed the door on my foot."

Halla caught me with her huge strides. "You should be sure. I will find out who is in your house."

"Slap my mother and her dog too! Don't bother! It's not your concern! Go help somebody else!"

Halla closed her eyes as she paced beside me.

"You're a horrible stick of a woman!" I felt I might be ranting a little and took a breath.

"Yes," she muttered. "I am horrible. It is well-known."

The rain had begun slowing. Halla was engaged in sorcery now, but I couldn't guess what. Maybe she was torturing the ghost until it talked or was throwing a party for other gossipy ghosts. Perhaps she was disguising herself as a fetching ghost companion and whispering secrets. I figured she wouldn't be so imposing facedown in the mud, so I tried to trip her. She skipped over my foot, eyes still closed.

Halfway to the town square, Halla opened her eyes and said, "Domov."

I rubbed my chilly arms and said, "What?"

"It is a type of minor spirit."

"I know what it is! Why are you talking about it?"

Halla peered at me sideways. "A domov is inhabiting Lin's house."

"The hell you say! You can't know that."

"I do know that. In fact, every home in this town is inhabited by a spirit. Domovs, kikivs, gegs. Even a haggit."

All of those tricky creatures did inhabit buildings, mostly homes. They didn't intend ill, but some were feistier than others. People had been known to take their own lives after living with a haggit for a year or two.

"Bullshit! A stubby little domov? They hide spoons and turn up the corners of rugs!"

"All of these spirits arrived when you did."

I grasped the hilt of my sword. "Shut up! Just shut up!"

Halla shuffled three steps away and cocked her head at me.

"No plain hearth spirit can haunt like I've been haunted!" My jaw was hurting, and I tried to relax it.

"Bib, I am not lying to you." Her voice was even, but her forehead furrowed.

I stopped facing her. The anger washed out of me like rainwater. "So . . . that's why old women sneer at me and little boys pee on my house. They all hate me. I guess they should too. You're not making this shit up?"

"Oh, she's not knitting excrement. She knows about these things!" A man's bouncy voice came from down the lane. Nothing stood there except for an upended barrel and a graying hound that lolled its tongue at me.

I glanced at Halla. "Spirit?"

Halla peered past me. "Your fault, then."

"Like hell!"

The hound said, "Don't bother fighting unless you're going to kill each other! Dismembering would be better." The beast's mouth moved, and a perfect human voice came out. Perfect if one liked the sound of jovial assholes.

I faced the dog but didn't know what to do after that. I could kill it, listen to it, go buy it a beer, or walk away. No action seemed more promising than the others.

The hound saved me from needing to decide. "I saw you sitting here and couldn't resist chatting and then whacking you around. Sorcerers have been so scarce! You, little person, pay attention to great, hulking Halla. Her hokkat slithered all over this horrid town and told her what it knew. All over town—it was a notable event, like a birthday party. At least I noticed."

A hokkat was another kind of spirit. "Halla, what does the dog mean?"

Halla shook her head. "It is lying."

The dog yawned at Halla. "Your hokkat is a boy, did you know that?"

Halla stared, her face like a block of slate.

The dog said, "Well, he is! You should find him something to screw right away. He's frustrated, I can tell. It shouldn't be hard—they aren't fastidious. A she wolf bound to a linden tree under a full moon. That's traditional, if you care about tradition. You sorcerers tend toward the iconoclastic, I know. If you don't want to go to the trouble, perhaps he can mount an old boot or something."

I ground my teeth. "What hokkat?"

Halla said, "Do not believe it. You should listen to me instead of the talking dog."

The hound sat on its haunches and looked from one of us to the other.

Halla scrutinized the dog. "Are you one of the gods?"

"Do you want a bone?" I added.

Halla gave me a slow stare.

The dog laughed and wagged its tail. "Bless you for the compliment, but no, I'm not a god. Nor do I want a bone. Pay attention to me now!" The beast swung its head and hit me on the back of my thumb with a flying string of slobber. "Now, little person, decide which half of this town will be destroyed. Hurry and tell me—it's going to happen in a few minutes."

I didn't decide anything, and I didn't tell the creature anything, either. I drew my sword, leaped forward, and thrust my blade right into the air where the dog's head had been an instant before. I thrust again, and it dodged. I slashed, but the hound slipped away as easily as if I were tossing baskets of flowers at it. Halla threw a knife, but the dog shrugged out of the way. The hound landed with a gentle bounce, its tongue hanging out the side of its mouth.

I pulled a sliver of my magical power out of the air and threw a yellow band around the creature's neck. The thing wasn't a spirit; it was a possessed beast with no name of its own. I didn't need to know anything about it to bind it. The yellow band touched the dog's loose neck skin and crumbled to drift away like fog.

I glanced at Halla. "Can't bind it. Do you have any ideas?"

"You are the smart one."

"Krak and all his whores!" I yelled at her.

The dog laughed, rolled over, and wiggled like we'd just tickled its belly.

Halla spun and picked up the barrel like it was a serving platter. I thrust at the dog again, and it dodged, but Halla was already running toward it. As she slammed the barrel down, the dog shot out from under it and sprinted right between us. It stopped a few paces down the lane and began cleaning its rectum.

After a few seconds, the beast said, "Huh. Won't try that again. Hail the mighty sorcerers! That was entertaining. Don't be shy, it really was! You almost touched me. To reward your valor, I have decided not to destroy half of this squalid habitation. So, have good cheer! Lie with your women, or your men if you wish. You won! I will destroy only one house." The creature sagged, turned in a circle like a regular old unpossessed dog, and lay down on the mud to sleep.

I stood over the thing, not sure what to do. "You wad of rat guts! Go away, and don't come back!"

The dog raised its head again to stare at me. "Oh, no. You shouldn't have said that."

Halla smacked me on the arm hard enough to bruise.

The dog tilted its head at Halla. "Charming damsel, I am entertaining your boys so sweetly. I anticipate a fratricide soon." It turned its head toward me. "And who are you?"

I sure as hell wasn't going to give it my name. "I'm Paul, the town burgher."

"You're so funny! I love it! No, you're . . . the Murderer?" After a pause, it laughed. "You're the Murderer! Oh, how things have changed. I just can't believe I found you. Now I'm going to kill every sad person in this pokey town. Unless you stop me!" The dog bounded away down the lane, its voice fading as it left. "It's your job to stop me! Meet me in the . . . oh, the town square, I suppose it would be. The good old Murderer! This is going to be so much fun."

I glared at Halla. "You did this! It came here because it noticed your hokkat!"

Halla glared back. "You made it worse. You invited it to return!"

I sneered and fetched Halla's knife, then I turned to follow the dog. Halla caught my arm.

"Wait. The talking dog said it found you. Perhaps you are in danger." Her eyes softened. "I am here, so let me help you."

"Horseshit! You didn't march your ass up to my house after ten years to protect me from a talking dog we've never met."

Her nostrils flared. From my angle, they looked as big as canyons. "You were easier to convince of things when you were drunk most of the time. Fine. I need your help to rescue children. They are imprisoned by . . . well, by something that possesses dogs."

"Do it yourself! You're a big, strong girl. I have to go save a bunch of people who hate me."

I turned, but her hand stopped my arm as if I were chained to a tree. She said, "I came here for your help. I must have a diversion. Created by someone I trust."

"Buy a dog. That doesn't talk!"

"The diversion will not be dangerous."

"Then buy a little dog!" I stomped her instep, yanked my arm free, and ran down the lane. I heard Halla trying not to curse and doing a piss-poor job.

THREE

Halla and I first met when I was a young man and she was hardly grown. On that occasion, she wept on me and then tried to kill me.

I had hired a boat captain, or at least a rancid piece of tooth cheese that owned a boat, to sail me up the coast. While the man patched his sails, or summoned an air demon, or whatever he did to get his collection of sticks and snot to move across the water, I lounged against a stack of crates on the dock.

An enormous, crying, black-skinned girl ran onto the dock from the road, carrying a dead dog in her arms like it was a baby. While tears ran down her face, she asked me who owned the dog, and I expressed ignorance. She then sagged against me and dripped tears onto the top of my head, which I found disturbing. I had not been raised to engage in such behavior with strange girls.

Before I could do anything about it, the boat captain stepped onto the dock and pointed at the dog carcass. "That'll teach that goddamn cur to bite me! Throw the shitty bastard back in the ditch and piss on it."

Halla accused me of protecting that horrible man. At least, I think she did. She was slamming me against the stack of crates over and over, so I suppose she could have been describing how she would kill me if slamming didn't work, or she might have been admiring my pretty blue eyes. I managed to gasp out an offer to help her kill that awful dog murderer.

We tossed the captain off the dock, and he sank. My promise to help kill him had been a convenient lie, so when he splashed back to the surface, I threw him an empty cask to cling to. Halla and I stole his boat and sailed two miles up the coast before the boat sank just like its captain had.

We traveled together for most of the next eight years.

As I ran up the lane in Bindle, I heard the possessed dog barking ahead of me without letup for two annoying minutes until I reached the town square. It was grandiose to call that bare expanse of black mud and scattered gravel a town square. It was square and existed in a town, but that's as much as I'll allow. The next town up the road, Hackpipe, had built themselves a charming town square thirty years before. Bindle's citizens immediately tore down half a dozen buildings to create a square of their own, twice as big. They bragged about it, even though it was as empty and awful as a dead man's eyes.

The rain had squeezed down to a drizzle. That was still wet enough to discourage all but about fifty citizens from coming out to judge me. The old hound was running around the space, barking like a mad thing and snapping when somebody got too close.

I ran to the middle of the square, drew my sword, and shouted, "All right, I'm here! To preserve Krak's ears and mine, shut the hell up!"

"Murderer!" The dog squealed like a happy child and trotted to within ten feet of me. "It's a fine day to be a gigantic, goddamn hero, don't you think?"

All the citizens in the square froze when the dog spoke. A couple of them ran off while the rest edged away.

The dog shook its shaggy head. "Now, I'm going to kill every person in this town, but first I'll award you the chance to talk me out of it."

Paul, Sam, and Tettler ran toward me out of the gathering

crowd. "Bib! Stop this, whatever this is!" Paul yelled. "Take that demon away from here, and don't come back!"

"Stand away, you insects!" the dog shouted, pointing its nose at Paul. "Back up right now and be quiet. I do not give you leave to speak in my presence."

Tettler's mouth fell open. "It's a goddamn talking dog."

The beast leaped onto Tettler's chest, knocking him on his back in the mud. I ran to skewer the creature, but before I arrived, it seized Tettler's throat in its teeth and tore out a big bite. I thrust, but the dog bounded aside while Tettler gurgled and spouted blood.

"Now, what did I say about speaking in my presence?" the dog said with its bloody muzzle. It glanced back and forth between Paul and Sam. I thrust again, but it leaned out of the way without stepping aside.

Neither of the men moved or squeaked.

"That's right. It's not allowed." The dog shook its head, throwing off droplets of blood. "Murderer, you crusty old sorcerer, what will you give me to save these people?"

I decided to accommodate the hound for a bit. Maybe it would get distracted and I could kill it or hurt it. Hell, it would probably have to fall down and break three legs for me to touch it. "Dog . . . should I call you something else?"

"No, Dog is just fine."

I shrugged. "Dog, I sure as shark bait don't intend to give up anything of my own. After all, I didn't invite you here. You had best bargain with the people of this town and allow them to save themselves."

Dog giggled, and my neck hair stood up. "That is wise. I have heard that the Murderer is wise! Doesn't everyone think the Murderer is wise?" It gazed around at the crowd, but nobody spoke. Dog shouted, "The squalid creatures in this unhygienic habitation shall pay me to secure their survival. However, the Murderer will bargain on their behalf."

I stepped back. "That is a foolish idea, and I will not do it!" I didn't intend to get even more caught up in this, whatever the hell *this* was.

Paul didn't speak, but he shook his head so hard that his long hair whipped almost straight out from his skull.

Dog swung around to stare at an old woman at the front of the crowd. She coughed, bent over, and fell onto her face, limp. Three people knelt to turn her on her back, and they murmured as they poked and listened. I ignored them, since I had no doubt she was dead.

Dog grinned. "Do you want to see how many I can do at once? While defecating?"

I held up my hand as I gazed around at the terrified people scrambling back. "Wait! I need to talk to Paul here without you making his heart fly out of his mouth or something."

The dog sat on its haunches. "Go ahead, if you just have to."

I stepped close to Paul and muttered, "What can you pay?"

"You piece of filth!"

"Yes, you're my hero too. What can you pay? Think in terms of things you can give up, things you can do, or things you can agree to have done to you."

Paul sneered at me, but his face dropped as he gazed at the dead woman. "We can pay some gold, I suppose."

I turned to Dog. "If you spare all their lives, they will give you all the gold in town."

"Wait—" Paul whuffed as I elbowed him in the stomach.

Dog walked in a circle. "That's disappointing. You're hardly showing any imagination at all. I can already get all the gold I want."

"Come on, look at who's involved in this deal." I jerked my head at Paul and then gestured around at the crowd, now over a hundred people slightly more curious than terrified. Halla had shown up behind me at some point, holding a spear longer than she was tall.

"I see what you mean," Dog said. "But I won't give them all back in exchange for mere gold—the gods would laugh. I'll give up everyone except the youngest person in each house. Those I shall be forced to destroy." Dog giggled again and frisked like a puppy.

I leaned toward Paul again. "What else have you got?"

He scowled. "What do you mean? Build it a kennel or something?"

"Good idea." I turned to Dog. "To save all the youngest people in each house, this town will build a temple to the god or goddess of your choice. A big one." If Dog was touchy about the gods laughing at it, maybe sucking up to the gods a little would please it.

"I like that! Not enough to give back everybody, of course, but I do admire the idea." Dog paced around the square, forcing people back. "I'll let the young people living between here and the river survive. I'll still destroy the youngest in all the other houses. Oh, oh, build the temple right here! In fact, knock down a few of these appalling structures around us so you can build a bigger temple. Lutigan . . . yes, a Temple of Lutigan!"

I put on the greatest fake smile I could manage. None of the gods liked me, but Lutigan hated me more than any of the others. I turned to Paul and murmured, "What else?"

He raised his eyebrows and shook his head. "You can't think of anything? Do you want me to think of something for you?"

Paul's eyes got wide. "No! Um, we'll stop the . . . we'll turn away travelers for a month."

That would hurt any town on the Empire Road. "Dog, these fine people will tell travelers to go to hell for the next month, if it will save everybody who's left."

"Maybe . . . it doesn't exactly make my crotch tingle." Dog stared around at the crowd. "All right, I feel generous. I won't kill the youngest ones living between the river and that big road. I'll just take them away with me. That's a lot better than death!"

"Let's not settle on taking anybody away just yet," I said. "To clarify, we're bargaining over two batches of young people now. You're talking about taking away the ones between the river and the road but not killing them. What about the ones south of the road?"

"I'll take them away too."

I decided to chip away at his position. "For the current offer of 'telling all travelers to screw themselves,' you could take away just half of the young people living south of the road."

"Done!"

I closed my eyes when I realized what I'd said. I couldn't take it back, and I didn't want to see. I heard the screaming, though.

After a couple of breaths, I stared around. Dog was waddling away from me, head down, just an old dog again. I saw several clumps of wailing, struggling people scattered around the square and a few more clumps searching around in panic.

Thirty feet from me, a dead boy of about ten years lay on the ground with a woman kneeling over him. A man beside him screamed and struggled while two men held him. The bottom half of the boy's body was missing, as if it had been cut in two at the waist with a fine wire.

Other people were shouting names in that tone a mother uses to call her children home.

Halla grabbed my arm and pulled me out of the town square, shoving through the crowd.

"I can't just leave," I muttered.

"They will tear you into many small parts if you stay. Where is your horse stabled?"

"At the inn."

Halla nodded and hauled me around a corner toward the inn. I stopped short when I saw half of a young woman lying in the street, intestines poking out from the bottom of her torso. Her eyes were open, and she was smiling—dead before she felt anything at all, I hoped.

Halla didn't speak, but she dragged at my arm until I followed her.

We met several people who were jogging toward the screaming at the town square. They passed us without pausing, although everybody eyed Halla as they went by. Five minutes later, we reached the inn and ran around back to the stables. The stable boy's torso and head lay on a small pile of bloody hay, as if he had lain down for a nap.

I had told that damned rutting dog to take half of the young people south of the river, and he had—the bottom half. It was the sort of ridiculous mistake that kills sorcerers. In fact, about a third of all sorcerers destroy themselves with such a slip before they turn twenty-two. By rights, I should have been dead for being so careless, but all these young people died instead.

I wandered back out into the stable yard with some idea of going to talk to the families, but I stopped there since nothing I could say would help anybody. A hundred people would grab me and kick me to death. They already hated me before I let their children get stolen or slaughtered like pigs.

Halla led me back into the stable and opened my horse's stall. "Saddle it. Hurry."

Without much thought, I began saddling the animal. "Do you think the dog took the others away? The ones it didn't kill? Took them in a flash?"

"Yes." She didn't hesitate or look at me as she tossed on her saddle blanket.

We continued our work for a minute while I thought about that. "You sound definite on that point."

Now she did look at me. "This being stole my nephews in this way. I think it called the house spirits to carry away this town's children."

I felt my face heating. "What kind of pus-filled road apple does this?" My anger made my horse stamp, and I forced a deep breath.

"I do not know. We should go find out and kill it. I already asked you to help do that."

I threw my saddle up onto my horse. "Fine! I'll come!"

Halla frowned. "Also, you should forget Lin's house."

"I . . . I don't know. Let's kill this damn ass-licking thing first. Maybe when we bring the kids back, things will be . . ." It was sounding stupid even as I was saying it.

Halla's voice was normally about as emotional as a grinding wheel, but she sounded almost tender now. "The house will only distract you. Put it behind you, Bib. Lin and your girls are gone. You love them, but they can never love you again."

I gaped and then yelled, "Go drown in a river of bacon grease, you twitchy pole! I'm going to catch a bear and make it eat you. You'd better ride out of here fast!"

Both horses whickered and stamped. Mine almost stepped on me.

Halla let one hand slap down onto her saddle. "You are not coming with me, then?"

"Of course I'm coming! Where is this damned entity, or whatever it is?"

"I don't know. Yet." She examined her saddle and ignored me. "But I know of an oracle who can help."

I stared at her for five full seconds. "Fingit's belly and bowels! You know better than to credit such a thing as an oracle. Maybe you're a demon in Halla's skin and I should kill you! Stupidest thing I've ever heard." I paused when the image of that dead girl in the street jumped to mind. "Well, go ahead and tell me about it, since you're talking."

"I wouldn't say she is the sort of oracle that books describe, but I hear she knows things. I have learned of her from more than one source."

"If she's such a peach of a diviner, why haven't I heard about her?" I mounted and kicked my horse into a walk.

"Because you have been killing men over gold," Halla said from her horse behind me.

We trotted our horses down to the Empire Road and headed east. I saw no call to wear out our mounts unless I spotted somebody chasing us. When we reached the tavern, only Whistler stood out front, and he watched us pass by him going eastward. I didn't speak, and he didn't, either.

Half a minute later, Whistler bellowed, "They're headed down to the river! I saw them riding west!"

FOUR

Ten minutes after Halla and I rode out of Bindle, she frowned at me. "I thought I would be required to hit you with a rock and carry you out of that town. You are too softhearted."

My mouth hung open for a moment. "You are like an iron boot! Sympathize with them a little. Your children have been stolen just like theirs." I couldn't easily recall the last time somebody accused me of softheartedness. I wondered what Halla had traded away to the gods these past years that had left her so harsh.

Halla stared down at her horse's neck. "Yes, you're right. I was thinking about myself and no one else."

"You remember that." I waved my hand like I was chasing away a chicken. "Your six-year-old self would be disappointed in you. I bet she was a tender, neck-hugging, weepy little thing kissing her bunny rabbits before bedtime."

Halla scowled at me and then turned away. "Kissing bunnies. How did you know? It is as if you were there watching me."

I laughed, and although she didn't look at me, I liked to think she smiled. "Where is this oracle, then? I hope we're not riding straight away from her."

"She will be at the Eastlands Crossroads Fair until tomorrow."

I had been to that place when I lived in Bindle. "Fine." I kicked my horse into a faster gait and prepared for hours of mud flying up at me from off the road.

Halla shouted, "Not that way! We ride straight across the grassland. That will regain the time you threw away in the stables complaining about this journey."

I turned to follow her, and we traveled fast enough to make conversation inconvenient. She didn't seem to mind the silence.

We rode across short, fresh grass stretched as flat as a sheet in all directions. It supported a meager collection of solitary trees, huge and bare. Bindle withered behind us. The Pip River ran through Bindle and now it flowed the same direction as us but half a mile to our left. At last, it curved and blocked our way. The river hurried along, fat with rain, but even at its greatest flood-fed width, a man could slog across it in less than a minute. We splashed across, hardly slowing down.

By midafternoon, the sky cleared. Neither the sun nor the gigantic, gaunt trees had shown me any polite strategies for asking my next question. At last, I bit down and asked, "So, have you spoken to your mother recently?"

Halla stiffened, but she didn't falter. "It pleases me to say I have not. It fills me with suspicion that you asked."

I coughed and gazed straight ahead as I tried to decide how much more to say. When talking about gods, it's better not to say much. It's often best to say nothing.

Every sorcerer ends up claimed by a god. Harik had claimed me. Such a relationship sounds like it might be unpleasant for the sorcerer, and it almost always is. It's about the same as a farmer owning a willful pig, except that the farmer wields unthinkable power and whines a lot, and the pig gets butchered alive over a space of years.

The Goddess of the Unknowable, Sakaj, had claimed young Halla over twenty years ago. Few people regarded that fact with the astonishment it deserved. Sakaj tended to leave her sorcerers, her "daughters," wrung out, crazy, or dead before age twenty. But even as a softhearted girl, Halla had made watchful bargains, dripping with suspicion, and she thrashed over every point like a rabid squirrel with the only nut in the woods.

Sakaj had claimed my daughter too, but Manon had been too young and foolish to be attentive. Sakaj had squeezed out everything Manon loved, and everything she hated, and just about everything else that made her a person.

I said, "I talked to your mother this past winter. Krak and Harik too."

Halla shifted in the saddle, trying to readjust her seat without appearing uncomfortable. "What did she say?"

"Nothing of great consequence. When Krak is present, it doesn't matter what anybody else wants to say. Your mother ruined my little girl, though." I coughed again to cover any strain in my voice.

Halla squinted at me. "Your daughter was a sorcerer."

I nodded.

She stared down for a few seconds, her brow furrowed. "So . . . you had to kill your daughter. Because my mother took her."

"I didn't have to!" I barked. I leaned back and lowered my voice. "I guess I could have done something else besides kill her, but I didn't do something else." I kicked my mare, and Halla let me ride on ahead.

I convinced Halla to camp for the night rather than push through. The fair lay eight hours ahead, so we would arrive well before dawn unless we stopped. I didn't care to shake the oracle out of bed. I had some experience with truth-seers, and if we vexed her, she might tell us a bunch lies and get us killed.

We made camp before the moon rose. Although it was dark as hell, we didn't build a fire. Anybody who wanted to harm us could have spotted a campfire ten miles off across that flat grass. Of course, anybody who could magically possess a dog, and do it from who the hell knows what distance, could probably find us by starlight if he wanted.

Chewing a bite of dry bread, I mumbled, "I'm tired of calling this son of a bitch the dog possessor. I'm going to call him Lord

Floppy-Ass, Bane of Bindle Town. For the sake of efficiency, I'll refer to him as Floppy-Ass."

"You still cannot help yourself. You must name everyone and everything. It is a weakness." Halla said it with no frustration in her voice. In fact, she said it with hardly any interest.

All those miles of darkened grass and trees had bored the hell out of me. I decided to poke Halla into an argument. "You may hold that opinion, but you're wrong. You think a silly name will make me underestimate him. Actually, every time I call him Floppy-Ass, it will scrape off a smidge of his self-confidence."

Halla grunted in the darkness. "He cannot even hear you."

"He doesn't need to! There are six words in the name I gave him, and six is a shitty number. Three of those words contain four letters, and four is an even less auspicious number. Floppy-Ass has nine letters, which is an especially repugnant number—and that's the name I'll call him all the time."

Halla stood. Under the starlight, I could make her out scanning the distance. "You should spend this time sharpening your sword, not playing with words and numbers."

I smiled so she'd hear it in my voice. "If it's so pointless, why did you choose a name with five letters? Five is a powerful number, you lumbering, terrifying bunny-kisser."

"I did not think about numbers at all. If you keep talking about kissing bunnies, I will stab you."

"Five is an auspicious number all right. The only number that's stronger is three." I grinned. "Isn't it?"

She walked away, I assumed to keep watch.

"You go on and wander in the dark," I called after her. "Don't feel inferior because I was the first one to strike a blow against Floppy-Ass."

I checked that our horses were properly hobbled, and then I lay down to stare at the stars and maybe sleep.

Halla woke me after the yellow, gibbous moon had risen, and I took watch. Two calm, boring hours followed. I wished that I still drank, not that I would have drank on watch. It just would have been nice to contemplate a future drink. The moon was well up in the sky, and it washed the whole landscape from green into gray.

I spotted movement off to the west. The wind was calm, so I felt certain it wasn't some blowing brush. "Halla."

She rolled to her feet with hardly a sound, her weapon ready. I pointed west.

After ten or fifteen seconds, she shook her head. "What do you see? An antelope? Lion? Swarm of bees?"

"Hah! You may as well have both eyes put out. It's two horses, one with a big rider."

Halla hissed. "If you see them so clearly, what are they wearing?"

"Clothes. They'll pass west of us unless they swing this direction."

Halla knelt. "Let them pass."

I knelt with her and watched for another few minutes. Then I stood up.

Halla's raised eyebrows stood out in the soft light.

"It's Whistler. And a woman on the other horse, or a big child."

I shouted and waved. The riders stopped and scanned the area until they spotted me waving. They rode toward us.

I glanced at Halla. "Aren't you going to say we should kill them?"

Her shoulders dropped a little. "I will wait to say it. Maybe they will decide to go away. Maybe they will stay here and build a farm together. This would make a nice farm."

I turned to her with my mouth open. "That sounds almost sympathetic."

Halla shrugged. "There is plenty of time to kill them later."

Whistler's horse blew and slobbered when he arrived. The woman joined us a moment later riding a side-stepping mule that looked as if it would feel more comfortable pulling a wagon.

I barked, "Lutigan's piles! I'm going to break your gawky neck, Whistler!" Actually, he was much more physically imposing than me. "Why'd you come? I figured everybody was still at the party to celebrate my leaving town." As soon as the words were out of my mouth, I saw those cut-up children back in Bindle. I swallowed and took a breath.

I squinted at the woman. "Why, you straggly little goat-knocker! Bea, are you possessed by some very stupid demon? That's the only reason you'd be following us. I'll have to cut off your hands and feet if you don't ride right back home."

Bea was a bar girl in the Bindle tavern, a wan, young widow with hair so dark brown it was almost black. Although I was a monstrous killer, she had sometimes smiled at me with kind eyes. I might have pursued her for a friendly romp or two before I left town, but the thought of such frolics left me empty these days.

Bea stared at me while her mule stamped.

At last, I turned to Whistler. "Why the hell are you here? Before you speak, understand that no matter what you tell me, I plan to chase you off anyway since you're so plug-iron ignorant as to bring her with you."

Bea slid off her mule while I was chastising Whistler. She walked toward me like she'd been planning her approach for a week. Her cheeks shone bright and slick with tears. In a throat-chafing voice born in her gut, she roared, "Give him back!" Then she hauled off and aimed a brutal kick at me. I'd have limped for a day if I hadn't stepped aside.

She bellowed, "Running off like a coward! Murderer! Coward and murderer!" She lined up for another kick, and I skipped back.

I said, "Bea, I'm sorry I let that thing take your . . . "

"My baby!"

"Your baby."

"Give him back," she grated.

I raised both hands. "I didn't take him, or any of them! But I am headed, right now, to get him back. The others too." I glanced at Halla, who stared at Bea with no expression.

Bea raised her chin. "I don't trust you!"

"Normally, that would speak well of your instincts, Bea, but not in this case," I said.

"Maybe you mean to get him, but you're the kind who goes in for one drink and can't find his way out for a week."

"Two weeks," Halla said.

I ignored her. "Bea, I feel for your difficulty. You can't understand how much. But when the first arrow strikes, it will be in your heart. Or the first cut from an enemy will lop off your head. I see you're brave, but you'll be among hard killers and sorcerers. You'll have no hope, and I will not haul you along to who the hell knows where just for you to die when you get there!"

Bea wrinkled her nose like she smelled something bad. "I'll follow you."

I glared at Whistler. "Look what you're making me deal with, you squatting, box-brain, corncob-for-a-dick idiot!"

"Sorry." Whistler didn't appear scared, or even too sorry.

I stepped closer to Bea and risked a shattered kneecap. "I know that you're a widow—"

Bea cut me off hard. "Yes, he's dead. My other boys are dead too, and all my people. If Tobi's dead, I'll go on and die too."

Halla stated, "You will not come with us. We are stealing your mule."

The young woman shouted, "You can't leave me, you nasty woman! Just you try it! I'll catch you if I have to . . . sleep with a man and kill him and steal his horse!"

It bemused me that Bea had arrived at that as the first solution for her predicament. "Whistler, turn around and take her home. The path is probably choked with dangerous foxes and badgers and cows."

Halla spoke from behind me. "I would like to keep your manservant. When the dog possessor tries to kill me, I can hide behind this man, who will be killed instead. Let him stay."

I waved a hand at her. "Don't be humorous."

"Oh, no." Halla examined Whistler and then me. "I am not being humorous."

Whistler smiled at Halla, his brown teeth looking normal in the moonlight. In his gravelly voice, he said, "You see, Bib? You need me. It's fated by the gods."

"What horseshit!"

Actually, it might not have been horseshit. The gods might have been fating us to do all kinds of things, and I would never have known it. But it pleased me to say horseshit because Whistler was making me mad and I hated the gods worse than a stick in the eye. "We may be going to get our damned heads cut off! You don't know."

Whistler laughed. "Bib, since you showed up, I've gotten richer than I've ever been in my life. Richer than anybody I ever knew."

"Don't you have enough money already, then?"

Whistler cocked his head and stared at me as if I'd said he had already had enough sex and needed no more. "No. Bib, you are lucky. Or at least I'm lucky when you're around, and that's good enough."

Halla cleared her throat, and I knew the argument was over.

"Well, come on, then." I pointed at Bea. "You go home."

Bea stiffened for ten seconds and then slumped. "All right. But you promise me that you won't fail. Or die."

"Well . . . I promise that if I have to do one, then I'll do the other as well." I was lying right to her face, of course. If death seemed likely, I would run like hell and not worry a jot about failure.

Whistler leaned in to say something to Bea. She stumbled against him for no damn reason at all, except to press herself against his body. She gazed up at him. "I could be useful on the trail. I can cook and gather wood. I can set a fine snare."

Whistler glanced at me. My expression must have been monstrous, because he shook his head and stood her up straight. "It's too dangerous."

Bea turned toward me. "Can I at least wait until the sun is up before I leave?"

I snapped, "You can wait until Krak sings on your birthday for all I care, as long as you don't follow us."

Bea walked off toward the horses, letting her hand linger on Whistler's arm. She sat down close to the mule, facing away from us.

I continued to keep watch until two hours before sunrise, when Whistler walked up to me. He normally favored his right leg a little, so I knew his step. He cleared his throat and pointed. "Bib, something strange is out there."

"Go kill the shit out of whatever it is."

"I don't know whether it's that kind of strange. I mean, maybe it's not strange like a wolf you can club, but maybe it's strange like a ghost or something."

I peered out where he had pointed. Something sure as hell was there. After a few seconds, I noticed small things moving through the grass, almost too subtle to see. Then two eyes glowed green in the moonlight. Several more somethings joined in, their eyes bright under the big moon. The horses started snorting and stamping.

"Halla!" I pointed and drew my sword.

Several of the things stopped moving, and I scrutinized them. "They're plains cats."

A plains cat bulked about twice the size of a house cat. It dined on rats, gophers, and inattentive snakes. I couldn't count the waving tails in the grass, but I saw forty or fifty glowing eyes.

From behind me, Bea gasped. "Where did all those damned eyeballs come from?" She bent and grabbed a long stick of firewood.

I turned and saw another seventy or eighty eyes out past Bea. I scanned the whole area and estimated more than two hundred eyes. It might have been three hundred. Once the number of cats ripping into your flesh exceeds a hundred, the exact total is mere curiosity.

I swiveled my head in all directions. "I'm not so tired as I thought."

Halla was gazing around too. "Yes, I could ride away right now if necessary."

Whistler was already saddling Bea's mule. "We're not leaving her behind!" he snarled over his shoulder.

I didn't have any idea of contradicting him. All of us saddled our mounts in a hurry and rode away into the darkness exactly as fast as a scared mule. None of the eyeballs chased us, so I suppose we left the plains cats behind. I didn't see any more before sunrise, but I turned in the saddle to check now and then, just to be safe.

FIVE

I have found that murdering somebody becomes far easier when you know where they are. Knowing other things about them helps too. Are they an innately supernatural being or some perverse sorcerer? Also, understanding what they want and how many ways they can kill you may prove decisive, although it is rare to possess all that knowledge.

We didn't know any of those things about Floppy-Ass, but I hoped that this oracle would.

We arrived at the fair before midmorning. It stood surrounding the crossroads and spread three hundred paces in every direction. It lay within walking distance of five villages and two dozen outlying farms. Hundreds of people wandered and jostled around. The fair ended today, so everybody would come. People had raised a few simple canvas tents, others had set up rude stalls, and one wooden cabin had been knocked together, to be as easily knocked down when the fair ended.

If today's fair was like every other I had seen, most people would crowd themselves around the tables and stalls where farm wives sold food to their neighbors at one price and to strangers at a higher one. Some stalls displayed leather goods, clay pots, clothes, or knives. The people running those stalls were often travelers and cheated everybody. All the fairgoers appeared poor but tidy. They had probably worn their best clothes. A number of cutpurses would be slipping through the crowd, and somebody caught alone in a quiet place might get beaten and robbed. The smells of woodsmoke, cold mud, and charred, dubious meat floated everywhere.

Just about everybody looked to be enjoying it.

Bea walked along beside Whistler, her arm in his. At first light, I had told her to turn around and ride off home, but she had begged to go with us to the fair. She intended to buy small, practical things for her neighbors to ease their pain a little. I told her she was a poor woman and that was horseshit, but Whistler insisted it wasn't safe for her to go home yet. Just because the sun was up, that didn't mean those cats had melted into the ground. Halla didn't seem to care, and I was getting bored with Bea's stubbornness, even if I sympathized a bit. I waved her on to follow us and told her to duck when sharp things started flying through the air.

I smacked Halla on the shoulder. "Where's the oracle? You're the one as tall as a damn ship's mast." Although people seemed happy, I didn't like how the fair felt. It was ridiculous of me, and I couldn't point to anything wrong. The lack of evident threat convinced me that something bad was about to happen.

Whistler was eyeing a table full of something that had been killed, stewed, and piled onto slabs of bark. He grunted, "We don't need to wear out our feet getting to this oracle right away, do we?"

Halla ignored him. "I think she must be in that wooden building."

"If you think it, it's just sure to be true then, isn't it?" I stepped aside to let a short, fat man march between us.

Halla pushed through the crowd, and she didn't have to push hard. She stood out. I glanced back to find that Whistler and Bea were gone. If they never returned, that was fine with me. Within a minute, we smacked into a ring of people watching something.

Halla glanced over and said, "Juggler." She frowned like she'd bitten into something rotten. She had never appreciated entertainment of any sort, and she started shoving her way around the circle.

Between the weaving shoulders and heads, I saw a thin man wearing a red mask, juggling four knives.

"Hey!" the man shouted. He tossed a knife toward Halla, not hard enough to knock over a chicken. Halla caught it as the juggler tossed another knife. Soon she held all four knives.

"Throw them back!" the man shouted.

Halla gathered all the knives into her left hand and pushed on through the crowd.

"Wait! Throw them back!"

"Thank you for the knives," Halla called over her shoulder. She muttered to me, "Maybe he will go do something useful now."

Whistler appeared beside me. Bea stood beyond him examining cloth at a stall run by a pretty, auburn-haired peasant woman. He whispered, "I bought this love potion." He held up a tiny clay jar. "Do you think it's real?"

"Ask Halla to drink it. If you live, it's real."

"Shit. I'm getting my money back." He slithered away through the crowd, muttering.

A big open area, eighty paces across, stood in front of the shabby wooden building. The builders had roofed the crude cabin with warped poles, which would never keep the rain out and would hardly block the sunshine. On one side of the clearing, a throng of men watched two wrestlers and waited their turn. On the other side, a young, sandy-haired man stood in front of a large, pale-green tent and offered to show people his horrible, flesh-shredding, disemboweling lions for the price of two copper bits. The man wore a nice blue jacket, which stood out in the plain-dressed crowd.

I heard Halla say, "Show us to the oracle."

A woman's tight voice said with a slight accent, "No. I deny you entry. You're impolite, and the oracle despises impolite people. Go on now, go away. Shoo."

I turned to see what was happening. Halla glanced at me with raised eyebrows. A starkly beautiful young woman, not much older than a girl, guarded the door. She had black hair, strong features, and wheat-colored skin.

Before I could speak, Whistler stomped up beside me. "She won't give me back my money. Will it bother you if I kill her?"

"Yes, it will. How many dead men have you robbed? And now this old grandmother cheats you out of a few bits that you'll never miss. You're a wealthy man! Don't you feel shame?"

Whistler stared at the ground. "I guess I do, a little." He turned away, and I heard him mutter, "She's not that old."

I turned back to the door guardian. "May I please visit the oracle, young woman? I promise to be polite and pleasant. I have a present for her to show my respect."

Halla cocked her head. "You have a present?"

"I do if you give me those knives." I turned back to the young lady and smiled my most woman-stealing smile.

She frowned but nodded. "Tell me your name, and I will lead you to the oracle."

"My name is Gundersak the candlemaker. May I ask your name?"

"No." She held aside the heavy cloth hanging over the door and waved me in. "Go to the right."

I turned right. I hadn't expected the interior to be so dim, but it was a cloudy day.

"Go straight," she said from behind me.

Within six steps, I entered a small room, just big enough for a nice table and two chairs with a small cabinet in the corner. A lantern hung from a beam, and another door stood in the left-hand wall.

"You have to prepare yourself to meet the oracle." She pointed at one of the chairs.

This was a dispiriting sign. It was clear that she intended to extract details from me that the oracle could use when she divined my fate. Most men talking to a pretty girl for a few minutes would give up their fears, their desires, and how much gold they're carrying. If the girl was clever, they wouldn't realize they'd been interrogated. That didn't help me a damn bit, though.

I figured I might as well stay, so I sat. Maybe this oracle would shock me.

The young woman fetched two wooden cups from the cabinet. Then she lifted a pot from a smoking brazier on the table and poured liquid into both cups. Sitting, she blew on her cup and took a sip. "Drink this tea to purify yourself." She sipped again. "It's safe."

It would take a horrifying, rapid poison to kill me before I could heal myself. I took a couple of sips and smiled. "So, the oracle is coming here to join me, eh? That's awfully accommodating and sweet of her. Do you have any bread?"

"No, but we have some nice bacon." She grinned and for a moment looked fourteen years old.

My mouth started watering, but I wasn't there for a tasty breakfast. I sighed and held up a hand. "I'll pass. It would ruin this fine tea. How long do you think I'll need to wait?"

"I see you have red hair."

"Not much."

"You must be from the Island of Ir. My grandfather told me stories about it."

"Hope they were interesting." Clearly the interrogation was starting.

"That's a beautiful sword."

"I stole it off a dead Northman in a ditch."

She pulled the chair around and sat close to me. "Where was the ditch?"

I sipped my tea. "It was just uphill from the lake."

She grinned again. "I love lakes. Which lake?"

I craned my head at the door I hadn't been through. "I feel fairly pure now. Maybe I should just walk on through and find the oracle."

"Wait," the young woman said, calm and sitting straight. Then she leaned in fast, headed straight for my lips.

I caught her by the shoulders and pushed her back a few inches. Nothing was going to happen, but I didn't want to hurt her feelings. "Miss, I can understand your being overcome by my pretty face, but I must tell you that I'm about a thousand years older than you."

"I don't care about that."

"Well, I'm sorry, but I do." I pushed her farther away.

"Don't be stupid. You want me. You do, don't you?" She sounded a little uncertain there at the end.

"Of course, any man—" I blinked when the point of a sharp knife pressed against my right testicle.

She showed me her teeth and murmured, "How much do you want to speak to the oracle? Enough to sacrifice one of these?"

I realized that I should have gone ahead and slept with her. Now she was tickling my groin with sharp steel, and I ought to kill her straight off. It was bad practice to let someone live after they demonstrated their willingness to make holes in my body. And I would never fulfill my debt to the God of Death if I started being merciful.

But I had seen too many girls die recently. If I killed one today, I thought I might lie down and die myself. I wouldn't really lie down or do anything like that, of course. I'd cut her throat and move on to the next murder. But I didn't have to kill this girl today, and I decided that I wouldn't. She had chosen a lucky day to threaten me.

I didn't even twitch as the woman shifted the point of her knife to my left testicle. I cleared my throat. "I want to make sure I understand you. The price you'll charge me to see the oracle is one of my balls?"

She nodded. "You shouldn't have been pushy. I could take them both, if you want an extra five minutes."

"I prefer to leave here intact. Please tell the oracle that I regret she missed the pleasure of my company and my sterling wit. Go on and tell her that. My friends and I will wait outside to help you tear down this little building tonight. I feel certain the oracle will come out before this place clatters down around her. We might exchange a word or two then."

The woman tensed. "Maybe we can bargain. I could take a finger. Just to the first knuckle."

That might have been a good bargain for me. I was carrying far more than enough power to heal that sort of wound in a minute. But I disliked the idea on principle. I would rather cut off this girl's hand and throw it at the oracle's feet. "I'm afraid not, dear."

"If you're going to call me 'dear,' why didn't you screw me a minute ago?"

"No part of my body is on the block for trading. I will share a bit of my reservoir of wisdom." I thought of the four fools I'd killed in Bindle and smiled. "I earned it with bruises and broken hearts."

She didn't smile back. "Your reservoir of wisdom is probably full of rats and urine. How about this for a bargain? Say you do a favor for me. I can claim it anytime within a year. Assuming you're good for anything. Or are you only good for underperforming?"

I paused. She had let me make the first offer—I wanted to see the oracle. She had staked out an aggressive bargaining position—my testicle. Now she let me think I was wearing her down, when in fact she was demanding a useful prize—a favor from me.

She bargained like a sorcerer.

"That is a mighty tempting offer, miss, but I fear you might ask me to do something distasteful. Instead, why don't I introduce you to Harik, the God of Death?"

The woman shoved herself away from the table fast, went over backward, tumbled through the door, and came up on her knees.

From deeper within the little building, an old woman's voice called out, "Pil, I'm ready. Send in the next soul."

Panting, Pil stood up and jerked her head toward the doorway, the knife still in her hand. "You go first. There might be spiders."

I laughed at her. "Go first? You may as well ask me to cut off my own head."

Pil sighed and walked down the hallway in front of me. After a left turn and then another, we walked into a small, dim room about six paces square.

The old woman sitting behind the table wasn't so much shriveled as she was collapsed. Her back curved so far forward it pushed her head toward the table so that she had to look nearly straight up to see me. Considering her infirm back, her face wasn't half so wrinkled as I thought it might be. Her blouse was blue or maybe purple, and she gazed at me with loving eyes.

Without breaking eye contact with me, she said, "Back to the door, sweetheart."

Pil didn't move.

"I know everything about this sorcerer," the oracle said. "You go back to the door."

Pil left the room as if she were dragging a weight.

"You're here about an enemy," the oracle said in not much more than a mumble.

I had met a lot of soothsayers, and considering Pil's prelude, this one didn't impress me. "If you say I am, I guess I am."

"A powerful enemy. You bring with you your companion from the farthest east."

That was a true statement. Halla's people lived in the easternmost part of the continent. "Go on."

"I can see your enemy. He's very powerful but can be killed."

"Just about everybody can be killed." I started tapping my foot to see if it would make her nervous.

"And he can too, but it won't be easy. Your companion—" She coughed. "Companions will fight loyally beside you." The oracle nodded. Her neck was so bent, I thought her head might pop off.

"Sure, they're the most loyal, bravest, and sweetest-smelling comrades in the world."

The oracle chuckled but glanced at my tapping foot.

"None but you can defeat this enemy, Bib the sorcerer. I will help you if you honor the gods with some gold. He rides fast to the northeast, away from you, toward Cliffmeet and the Northern Stretch. You must rush if you wish to overtake him!"

"Rush, huh? Well, that makes sense. I've never overtaken a single foe by failing to rush." I shook my head and bellowed, "Halla! Come on in here and meet the oracle."

The oracle didn't show even a tiny sign of discomfort. "I foretold that you would distrust me, as you distrust the God of Death—"

That was enough for me. She was just another scoundrel who stole poor people's money and gave them hope that wasn't worth a damn. "You are full of seven kinds of dog shit and your mother's shit besides!" I took a step toward her, and she flinched.

A scream came from the hallway, and then a geyser of profanity from what sounded like Pil. A few seconds later, Halla strode into the room carrying her spear in one hand and Pil under her other arm like a flailing, foulmouthed sack of corn.

"Now," I said, "who wants to tell us what's going on here? Keep in mind that people who don't tell us what's going on here are going to be killed."

The oracle sat straight up, her back and neck not bent in the least, and pointed at Pil. "It's her fault!"

Pil stopped beating Halla's leg and stared at the oracle, mouth open.

I raised my eyebrows at Halla and pointed at the oracle. "Whack her until she says something I like."

Halla dropped Pil on the ground, cracked her knuckles, and gave the oracle a little nod.

While the oracle was turning pale, Pil jumped up and rushed toward the old woman, raising an open hand.

The juggler in the red mask leaped out from hiding in a side room and tackled Pil.

The oracle pulled a knife as long as her forearm out from under the table and stood up.

"Stop!" Halla screamed. Dust drifted from between the wooden wall slats. Everybody stopped.

I cleared my throat. "Should we expect anybody else? The short, fat man who almost ran us down this morning? One of those damned lions?"

The juggler eased himself to his feet, hands raised. He pulled off his mask, and I recognized his lean, hard face.

"Dixon?" I said. "Why aren't you crushed flat?"

The sorcerer Dixon, who I hadn't seen since I killed him twelve years ago, shrugged and gave me a crooked grin. "You missed. You were probably drunk. Are you drunk now? Would you like to get a drink? I'm buying."

I nodded. "If I kill you and take all your money, technically you'd be buying."

Dixon grimaced. "To hell with you, then. You crushed my horse."

"I am sorry about that."

Halla said, "Wait."

I never found out what we were supposed to wait for. The oracle gagged and then bleated a short scream. Five small objects shot out of her abdomen, leaving five ragged holes in the skin. One of them whizzed past my head. Another knocked Halla's spear out of her hand, clattering to the dirt floor. Yet another smacked Dixon in the back of the neck and exited through a plum-size hole in his throat. It continued without slowing down.

All five objects punched holes in the wooden wall behind me and in the wall behind it, if the splintering sounds meant anything.

The oracle flopped forward onto the table and lay still, blood seeping out from under her body. Dixon lay on his side, his eyes open and glassy.

Halla looked at me, and I shrugged. We both stared at Pil. I said, "Well, sorcerer?"

Pil scowled. "It wasn't me. I'd have killed both of you." She knelt beside Dixon, held his hand, and brushed his hair back out of his eyes.

SIX

I honestly couldn't recall why I had tried to kill Dixon all those years ago. He had probably done some awful thing, but not so awful that I still remembered it. Or, maybe I'd done the awful thing. We were probably both just arrogant sons of bitches who thought we were always right.

Anyway, Dixon was dead now and had at least one person to mourn him. Pil wasn't crying, but her body was hunched with sadness. However, the world afforded her just ten seconds to grieve.

Screams filtered in through the gaps between the cottage's scarred wall slats. A few came at first, but dozens more joined within a few seconds. I hustled back to the door that led outside. That might sound foolish, but it was sound tactical thinking. Outside I could see whatever was happening and do something about it, hopefully something smart. Inside the oracle's shack, I knew nothing and couldn't go anywhere. I was as helpless as a chick in the shell.

When I stepped outside so many people were screaming and banging into each other, it sounded like surf against a cliff—too loud to be anything but plain noise. I saw thirty or forty people lying on the dirt, not moving. A hundred more ran, tripped, and bled in every direction. I couldn't see more than a fourth of the fair from where I stood, so the situation was probably a lot more dire.

Halla touched my shoulder from behind and shouted, "Where is your servant? I need him to stand in front of me."

"Let's find him and get to our horses, if they're still alive." As I said it, Pil ran past us and off around the corner of the building. Since that was the direction we needed to go, I chased after her.

I rounded the corner and nearly tripped over Pil as she scooted backward on her butt faster than I could trot. I jumped over her and met a little hairless dog, about the size of a chicken. It must have been chasing Pil, but now it scrambled toward me instead. It looked wrong somehow. Another dog followed it toward us.

As I slashed at the creature, I realized it had only two legs. My cut didn't just kill it. The blade sliced right through the dog, and with a piercing pop, it flew into pieces smaller than my thumb. A blast of repugnant, bile-smelling air blew into my face, and some of the pieces hurtled thirty feet away. I peered hard at the other creature as it jumped toward Halla's face. It jumped high, and I saw it flap just before she destroyed it. It wasn't a dog—it was a ragged, featherless chicken.

I checked behind us and saw Pil swing a big knife and slam a chicken to the ground before stomping it into pieces. The creature made a gigantic, foul-smelling pop. Another chicken chased a teenage boy right past us. Now that I knew it was a chicken, I could see it wasn't just naked—it was missing some bits of flesh here and there. The horrible chicken was also missing feet, eyes, and a beak, but it had no trouble jumping onto the boy's head and knocking him to the ground. I ran toward this leaping death-chicken, which was pecking at the boy's eyes. Something zipped through the air from the middle of the fairgrounds and hit the ragged chicken on the back. Instead of hurting it, an empty spot on the chicken's back had filled in.

I skewered the chicken and dragged the boy to his feet while trying to figure out what the hell I had just seen. Five people lay nearby, unmoving with blood leaking from their bellies. I could see three more hideous chickens chasing terrified, scrambling fairgoers. I understood it then, even though I didn't want to know such a thing.

Before the attack, the chickens had been dead, which was horrible but not shocking. But they hadn't just been dead. They had been killed, cooked, chewed up, and swallowed. Now somebody was reuniting each dead chicken's body and doing it in such a rush that pieces shot straight out of people's stomachs, careless of what they tore up on the way to reunite.

"God damn!" I shouted. "I hope Whistler didn't eat breakfast!"

Halla stared at me. "I do not think that is our greatest concern."

Pil squinted at me. "Who's Whistler?"

I shouted into Pil's face, "Where do they sell the love potions?"

She nodded and ran off into the hell of the breakfast chickens with Halla and me following. I destroyed three more awful chickens in less than a minute, one of which Pil hurdled, before we reached the magical doodads stall. Whistler stood in front of it clinging to his sword with such fervor his arms shook. Bea and the pretty peasant woman crouched behind him in the stall, the woman holding a sturdy stick. When we drew close, Whistler swung wildly at Pil, who threw herself on the ground. Whistler glared at me with crazy eyes.

"Whistler!" I shouted. "Don't cut me in two! Look! I have skin and hair and everything!"

He didn't speak, but Bea ran out of the stall and grabbed his sword arm. She said something in his ear, and he let her pull his arm down. Then Whistler pointed past me with his other hand and screamed, "Mother kick me in the nuts! Look! Look out!"

I turned and found out that chickens were not the only creatures that people had been eating for breakfast. A burly, skinless, eyeless pig rampaged through the crowd. For a beast without teeth or claws, it created a surprising amount of carnage. The flesh-gaping monster pointed its snout straight at me and charged, but it tangled itself among the bodies, living and dead. The pig tumbled and skidded sideways across the bloody mud.

That was lucky. It would've been luckier if the repugnant pig hadn't had three friends who seemed to hate all mankind just as much as it did.

Fighting a trio of unclean spirit pigs sounded like more work than I cared to do before lunchtime, and I was getting queasy remembering the bacon I'd almost eaten. I dropped my sword, and with both hands, I reached into nothingness to pull from my reserve of power. I formed it into yellow bands suitable for grabbing onto spirits, animals, and supernatural pigs, I hoped.

Halla stood to my left and Pil stood to my right, both closer to the pigs than me. Whistler was somewhere behind me. I whipped bands around the lead pig's hind legs and yanked it to a skidding halt that slung chewed-up pieces of pig flesh off its body. The bands would hold it down so long as I didn't dismiss them—or get killed. Using both hands, Pil manipulated the air, a bit tentatively, but a pig went down and that's what mattered.

I didn't know why, but Halla did nothing but stand still with her spear poised like some magnificent, aggravating statue. However, a clay jar sailed from behind me and bounced off the nearest pig's head, with as much effect as throwing a pillow. From behind me, I heard Bea curse the jar. Then Pil shouted, "Stop! Just you stop, you nasty monster!"

I glanced over at the pig that had fallen and skidded. It was back on its feet, and two friends had joined it. I began pulling bands of power as fast as I could while wondering whether reanimated pigs traveled in herds. No matter how many we killed, more seemed to come running.

By now, seven nasty, greasy-fleshed, mindless pigs charged us. To my right, Pil stopped another pig, which trembled and might have farted mystic gas as it strained against the bindings. I dragged a huge pig over onto its side, and I didn't pause to appreciate how it bounced.

I kept pulling power like a crazy man, and I dragged down another hell-swine. Pil appeared to be pulling bands for another pig, but she was definitely slow. Halla leaped toward the two pigs on the left side and whipped her spear in a double arc hard enough to smash a barrel. Both pigs exploded in clouds of repulsive air with chewed-up pig bits flying in all directions. Halla staggered backward.

About a plateful of demon-pork flew past me and slapped the side of Pil's face. She lost her concentration, but the pig she'd been focusing on kept charging. I didn't have time to haul it down. A clay jar bounced off its skull, and Pil screamed as the pig barreled into her. She flew backward at least ten feet past Whistler, who stood rooted with his sword raised, shaking all over.

I realized only two chewed and semi-digested nightmare-pigs were left to pound us flatter than dirt. One of them was Whistler's problem now. Halla seemed to have been stunned by a face full of pig gas. I had just enough time to bind that last damned pig, so I stepped back to gain a bit more time. That was the dumbest thing I'd done all day, because I slipped on a dismembered pig snout and fell to one knee. I bobbled away the power I'd been pulling.

I stared into the eyeless face of the monster pig charging me and prepared my awkward ass to roll aside. I wanted to wait until it was too late for the pig to veer after me. Just before the moment arrived, a jar hurtled past from behind me and broke against the pig's foreleg. I don't pray to the wicked gods, but I thought about offering Krak a casual thanks that the jar hadn't hit the back of my head. I rolled to my right, and the pig scraped against my left calf as it passed.

The pig scrambled to turn and rush us again, but Halla sprinted around me and drove her spear all the way through it. The pig exploded into bite-size pieces. Enough for three breakfasts slammed into me like stones. I grabbed my sword and spun toward Whistler just as he landed a ferocious cut on the last pig. When it exploded, he staggered but didn't fall. He leaned on his sword and panted as if he'd just climbed a mountain.

Halla pointed at Whistler. "Manservant! This fight has not ended. Go find every pig still whole and struggling. Make sure they are all dead. I mean, more dead."

Whistler grunted and trotted back toward the field of twice-slaughtered swine.

I ran toward Pil. She lay on her back, arms splayed, legs up so that her knees were almost in her face, and both boots knocked off. Bea and I lowered her legs in a slow, smooth arc. Her chest was shattered, and so was the lower half of her face. Both arms appeared broken, and maybe one leg as well. She drew tiny, ragged breaths, but that couldn't go on much longer. She was probably too far gone to save.

"Hurry, we must find a true oracle." Halla said it as if I were kneeling over no more than a fallen bird.

"They're probably never was a damn oracle." I didn't glance away from Pil as I said it.

"Perhaps someone here knows. We should find some people and question them."

I prepared myself to rage and yell at her, to throw some rocks at her or maybe a boot. But that all drained away. There seemed no point in being angry.

A shadow slid over Pil's face, cast by the thin, young man who had been charging people to look at his lions. He rubbed his hands together. "Excuse me. I need to talk to you."

"Shut the hell up." I touched what was left of Pil's rib cage as gently as possible.

The lion barker said, "I do beg your pardon. I didn't think all this would happen today. So, I need to talk to you."

I growled, "Be quiet, or go to perdition, you drooling ass-dragger!" Right in that very moment, I decided to save Pil, just to spite whichever god had burdened me with this annoying pissant.

The fellow stepped back. "I can tell you about your enemy."

Halla slammed the butt of her spear against the ground. "You are the oracle?"

The young man said, "That's a bit grandiose. At least it sounds that way to me."

I sneered without looking up from Pil. "Well, oracle, are you any good? Or are you as full of shit as that last oracle?" I touched the dying girl's splintered jaw. "How many oracles do you have around here, anyway? Oh, hell, you can just wait right there until I'm done."

"Hold on a moment," the oracle said in a stiff voice. "I don't care for abasement and animal sacrifice and all that, although a little gift is nice. But you are pushing the bounds of politeness. I needn't share my wisdom with you unless I care to. If you act rudely, I may just tell you to go away."

Halla gritted her teeth. "Bib . . ."

I glared at her. "I'm busy here!"

"We're very sorry, oracle. Please forgive us." I heard the smile in Halla's voice and glanced up to see the uncomfortable thing sitting on her face. I also saw the carnage behind her. Corpses pocked the ground like bloody mushrooms. The wounded staggered and fell. The grieving knelt beside the dead and wept. One of the tents was ablaze, and black, fatty smoke rose from it.

I turned my attention back to Pil. Behind me Halla cleared her throat. "Well . . . oracle, would you like a beverage while you wait?"

I heard the oracle say yes, but I never learned what Halla brought him. I knelt over Pil, pulling green bands and sheets out of nothingness and using them to rebuild her chest. Every time I took a pain away from her, it appeared inside me, although not as great. Sorcerers have long argued about why healing produces pain for the healer. Some have fought and even killed each other over the question, which says more about the folly of man than could any thousand sermons. Myself, I believe the gods made things work that way to discourage us from being nice to one another.

When I had saved Pil from the risk of expiring with her next breath, I restored the structure of her chest. I gave her body the right push toward recovery and the power to recover once pushed. A band of invisible knives slowly cinched around my ribs. I could hardly draw a breath without my eyes rolling up.

Then I wheezed and sweated as I addressed Pil's smashed face. I found the work tricky anyway because of her peculiar beauty. I wanted to restore it for her. Not many of us are given something truly remarkable, and losing this would be a damned shame for her.

I believe I did a near-perfect job. My face felt like it had been stomped, hit with hammers, and then pulled apart with white-hot pliers. I finished by repairing Pil's arms and leg, which required the least delicate touch. It added some nice throbbing limbs to my final mix of pains. I would have enjoyed passing out, but that didn't happen. The pain would fade within a few hours, or at most a day, so I hissed a lot and eased myself into a period of lying in the dirt, trying not to move or breathe.

The oracle would just have to wait on me. I hoped that Halla had plenty of whatever he liked to drink.

SEVEN

I once adored soothsayers, oracles, and even scabby village healers if they had a bit of the Sight. Whenever a drunkard or whore told me about some pure, transcendent seer, I would search her out, ready to make detours that would infuriate my companions. But contrary to common wisdom, future-tellers never lived up on mountains or out in swamps. They lived within walking distance of people who wanted their futures read.

That should have warned me that being an oracle was less of a mystical calling and more of a mercantile operation.

Whenever I dragged my comrades in search of a seer, I would describe how knowledge of the future would be an important tactical advantage. That was crap, of course. I just wanted the soothsayers to tell me where to go and who'd be waiting for me when I got there. Or where *not* to go and who could eat dirt because they missed the chance to do me harm. The predictions mostly came true, if I looked at things the right way and ignored a few details.

One cherry blossom–fluttering day on which nothing bad could possibly happen, a tiny old fortune-telling woman promised me, with unimpeachable certainty, that the road east was clear and safe. I traveled down that road, where about fifty ruffians caught me and tortured me for quite a few hours before I managed to slip away.

I ran back to the village bare as a baby pig, begged a sheet to wrap around my nakedness, and charged into the old woman's house to strangle her. I found her already dead on her kitchen floor, killed by some malady that left a carpet of sores on her face.

Knowing that the gods didn't care about me, or her, or those torturing sons of bitches, I praised her death as a random occurrence. Then I swore off oracles and resolved to travel into the future like everybody else, full of apprehension and unjustified optimism.

At the fairgrounds, most of the pain from healing Pil had eased by midafternoon. I sat up and found the girl holding my hand. "Don't think anything special about my helping you, young woman. I would have done the same for a kitten or a moneylender."

Pil stared at me blank-faced, held my right hand tight, and didn't speak.

I realized that my left thumb was tingling. When I wiggled the digit, it went numb. But I had just been through a hard fight and an even harder healing, so I put it out of my mind as a random hurt.

Halla leaned over Pil and me. "You are being a foolish girl." She dragged at Pil's arm, but she hung on. Halla used both hands to pull the girl off like a tick.

Pil flailed, hissed, and threw herself toward me. She pitched such a silent fit that we at last let her hold on to my arm. It was a discouraging development, magical for sure, but not the problem biting us hardest just then.

Finally, Halla, Pil, and I walked up to the oracle's dingy tent flap. I had thought the tent was a pretty pale green, but the canvas was just thin and faded from a decade or two in the sun. Whistler was off wandering around the fairgrounds, scavenging the corpses, while Bea watched and looked disgusted.

Halla leaned toward the tent flap and called out, "We are ready."

No sound came from inside the tent.

Halla said louder, "We are ready now!"

When nobody answered, Halla closed her eyes and nodded. "Thank you for waiting for us, oracle. Many people may die, and Bib has delayed us foolishly. I know that a wise person like you would not risk even more deaths than does foolish Bib. Please help us. We are ready."

I said, "Hell, you could've said that the first time."

Halla stared at the closed tent flap. "I did. I thought that everything before 'We are ready' was obvious."

"Enter!" came the oracle's voice from inside.

We pushed into the dim tent, lit by three lanterns. It was the size of a small farmyard, and I could have walked across it in ten steps. The air smelled cool, musty, and dry. The oracle's elderly lions lay across the tent from us, staked out, lazy, and no more interested in us than they would be in four grasshoppers. Each was the size of a large hound.

The oracle stood with his back to us, raking hay and probably lion scat from in between the beasts. "Find a place to sit. I hate to let this build up. By the way, your entreaty was remarkable. Obsequious and uncaring at the same time."

The tent held no obvious chairs, benches, or stools. Some boxes and large sacks had been dumped in one corner, so Halla and I each seated ourselves on a box. Pil knelt beside me, crushing my arm as if it were the only thing keeping her from floating off into the sky.

The oracle joined us within a minute, plopping down on a big sack full of something soft.

I glanced at Halla and then back at the young man. "Do you need us to do something? Say anything? Pay you anything?"

"Nah," he said.

He picked a small canvas bag off the ground, dug inside it, and pulled out four semi-withered winter apples. He tossed one to each of us. Pil didn't try to catch hers. It bounced off her collarbone, and she watched it roll away.

The young man shook his head. "I'm sorry, that was careless." He fetched the apple, brushed it off, and set it on the ground in front of her before patting it twice as if it were a little dog. He passed us each a wooden cup, pulled out a bottle of wine, and dropped the empty sack at his feet. He must have had a good idea of exactly how many apples and cups he'd need.

"I wish we could drink from glass, but the road is jouncy. Jerky and bouncy." The oracle smiled as he poured, bit into his apple, and gazed back and forth between Halla and me.

Halla examined her apple. "Is this part of the ritual?"

"No. It's part of dinner." The oracle took another bite and kept talking around the mouthful. "I'm hungry. You are too. I don't need prescient powers to know that. Bib, you've been lying on the ground like a forgotten turd for eight hours."

The wine was mouth-puckeringly sour. I didn't offer to feed Pil or hold her cup. If she wanted a drink, she could let me go with at least one of her own hands. Halla drank the wine as if it were water.

The oracle wiped his lips with a plain, dingy handkerchief he had pulled from his sleeve. "Now then, I can't see your enemy in detail, or tell you his greatest weakness, or anything along those lines. That's not how this works, just to be clear. I don't want any complaints later."

I glanced at Halla. "All right."

"First of all, he lives on a mountain. That never bodes well, you know. It's not good for you, I mean. He possesses vast physical power."

"How vast?" Halla asked in a calm voice.

"Well, that's hard to say, isn't it? We'd need some frame of reference. A mountain is vast, but is it vast compared to an ocean?"

I put as much false politeness in my voice as I could—which I guess probably wouldn't fool a real oracle. "This could be the very knowledge we need to prevail, sir. We'd be obliged."

The young man frowned so hard he almost pouted.

Halla said, "Compare his power to ours."

"Oh!" The oracle grinned. "He could kill you both at the same time. Easily. One hand for each of you. You know . . . you're not fated to meet this fellow. You can still choose. I'd consider forgetting about him and doing something else this spring."

"We have no choice." I held up a clenched fist. "We heard that he called Halla's mother a rancid bitch. What else can you tell us?"

"He's awfully unhappy. That may not be germane, but you never know." The oracle closed his eyes and scratched his ear. "Let's see . . ."

Halla leaned forward. "Where is he?"

A familiar voice joined us from the center of the tent. "Oh, this is such a sad, whimpering sight," he said. "I ought to devour you right now and save time."

I stood and saw one of the lions stretching and tugging at its tether. The oracle tried to jump up and turn around at the same time, and he fell into Halla's lap. She rolled him onto the ground like he was a melon.

The lion yawned, showing yellow fangs the length of my finger. "You seem awfully pathetic, though, too pathetic to eat. If I see you in this state for much longer, I might be ill. Run around and look industrious for a few minutes." The lion shrugged to pull at the tether, and its stake popped out of the ground.

I strode toward the lion, but Pil clung to me, as solid as a box of horseshoes. I ended up striding only one step, and I appeared less bold than I might have. "Hello, Floppy-Ass. I like you better as a dog. To be honest, you seem a little effeminate as a cat."

The lion's ears flicked forward. "Floppy-Ass? It doesn't exactly bewitch me."

Halla had shifted to one side, her spear relaxed in her hands. The oracle was on his feet and had crammed himself as far as possible into the corner, goggling at the lion.

Floppy-Ass bounded onto a box four feet in front of me and sat on his haunches. "Did you adore breakfast?"

Halla said, "Bib's wife could cook better. With a stick and a bowl of dirt."

"I labored over that breakfast! The Symphony of Irredeemable Beasts! I toiled, although I'm sure you didn't deserve it."

I tugged at Pil again, but she hung onto my sword arm.

Floppy-Ass rumbled a growl that would force any human being's sphincters to slam shut. Then he lifted his head, squeezed his eyes tight, and scrunched up his nose. A sneeze shot out of him, echoing off the tent walls and spraying me with lion snot. Another sneeze followed, and a third right after that. The lion shook its head, glanced left and right, and wandered back toward its spot across the tent.

The oracle was panting. "I didn't foresee that." He strolled around the boxes and bags toward the center of the tent.

Halla raised a hand. "Do not be concerned, oracle. The creature could have already killed you if it wanted to."

I added, "We'd be wading in your entrails."

The oracle hit the tent flap at a run and burst outside.

Halla scowled at me and sprinted after the young man.

I dragged at Pil with both hands until I got her half scrambling alongside me. When we pushed outside, I saw that the oracle had run only twenty paces before Halla caught him. She held him up by the back of the collar and the left arm. I dragged Pil ten steps before she seized my leg with both arms and hauled me to one knee.

The other lion ran out of the tent. "I chose to change bodies! That other lion was uncomfortable. She probably had a plague or a blight. I wouldn't be surprised if you all drop dead!"

I glanced around to see whether things could get any crazier. My gaze locked onto Whistler and Bea. They stood together motionless, gaping at the chaos.

Halla eased the oracle down but held on.

Floppy-Ass harrumphed. "If I were you, which is a repellent thought, I would devote my energy to being as interesting as possible. Yes, I would pursue that with greatest industry if I wanted to enjoy even—" Floppy-Ass sneezed twice. The second sneeze made my ears ring. Then the lion collapsed onto the ground, grunted, clambered back to its feet, and waddled away, head low.

I pulled Pil and myself to our feet and glared at the oracle. "Do you have any more lions in there? Or venomous serpents?"

The oracle gazed at the tent flap blankly and shook his head. "No. I was going to buy a horse. To feed the lions."

A man's voice from behind me said, "You'd be fortunate to be slain by a viper! You should pray for it, really."

Everybody turned around. At least eighty corpses had stood up and were trudging toward us without a bobble. A few heads had been smashed, probably by those horrible pigs. Two corpses dragged their guts behind them.

The closest corpse stared right at me. "I hate lions, anyway! Did you know that? My famous hatred of lions dates back—"

Two dozen corpses behind him collapsed like empty sacks.

The blabbering corpse looked around. "Krak damn it with piles and iron rods! You should not take any of this as a sign of weakness!"

Several dozen more corpses flopped down.

"Well, shit." The rest of the bodies, including the cursing one, crumpled.

Halla scanned the open ground and the twice-killed corpses. "Perhaps if we wait here, our enemy will destroy himself and we can go home. Or at least go away from here."

"Son of a bitch!" Whistler shouted, rubbing his neck.

Bea squeaked, "Ow! Ow!"

A big red wasp landed on me and stung me on the right nipple. "Weasel-humping, greasy-ass crotch of Lutigan on fire!"

"Back in the tent!" Halla was already running when she said it, hauling the oracle behind. Beyond her I saw a little cloud of black dots flying toward us, and in five seconds, it grew twice as big.

I began pulling white bands with one hand as another wasp stung me on the elbow. I thought I might convince these bugs that stinging us to death would be less fun than doing any other thing at all. Before I did much in the way of magic, though, every single hornet dropped out of the air. The ones that hit the ground near me walked around wobbly.

I didn't know whether to stand my ground, run inside the tent, or find a fast horse. I let the white bands fall away, the power lost. I drew my sword for no good reason except that I couldn't think of anything else to do. "Halla, come on out here. Maybe some wagon will roll toward us, set itself afire, and burn up before it runs us over."

The oracle strained against Halla, which was like trying to pull his arm out of a shark's mouth. "You may as well release me!" the oracle shouted. Halla lifted the young man partway off the ground as he yelled, "I won't tell you anything now!"

"Come on," I said. "After all this shit, you just have to help us."

Halla said, "There must be a code or obligation that binds you."

The oracle tried to tug away from Halla again. "There is not. Nothing like that."

Halla nodded. "Does fear of death bind you, then?"

The oracle sagged. "Fine, I'll help you. I can see there are extraordinarily bad things happening. I want only one thing. After I've enlightened you, go away and never look for me again. In fact, if you see me someday buying kumquats in the marketplace, pretend we've never met."

A minute later, Halla and I sat inside the oracle's tent again. He sat with his jaw clenched and his eyes closed for a minute. "For one thing, your enemy is protected by divine magic."

I considered that for a few seconds. "If he's a god, then he's a sorry specimen. He can't even keep control of bugs."

"Are you interested in my vision or not? I have a lion to recapture."

Halla whacked my shoulder. "Yes, we are interested. Ignore him—he is stupid."

"Your enemy isn't a god, but he has access to divine magic. Just like you. And that's what he wants." The oracle pointed at me.

I touched the pouch inside my shirt, which contained a little magic book created by Harik, the God of Death. "Do you mean he wants this? This book?"

"I don't see anything about a book. He wants to kill you, Bib. He wants it very badly."

"Hell, what did I do?"

"The signs are unclear. Many people just want to kill you, though."

I gaped. "That's in the signs?"

"No, I can tell because I've spoken to you for fifteen minutes. Your enemy is to the north."

I gazed at the tent's northern side. I couldn't help it. "North?"

"Sure, north. Farther than a mile. If you see ice, you've gone too far."

"Nothing else?" Halla said.

"Nothing else. Now go away."

EIGHT

When sorcerers bring a person back from the lip of death, they sometimes create a peculiar connection. Scholarly sorcerers have created a complex magical construct to explain this. They have given the phenomenon a pretentious name and written a couple of books about it. One of them is illustrated. I've never given a shit about any of that, because it neither prevented nor resolved the main problem.

When linked by this connection, the revived person becomes terrified that he will drop dead unless the sorcerer is touching him. It rarely occurs, and when it does, it usually fades within a day or two. I have experienced it a few times from the sorcerer's side, and it never lasted more than two days. In one case, by the second day, the recently healed did not even need to touch me as long as I remained within six inches of him.

That illustrated book does document vanishingly rare cases of connections lasting longer than a few days. Strictly speaking, nobody had ever seen a permanent connection. Sorcerers have recorded a few connections that lasted, undiminished, until one of the parties died, but those could not technically be called permanent.

Once the oracle had dismissed us, Pil had not released me for even an instant. She preferred to hold my hand, but I could eventually convince her to hold on to my arm instead. Occasionally, she clamped my hand in both of hers, and to hell with what I wanted. She wouldn't speak to anybody but me. She wouldn't even say much to me and wouldn't look me in the face. I had never experienced that behavior before, and it worried me.

Our connection would produce some interesting logistical consequences. Pil would be riding on my horse with me for a while, no doubt. Her home and family might be waiting just over a gentle rise, but if I went the other way, she would go the other way too.

When the oracle dismissed us, the sunset had faded to a few yellow strips of sky. None of us could stomach the idea of eating any food from the fairgrounds. Bea had snared two rabbits, and we ate them with some of our bread, which hadn't gone too stale yet. Halla dug a piece of gristle out of her teeth with a thumbnail. "We cannot just ride north. It is foolish."

"Hell, you're the one who put so much faith in the oracle," I said. "Are you changing your mind just because I agreed with you about listening to the lad? Dammit, you're aggravating!"

"I am not changing my mind! I have not decided anything, so I can't change my mind. Can I?" She threw a stick into the fire so hard it bounced out the other side.

"So, where do you want to go, you great monument to no fun?" I leaned toward Halla, and Pil pulled my hand back toward her.

"We will go to the Fat Shallows and scout. Bad people from everywhere can be found at the Fat Shallows. They know things."

I sneered. "The Fat Shallows? It's a shit pot with a couple of boats in it. I guess you want to catch mackerel, because that's all it's good for."

"We cannot just get on our horses and ride north. It's foolish."

"Yes, we can! Watch me!" I laughed at her. "Whistler and Bea are coming with me. Pil is sure as hell coming with me. Take that, you oaf!"

"Oaf? Have you used up all your words?" Halla stood up. The poor light caused her head to fade into darkness, which made her seem about twelve feet tall.

"The oracle said north!" I yelled. "The oracle did not say go to the lousy Fat Shallows! And sit down. Looking up at you makes my neck hurt." I chuckled, since I was kind of enjoying the argument.

Pil leaned close to me and whispered, "Isn't Fat Shallows due north from here?"

I grinned and whispered back, "Oh, hell, I guess it is."

"I heard that. Good!" Halla grunted. I had forgotten what fine hearing she possessed. She sat down with her back to me. "I am glad everyone agrees with me."

She might have been smiling, at least a little. I hoped so. We'd had plenty of horrors that day. I got up and walked forty paces away from the fire, Pil squeezing my hand hard. I waited two minutes for my night vision to return.

"Pil, you're just fine, you're safe, and you don't need to worry. You can let go of me anytime you want to." I didn't say that she'd better want to pretty flipping soon.

The girl glanced at me and then stared back down. Of course, darkness hid her face, but she hunched against my side with her back to the rest of the world, as if she thought the trees or the air might tear her apart.

I patted her hand and began walking circles around the camp, watching for anything that might mean us ill.

At the end of my third circle, my stomach flopped over and something hauled my spirit upward out of my body. For a moment, I felt it would be a relief to vomit. Then every sensation of sight, touch, and smell vanished. Some god had brought me to his home to bargain, or at least to pile abuse on me, and I knew with near-perfect certainty which one it was.

A smooth, precise voice cut through the nothingness. "Murderer, you are not allowed to have any more children. We agreed upon it, agreed with crystalline specificity." Harik, God of Death, always reminded me of a banker looking at your last coin.

"Mighty Harik, I have no children anymore. I understand that to you it may seem like I do, maybe because you lack kids of your own. That swamp of emasculation between your legs must be a bother at times."

I imagined drawing my sword. It had been forged by some slope-brow, floppy god at some point in history, or by some god's ass-kissing lackey, and they had bestowed upon it a name so trite that I could hardly bear to say it without banging my fist against something—The Blade of Obdurate Mercy. As a weapon, it was exactly as magical as a butter churn in the world of man. In the Gods' Realm, it allowed me to see as the gods see.

My sword's point swept through the air, wiping away the nothingness like cobwebs. My breath caught. A double rainbow circled a full, chalk-white moon trapped in a star-pricked sky. Moonlight drifted down and struck tiny sparks wherever it touched something sharp or angled. A massive field of fat, silver flowers flowed downslope into the distance, their faces turned down. The blooms fluttered in waves, as if creatures were running around beneath them, close to the ground. On the other side of me, a light, open forest of straight trees swayed. They weren't swaying with the wind. Instead, they moved in and out as if the entire forest was breathing.

I fought off the urge to lie on the dirt and curl up asleep. Instead, I stood straighter and glanced at the shadowed, marble gazebo above me. Harik was sitting in there someplace, whether I could see him or not.

Something made a sound to my left, and I spun that way. It was a foolish thing to do, since I couldn't harm or affect anything in this realm. The thing sighed, and I saw Pil standing there, staring around at nothing, since she had no sight in the Gods' Realm. A sorcerer herself, she must have clung to me and come along when Harik seized me. It wouldn't have been hard for a sorcerer to do, even a disturbed one.

"Pil, stay calm." I would have told her to take a deep breath, but she couldn't perceive that she was breathing. "I'm taking us back right now."

"Don't." She looked up and then down, wide-eyed. "How did you know I was here? I didn't say anything."

A chuckle came out of the darkened gazebo. "She is already questioning you with vigor, Murderer, but she cannot conceal her fear of being without you. Tell me again that you don't have a child."

I pointed my sword at the spot where the god's voice seemed to be coming from. "She is not my daughter, you celestial dimwit!"

"Perhaps not. If she survives to the end of the week, I will be convinced. Murderer, you dispose of daughters as if they were empty wine cups."

Pil spoke up before I said something really appalling. "I am not his daughter!" she said to a tree directly away from the gazebo. "Bib, is that really the God of Death? I've never heard him speak before. What does he like? Weapons?" Pil focused on the treetop. "What do you like, Mighty Harik? Sacrifices? Jokes? Things that are just dead?"

I waved at the gazebo. "Harik, we'll be going now and let you get back to whatever unnatural shit you were engaged in."

"No!" Pil shouted.

"Listen to her, Murderer. You may not go until I give you leave, you oily spot of arrogance. You must be chastised." Harik leaned forward into the moonlight, showing his face, a stretch of his void-black robe, and one arm swathed in muscles. His face was beautiful in a particular way, as if unimaginative teenagers had designed the most gorgeous face they could think of.

"All right, Harik, call me a son of a bitch or whatever else you need to say."

"Bib!" Pil yelled, jerking around and trying to face things her nonexistent vision couldn't see. "Be nice! Don't make him destroy you!" Her voice edged into panic as she gaped back at the tree. "Mighty Harik, destroy me instead! Well, no, don't, but if you really must destroy somebody, don't destroy Bib. I mean, it would be much better if you destroyed somebody else altogether, but if it's one of us, then make it me."

Harik leaned farther forward into the light, his eyebrows furrowed. "What?"

I said, "Pil, didn't Dixon teach you anything? The gods don't kill sorcerers. They fool sorcerers into getting themselves killed. Harik, send her back before she agrees to something fatal."

It might seem that standing before a god and saying "Destroy me!" as Pil had just done would constitute agreement that you should be destroyed, but that's not so. Telling a god to destroy you isn't a trade by itself, no more so than telling a god to give you a golden ship with magical singing dolphins to accompany you wherever you sail. Something meaningful must be offered and agreed to on both sides, otherwise no deal has been made.

That was the rule. The gods had been known to break the rule if it seemed like fun, however.

Harik examined Pil and then glanced back at me. "I don't think I will send the Knife back yet. This is too entertaining."

My eyes widened. "What did you call her?"

"The Knife." Harik snickered. "Ponder that for a while."

I hung my head. "All right. Pil, please hush. I promise that if something deadly comes along, I will throw you in front of it and save myself."

Pil's voice quavered. "That's . . . I know I'm acting crazy, but I can't stop."

"It'll all be fine, don't worry. You'll be mashing my hand off again in just a minute. Harik, go ahead and tell me what a bad fellow I've been, you nipple-scraping nugget of filth."

Harik frowned. My insult might have made him a little bit angry, but he said, "Besides our agreement that you shall have no more children . . ." He glanced at Pil and raised his eyebrows. "You have also promised to take my book to the northern kingdoms. You have not done so, nor have you shown an inclination to do so."

"Where in the northern kingdoms, Mighty Harik?"

"That has not yet been revealed to you."

I shrugged. "So, I can just sail up to the northern kingdoms, pitch the book onto whatever beach I land on, and sail away?"

Harik lowered his eyelids. "No. You may not. You shall deliver my book into the hands of the person I select. You shall exercise care, as if it were made of crystal."

"Oh, hell. I've been carting it around in a saddlebag with the bacon and a spare bridle."

Harik leaned back and disappeared into the gazebo's dimness.

"You may dispense with your limp attempts at humor. You carry the book right there near your heart."

"I don't intend to ride around in circles all over the northern kingdoms until you direct me to a particular man or woman. Or barnyard animal. Once you do direct me, I will proceed with the greatest diligence to get shut of this horrible book. As a mark of my pure intentions, I will ride north in the morning, just on faith."

Harik chuckled. "You intend to ride north in any case. You seek to kill Memweck."

I tried not to pause at that news. I smiled instead. "Yes, we intend to kill the holy hell out of Memweck. Then we'll have a party and maybe a holiday at the beach. I hope Memweck isn't a friend of yours."

"He is not."

I walked a couple of steps toward the gazebo. "Well, then, would you like to say nasty things about him? Gossip a little?"

"I would not. Go to the northern kingdoms and put Memweck out of your thoughts."

I laid my sword over my shoulder. "I might do that, except he stole a bunch of babies and children."

Harik moved into sight again and stepped down one step. If we had reached toward each other, we could have touched hands. "Murderer, allow Memweck to take whatever he wants. Just deliver my book and ride away."

"So, Memweck's in the northern kingdoms too! Like the book!"

Harik paused. "No, he's not."

"Where is he, then?" I had only been needling Harik about Memweck's possible location, but Harik sounded guilty when he denied it.

"You have no reason to know that!" Harik's upper lip curled in a scowl.

I opened my mouth, but he cut me off. "Although I despise you in almost every possible way, you cannot doubt that I value your continued existence, the murders you commit, and the trades you have left in you. Listen when I tell you to leave Memweck alone."

I hurried to make sense of that. I had never heard of Memweck, so he wasn't a god. He wasn't a sorcerer. Harik wouldn't look all dire and solemn about some shitty sorcerer. He could be a powerful spirit, like an ocean spirit, or maybe a mountain spirit.

Or, less likely but more terrifying, Memweck might be some type of void-walker, solitary and unpredictable beings that moved between worlds whenever they wanted. They could look like just about anything: a bear, a chubby old lady, or a sack of apples, with almost any powers imaginable. The chance of this was tiny, but one might have decided to drop out of the Void into the world of man for a brief rest of three or four centuries.

I smiled at Harik again. "I understand, you dripping toad. Well, if I'm to arrive at the northern kingdoms in good book-delivering condition, I might need some more power. I think I have plenty, mind you, but it might be wise not to be caught short. Mighty Harik, may I prevail upon you to make me an offer?"

"I offer you nothing, Murderer. I know that you will use any power I grant you to seek out Memweck. You will be crushed flat and then pulled into shreds. Then he will burn the shreds, or merely cook them and feed them to wild beasts. Much depends upon how bored Memweck is when you find him."

"That's a shame, because an oracle says that Memweck wants to find me and kill me. And not just any sorcerer will do for him. Floppy-Ass Memweck wants me and no other."

Harik sat quietly in the dimness of the gazebo for a full fifteen seconds. He might have been thinking, or making faces at me, or biting his divine fingernails, I don't know. At last, he said, "Well, that's something to think about. Goodbye, Murderer."

Harik hurled Pil and me back into our bodies. We collapsed onto the vigorous young grass. She never let go of my hand. Nothing else had moved, since no time passes in the world of man when one is in the Gods' Realm.

We sat up. I could make out the outline of Pil's face turned toward me. She whispered, "That was nothing like visiting the gods with Dixon. Nothing at all. You were so mean to Harik. I wonder what Fingit would say if I called him a runny toadstool?"

I held my hand in front of her face. "Ease up, woman." I tried to flex the fingers of my left hand, the one that was dripping blood as she dug in her nails. The forefinger had gone numb, joining the thumb.

Pil stopped with her mouth open and relaxed her two-handed grip.

"That's good. Less crushing, more letting go. More talking too."

Pil let out a long breath. "Why Floppy-Ass?" she whispered.

"Oh, his full name is Lord Floppy-Ass, Bane of Bindle Town."

Her voice brightened. "That's brilliant! There are some awful numbers buried in there."

"Why the Knife?" I asked.

Pil didn't answer right away. "I don't know. Not at all. I like knives, but I don't think that's it." She leaned back and let one of her hands drop.

We stood, and I pushed her other hand up on to my forearm. She didn't fight it. "That's phenomenal. Wonderful. By tomorrow night, you won't be touching me at all. You might not even care if I exist."

NINE

After Pil and I completed guard duty, I slept just a few hours, so the next morning came hard for me. I yawned all through examining Whistler and Bea for hidden sorcerous talent. It seemed unlikely, but in the past three days, sorcerers had been falling out of the damn sky. First Halla had arrived to conscript me for her rescue attempt. Then Dixon and Pil happened to be swindling people at the fair when I showed up. Coincidence was statistically possible of course, but less likely than divine intervention or some drunk sorcerers playing a practical joke.

Neither Bea nor Whistler proved to be sorcerers, so it was time to send Bea home. Whistler could come along and die saving Halla's life if he chose. Whistler saddled Bea's mule while she watched, not speaking. She didn't even give me any mean looks.

I waved a hand toward the mule, and Bea mounted. "Go on home, Bea. People will think you've gone off to foreign places where they drove you crazy. They'll never again drink from a cup you've touched."

She stared at me. "No. You go on, and I'll follow. Go on."

I raised my voice. "You won't be any help, and hell, you'll probably be killed!"

Bea leaned forward in the saddle. "Maybe, but I know you for a liar. You won't save my boy unless I kick you in the butt all the way there."

I patted the mule's neck. "Bea, I'll save your boy if I can. But he may already be dead."

Bea swallowed hard. "He probably is, you ass."

I hadn't expected her to say that. I had expected her to cry or yell at me—something to make it easier to shoo her on home.

She pushed her near-black hair out of her face and went on: "I'm going. You probably can't save him even if he is alive. I know it. I just can't do anything else but go. If you steal my mule, I'll walk, and I'll damn you every step."

I considered Bea's problem from a different perspective—mine. Hell, if I were Bea, I'd go anywhere, kill anybody, and be happy to risk dying. I felt a bit ashamed for assuming she'd do it differently. I frowned at her and then spit on the grass to cover up how ashamed I felt. "Shit, woman! I wish you'd said something besides that. Well . . . come on and die, then. It's not up to me to keep you from it." I turned to Halla before she could bitch at me about it. "Don't you say a damn word! We'll go save her boy. We'll save your boys too. Hell, we'll save all the goddamn boys while we're at it!" I spit at the ground again, just in case I had missed the first time, and I took Pil with me to saddle my horse.

It would not have shocked me if Halla engaged in some stiff, sarcastic criticism about Bea. Instead, she stared at the young woman for several seconds, then walked to the mule and handed Bea a long knife from her belt. Bea grabbed the knife like it was a snake that might get away, but she didn't speak. Halla walked back and mounted without comment.

I convinced Pil to hold on to my shoulders as we traveled, and on the sunny, brisk ride north, she clamped on like an owl grabs a field mouse. The trail soon curved through short, treeless hills smelling of new grass. Occasional shallow streams rushed along the valleys, and we rode our horses splashing down them.

The border between the Empire and the Kingdom of Lakes lay someplace in those hills, but nobody much cared where. The

Kingdom was really just another province of the Empire, and its king had no more volition than a rosebush.

Two hard days traveling north from the crossroads fair would bring us to Fat Shallows, which squatted on the coast by the wetlands. Halla wanted to ride there because we didn't know some things, and maybe somebody there would. That was her peerless logic. I did not in any way want to go to Fat Shallows, since its only purpose was to smuggle things back and forth to the northern kingdoms. I preferred to continue aggravating Harik by not going there to deliver his book.

Yet Harik had bumbled into implying that Memweck lived someplace in the northern kingdoms. My long experience with the God of Death told me that the condescending ass-wart had let that slip by accident and not as a ploy to herd me north. Gods could be as foolish, careless, and greedy as any human. It was the only reason any sorcerers survived more than a few weeks.

But I couldn't bear to admit to Halla that she was right, at least not without a struggle.

For half a day, I argued with her about our destination, claiming we should turn east toward the Empire. Our arguing resembled me screaming abuse at a big tree stump that only knew how to be sarcastic and say no. After two hours of this, Whistler joined us and offered to break the tie. He retreated when I threw a water sack at him and Halla threatened to drag him behind her horse all the way to the ocean.

Two minutes later, Whistler caught up and handed me the water sack. He sucked the inside of his cheek and squinted at me. "Bib, I don't want to be insulting, but throwing that sack was stupid. Or, maybe I do want to be insulting. My point is I don't remember your being so reckless back in town. I don't care whether you apologize or spit on my shoe. Just don't throw shit at the wrong person and get us all killed."

Everything the man said was true, so I nodded. "Whistler, I apologize for treating you so harshly." I said it with as much sincerity as I possessed. "You can't help being a greedy piece of shit, no more than I can help being a murdering asshole. It wasn't right of me."

Whistler sniffed. "Spit on my damn shoe next time." He nodded at Pil. "Beg pardon, but what the hell's wrong with her?"

"She's stunned from being exposed to my shattering wisdom. If she lets go of me, the mysteries of existence may drive her mad."

"That sounds awkward."

I shrugged. "She should be done in a day or two. There are a lot fewer mysteries than most people think."

"Huh. Don't let her stab you in the back. We don't know a thing about her."

I glanced over my shoulder. "Pil, what were you doing with that bastard, Dixon?"

Pil spoke out strongly: "That bastard Dixon was training me. And teaching me crime."

I hadn't expected an answer, and certainly not such a bold one. "What was that dog training you to do?"

Like she was stating an interesting fact, Pil said, "That dog was teaching me to be a Binder."

Binders used sorcery to create or enchant all sorts of objects, anything from a loop of twine to a ship's rudder.

"Where do you come from, Pil? Where'd Dixon find you?" I asked.

"Dixon found me in the cellar."

Whistler asked, "What cellar?"

Pil turned her face away from him and didn't answer.

I opened my mouth to ask Pil about the cellar, but I realized she was crying against my back. I didn't know everything about our near-death connection, but I supposed it could be making her answer questions she preferred not to answer. If so, that created a rare opportunity. I could find out every helpful thing Pil knew and be sure she wasn't lying.

Of course, Pil would never trust me again. She might even try to kill me. But hell, she probably didn't trust me now, and she was right not to.

In the end, I decided that the girl might know something that would save me from discomfort or indignation but probably not death. "Pil, I didn't mean to upset you with all these questions. Just ignore me or tell me to go to hell if I ask any more for a while."

Pil yelled, "Dixon was not a bastard!" and stopped talking.

Later in the morning, we halted under two budding trees to rest the horses. Pil's hand came off my shoulder and stayed off when we reached the ground. However, she did keep her body within three inches of mine, which overall proved more awkward than holding hands.

Pil whispered to me, "Why did I answer all your stupid questions? And cry?" She gritted her teeth. "Did you do something to me?"

"Not on purpose," I whispered back. "Wait. In a day or two, you'll be lying to me about everything."

Once we had ridden on, Whistler edged over to pace Bea, who was trailing me. I heard him clear his throat twice. "I can help you sharpen that knife," he said.

"I think it's sharp enough as it is," Bea said. I glanced back to see her staring straight ahead.

Whistler's shoulders slumped a little, but then he smiled, showing his brown, crooked teeth. "A knife can never be too sharp."

Bea didn't answer. She guided her mule away from Whistler and rode up beside me.

I glanced back again and saw Whistler's face drooping. He stared upward as if he were figuring numbers in his head. Then he caught up to Bea and smiled. "You'll need a sharp knife when we get your boy."

"For what?"

Whistler's jaw opened and hung there for a second. "Cutting ropes. Jamming it in some nasty fellow's liver. Lots of things."

Bea stared at Whistler the way she'd stare at a dog humping her leg. Then she kicked her mule to join Halla farther forward.

"We could talk about beer!" Whistler called after her. "You probably know a lot about beer."

Bea didn't show that she heard him.

Whistler sighed, his cheeks sagging. "What did I say wrong, Bib? She liked me fine yesterday."

"I can say only one thing, young man. Go talk to a fence rail about romance, because you'll get better advice than I can provide."

After midday, Halla and I continued our earnest discussion about strategy, and I enjoyed it. The highlight was my calling her a puckered sore of a woman. After that, we rode on north and ignored one another.

Late in the day, Pil, still riding behind me, jerked upright. She began talking about the weather, cloaks, the fat man in Pasra who sold pretty clothes, how nice it would be to take a bath, and just about every trivial thing she had seen and done in the past few months. I didn't ever answer her, and she didn't seem to care. After an hour, she shut up in the middle of a sentence.

Pil's voice shook as she said, "I don't know why I said any of that. Am I going crazy?"

"Nope. Whistler there is twice as crazy as you. Compared to you, Halla is a screaming maniac."

I explained to her my theory that our connection was causing both her undesired honesty and her flood of drivel. I thought the explanation might comfort her, but she blamed me for the whole situation and didn't stop shivering for quite a while.

We halted half an hour before sunset. Our evening consisted of the same arguments Halla and I had engaged in during the day, but with more fatigue and less patience.

The next morning, Pil tried to mount her own horse, panicked, and was thrown when the horse spooked. Before anybody could reach her, she jumped up, ran, and threw her arms around me, trembling the whole time.

Halla retrieved the spooked horse and brought it to Pil. "Listen. This problem will go away and you will be fine, so stop making so much noise. Noise is dangerous. If you keep making noise, I will break your jaw."

"That'll calm her right the hell down," I said.

Pil ignored us both and mounted behind me for what looked to be another beautiful, chilly morning. The grassy hills had become steeper and dotted with small stands of rangy trees. We traveled through the valleys as much as possible to avoid climbing up and down hills.

After midday, six horsemen came into sight just a hundred paces away as we rounded a hill. They wore red and silver, the Empire's colors, and one of them waved as he rode toward us. Another of them hung back and sounded a horn. The call didn't sound like a "charge" to me, but I wasn't an expert on imperial battlefield communication. It could as easily have meant "find people to torture."

The horsemen trotted toward us, so we matched their gait until we reached speaking distance. The men rode decent mounts, and they carried curved swords and long spears. Not one of them had blond hair, the mark of a true Empire dweller, but that didn't surprise me. The whole area had been conquered by the Empire just a century earlier, and these dark-haired, light-skinned locals had been imperials ever since. They worked in all parts of the Empire's economy, becoming soldiers, boot makers, tax collectors, prostitutes, and blackmailers.

A blocky soldier with a mustache like a squirrel's tail nodded and then coughed. "Corporal Hullet, Fourth Frontiers, making the roads and lands safer . . ." He faded off into mumbling so quietly that I couldn't hear the rest, although he behaved as if we could hear everything he said. He kept a gentle nod going the whole time.

I waved and pushed my smile up near the point of ridiculousness. "I'm Elder Fank, patriarch of my family here, the Fanks. We are in search of a new farm."

Hullet raised his bushy eyebrows.

"Our old farm burned down. We couldn't pay the taxes, so the baron burned it and ran us out, may he eat fish heads in hell."

Three more horsemen rode over the hill to our right. Hullet waved at them. To be polite, I waved too. Then ten horsemen cantered around the hill behind us, boxing us in. Hullet waved at the new bunch.

I turned back to Hullet, who pointed at the hill to our left with no horsemen on it. "That'd make a good farm, right? Unless in winter you like your ass in the . . ." He trailed into a mumble.

One of the three soldiers above us on the hill, a woman, called out, "Corporal, don't talk to people anymore. I warned you, you're terrible at it. Go help your trumpeter clean his horn. Maybe you can run your mustache through it."

Hullet looked down, nodded, and turned his horse back toward his men. The woman examined us while scratching her blonde hair. Her whole family was probably blonde and came from the original lands where the Empire began. Everything about her seemed stretched. She was thin and tall. Her face was narrow and long, and it opened in a huge grin that seemed to cut her head in two.

The woman yelled, "Aren't you going to thank me?"

I waited a moment, but she appeared to be serious. Maybe it was some sort of strange Empire test. "I would love to thank you, General. Thanks for the beautiful day, and for not ordering your men to kill us, and for letting us continue our journey a couple of minutes from now."

"No. No! Thank me for saving your lives!"

I glanced at Halla.

The woman pressed on. "From the bandits! We killed ten of them just a few miles from here. You're making me wish I hadn't."

Halla shrugged. "Thank you."

The woman rubbed one of her eyelids. "That's all I get?"

"It's all you asked for," I snapped. "We appreciate not needing to slow down and kill those bastards ourselves, but we didn't ask you to save us. I wouldn't have asked unless we faced more than that. Maybe . . ." I shrugged at Halla.

"Sixteen." Halla didn't look away from the blonde woman.

I nodded. "Unless there were sixteen of those criminals. Even seventeen."

The woman smiled like a girl with a new puppy. "You should escort us, then! I'm Captain Leddie. What are you talking about, me being a general? Although I could be, if I wanted. Yes, you come along and escort us, that'll be fine."

Despite our big talk about killing sixteen or maybe seventeen bandits, escaping these soldiers would require hard fighting. We wouldn't all survive. Maybe none of us would. I should just cut off Bea's head the first thing and save time. I felt a bit responsible for her, since I had allowed her to come with us. Also, until Pil stood on her own, I had a shade of responsibility for her.

Before I could suggest alternatives, Halla said in an even voice, "We will protect you from bandits. We will protect you from wild dogs and fish too, since you are weak and afraid."

Between Halla and myself, I was considered the diplomatic one. Even I sometimes found that idea terrifying.

Leddie chuckled. "Oh, you are exactly what I've been looking for. Don't tell me your names. I want to think of you as Creaky, Frumpy, and three sacks of meat riding on horses." She glanced back and forth between Halla and me, at last settling on me. "I'm joking! By Lutigan's swinging phallus, do you even have a sense of humor?" She pointed at Halla. "Act more like her. She's hilarious."

I smiled and shifted in the saddle so I could draw my sword faster, should it be required. "We may not be going the same direction as you, Captain."

Leddie sat up in the saddle and scanned the horizon. "Which way are you going?"

"We were just debating that when we met you. We might decide to go in just about any direction."

Leddie gave me a careless wave. "Come north to the garrison with us while you work that out. You'll protect us, I'll feed you, and you can meet my commander. He'll just love you. I bet he'll throw a party. He can throw a party that will make your tits pop off."

I heard hoofbeats from someplace, but I didn't see any horses for a moment. Then three dozen mounted soldiers rode over the hill to our left and halted so that we were surrounded.

I surveyed the horsemen. They appeared dirty, hard, surly, and well-armed, like soldiers on patrol. I raised my right hand and smiled at Leddie. "Captain, consider yourself under our protection. If my tits don't pop off, I hope your commander won't see it as a sign of discourtesy."

TEN

I detest military ventures. That might surprise some people, since war is known to involve a lot of killing. But I prefer to kill people I think should be dead, not the people some old fart with a fancy hat tells me to kill. Also, orders and battlefields lead to indiscriminate killing where personal fighting prowess may not mean shit.

Wars are ridiculous for other reasons. The people in charge hate it when soldiers run away, even though running is often a successful tactic. They like to capture useless places just so they can brag that they captured one. Often, the useless place is where the biggest bunch of enemy soldiers is waiting, wondering why the hell they're defending a spot no sane person would take on a bet.

Too often, the whole business is men with shiny buttons and clean hands telling other men to go get killed.

Leddie commanded her troop of horsemen less expertly than I would have expected of an imperial officer. She ordered them to form a northbound column, but that produced a pot of confusion that boiled for five minutes. Men shouted contradictory orders while a couple hundred hooves stamped, and one man fell onto a nearby horse's rump before getting kicked. Leddie sat her stallion on the hillside and watched it all happen, and she never gave anybody a hard look.

The mass of men and horseflesh finally got moving, all fifty-two soldiers and her. She used her horsemen to surround us, placing Halla, Pil, and me in the center of the column, while Bea and Whistler rode behind us.

Leddie grinned as she paced me. "This is the perfect post for you! From here you can kill our enemies no matter where they attack from."

"Hell, shut off this crap about us protecting you." I scowled at her. "We're so blocked in we'd have to cut through five of your men just to shake hands with somebody who wants to kill you."

"Where do you plan to take us?" Halla put her hand on her spear, which pointed backward and upward from a sheath fixed onto her saddle.

"I told you!" Leddie leaned over and slapped Halla on the shoulder. "To the garrison to meet my commander! If I have to keep repeating myself, this is going to be a long ride."

"We heard you." I shook my head. "We just have doubts."

"Because you are a liar and a coward." Halla stared at the woman.

"You are the most ungrateful people whose lives I have ever saved from bandits." Leddie rubbed the back of her neck as she stared at Halla.

"We'd be more grateful if you would just let us go on our way," I said, wondering whether I could stab the woman in the back and then get away without her troops killing us all. I decided it was unlikely.

Leddie turned to me and jumped to a new topic as if we were already in the middle of discussing it. "When you duel, is that the sword you like to use? It looks a little effeminate. Do a lot of people make fun of you for that?"

"No, and not a single complaint from the dead, either." I winked at her. On the other side of Leddie, Halla had produced a knife from someplace. She hid the blade against her forearm and started edging her horse closer to Leddie. I tried not to glance straight at Halla while she did all this.

Leddie spun her head back to Halla, who relaxed. "You probably don't duel. You're too tall. Tall people are hopeless at dueling. I'm almost too tall myself."

I couldn't see Halla's knife anymore. Trying to kill Leddie was a desperate move anyway, one we didn't need to make yet, and I gave Halla a tiny headshake.

"Why do you want to duel, anyway, Captain?" I said it to get Leddie's eyes off Halla.

Leddie chuckled. "To see who's best, of course."

I regarded her. "What if you already know you're the best?"

Her eyes widened for an instant before she laughed. "Nobody can know that sort of thing. It's always changing. Maybe the best fighter today will be hungover tomorrow and not be the best anymore. No woman can be the best every day. Or man."

I waited, but she didn't laugh like it was a joke. "Do you write all this down on a big wall every morning? The side of a warehouse someplace? I mean, is that where you write down who is better than who else that day?"

"Don't be an ass! That's a ridiculous question."

"No, it's ridiculous to even think about this 'no man can be best every day' crap, you nasty-ass sack of horse balls." I frowned at her as if she were a toddler painting the wall with her own excrement. "Worry about being better than the one you're fighting and forget all this bullshit swordplay philosophy."

Leddie's eyelid twitched three times. Then she laughed at me again. "Well, how does that help me? It doesn't. Not at all."

Halla gestured around us. "You have fifty men here to help you. Or, you could hire a bodyguard."

Leddie snarled up into the sky. "Gods, am I the only one with a brain here? Guards leave. Soldiers die. Then you're stuck with nothing but your own skinny butt."

"Hell, Captain, what are you afraid of?" I didn't think I'd get a real answer, but asking cost me nothing.

The woman's face rewarded me by going pale. I saw the pulse in her neck speed up. "Nothing." Then she reached her hand out to me.

I glanced at Halla, whose face didn't offer me a twitch of help. I gave Leddie my hand, and she kissed the back of it, leaving a good smear of spit.

Leddie dropped my hand and grinned. "You're a lamb, Creaky, just a lamb. I'll remember that you cared." She kicked her horse and rode toward the head of the column.

I lowered my voice. "She looks terrified when she's not afraid."

"I should have killed her." Halla grunted. "These men would not expect it. We could escape."

"She's spun so tightly she'll fly to pieces soon."

"Before sunset would be nice." Halla replaced her knife in its sheath, which turned out to be behind her back and under her tunic.

The short, green hills seemed to stretch forever, but I knew we were less than a two-day ride from the ocean. I spied a dark-green spot in the distance, farther than most individuals could see. "Look at that."

Halla shaded her eyes with her hand, pretending to wipe off sweat. "Yes, something is there."

I knew she damn well couldn't see it. I could hardly see it myself. "How far do you think it is?"

She grunted and kept examining nothing.

"It sure has grown, hasn't it?"

Halla faced me and stuck out her chin. "Fine! Describe this tavern, or brothel, or whatever it is that thrills you so much."

I lowered my voice. "Don't ever call me old again, you towering twat. That's the southern end of the Graplinger Bog. I think it is."

Halla paused. "Then the sea is not that far now."

"And the bog stretches a fair bit of that distance. If we keep on this heading, I think we'll skirt it."

"Have you ever crossed it?" Halla asked.

I shrugged. "Not all the way through."

She nodded. "I have never put a foot inside it, either."

"Smartass."

I heard hoofbeats closing from behind, and Whistler rode up to pace me. He glanced back and murmured, "That soldier finally stopped bragging about his dick's adventures and left me alone. I was an imperial soldier once."

I glanced at him. "Good for you. Do you want to reenlist or something?"

"I'd rather have my head sliced off. But listen, imperial horse soldiers are prissy about their looks. They always tuck their cuffs into their boots." He nodded toward one of the riders off to the left.

I glanced at the man, and then I checked the soldiers ahead of me. I didn't see a single tucked cuff. "This outing has become much less entertaining. I can't think of any nice motives for pretending to be soldiers. We should thank Leddie and leave."

Halla had stopped searching for the distant bog and was examining the head of her spear. "For a farewell gift, we should kill her."

"That right there is why people don't invite you places. Whistler, stay ready to break to the left and ride like a wild man. It'll happen close to sunset. Be good till then. No singing songs or playing grab-ass before the escape."

Whistler rolled his eyes, nodded, and dropped back.

I evaluated various plans against the meager facts I knew about Leddie. Maybe she was just pretending to be a rollicking madwoman and really was no more disturbed than my horse. She gave a fine theatrical performance, but she didn't act crazy every minute. It would be easy to underestimate her.

I chose a plan and I hated it. Its main flaw was that all of it depended on me. When I had asked Halla how she could contribute to the escape, she shrugged and turned away. Then I asked Pil how she could help, but her answer was less encouraging than Halla's. She rested her forehead against my back and sighed.

When I dropped back to confer with Whistler, a soldier who I had pegged as a sergeant charged up and whipped me with a coil of rope. He shouted, "Get the maggot-screwing hell back up there, you asshole-licking pot of piss! I saw you with that galloping ballsack, with your heads mashed together like two horse turds full of rot and bloody oats!"

The man pulled in a breath and kept yelling. "I'll be fried like a goddamn diseased chicken before I let that flesh-sack of tears, snot, and bile that is your pathetic self talk to that pig-screwing, overripe man whore again! So get back into place! Into your pissing-precise, straight-as-the-Emperor's-dick, unmistakable-even-to-blind-cockroaches place in the line of march, assigned to you by the wretched weeping gods themselves! Or by their all-seeing, virile, pissant-crushing, destroyer-of-whimpering-dreams representative on Earth! Me!"

The man was a credit to sergeants everywhere. However, because of him, I could no longer chat with Whistler, and the escape's hard parts fell to me whether I liked it or not.

My other qualm was that the plan was cruel to horses, or at least it might be. I didn't expect any injuries, but what I expected was rarely the same as reality.

We rode closer to the bog as the day progressed. The hills dwindled in a shocking hurry, leaving us on flat grassland blotched with thickets of trees. By the time the sun stood close to setting, the bog lay no more than two miles to our left. I judged that thirty of Leddie's horsemen could reach us within fifteen seconds. I needed to make sure that during those fifteen seconds, they would be worrying about something besides us.

I reached out into nothing and pulled a yellow band of power from my reserve. I pulled a second, and a third, and so on until I held fifteen of them. I whipped them out to horses all around us, and I convinced each beast that the horse closest to him was an awful threat that should be kicked right away.

When this hell for horses broke loose, complete with kicking, neighing, biting, stomping, and men cursing, I wheeled my horse left toward the bog and kicked its ribs hard. Once in the swamp, we could keep Leddie chasing us forever, or until her men were sucked down by the swamplands, one by one. I hoped we could. I had been spending power more freely than I liked and was feeling a bit pauperized.

I peeked over my shoulder to see whether everybody was following, but Pil had become such a familiar burden that I forgot she was right in my way. I slowed to turn and peek around her. That's when something ragged hit me hard on the skull. I felt myself fall and bounce on the grass, but I didn't feel anything after that.

ELEVEN

I didn't know whether the pain in my head or the pain in my hands woke me. It was probably the hands. I sometimes have nightmares about losing my hands. Again. A miserable dog's whang of a sorcerer once cut them off. Considerable effort was required to repair that situation.

I could see light from a nighttime campfire close enough to toss a stick into, if I'd been free to toss anything. My butt rested on something low, maybe a stool, and my back leaned against a tree. Something weighty dragged both my hands straight down at my sides.

Leddie's fake imperial sergeant leaned over me. "Awake?"

I nodded. Leddie stood behind him grinning.

The sergeant stomped on my toes. "Goddamn sorcerer."

"Shit! Krak's pits! I'll ram that foot in your ear and pull it out your nose!" I would have jumped up to pummel him but for the chain running across my chest, pinning me to the tree.

Leddie pouted. "Creaky, I think you're just mean. You ran away and hurt my feelings! It's as if you don't love me anymore."

I smiled, showing her as many teeth as I could. "I hope you have this much fun when I cut your throat."

She nodded at the sergeant, who seized me by the head. Somebody else stepped up and yanked open my mouth. I tried to bite him, but he evaded while cursing me to both Krak and Lutigan. I didn't even slow him down—maybe he grew up feeding wolves by hand. Leddie leaned in and blocked out most of the light, but I saw her holding a cup, and I flailed like a carp on fire. She poured something cool and as sweet as honeysuckle into my mouth while somebody else slapped me hard on the shoulder. All the slapping and blasphemy distracted me, and I swallowed some of the stuff before spitting out the rest.

Leddie stepped back. "First time I've tried this. I hope it doesn't kill you. They say you should breathe deep, or you'll get a tummy ache."

I spit some more of the dubious fluid out. "Don't worry about my comfort, you ass-wrecking sow! Stab yourself in both eyes if . . . you . . . yellow . . ." My head shivered and plunged down through my body into the earth before I passed out.

Sometime later, I heard people talking far away. I kept my eyes closed and my breath even. Leddie had been right: My stomach hurt like it was full of shattered glass. I twirled the tip of one finger to pull a band of power, but it was like moving in thick mud.

"He's awake." The sergeant grabbed my head again. Leddie's thugs pinned me and held my mouth open.

"Hope you remembered to breathe!" Leddie sounded as jolly as if she were reminding me to take my cloak with me while picking apples. She poured the nasty crap into my mouth again. Instead of swallowing, my body vomited right back into her face.

Leddie shook her head, wiped herself with her sleeve, and shrugged. "Sharpen your manners. They'd better improve if you ever want to be my guest again." She reached behind her as I concentrated on pulling power to do something fatal to her and all her men. I wasn't sure what yet and was hoping for inspiration in the next few seconds. But the thick resistance against my fingers slowed me down.

Leddie brought out another cup and poured it into me. I choked and tried not to swallow the stuff, but some of it seeped down. I thrashed, and one of the soldiers kicked me in the shin. My head plunged, and I passed out again.

When I woke up, morning hadn't arrived yet. Or maybe a whole day had happened while I slept. Somebody had moved me, and I was sitting on the thin grass with my back against a big tree. Manacles clamped my wrists, and they seemed linked by a chain that ran all the way around the tree behind me. Some sort of heavy gloves covered my hands, and I couldn't wiggle my fingers the tiniest bit.

I hadn't successfully pretended to be unconscious yet, so I said to hell with it. I pulled my hands forward hard. The chain allowed me a foot of movement with one hand or the other. My right hand seemed to have been shoved into the middle of a rock big enough to smash out a man's brains. Or, maybe somebody had transformed my hand into a rock.

Leddie stomped up and stood over me. "Now that you're done exploring, how could you be so reckless? And selfish? You're ruining everything!"

"Well, if I knew what 'everything' was, I could try not to ruin it so much." I wanted to scream at her and kick her a few times, but that didn't seem likely to lead to the long-term satisfaction of cutting out her heart.

Crossing her arms, Leddie grimaced at me. "All right. I work for a sorcerer who exists beyond death. He wants to build an army to conquer the world, and he needs to sacrifice you to do it. All the signs say so."

"Really?" I said, deadpan.

"Yes, really! So just behave yourself, or I'll kill you and bring him your head and liver. That'll be almost as good."

I nodded slowly. "So, this dead sorcerer . . . wants to sacrifice me. Because of the signs."

"Yes!" She glared at me for a few seconds. Then she shook her head and laughed. "No! Hell, I almost had you believing it! If I had a totem or a magic glass, that would have sold it. You almost believed it, though, right?"

I grinned. "Almost, you howling gobbet of scum. What's really going on?"

Leddie stepped in and kicked me in the crotch. I groaned and slid sideways as far as the manacles allowed while she knelt in front of me. "Do you think I'm going to tell you everything about everything? You're not so smart, but you're smarter than that. I'll tell you one single thing, all right? One. All right? One, right?"

I nodded and wished I could puke on her again.

"If you knew what's really going on, you'd be galloping your ass home." She patted my cheek. "Too late now!"

Leddie swaggered away toward a tent in the middle of the camp but turned back toward me when she arrived. She held up the gold lump from my pouch. "This almost makes me think you do still love me." She blew a kiss at me and pushed on into the tent.

Less than a minute later, a hiss came from around the tree trunk. "Bib!"

"Pil?" I whispered. I peered over my shoulder but couldn't see around the tree trunk.

"Yes. They manacled us to each other around this big tree," she said in a garbled whisper. "I wish this magic connection between us would cut it the heck out. If it hadn't been for you and it, I may have gotten away."

"What happened?"

Pil sighed. "Somebody knocked you out of the saddle with a piece of wood. I mean, they threw a stick of wood, and it smacked you on the head, and you fell hard enough to bounce. I fell on top of you—I'm sorry about the bruises—and they grabbed us both."

"And when they separated us?" I could imagine significant furor.

Pil was silent for a few seconds. "I panicked, a little. Well, I panicked a lot, enough that I kicked a few and bit one, but that's all right. They're our enemies, so it was worth it." The faster she talked, the more she slurred her words.

That worried me a little. "It was worth what?"

"They hit me a few times, which you figure . . . that's what they do, right? They hit people, so they hit me and kicked me some—two of them did. Not too long, probably. I didn't count off the time."

"What in the name of Effla's thousand lovers did they do to my hands?"

"Oh, that was clever! They put your hands into pails full of plaster and kept you sleeping until the plaster set. I've never heard of that. Is it a common way to make a sorcerer helpless? Dixon never mentioned it."

I had never heard of it, either. "I didn't credit Leddie with that much imagination. It's a useful tactic. She keeps me tame, and when she's done with me, she can just pitch me into a pond and watch me sink."

Pil took a deep breath. "I think they want you for something, or that's what that tarty blonde said, anyway, but I didn't hear anybody say they want me for anything." She paused. "They're going to kill me, aren't they?"

That was an accurate assessment, but I saw no need to frighten her about it. I prepared to lie like a boy with sticky hands. "I don't think you—" I stopped when I saw Leddie walking back toward us, and I hissed at Pil.

Leddie knelt beside me and grabbed my hair. "Three drinks, and I'm ready to slap caution on the ass. Bib—yes, I know your name and everything about you—why oh why are you this way? That's the question I yearn to ask. How can you kill people who are faster, smarter, meaner, more desperate, and prettier than you? Any of a hundred people should have killed you. They couldn't have failed to kill you! But here you sit, dirtying up the ground. Can you make me understand it?"

"This is a poor venue for philosophical discussions. Set me loose, and I'll find us a tavern with a contemplative atmosphere."

"This is the only venue. It might be your last," she said in a quiet voice.

A lie would be simple. The truth would be a better weapon. I grinned at the woman. "Although I am not inclined to be frank, you dripping dog's ass, I will say what I can. Apart from a jingling amount of luck, several things have run in my favor. I never hesitate to run away. When steel fails me, I can use magic. I have a strong preference for being alive, and goddamn it, you sucking cow's gut, why are you wearing my sword?" I nodded at my scabbarded sword on her belt.

Leddie blinked, stood up, and crossed her arms. "It's a good sword."

"Swinging that effeminate sword won't make you invincible, Leddie. Wearing it like a magic charm won't do it, either. Did you pay attention to anything I was saying?"

She nodded.

"Fine. None of what I said means anything."

I paused to see how anxious she was to hear me talk. She must have been fairly antsy, because after a couple of seconds, she snapped, "Go on, then! If I like your answer, I might bring you to my master with most of your parts intact."

"Here's the truth, then. You want to live. You want to kill me. Maybe killing me is your only goal. But I don't have goals, and I don't merely want your life. I crave your life. I hunger for it, and that's all there is."

"How do you get that?" She clenched her teeth.

I shrugged a little and went on like I was commenting on tonight's beer. "Kill when it will do the most good."

"What does that mean, you smug turd?"

"Know that your killings are pure and good. Know it in every part of you. Later, you'll understand that you were wrong, that all the killings were just selfishness that didn't do a single good thing. But it won't matter what you understand. You'll have made yourself into a killer, and you can't unmake that."

Leddie whispered, "How long did that take?"

"Oh, about ten years."

She stared at the ground and mumbled, "I don't have ten years."

I showed her my teeth. "Well, that's a damn shame."

Leddie stared at the stars.

I snickered. "Woman, did you believe all that bullshit? Hah! I didn't even have a magic glass to wave around! I'm astounded by your gullibility."

I figured she'd be pissed and maybe kick me some more. But I hoped she'd be so enraged she'd do something stupid. I didn't expect the woman to beam down at me like I was her favorite sweetheart. "I could kiss you! I could mount you if we had some privacy! Now I know I've made the right decision." She turned without spouting any more craziness and walked back to the tent.

After a few moments of silence, Pil whispered, "I don't want to make light of your morality and guilt problems, but can we figure out how to escape before they kill me? Please?"

"Hush for . . . wait! Pil, you're a sorcerer. Can you do anything immediately helpful?"

The closest soldier swung around to peer at us. I hissed at Pil and then held my breath. It was a useless act, but my repertoire of useful acts had grown thin. After ten seconds, he walked off closer to the fire and sat on the ground, rubbing his hands to the heat.

I whispered, "All right, Pil, go ahead."

Pil whispered, "No. If I had time, I could enchant this chain so I can kill you better with it, but not tied up in the dark on my butt."

With plenty of leisure and materials to work with, a Binder was a horrifying enemy. I once saw a Binder stab a powerful sorcerer and his two bodyguards to death with a spoon she had enchanted for that purpose. However, it had required two days, a forge, and ninety silver coins to create that spoon.

I nodded even as I told myself she couldn't see me. "Fine, just be ready to kick somebody and run like hell. Now, be silent while I plan."

Pil wasn't silent. "I can break my thumb if I need to. I mean, I obviously don't want to, but if it will help us get away."

"Harik's ass, why?"

"To get out of the manacles."

I wished she could see how disdainful I looked. "That's mighty sweet of you. Whoever told you to break your thumb to escape manacles is an asshole who hates you. You'll end up in manacles with a broken thumb. Now, be still."

No matter what Leddie claimed, I felt confident she didn't know everything about me. If she did, she'd have made a more vigorous effort to crush my toes. Sorcerers pull and direct magical power with their hands, or really their fingers, and that's how I generally did it too.

However, I had once been temporarily without my fingers for most of a year, and I had taught myself to use magic with my toes. My toes were now out of practice, and I had never done magic with them while my boots were on, but that wasn't the moment for doubts.

I wiggled my toes in what I hoped was a mystical manner. The boots did constrict them a bit. After a couple of minutes, I tried with the toes on the other foot, without success. Maybe now was the moment for doubts.

The soldier who had glanced at us earlier still sat by the closest campfire. I called out, "Hey!"

The man sighed. "Shut it, finger-waver."

"Come here! I have some information."

"Of course you do. I have a dong that whistles." He spat into the fire.

"Really! Come here! Do you want the sergeant to get the credit?"

The soldier stood and trudged toward me. "Come here? Come here? I'll come there and kick in your teeth. What's this gold-plated information?"

"Well," I said, lowering my voice, "it *does* have to do with gold. Is the captain sharing that giant lump of gold with everybody?"

He squatted down near me and grunted, "Shut it."

"Unfair, right? I have some more gold that I'll give you if you do a service for me."

"Where is it? In some whore's britches?"

"I have it here. Just a service." I held my breath.

"Right, what?"

"When they unchain us, 'accidentally' let my friend loose."

The man rubbed his nose and cheek. "Sure, easy. Where's the gold?"

"Thank you! Thank you!" I thought I might be too obvious, but he seemed as stupid as a knothole. "I keep a gold coin hidden in my right boot. An imperial wheel."

The soldier latched onto the boot, yanked it straight off, and upturned it. The hypothetical coin did not fall out. "Where is it?" He shoved the boot in my face.

"It's not there? Harik, I hope it didn't fall out. I'm sorry!"

"Cheap, lying piece of crap!" Then he stomped my unshod right foot.

I had assumed the soldier would kick, punch, or stomp me. I wished he hadn't stomped my foot, which was smarting, but at least he hadn't set me afire. I had considered that unlikely but possible.

I reached out with my bare toes and found I could grip magical power, so it had been worth it.

As a Caller, I could only work with things that typically move. It doesn't do much good to call things that can't move to answer. I could rile up animals and coax broken bones to heal and fool water into falling on my enemies like it was the heel of Krak. But as far as iron, stone, and dirt were concerned, I was no more influential than a butterfly. The iron manacles and plaster mittens were out of my reach.

Our escape would probably be loud, so we wouldn't be able to wriggle away like grateful snakes. But I felt I could contrive something that was superior to my earlier horse-kicking escape plan, which could only have failed worse if my horse had stumbled and crushed me to death.

I didn't tell Pil I had an idea yet. I wanted to think it through rather than rush to the escaping part. Maybe I could come up with a vengeful attacking part at the same time. Why limit ourselves?

Before I finished the details, I heard two soldiers trudging toward us. A little, slow man said, "There is no ding-dong-damn reason this can't wait until morning." He pointed off into the darkness. "There's animals out there. And holes."

His big companion bounced along, jittery even after a day of hard riding. "Hell, that's even better! We'll fling her in a hole all bound and let something come eat her up!"

I saw the outline of the slow one stop. "I didn't bring my knife."

"What kind of ignorant piece of shit walks around without his knife? Here, use mine."

The slow one cleared his throat. "I don't like your knife. The handle hurts my pointy finger."

The jittery one spouted abuse of some kind, but I lost interest in the conversational details. That soldier's pointy finger wouldn't save Pil from a slit throat for long.

"Pil!" I whispered. "Be ready to roll to your right, fast, when I tell you!"

"Fine." Her whisper was strained, but she didn't sound scared.

She should have been scared, since I was about to do something as dangerous as hell. I intended to rot a section of the tree trunk so that the tree would fall as if it had been cut with axes. Chained together, Pil and I sat exactly on opposite sides of the tree. If I rotted the trunk just a little in the wrong direction, it would break one or both of our arms when it fell. If I erred more than just a little, one of us would be smashed to death.

I didn't explain any of that to Pil. I said, "Scoot a little to your left."

The soldiers weren't quite yelling at each other, but their spirited discussion had somehow evolved to include a redheaded whore in the Old Quarter.

"A little more," I whispered.

Pil scuffed the dirt on the other side of the tree, and it made a scrunching sound.

The slow soldier gasped. "What was that noise? Do you see something?" He stared right past me into the darkness.

"I don't see nothing." The other one's voice quavered a little.

"Bugger this!" The slow one turned toward the camp. "I'm getting my sword!"

The jittery one strode after him. "You can't even get your knife, you pokey turd!"

I let out the breath I was holding. "All right, Pil, wait for my word."

I wished that I could press my toes against the tree trunk for this. Direct contact improves power and control. Since I couldn't bend like an orangutan, I put that thought away and pulled with my toes to force a blue wedge of power through the trunk, low to the ground. I flinched at the sound of the two soldiers walking back toward us.

Adjusting the blue wedge and the rot within it, I gave the rot a twist and the tree trunk gave way. The big tree, which had just started to bud for spring, creaked like a small herd of dying cattle and leaned toward the camp. The two soldiers froze, saw the tree, and sprinted away from us.

"Now, Pil!"

As the trunk separated, we rolled away from the falling tree. Something whacked me on the head, but not too hard. I glanced back but didn't see whether those soldiers had been crushed when the tree slammed against the ground. I did see that the great network of limbs and branches had obliterated two campfires, whooshing embers up in all directions. Embers and stars provided our only light, leaving the camp in near darkness.

I shook my head and crawled to my feet along with Pil. We were still manacled to the other's opposite hands so that we faced each other with only four feet between us.

"You're hurt," Pil whispered.

I made a face she couldn't see. "Screw it." For two seconds, I contemplated my sword, which I hoped was now attached to Leddie's mangled corpse, squished flatter than a biscuit. This might be the best time to steal it back. "Come on, Pil! Grab my boot!"

Pil had no true choice but to follow or fight me. We traveled facing each other at a skipping sidestep, and she came along, but not graciously. "No! Let's run! Run, you ratty old man!" I guided her along toward the place I'd marked as the tent's location. She lowered her voice but kept cursing me.

I tripped on a branch, and when I recovered, I found tent canvas under my feet. Soldiers had begun shouting from all around the camp, so I rushed to find any edge of the collapsed tent. After five seconds, the shouting had come closer, and in five more seconds, a man yelled almost in my ear, "Where's Jod? Anybody seen Jod?"

Pil grabbed my collar and hissed. "We'll be caught, and then what will you do? Knock down every tree in the forest?"

Pil was right. "Shit! Damn Leddie and damn me too!" I grabbed

Pil's hand and guided her away from the camp as fast as we could skip, shuffle, and trot in the dark while chained together face-to-face. I would have to come after the sword another time. Krak, Father of the Gods, was making me haul the damn thing all over creation, and if I lost it, he'd want to know why I'd been such a careless little squid.

We paused after ten minutes of fleeing. The eastern sky was just showing light, and I heard hoofbeats behind us. I felt confident we were headed toward the bog, but it lay two miles away across land as flat as any table. Our situation didn't offer too many advantages, but if we found a circumstance in which panting and cursing were helpful, I would carry the day.

TWELVE

Pil and I paused a quarter mile from Leddie's camp. I was limping and panting like a horse after a hard run, but Pil was pulling in deep, calm breaths.

"Damn you for being young," I muttered.

She ignored that. "It will be sunup in a few minutes. I mean, there'll be some light. Enough for us to show up like two big, blazing trees! In the middle of nothing!" Her slurred words came faster and faster. "We can't hide, or outrun horses, or fight all chained together. I—"

"Exhilarating, isn't it?" I chuckled for her benefit. I didn't really think it was exhilarating. It was pretty damn terrifying, and even depressing. Sitting in a tavern next to a pretty girl while I won a pile of gold in a dice game would be exhilarating. This was just a horrible, maybe fatal, pain in the ass. But I didn't want her to panic.

Pil didn't panic. She tried to kick me, missed, and snarled. "Stop being ridiculous. And go to hell."

"I'm not being ridiculous." I plopped down on the grass and stuck up one leg. "Pull off my boot."

Just after we fled the camp, Pil had taken a moment to reshoe me. Now she stood over me, an unmoving outline. I imagined her making a mean face.

"This is a poor time to stop trusting me, young woman. Step quick and pull off my boot! I can't do it with these!" I held up my plastered fists and waggled them.

Pil hesitated another second before grabbing onto my right boot and hauling it off.

"Don't lose it. I intend to walk away from here. Kneel down and put one of your hands on the ground." She muttered something that sounded nasty but dropped down. I pressed my bare toes against her hand just below the manacle, and with them I pulled a green band of power from the empty air. "We should be grateful to Leddie for helping us feel this alive. I may buy her a damn present."

"Ow!" Pil twitched but didn't jerk away. "What are you doing?"

"Not breaking your thumb." I did shift Pil's thumb, though, and I pushed it inward where the big joint met her wrist.

She tensed and raised her other hand, but she didn't say anything.

I smiled. "Good, hold still and don't hit me. If you distract me, your thumb might bend backward for the rest of your life. Besides, finer women than you have beaten the hell out of me."

"Are you all right?"

"Better than a chubby puppy. Be still."

I bent, twisted, and mangled Pil's thumb. "Slip that manacle off."

Pil eased her hand free with no more than a slight twist.

I patted her shoulder. "Down with your hand again. Don't dawdle, or Leddie's horsemen will run us down." I pushed my toes against her thumb joint, and she grunted. In a moment, I'd finished putting Pil's thumb back in place, a simpler task than crippling it had been. "Other hand, Pil."

"Hurry up, it's almost light! We should run!" Pil was squirming in distress.

I didn't answer. She was correct about the light.

Pil hissed as I shoved her other thumb into an unlikely angle.

She eased the cuff down, and it hung, which must have hurt like a scorpion in the eye. Then it was off, and I repaired the damage.

I leaned back, resting with my elbows on the ground. "Ah, that's good." I assessed the still morning air. It hung dense with moisture, and no wind at all eased through it.

"Bib, we're going to be trampled as flat as horse turds in about thirty seconds."

I snagged a white band of power from nothing using my toes, tried for another, and then fumbled them both away. I pulled again, held one, and then pulled three more before I whipped them out in four directions. I eased the moist air a few degrees cooler and added a breath of wind.

"Look, Pil." I pointed with my plaster lump at two riders outlined against the morning twilight, not a quarter of a mile away. Then woolly fog smothered everything for a mile around us.

Pil grabbed my arm and yanked at it. "I have your boot! Stand up, and I'll pull it on!"

I rolled to my knees. "Wait."

"Wait? Why? Why wait?" She slapped my boot against her leg.

I laid my plaster-encased right hand on the ground, raised my plastered left hand, and smashed them together. The crash sounded as loud as a ship's anchor dropping onto the dock. Plaster chips flew, but nothing broke.

Pil grabbed my arm. "Stop, they'll hear you!"

I shook her loose. "Oh, stop whimpering like my baby sister. They won't find us in this fog." I smacked my hands together again. The plaster on my right hand cracked a little, but the plaster on my left shattered and fell away. I flexed my left fingers. I still couldn't feel the thumb and forefinger at all. "Well, I was hoping to set free the other hand, but that's fine. Now the boot!" I stood and rubbed my hand against my shirt to knock off some clinging plaster.

Once I was reshod, Pil grabbed my arm again, but I pulled her back toward Leddie's camp. "I forgot something. Let's go back." I started winding the long manacle chains around my arms.

"What?" she yelped, and then she whipped around in case some soldier might have heard her and ride out of the fog.

I trotted back toward the camp.

Pil followed me. "Stop! Stop right there, or I'll knock you down!"

Without warning, I turned and grabbed her shirt front. "Will you stop acting like a little dog caught in a gate? There's a time to run, and we ran. There's a time to cut your enemy's throat. This is it. We have every advantage. The camp is the last place they'll expect us, and if they did, they couldn't see us coming. You're a sorcerer, so stop whining. I'm embarrassed for you on behalf of all the sorcerers throughout time."

The fog happened to lighten around us for a couple of seconds, and I got a good look at Pil. Her face was beaten to hell. Whoever kicked her had broken her nose, split both lips, and blackened both eyes, one of which was swollen shut. She stared at me with her one good eye for a couple of breaths. Then she nodded and smiled, showing two empty places where teeth used to be. I trotted back toward our enemies, and I heard her following along.

A few spooked soldiers still yammered and shouted around the camp. Although I rarely get lost, even in the dark, the sounds helped guide me. When they sounded close, I slowed to a walk. Pil creeped along behind me, touching my shoulder. Ahead of us, two men were yelling at each other to find something for putting out the fire.

I found those two confused, screaming firefighters standing together along with one quiet man in between them, shaking his head and frowning. I jumped out of the fog and knocked one man's legs out from under him, then I smashed his head with the club of plaster around my right hand. Neither his skull nor the plaster survived. I grabbed the knife off his belt with my liberated right hand and jumped at the silent man. He was still looking around, trying to figure out what was happening, and he never did because I stabbed him in the heart.

I turned to the third man. Pil was kneeling on his chest, her hands wound in his hair, bashing his head against the ground. I cut his throat for her, stole his sword, pulled two more white bands, and freshened the fog. That required expending a good chunk of my remaining power, but the sun was up and I had no better options.

Long chains still hung from the manacles on my wrists, but I sure as hell wasn't wasting time and power to free myself. I handed Pil the sword. She handed it right back and took the knife from me. Then I gathered the chains up into each hand, turning them into big iron fists.

The soldiers had been talking about a fire. I heard flames snapping from ahead, so I figured the campfires had set the fallen tree ablaze. We padded through the fog in near silence until we ran across a man who seemed to be wandering by himself without purpose. I punched him in the face when he turned. He collapsed limp, and we moved on almost without slowing down.

We reached the fire, which was modest but promised better destruction as it spread. Two men flailed at it with blankets. I clubbed one from behind, and Pil crippled the other's arm with a thrust. She stared at him as he groaned.

"Kill him!" I snapped. "Stab him. Or knock him down and break his neck!"

Pil squinted at me as if I were speaking in the language of baboons.

"Goddamn it, Pil, don't let him pick up his sword!"

Pil jerked around toward the soldier, who had knelt to snatch up his sword with his unwounded arm. She swung her knife in a wild cut that glanced off the man's skull, and he dropped to his hands and knees. He crouched there, wobbly and shaking his head. Pil hesitated again.

"Fingit's balls on fire!" I knelt and punched the man's skull hard enough to kill any regular person. "Come on."

The half-collapsed tent lay partway under the flaming tree, and I cut through the canvas tent-side using Pil's knife. She held it open while I pushed inside. Enough firelight leaked in for me to see a small, crushed table and a cot. My scabbarded sword lay on the ground beside the table, and I grabbed it. Blood covered the cot, but I didn't see Leddie, either alive or smashed to death. The gold lump lay on the ground beside the cot.

"I bet she was lying there admiring it." I laughed. "The price of avarice."

"What are you saying?" Pil hissed. "Are you laughing? Have you lost your wits?"

"I'm sounding the retreat now," I muttered.

"Do you mean we're not going to kill them all?" Pil sounded a little hysterical, and her one good eye appeared too bright, but it was hard to be sure through the fog, bruises, and dried blood.

"We'll let a few live till tomorrow, in case we get bored." I led her out of the camp at a lope toward the bog. Hoofbeats and shouting sounded through the fog, mainly ahead of us.

We jogged on for fifteen minutes, stopping twice to wait for riders to either pass by or stumble onto us. I paused once to pant and freshen the fog, which wanted badly to thin and blow away. I tried to run faster but seemed to slow down instead.

Keeping the fog in place would take just about all my power, so if I wanted to keep a reserve, I'd have to let the fog drift away. I struggled with the decision for a minute. Then I said, "Prepare to be seen, Pil. This mist will die away in a few seconds." I let the fog dissipate and saw we were still half a mile from the bog.

Clear daylight showed me six pairs of riders crisscrossing the miles between the camp and the bog. One pair was within a quarter mile of us, and they wheeled our direction. I sprinted toward the bog, and Pil followed. The chains clanked with every step. My sprinting faded into over-optimistic jogging within twenty strides, and my vision blurred in and out of focus.

About the time I thought I might die just from trying to run, the two riders closed with us at an angle. One charged Pil, who avoided a beheading by throwing herself onto the ground. The other charged me. I dropped the chains and breathed deep as I waited for him bare-handed. At the last moment, I ran toward the man, sort of amazed that my legs would obey. I barely avoided tripping on the chains, grabbed the man's arm as he swung, and threw him out of the saddle. His horse ran on before I could grab it, so I drew my sword and stabbed him in the throat as he lay on the ground.

I turned, but the other soldier didn't come around to attack again. He was riding away toward two of his comrades half a mile distant. I scanned to make sure there weren't another eight or ten of the bastards about to run us down. I was panting like an old ox when Pil arrived and reached out to steady me, but I shook her off. Then I spotted Halla and Whistler galloping toward us from the bog, leading two horses without riders.

Halla and Whistler reached us before the three soldiers organized themselves to attack. I pulled myself into the saddle and held out my hand to Pil, but she ignored me and mounted the other horse. The four of us rode like the wind afire and reached the bog ahead of the soldiers.

Only patches and wisps of fog clung to the marshy ground, and they probably would have lain there even if I hadn't fiddled with the weather. Whistler led Pil down a path between two swampy patches. Halla and I stayed behind on our horses and observed the riders. The three horsemen approached the marshy area with some caution, and we retreated into the swamp. They didn't follow us, at least not yet.

Halla glared at me, frowning, and then turned away. "I couldn't find you. You should not have called a fog if you wanted my help."

"I didn't need your goddamn help! Your gigantic ass would just have been in my way. I didn't need rescuing at the end there, either. I could have killed another seven or eight of those rascals." That was a damn lie, of course. Any one of those horsemen might have run me down or cut my head in half. Fighting a mounted man was a chancy business. I took a breath to yell at her some more, but I forgot what I was going to say.

We reached a narrow, uncertainly squishy stretch of dirt in the marsh, and we all dismounted. Halla peered back the way we came. "I will wait and kill them."

"Not without me." I knew it was a foolish statement the moment it left my mouth. To cover my foolishness, I did some more foolish things. I held up the chains and shook them. "I wish I'd discovered chain fighting when I was a boy. To hell with swords and axes."

Halla stared at me. Whistler and Pil did too. Bea stood behind them, splashed with mud as if she'd fallen when everybody ran into the swamp.

I glanced down at my manacles and chains. "All of you can go to hell." I crossed my arms to be defiant, which jangled the chains, so I dropped my arms again. I was just arguing to be contrary. Actually, I was sweating and felt like shit.

Whistler rubbed his mouth. "Bib, look at your arm. The other one."

"I know it's bloody! You always get bloody little cuts in a fight!"

He pointed. "No, farther down."

Blood soaked my left arm and my left trousers leg past the knee. When I bent my head to examine it, I realized the top of my head was sore. Without thinking, I reached up to touch it, but before I got there, I encountered something that felt like the end of a belt.

"Bib, your scalp is hanging off. Not the whole thing!" Whistler hurried to add that part. "But it doesn't look nice."

I found myself sitting on the ground and wondering how I got there.

THIRTEEN

As I sat like a dim mule with my scalp dangling toward my left ear, Bea put her hand on my unbloodied shoulder. "Let me see it. I can fix it." She swallowed and didn't look too damned confident. "It must hurt."

"Well . . . it didn't much until you said something."

When I had knocked down that tree to escape, a broad, sharp splinter must have smacked me on the skull. I reached up to touch the wound, but Bea pushed my hand back down.

Halla and Whistler walked back down the path to prepare an ambush for the soldiers.

"I'll come too," Pil said, adjusting her grip on her knife.

I pretended like I was going to stand up. "Hell no. You'll just get killed."

Pil glared at me. "Is that what all the sorcerers throughout history are saying? Or just you?"

"I am empowered to speak for them."

"Isn't this the right time to cut our enemies' throats? It certainly seems like it. Their throats are going to be coming up that path, which sounds convenient to me."

Halla stood behind Pil, leaning on her spear with her eyebrows raised at me. Pil was a sorcerer in her own right, and I had no business telling her not to go get killed. "Well . . . I wish you wouldn't go."

Pil ignored me and followed Halla back toward a bend in the path. Bea fussed over my scraped skull.

"Shit! Nobody listens to me." I closed my eyes and pretended I was someplace with a big fire and plenty to drink. My head was telling me I was falling over backward, but I decided it was lying.

"Hm?" Bea patted my arm. "I'm sorry, I'll be more careful." She said it, but her fingers kept poking and mashing, not a bit gentler than before. "You look a bit like a mongrel with a flop ear." She giggled and stifled it.

I let my mind drift.

A man screamed from someplace down the trail. More men shouted, and weapons clanked, but I didn't hear a woman scream. Of course, Pil couldn't scream if she were stabbed in the throat. Or gotten her head cut off. I tried to stand up again, but Bea pushed me back down, and she didn't have to strain to do it.

Soon, Pil, Halla, and Whistler walked back toward us from the ambush. Blood covered Pil's shoulder and spattered her chest. She stared at the ground, but she walked steadily.

Halla stopped near me and lay her spear across her shoulder. "We should leave before any more come."

Whistler spit on the ground and glanced at Halla. "If we had hung their heads in the trees, then their friends might have thought all this fighting was a bad idea. You should have let me."

Halla's head swung toward Whistler in a greased arc. "You fought well, so I will answer you. Hanging their heads was a bad idea for many reasons. At least four. You did not fight well enough for me to tell you what they are. Bib, can you walk?"

"Hell yes, I can walk."

Halla frowned at Bea. "Why is he not bandaged yet?"

"We don't have anything even a little bit clean to cover that with." Bea's cheeks were turning pink.

"That's a limp excuse," Pil said.

Bea took a step toward Pil. "How do you know? From bandaging your horse?"

"Hey, that's not nice . . ." Whistler shut up when Pil and Bea both glowered at him.

Halla twisted around to unlace a large pouch on the back of her belt. I hadn't given it any thought. Maybe she carried the fingers of her enemies in it. Now she pulled out a huge, yellow chemise that shouldn't have fit in that pouch except that the garment was made of fine silk. She shook it out, and I saw detailed, green embroidery at the collar and cuffs. It probably cost more than every stitch of clothing our group was wearing, including our boots.

I wondered why she was changing clothes out here in the middle of the swamp. Then a moment too late, I realized what she was doing. She started cutting the big shirt into strips. Everybody stared and let her do it.

"Don't," I wheezed. Halla glanced up, and I went on. "I have to heal this. I can't guess what kind of filth is floating in this swamp air. If we just bandage it, my head will rot off in a day."

"Why didn't you tell me that before, you ass?" Bea said.

I gazed at Bea and shrugged. "I have no idea."

Halla stopped, chewing her lip. Mounds of yellow silk and silk strips dangled from her hands. Without commenting, she twisted around and began stuffing it all back into her pouch.

I closed my eyes to begin pulling my scalp back together, but then I peeked at Pil with one eye. "Pil, are you all right?"

The young woman stared up from the ground. "Sure." She smiled at me, shrugged, and shook her head all at the same time. "Everything's wonderful. I'll tell you later how I killed him, you know, after your head's not about to fall apart. I'm glad I did it. I'm glad I killed him, I mean."

My manacles and chains complicated the healing somewhat. I pondered removing them the way I had Pil's, but I was already regretting the power spent to heal my scalp when I had so little in reserve. My survival was the most worthwhile of causes, though. The healing didn't improve the pain much, but my faculties cleared remarkably.

Halla stood over me until I finished.

I patted her arm, and she only flinched away a little. "I owe you one silk nightgown."

"You do not. There is no debt."

"Thanks just the same."

"Put it from your mind." Halla peered toward the horses.

"All right." I nodded and wished I hadn't. "It's just a lemon-colored nightie. But thanks."

Halla stiffened. "Stop."

I grinned and poked at her arm but missed. "Why don't you want me to offer you a little gracious thanks? Will it make you cry big, embarrassing tears? That can't be it. I won't accept it." I realized I was feeling more light-headed than I'd thought.

Halla turned away from me. "Very well. Do not accept it. Do not accept that you are an ugly, old man now too. Also, go back to your cursed house and do not accept that your wife and children are dead forever." Then she pushed past me toward her horse.

I expected I'd yell at her, call her a whore's crusty ass crack, and maybe throw whatever objects I could reach. But all the anger fell out of me instead. She wasn't who she had been before, so this was what I should expect from now on.

Well, to hell with that shit. Maybe she was a grim chunk of brutal iron now, but she'd have to prove it to me. I'd poke her with a stick all the way to the northern kingdoms and back until she either laughed or broke my arm.

I followed Halla into the bog, leading my horse. We had entered the southern part of Graplinger Bog, which forced a decision on us. We could tramp fifteen miles north through it toward the sea and Fat Shallows. Or we could walk inside the edge of it a few miles north and then pop back out. Leddie's hooligans couldn't be everywhere waiting for us.

Sadly, the bog was perilous to about the same extent everywhere, including just inside the edge. The path led deeper into the swampy lands, not along the edge, and I didn't fancy skipping off across the marsh to get sucked underwater and eaten by a hundred spiny little fish.

Because we didn't have any better strategy, or a strategy at all, we followed the path northward, deeper into the musty, rot-smelling swamp of stale water, sharp grass, and low, mossy trees. I am ashamed to admit that even though I am a Caller and should appreciate nature, swamps do not enchant me. The Graplinger Bog struck me as one of the most depressing I had experienced.

As we walked, I shifted from blaming the swamp for my unhappiness to blaming my companions. I scrutinized each of them from the corners of my eyes and got more pissed off about my situation. "May all of them eat snake heads off their mother's clean floor," I murmured. Why was I with them, anyway? To be their loyal companion? Bugger that. I could bring back those kids, and that was worth doing. And at some point, Harik would demand I take his book across the sea. Despite my intentions, I was headed in the right direction for that. So, screw everybody else. Halla too. Let somebody else poke her with a stick.

I made myself breathe deep and admitted that my attitude might be improved by a hot fire and a few drinks.

What I really wanted was to kill the shit out of Memweck, whoever he was. I would carve out his heart and feed it to the nastiest rats I could find in the Empire's sewers. I savored that thought for a few seconds and then shook it away to concentrate on the boggy muck around us. It would be cruel and sad for Memweck to be saved by some slimy, callous beast that seized my foot while I wasn't looking.

Half an hour later, we set our horses loose after picking through the packs and bags for water, food, and useful items. The path was narrowing, and we'd never be able to lead the horses across the bog without broken legs or horrible sinkhole accidents. They could wander back out and make friends with Leddie's horses.

Before the horses were out of sight, Halla dropped back beside me. She cleared her throat, an uncommon sign of discomfort for her. Staring straight ahead, she said, "I am sorry." That was all.

Maybe she meant it. Or maybe she said it to mollify me and avoid problems. Maybe she would rub up against a fallen tree and say she loved it, if that would move it out of her way. Maybe everything she'd said and done since she returned had just been to manipulate me. "That's all right. Your meanness made you apologize to me twice in the same week. You've never done it twice in the same year before this."

Halla didn't comment on that. She walked faster to outpace me, but I kept up by walking fast and jogging a little, even though my head wasn't pleased.

I chided myself for my earlier whining, which was unworthy of a sorcerer. Now was a good time to start poking Halla. "Let's return to the subject of your fleeing into the night, with no message or even a dead chicken on my porch, and staying gone for ten years."

"No."

"It was uncivil behavior in a guest."

"No." Halla sped up. I was almost running.

I stared at the side of her head and raised my voice. "I killed two horses looking for you!"

"This is tiresome. Go bother your manservant."

"Bett drew a picture of you and then burned it."

Halla shook her head. "She did not."

I touched her arm. "No, she didn't. You hurt Lin's feelings, though."

Halla's voice was steady. "You hurt her far worse."

"All right! I'm going over to the other edge of the trail and walking along until I kick a hundred snakes, or frogs, or muskrats. Then maybe I'll be able to continue this conversation without smashing in your head!" I shook my manacles and chains at her while edging to the other side of the path, a full six feet away.

After two silent minutes, Halla slowed down and said, "I thought my meaning was clear."

"When you left? Yes, you were clear that my buckle was rusty!"

She finally met my eyes. "It was. Next, you might let your sword rust, and then your attention wander. And then you would die."

I gaped at her. "You meant nothing of the kind! It's a story! You're making that shit up!"

Halla stopped short. Her voice was stiff. "Yes, I am making it up now. But if I had not cared at all, I would have said nothing."

That might almost have made sense, but it didn't explain anything. "Your blabbering just now made me miss kicking two frogs! Just . . . hush and let me be mad."

Halla walked off, and I let her walk. I couldn't decide whether it had been a successful stick-poking.

Late in the afternoon, the path became narrower in a hurry. Soon, Halla nudged me and nodded toward a spot twenty feet off the trail. I peered and spotted a deadfall trap mostly hidden by reeds. It was about the right size for catching a swamp rat or an opossum.

I flexed my numb fingers, nudged my sword loose in the scabbard, and started wrapping my chains around my arms. Somebody lived close by, and if they didn't like swamp rats, they might not like me, either.

We spotted more traps during the next ten minutes. Halla stopped and turned her head. I stopped and heard it too, a rhythmic clank of metal hitting metal, filtered through some unknown distance of reeds and moss-dripping tree limbs.

"Trap?" I whispered to Halla. "Or just careless?"

Whistler poked his head right in between us. "Maybe he's so ferocious he doesn't care who hears him. Maybe those are his balls banging together."

Halla nodded at Whistler. "Go find out. We will wait here."

Whistler stepped back. "I might not know exactly where to put my feet so as not to get sucked down."

I said, "If you're cowed by a stretch of muddy trail, then you're likely a piss-poor disappointment as a swamp fighter."

A man's far-off voice sounded resonant and clear from someplace ahead of us. "Hurry up! I've been smelling you for the past hour." The man laughed. "You smell like Lutigan's asshole! Stay on the left side of the path. That's important!"

I shouted, "Who are you? And how do we know that walking on the left won't kill us all?"

The man laughed again, so amused that I almost wanted to laugh with him. "If you're cowed by a stretch of moist dirt, then you should go home. You're not brave enough to eat snakes with me."

I didn't call him a lousy son of a bitch or anything like that. Instead, I examined everything around us, starting with the tree limbs. Less than a minute later, I found it, a small, complicated nest of strings woven into tree branches twenty feet above us. I hissed at Halla, pointed up, and mouthed the word, "Hex."

Most regular people talked about hexes and witches quite a bit. Sorcerers were mere rumor to them, but they likely knew a few witches, and popular thinking had witches running around hexing people and animals and just about anything they chose.

The notion that witches hexed things was crap. Witches were folks who understood a lot about how things worked and learned a great number of practical things. They performed magic that was tied into the world, less powerful than sorcery. No witch could burn a sailing ship to ash within a few minutes. On the other hand, witches didn't rely on the gods for power. At times, I thought of them with great envy.

The people who made hexes called themselves "hexers." They claimed it was a simple and dignified term. I thought it was damned unimaginative, but they didn't ask me. They relied on inborn ability, craftsmanship, and death—specifically, pulling the guts out of creatures such as rabbits and roosters.

Some people think that sounds awful, but not me. Compared to the things I've done to gain magical power, disemboweling a little bunny rabbit is wholesome.

A hex was a complex object, like a puzzle or a drawing built to create a certain effect. A hex scratched onto a stove could make food taste better. A different hex hidden in a cupboard could make every person who walked past stub their toe. Those were simple hexes.

More complicated hexes might give people nightmares, keep a baby from crying, or blind a person for a while. If this snake-cooking fellow had woven the hex above us so he could listen through it, that was a mighty crafty hex.

The man shouted, "Have you drowned? If not, you can come on and share a meal with me, or you can go back the way you came." The voice laughed. "Or you can sit yourselves down right there and suck swamp grass. I don't recommend that. Leeches hide among the grass blades."

Halla scratched her chin. "I like snake."

I followed her down the left side of the path.

FOURTEEN

The path sank underwater twice in the next ten minutes, but it resurfaced before we wandered off it and drowned. I counted three hexes aimed at the right side of the path, and I might have overlooked some. Along the way, the smells of woodsmoke and cooking meat began weaving into the mushy scent of swamp rot.

We stumbled onto a sunlit mound of semidry earth, big enough for a whitewashed cottage, two small, red outbuildings, and a chicken coop. A fire and a clay oven stood in the center of it all, while tight stacks of crates snugged up against the outbuilding walls. It might all have been picked up from a prosperous town and dropped there.

A rangy, graying man taller than Halla beamed as he ambled toward us. He wiped his hands with a white rag and then stuffed it into his leather apron. A shaggy brown hound trotted along behind him. The only weapon I saw was a tall bow leaning against the cottage, although the man held a long smith's hammer.

"Welcome to the Button! I'm Peck." He laughed as he stopped a polite distance from us.

Bea pushed past me. "Has anybody brought some stolen children through here?"

Halla and I both stared at her.

She waved us away with one hand. "Why spend an hour standing around with Bib claiming some ridiculous name and trying to find things out but not ask questions? Let's get on with it."

Peck chuckled. "This sort of thing is what made me decide to be a hermit. That and the amphibians. Sorry, I didn't see any stolen children. Please stay for supper with me before you keep on chasing them, though."

I glanced at Halla, and she gave me a tiny nod. I made a face and shook my head in response.

Turning to Peck, I said, "That is a kind offer, but I prefer not to eat snakes off a hexed plate." I waved and walked straight past him. "We'll go on our way and leave your supper uninterrupted."

Whistler muttered, "The bacon I'm carrying around has almost putrefied."

Peck caught up and fell in beside me as I walked. "I understand, and it seems like forever since I met anyone who knew anything about hexes. Stay, and we can discuss learned matters. You can lay your food straight onto the bare table if you like."

I snorted. "If you're so anxious for companionship, why do you live in the middle of a damn swamp?"

"Are you yourself a hexer?" Peck asked, ignoring my question. "Or perhaps a sorcerer?"

"No, I carve wooden legs for a living." I jerked my thumb back at the others. "But all of my friends here are sorcerers."

Halla gazed across me at Peck as we walked past the cottage. "We are not concerned with your hexes. But the snake smells good. Bib . . ." She stared at me and then at the manacles on my wrists.

Peck nodded at the manacles. "I wanted to ask you the story of those, I admit, but I didn't want to come across as rude. I'll be happy to strike them off, if I can keep them. Iron is an uncommon commodity here in the bog."

I stopped near the edge of the mound and sighed. I didn't know where the path picked up again, or if it even did. I'd been marching straight across and hoping something good had happened. "Peck, that sounds like a fair trade, if we can do it before supper."

"I would prefer that." Peck chuckled. "You're less likely to slip and drag some of my good snake onto the floor."

Whistler made a sick face. "Leave it there."

The tall man led me to an outbuilding at a bouncing walk and pointed at a small anvil. "Lay 'em up there." A tiny forge and a table full of smith's tools stood nearby.

I forced myself to lay my left hand out. "Did you cart all of this here yourself?"

"Mm. Some." Peck selected a chisel. "I hired the rest of it done. I had to kill the porters afterward, of course, and throw their bodies into the swamp. Hold still now. Don't move a jot."

I whipped my hand off the anvil.

Peck laughed until his eyes watered, and his grimy fingers left smudges as he rubbed at the tears. "Sorry, but you looked awfully serious about everything. Of course I didn't kill them! I met them partway and hauled things the rest of the distance myself. Now lay your hand up here."

I took the chance, and within two minutes, the manacles lay on the ground. Peck wound them up and stowed them in a solid-looking chest.

Back outside, everyone but Halla loitered, shifting from foot to foot and murmuring. Halla stood as if she'd been planted and was waiting to sprout fruit.

Whistler hefted his pack. "It was nice to meet you. Have fun eating your snake."

I laughed. "Thank you, Peck. Sorry we can't stay for supper."

Every smidge of happiness fell off the man's face. "I wish you would. Really do. If you don't like snake, I have some day-old swamp rat. It's damned chewy, though."

"It would please me to stay, but every minute we tarry is a minute of torture for those children. Um, where's the path north?"

"Wait!" Peck shifted to stand in front of me. "Do you care about a secret path out of the bog? It would shorten your trip north by half a day."

Bea ran up beside me. "Yes! If it saves time, show it to us!"

Peck gave Bea a tiny bow. "Showing it to you would give me pleasure. After supper."

Bea kicked Peck hard in the shin. "Not after supper. My baby may be dying. Now!"

The hound ran toward Bea, growling.

The hexer jumped back, hopping a little, and whistled at his dog. The dog sat and watched Bea like she may grow claws and horns. Peck made no move toward a path, secret or not.

Bea tried to kick him on the other shin, but he held her off with one arm. She screeched, "Let go, you criminal!"

Halla grasped Bea's arm and held her in place. "Eating snake does not take much time."

Bea curled her lip at Halla and lowered her voice, but every word fell like a marble in a quiet room. "Your children may be an hour away from dead, but you whine about supper? What kind of woman are you?"

Halla froze, still holding Bea's arm. Then she let the small woman go and gazed at the ground. "I am ashamed. I am a woman who is ashamed. Thank you."

Peck was rubbing his shin and glaring at Bea. I edged closer in case the man tried to hit her or kick her in return. Instead, he straightened and smiled. "I suppose you're in a spanking hurry to travel on, that your task is more important than a good snake stew. You ought to sleep here for the night, though." He shifted his gaze to Halla and me. "You can set off rested. Besides, you'll want to travel through the bog as little as possible in darkness. Does that make sense?"

Suddenly things *did* make sense. I had been looking for treachery, but Peck was just lonesome and wanted to share a meal. Well, if he desired company, he shouldn't live in the middle of a damn swamp. I turned to Halla. "We can get out of this smelly, sucking hole half a day sooner than Leddie's men expect."

Whistler said, "To hell with Leddie's men. Beg pardon." He nodded at Bea. "This place smells like a sick pig that's passed through an alligator. Let's cross it as fast as possible."

Halla nodded. "Peck, show us this secret path."

The hexer threw his head back and laughed. "Wonderful! You can stay for supper!"

"No, we will leave now," Halla said. "Tell us about this path."

Bea stepped up beside Halla and nodded.

"You seem set on this, and that is damned unfortunate." Peck crossed his arms. "You'll all stumble off the trail and die as soon as the sun sets, and that's an unlikely path to victory. Think of those children. No, I'll have to guide you. And there will be a cost." The man chuckled.

That was to be expected. Even hermits needed to buy things now and then. I made a show of digging in a pouch that I knew held no coins. "We can scrape together a little silver between us. We might find a smidge of gold deep in a pouch someplace, but I couldn't promise it."

Peck stopped smiling. "I don't need gold. The toads and raccoons don't care about it. I need help with a problem."

I should have ignored Peck at that point, just pretended he never lived and gone off into the swamp without him. But everybody else started asking about his problem, and Bea promised straight-out to help him before she heard a single detail. Whistler backed her up half a breath later. Peck started explaining things, Halla and Pil asked questions, and the whole situation flew beyond my control in less than a minute.

Peck's problem was lawlessness. For a few weeks, some broken-down bandits had hidden in the northern end of the swamp, popping out to rob passersby and then retreating into the marsh. Peck didn't give a damn about passersby, but he needed to bring in supplies for himself soon. He exclaimed over the wonders of the swamp the same way he'd talk about a beautiful woman, but it couldn't provide him with iron, flour, wine, salt, cloth, and a dozen other items that made a hermit's life enjoyable. Peck feared these bandits would snap up his supplies and maybe him too.

I saw a chance to regain control of the conversation. "I guess you want us to kill these people."

Peck chuckled, his eyes almost disappearing behind his high

cheeks. "If you can chase them away, that would be all right with me, but I wouldn't count on that level of cooperation."

"How many are there?" I asked.

Peck gazed upward. "Oh, it varies. I have seen as few as three and as many as six."

"You spied on them? Lately?" Pil snapped. "Is there any particular reason why you need us to go get cut up and murdered when you can just sneak in and hex the crap out of them?"

Grinning, Peck said, "I beg your pardon, but you may not understand the intricacies of hexing."

Pil raised her eyebrows. "I understand that cowards will risk other people's lives."

Peck's grin disappeared. "The secret way north starts a quarter mile down the trail beside the dead tree that looks like two geese. Good luck." He walked back toward his cottage.

"Pil!" Bea set her jaw. "Say you're sorry."

Pil blinked. "I'm sorry, Bea, but I can't say I'm sorry to that old rat-pile, because I'm not a bit sorry!"

Halla said, "Young woman, say you're sorry. You do not have to be sorry."

Whistler glared at Halla. "Nobody has to say a single thing they don't want to say, so go sit in a puddle."

Halla turned to me. "Control your manservant."

"Whistler doesn't work for me." I nodded at the big thug. "He's his own man. He's just here to save your life and die gloriously."

Peck started laughing behind us, a deep, joyful laugh that's born in the gut. "Never mind, miss, I don't need an apology. You people are more entertaining than dancing bears. I'll lead you along the short path. Just promise you'll help me dissuade those bandits."

FIFTEEN

I have traveled more than I've stayed put in my life. I've wandered, homeless, for stretches of months and years. When the gods went looking for somebody to ride around randomly and open the way for their return, they could hardly have chosen better than me.

I've passed through just about every kind of countryside and weather. So, when I proclaimed that the center of the Graplinger Bog was the most repugnant and awful place in the world, my opinion was not an idle belief. It was based on hard experience.

The air smelled like filth, and not the honest filth of a barnyard manure pile. This smell seeped all the way into the gut. It rose from excrement squeezed out by dank, slick beasts, churned together with a million nameless deaths that oozed up to the surface of the muck. All of it fermented in nature's chamber pot and squirted over everything that could be seen, touched, or inhaled.

Ahead of me, Peck chuckled. "Stay close, or the swamp monster will get you!" That was the five hundredth time he had said it in the past thirty hours, or so I estimated. The rosy bastard chuckled again. I slopped along the path, which was more water than dirt, and imagined shoving my knife into his jovial heart from behind.

We slogged onward, silent except for the squishing of our boots on the path. I flexed my left hand. The numbness had overtaken my whole hand and then spread up to my wrist. I couldn't cure it or even understand it. I admitted to myself that I would need Harik's help with it, or at least his mocking advice.

Sunrise pushed sickly, greenish light into the swamp and filtered through the nasty trees and foliage. An hour later, Peck stopped. "They'll be not far ahead," he whispered, "so keep yourselves quiet while I scout them." Peck turned, sliding his feet to quiet the sloshing mud. He had commanded his woolly dog to stay behind, I supposed to guard their home.

I touched Peck's arm. "I'll accompany you on this jaunt, Peck. I need to see these horrible bandits for myself. Besides, you might be leading us into a trap. I'll be walking close behind you, and if I think we've been betrayed, my knife will be in your heart before you hear me move."

"Foolishness!" Peck didn't so much frown as he pouted. "When you walk, you sound like a crippled toad dragging and bouncing its butt along."

"There is no other way," Halla grated. "You cannot go without him."

"I'll go home, then. Take your chances without me."

"Don't break our bargain." I shook my head, slow and sorrowful. "That's an awful thing. Some of the gods would hate to hear about it, if somebody were to tell them."

"I don't need gods for my work." Peck stood tall, but he bit the inside of his cheek.

"I've heard Harik say he loves to watch a good, creative hexer. The disappointing hexers . . . well, I never hear anybody talk about them again." I stared at the mud and shook my head.

Those were raw-boned lies, but Peck had never spoken with a god, so he didn't know the difference. He called me a damned bastard with rotting balls and then led me down the path, both of us sliding our feet as we walked. I followed him at a gliding pace for twenty minutes, and then Peck made us creep along until we neared the bandits' camp. Kneeling behind some tall grass, I examined them.

The camp was almost an island—a big, damp area separated from the path by a wide stretch of swamp water. I wouldn't have cared to rush across that water. There was a good chance I'd sink. A narrow bridge of dirt and swamp grass connected the island to the path we crouched on, and it seemed to be the only way in.

Nine ragged but well-armed men and women ate, slept, or walked around the camp, which had no fire. Two of them stood guard with bows. A tenth man sat on the dirt tied to a tree, his head dangling.

I figured if I sprinted to the dirt bridge, the archers could each fire at me once. They might manage two shots, if they were proficient. If we could attack by surprise, we might overrun the whole bunch. That seemed unlikely, though, since we had to cross that mud-slathered path, and the bandits could shoot arrows and laugh at us as we ran, slipped, and cursed all the way.

I jerked my head at Peck, and we retreated up the path.

When we returned to the others, Peck murmured, "We found them. Less than half an hour ahead."

"How many?" Halla whispered.

Peck hesitated. "Nine."

Pil growled. "What happened to three or six?"

Peck shrugged. "They're part of the nine."

"We can't attack by surprise," I said. "We have to run through the mud while two bandits shoot arrows at us. I admit it presents a challenge." I smiled. "But hell, we have three sorcerers and one shabby tree trunk of a hexer. They're just a few bandits sitting on their asses. Some of them look puny. They might have the swamp-wombles and spend the day squatting with their trousers down." I was overstating my confidence a little, but if we couldn't kill these sad bandits, then we may as well present ourselves to Memweck bound, naked, and oiled.

"No. No. Think about thith—" Pil swallowed and slowed down. "About *this*. Maybe we should go back into the bog and take some other path to some other entrance. Or, exit, really."

"That is a bad plan." Halla growled. "Very bad."

Pil flinched as if she'd been kicked.

I patted Pil's shoulder. "The grumpy woman is right—think about it. How many more soldiers does Leddie have?"

Pil stared downward and shrugged. "I guess I don't really know."

"No, you do not," Halla said. "I do not, either. It may be a thousand, or enough to surround the whole swamp. The sooner we leave the bog, the less likely there will be many men at every exit."

"That was incisive, Halla!" I patted her arm. "Almost brilliant. I don't know why you're not the general of all the Empire's armies yet. Now . . ." I rubbed my hands together like some charlatan cheating people of their coins. "It's time for all sorcerers to show what they're holding. Halla?"

She shook her head, as slowly and deliberately as a gristmill.

I examined her face, but she didn't give away anything. It wasn't for me to question her about sorcery, but if she had abandoned magic, that would pare down our tactical options. I sighed and raised my eyebrows at Pil.

"No, I'd need time. Krak, we've never stopped moving since I met you. " She slurred a little against the holes where her teeth had been. Her speech had deteriorated as her face and lips had swollen even more these past two days. The unclean air and water of the bog might be poisoning her. For all I knew, her face would fall off.

I sighed. "Well, Krak tear our skins off to wrap his mighty loins." I lifted myself to call on Harik.

The God of Death answered me without delay. "Murderer, do you promise to leave Memweck alone?"

"Yes, I promise, Mighty Harik, you immortal ass-flapper."

Harik hesitated. "Are you lying to me?"

"Of course not, Mighty Harik! I'll be a good boy. I'm headed toward the northern kingdoms even now, aren't I? And just to be certain I'm not caught short on power during the undoubtedly perilous trip, I extend to you the privilege of making the first offer on a new bargain."

"You shall wait until you have a greater need. If some part of your person is mutilated and dangling, you may call me again."

"I need to bargain now so that Your Magnificence doesn't screw me later on when I'm desperate."

I imagined drawing my sword, but before it cleared its insubstantial scabbard, Harik shouted, "Enough! I know you're lying, you nasty little toenail!" He flung me back into my body, driving me to my hands and knees in the mud.

I stood up, shaking the mud off my hands and looking around at everyone. "Let's go kill the bastards with steel, the way our forefathers intended."

Half an hour later, we neared the bandits. We had already achieved the real victory—we'd managed to sneak five people close to the camp without anybody hearing us. That feat would outshine the glory of any success we might earn in combat. Bea stayed back up the trail out of sight with orders to hurry back to the cottage if we were slaughtered. With luck, the bandits wouldn't pursue her, rape her, and maybe murder her.

My plan was as simple as milk and based on a lie. I explained that Peck would begin the attack by shooting one of the guards, then the other guard, and then anybody else who might jump up to fire arrows at us. I would hustle down the path with Halla and the rest behind me, leaving Pil to guard the rear. Then side by side, Halla and I would assault the bandits' camp, with Whistler just behind us.

That's how I explained it to everybody, but in fact the bridge into the camp wasn't as wide as I had described. Halla would have no room to fight beside me on the narrow bridge. That was good. I wanted to kill all those bandits myself, and I didn't want her to cheat me out of a single one.

Peck stepped out from behind a tree and fired an arrow right into a guard's heart, forty paces away. With my sword drawn, I ran past him down the path as fast as I could without tumbling like an apple across the mud. Halfway to the camp's entrance, somebody behind me slipped, hit the ground, and skidded. I dared a glance at the camp just as Peck put an arrow in the second guard's chest. She cried out before dropping straight down.

Two armed bandits raced me to the camp entrance. The rest either followed them or were grabbing weapons. One man in the front was bare-chested. One in the rear fumbled with his boots and then threw them aside.

I reached the bridge just ahead of the shirtless bandit, who swung his club at my head while I skidded and ducked. Then I cut him deep across the thigh, and he shouted some fine profanity as he staggered aside and fell into the water. His friend roared at me, charged, and impaled his throat on my sword.

The next bandit was twenty feet away.

Halla yelled from behind me, "Move up! There's no room!"

I laughed and shifted half a step, right in her way, and I lunged to stab the bare-chested man in the back as he knelt, panting in the water. I shifted over to face the next man, who looked older than me. Back in the camp behind him, a squatty bandit snatched up a bow, nocked an arrow in a flash, and fired. Then he stared straight at me and nocked another arrow.

The gray-haired bandit eased toward me, on guard with his sword. The bowman aimed at me, and I knelt low. The arrow whipped over me as the old fellow thrust at my face. I reached up for an awkward block, and he came back trying to cut my arm off at the shoulder. I almost fell to one knee as I dodged. I scrambled forward, grabbing the knife off my belt to stab him from inches away, but the knife slipped out of my numb fingers and sailed off into the water. Another arrow flew past, inches from my leg. I hadn't even seen it fired. My mature opponent punched me in the stomach with his free hand.

This was what I had schemed to get—all of them to myself.

I laughed and slipped a leg behind the old bandit's, threw him to the ground, and hopped past him. The man behind him wasn't prepared for me just yet, probably hoping his friends would finish me. I stabbed him in the heart before he moved. The gray-haired man I'd thrown down squirmed on the ground just behind me, so I stomped his neck and heard bones crack.

The squatty archer now lay on the dirt with an arrow in his chest. A man and a woman still faced me, the man tall and trembling, and the woman powerful with long, auburn braids. The tall one cut at my head as if he didn't really mean it. I slashed open his throat. The woman threw down her sword and backed up, her hands raised. I followed to kill her, but my collar yanked me back.

Halla dropped my collar, stepped around me, and knocked the woman down with the butt of her spear. "We might want to ask her questions." Halla pointed at the dying older man and the shirtless bandit, now facedown in the water. "You did not need to kill those two."

I grinned. "Oh, I needed to kill them, darling. I'd have killed this one here too, if you hadn't interfered while I was contemplating it. Hell, I may kill her yet."

I searched for Peck and Pil up the main path. Pil was kneeling over the hexer, who had an arrow in his forehead.

A great moan came from behind me. I swear it was as loud as a moose. I turned to see Whistler squirming in the mud with an arrow sticking out of both sides of his leg.

SIXTEEN

Pil ran, skidding all the way, to the spot where Whistler writhed on the muddy ground. When I got there, she was kneeling beside Whistler, so I leaned over her shoulder. She was feeling the flesh around his wound with such a determined touch that it probably hurt like hell. Halla was guarding and probably terrorizing the prisoners.

"I need help pulling it out," Whistler said through gritted teeth. Sweat covered his colorless face. "It needs to come out right away. I imagine it's covered in crud." He shot a glance at Pil. "Bib, will you do it?"

I knelt over his leg. "You trust me with that task? I might wallow it around in there to make you cry." I winked at him.

"I've watched you. You don't like it when people are in pain. You like it when they're dead, but not in pain."

It was a fair observation, so I laughed at him.

Quick steps came from behind me, and Bea arrived while I was still laughing. She dropped to her knees beside Whistler. "What did you do?" She reached into the mud for his hand and grabbed his filthy fingers.

Pil was holding Whistler's other hand. "Bib, I'll do it if you won't, but I know you can do it better. I don't want to do it badly and kill him." She glanced up, her jaw set. "I don't know, I think my heart would break."

It was a bald exaggeration to say Pil's heart would break, or so I assessed, but Bea looked as if hers might. Her body had sagged over Whistler's hand, and her face resembled a wet rag.

I sighed. "Fine. Bea, go beg some of that silk from Halla. Pil, you scoot back. Whistler, do you need a few seconds to prepare for this ordeal?"

Whistler shook his head, his face turning gray.

I broke off one end of the arrow and pulled the other side through, fast enough not to count as torture, but not so fast as to tear up his leg. Whistler shouted when I broke the arrow and called me a son of a bitch when I pulled the rest out. Then he lay on the ground, panting.

"Keep the wound out of the mud. Bea, hand me that silk." I cut some strips and started bandaging. "You better fashion yourself a crutch soon. I don't intend to slow down for you."

Whistler said something, but I didn't hear it. His wound was bleeding a lot more than I expected.

"Whistler, the artery is cut."

After a pause, he said, "Aw, hell."

"What does that mean?" Bea demanded.

"It means Bib could wrap a thousand shirts around my leg, and it wouldn't do any good. I'm going to die lying right here."

Bea pointed at Pil. "Why can't Bib save you the way he saved her? Ask Bib to save you."

Whistler blew a couple of breaths. "He will if he wants. I won't die begging."

I had just told myself I couldn't spend even a thousandth of a square of power saving Whistler. But now that he was acting so brave, I felt kind of miserly.

Bea turned her squashed-up face to me. "Please save him!"

Pil didn't join in but looked as if she'd like to.

I shook my head. "Sorry, ladies, I can't spend power I might need later. Maybe to save one of you." I had retained just a sliver for emergencies, and saving Whistler from death would eat almost half of it.

Pil frowned at me. "How many people have you killed these past days? You should save one now so the gods don't get bored watching you do nothing but kill."

"Pil . . . the gods never get tired of watching people get killed. What did Dixon teach you?"

Pil jumped to her feet so fast she almost slipped. "Well, would it just offend the gods to no end for you to change your mind and save somebody today? Save him and then not kill anybody for a while? Would that be acceptable? Or would Harik get mad?"

Harik probably would get mad.

And that by itself was a damn fine reason to do it. Without any more conversation, I lifted myself to trade, calling on Harik.

Harik did not answer. I called out to several other gods who I thought might stoop to speaking with me. None of them answered, either.

Discouraged, I returned to the exact moment I had left. I wanted to save Whistler, although it probably was a wicked thing to do, considering what a rascal he was. It would be a foolish act.

Although, how foolish would it be compared to hunting down some mysterious, snotty being of vast power? Or letting Bindle's children get stolen? Or working on a ruined house hoping a dead woman would come home? Or murdering a little girl? Hell, my life had been a bucketful of foolish acts.

Saving Whistler would fit right in.

None of that sloppy logic meant anything, of course. I just wanted to save him and was searching for a reason.

I didn't consider for an instant explaining my situation and asking everybody what they thought or telling them what it might mean. It was none of their business, not even Whistler's. My acts of sorcery were beyond their judgment. That may have seemed damned arrogant of me, but if they couldn't judge me, then they also couldn't be blamed for anything horrible I might do.

I knelt beside Whistler's leg and pressed my palm against the wound. "I'm healing you just enough to keep you from dying, and not a speck more. When we march out of here, you'll have to keep up. Although these devoted ladies might be pleased to carry you on their shoulders."

When I was done, I felt happier about saving him than I had expected. It surprised me, since I figured I'd be aggravated with myself for doing it.

Bea hugged me, and Pil smiled before she walked back up the trail. Then I found an almost-dry spot away from people doing things and lay down to sleep without asking anybody's leave.

I lay awake listening to every grunting, chirping, farting, death-crying creature within half a mile. I considered whether I had wasted my effort on Whistler, since he might get killed by something else before nightfall. I wondered what the prisoners might know and how terrified they were of Halla by now. I remembered how Manon had sounded when she was pissed off at me, and I thought up a few nasty names to call Harik the next time we spoke. I finally fell asleep not much before noon.

Sometime in the afternoon, I woke up because Halla was kicking my boot. When I peered up at her, she said, "I want to kill the prisoner, but I do not want to listen to you complain about it for a year. So, you kill her."

I dislike killing prisoners, although I won't hesitate to kill a man who has surrendered in combat. I admit that the distinction is vague, but a shackled prisoner is no threat to me. On the other hand, an enemy who tries to kill me and drops his weapon could try again if my attention drifts.

When I bind a prisoner, I'm responsible for his life. If the trees start burning, I can't leave him tied to one. But if a man does his best to kill me and then throws down his weapon, my only responsibility is making sure he'll never try again.

It almost makes sense. However, it's just some shit I tell people. In truth, I have found that I need a line between the people I will murder and the ones I won't. If I wanted, I could accept a man's surrender with one word, or even a nod, and then he'd be safe from me. So, the distinction is faint. But it's a reason to let people live.

That's a lie too, of course, one I often tell myself about my morality. In the end, my reasons for deciding who to kill and who to let live won't withstand harsh examination.

Despite all that, I have killed prisoners now and then. After twenty seconds with this woman bandit, I yearned to murder her. I felt ambivalent about the man her gang had tied to a tree.

The man, Vang, turned out to be one of Leddie's horsemen. In fact, he was the small, slow one who had been sent to cut Pil's throat. When I told him about that, he shrugged and said, "Sorry. I didn't much want to kill her anyway."

The woman, Affie, said she had been with these horrible, murdering dog-knockers just one week, and before that had led a blameless life of prayer and good works. She cried as she said, "I didn't have any single idea what kind of men these were, not a single goddamn one! I thought they were some nice traveling tradesmen, out fixing pots and saddles from one nail-dick town to the next. I never killed a single soul myself, not me, not a single rotten soul at all, and I didn't rob none, either. The deceivers tricked me! I'm the one who was hurt!" She dropped her face into her bound hands, and her shoulders shook like she was riding in a bad wagon on a rough road.

Vang belched. "Hell, woman, you're going to kill me if I have to listen to much more of your bullshit."

Affie snapped, "Shut up, you cross-eyed, thimble-balled son of a dripping bitch! You . . . you're the murderer with blood on your sword! And human flesh in your bag—" She glanced up at me before sneering at Vang. "Maybe it was a pig shank, but it could as easily have been a baby's leg! Couldn't it, you soulless throat-pounder?"

I might have appreciated Affie's vicious profanity more, but even after a nap, my head felt like a thumb that somebody had slammed in a door. I pointed at her. "You! Hush!" I turned to Vang. "Where are the rest of Leddie's little boys?"

Vang peered off into the swamp. "Well, I shouldn't say, I guess, since it would be traitorous and all." He shifted one shoulder and then the other up and down as if they were scales, and he grimaced. "But I guess you can't be a traitor unless you go against your king, and the captain and I ain't got the same king. I'm not sure she has a king. And she already missed two paydays, which doesn't make me love her too damn much."

"He's a liar!" Affie leaned toward Vang, and flecks of spit flew at him.

Vang sat up straight. "Which part was I lying about?"

"All of it!" Affie shouted. "Don't listen to that maggot slime! I'm the one who can help you!"

Halla stood tall over Affie. "Be quiet if you do not want to be thrown into that water."

Vang said, "The captain sent little groups of us off to watch the places where trails leave the swamp. If we saw you lot, we were supposed to ride hell for leather back to her with the word." He nodded at Affie. "Three fellows and I were guarding the trail north of here when this banded bitch sneaks up with some friends and whacks me while I'm shitting behind a bush."

"Oh, the untruths! Let me fight him!" Affie strained against the rope around her wrists. "The gods will see that the truthful are victorious!"

Halla thrust her spear into the ground between Affie's legs, a finger's width away from the woman's crotch. "Be silent. Speak, and I will cut you in a bad way. Speak again, and I will cut off one finger for every word you say."

Affie froze for several seconds before leaning back away from the spear.

Vang laughed until his eyes watered. "Thanks for that. I'll help you for sure now."

Halla and I combed a few more details out of Vang. Leddie had survived the falling tree, which I had suspected, although she'd been wounded in some way. She and her main force waited about four hours away, ready to run us down since we'd be afoot.

Whistler and Bea had dragged Peck and the eight dead bandits to the middle of the clearing and laid them in a row. Now Whistler was limping around, digging with a cracked wooden spade he'd found someplace. When I reached him, I saw that the three-foot square hole he had dug was nearly filled with water. He glanced up at me, reached into his shirt, and handed me something wrapped in dirty cloth.

I unwrapped it to find a dozen assorted coins, a nice ring, and a good whetstone. The cloth wrapping had been torn from one of the dead men's shirts.

"That's your share." Whistler nodded and then jammed the spade into the ground again.

"Hell, I don't need this."

Whistler shrugged and took it back from me. A moment later, it was rewrapped and stuffed into his shirt. He returned to digging.

I kicked a few pounds of mud off my boots, a futile effort. "Whistler, leave off that work. You'll open your wound, and I need you to take watch."

The man gaped at me. "I can't let them lie here. It's not decent."

I blinked a few times. "They weren't too damn decent themselves. Getting eaten up by bugs and alligators is good enough for them."

Whistler shook his head. "I can't let them lie here and rot. It's against the gods."

"Oh, but once they're dead, the gods are pleased for you to steal everything but their teeth?"

"No priest ever told me that taking a dead man's things would make the gods mad." Whistler glanced at me sideways. "Besides, is it worse to rob them or to kill them?"

I could have told Whistler how much the gods didn't give two shits and a blind horse about whether he let these bodies rot, but nothing good could arise from arguing religion just then. "You'll never get a hole big enough. This is a swamp—water would fill a bucket if you held it over your head."

Whistler examined the hole. "Maybe I won't. Or maybe the gods'll hold back the water. I won't know if I stop digging."

I left the man to dig and walked over to Pil, who was handling Peck's bow.

"May I take a look?" I asked.

She handed it right over. The bow was tall, and I would have thought it too strong for Pil. Once Peck was killed, though, she had snatched it up and may have saved my life with it. The bowstave was made of ash and was rectangular for most of its length, although tapered to a grip in the middle. A complicated symbol formed of triangles and waves was carved just above the grip.

I pointed at the symbol. "This bow is hexed."

"I know," Pil said.

I handed the weapon back to her. "Peck would have depended on it, so hexing it made sense. Have you shot a bow before?"

Pil nodded. "Although it's not as if I was the greatest archer around, I wasn't even average most of the time—which sounds odd, because average means averaged across all the times, but I think you know what I mean." She talked fast, and the slurring from her teeth made understanding her a challenge. "I wasn't truly all that good and I probably killed that horrible man today with a lucky shot." She clenched her teeth and scowled at the ground when she said it.

Peck and the two dead archers had left more than forty arrows behind. Pil snatched one off the ground, nocked it, and stopped.

"What's wrong?" I asked. "Is the hex something bad?"

"No, the hex makes the arrows fly true." She pointed across the clearing at a modest tree. Six arrows were clumped in a space smaller than my palm.

I nodded. "That's pretty damn handy. Hang on to that weapon, young woman. The world isn't full of fellows ready to have their brains scrambled so that you can have a hexed bow."

Pil bit her swollen lip and winced. "What do you think would happen if I took a hexed bow and enchanted it too?"

That was a novel thought. I couldn't remember seeing something that had been hexed and then enchanted. "It might be an irresistible weapon. Or it might turn into a snake and crush you to death. There's no good way to know."

"Yes, there is. At least I think it's a good way, or probably the only way. Would you like to find out? I enchanted it while you were asleep."

I almost said no. Something catastrophic might happen. It was an unknown endeavor. But I nodded and stepped all the way back to the water's edge. "All right. I want to see you shoot a dragonfly in the eyeball."

With a creased brow, Pil fired toward the tree she'd already used for a target. The arrow missed the tree trunk by two feet.

"Don't feel bad, Pil. It was an uncertain effort to begin with."

Pil pushed out her jaw, grabbed another arrow, and fired again. She struck the trunk right in the middle. The arrow bounced off.

"Entertaining," I said. "Not too handy."

Pil was already grabbing another arrow, and a moment later, she fired at the tree again. The arrow sailed twenty feet wide and a hundred feet into the marshy water, where it slammed into a shocked stork. The bird screeched and tumbled into the water, leaving a few feathers in the air. Pil already had another arrow in her hand.

"Wait!" I shouted.

The next arrow smashed into the tree and kept going, splitting the trunk all the way up. Half of the tree creaked, listed, and then groaned as it fell, hammering the water and soaking Halla along with the prisoners.

I expressed my opinion as an expert fighter. "Well . . . that's . . ."

Pil stalked over and shoved her reddened face right in front of mine. "It's a damn disaster, that's what it is. And I enchanted it! It came out of me! What have you done to me?"

I kept my voice matter-of-fact. "Not a thing, Pil. This was your idea. I was asleep."

Her chin trembled. "What did you make me do to myself?"

"First of all, let's squash this notion deader than that stork. Nobody makes you do anything to yourself, not the gods, not your old mama, and sure as hell not me. You are the architect of your own glory or destruction." I pushed her out to arm's length, and not too gently. "Second, there's probably nothing wrong with you. Hexing and magic just may not agree with one another."

Pil nodded as she grimaced. "I'll make something else then, something not hexed ahead of time, and that'll show me one way or the other."

"That's the right idea. Keep trying. But first pitch that bow into the next mudhole we see before it cuts somebody in two."

An hour later, Whistler and Bea had found a stout root from some unwholesome tree to serve him as a crutch. He experimented, slipping a few times before he found his stride and crutched along steadily. By the time we marched north on the tenuous trail, Whistler was moving pretty fast.

SEVENTEEN

For the twentieth time in ten minutes, Vang tripped on a rock or in a hole. Whenever he stumbled, he cursed, "Bloody piles!" or something like it. Now and then, he tossed in a "Raw bloody piles!" or "Your mother's bloody piles!" Once when he sounded like ten sacks of flour hitting the ground, he growled, "Bloody piles of the gods and their leg-humping wolves!"

I peered in the man's direction as he bumbled ahead of me under the merest starlight. "I admire a man who's loyal to his profanity, Vang. It argues that you had a happy childhood."

"Shit! Damned rocks! Damned ground! There's a reason I'm a horseman, you know!"

Halla's energetic whisper came from off to my left. "Maybe this man's friends have interesting curses too. They might be happy to teach them to you while they kill you."

"Coward," I answered, but hardly loud enough for her to hear. She was right to chide me. I had gotten bored with tramping across this dark, stony plain just north of Graplinger Bog. We were walking a huge circle around the place where Vang had said his fellow soldiers were sitting watch while they argued and gambled. The circle might not be huge enough to mask oaths and joking, however.

"Vang, quit cursing the gods and their fine rocks," I whispered. "If you need to express how much you hate existence, bite your lip or smack yourself in the eye."

Vang didn't say anything to that. Instead, he tripped again, but he stayed quiet.

Everybody but me had argued that we should sneak into the lookouts' camp and overwhelm them. Ideas for what we should do after that varied. Pil wanted to take a prisoner or two and question them in case the situation had changed since Vang was captured. Halla and Whistler preferred to kill everybody, steal their horses, and move on. Bea felt we should get as much information from them as an hour of torture could produce. She offered to kill them herself. Vang and Affie sniped at each other and didn't offer opinions.

I explained to everybody that if we killed the soldiers, or captured them, or tied them up in a tree like apples, Leddie would soon figure out we had escaped north. Then she and her horsemen would run us down like we were chubby young pigs. But if we sneaked past her sentries, Leddie may well assume we were still in the bog, and she'd continue waiting for us to break out.

Bea glared at me, but everybody agreed to follow my plan. I hoped it played out better than most of my recent plans.

Pil moved up to walk beside me, a presence in the darkness. She tramped along, not speaking.

After a while, I whispered, "Do you want something, Pil? Or are you just enjoying my energetic presence and fine, manly smell?"

Pil choked a little, and I hoped it was laughter instead of disgust. She whispered fast, "Not that. Yes, I want something, but it's awkward, really it is. I was wondering if you might agree to . . . if you would ever think about showing me a few things about things. About sorcery things, I mean."

When I didn't answer, she kept talking but even faster. "I don't mean I want to follow you around and do your bidding and that kind of crap, and I don't want to wash your clothes and clean every darn thing you own twice a week because it's supposed to teach me something. Just a few things I don't know, which I guess makes sense, because if I already knew them, I wouldn't ask you to teach them to me, would I? So, will you?"

I whispered, "You were Dixon's student. If I try to teach you something, any sorcerer has the right to kill me."

Pil paused. "Really?"

"Hell no! Screw Dixon and both his homely sisters! I don't think I can teach you anything useful, though." I thought little of Dixon as a person. He must have been a canny sorcerer to have survived so long, but he didn't seem to have served Pil well as a teacher. On the other hand, I wasn't sure I wanted to compare my teaching to Dixon's. After what happened to Manon, my history as a teacher was tarnished.

Pil sighed. "Don't say no. Just don't."

I sighed right back at her. "I won't say no, but I won't say yes, either."

"Good!" she whispered.

"I didn't say yes!"

She kept on as if I hadn't spoken. "I need help with manipulation. I'm clumsy."

"Not too damn clumsy with a bow." Pil had kept the cursed weapon, not caring that I had advised her to get rid of it. Twice more I had almost told her to throw it away, but I kept still about it. She was a sorcerer, and I had no right to give her orders.

Pil whispered on: "And that's the other thing, which Dixon didn't know anything at all about. I need to understand enchantments and creating magical things. After all, I'm a Binder and am supposed to make enchanted objects, so I have to know more, and Dixon—he tried, but he was just ignorant on the subject."

I glanced over at Pil's outline against the stars. Vang stumbled again and hit the ground with a grunt. "Pil, what makes you think I know a single rat-gagging thing about Binder magic?"

She smiled big enough for me to hear it in her whisper. "In the oracle's tent, you talked about carrying a magical book there under your shirt. Created by the God of Death. That makes you a thousand times more qualified to talk about magical objects than any person I've ever met."

I did not want to talk about the book, especially since Harik had been threatening me over it. "It's not the same at all. Forget about it."

She paused, and then words spilled out of her as if she were pouring them from a bucket. "It might be the same, you can't know for sure—of course I know you're the expert since I'm asking you about it, but maybe you need a new perspective, like from somebody who's stupid about all this, who'll see things you don't, or can't, but you could, if you just knew what they couldn't see. Like me. What does the book do?"

"Nothing good. Not a single damn thing." I said it softly, but I knew she could hear.

"But what not-good things does it do?"

I felt sick. "Nothing. Leave it alone."

"Well, it has to do something! Why would Harik make a book and then just have it do nothing?" She put her hand out in the darkness and touched my arm before moving up to lay it on my shoulder. I shrugged it off.

"Oh. I see." Pil sighed again. "It's that important, then. Well, just tell me about the book, and I'll leave you alone about everything else. I mean, we've saved each other's lives, so you should be able to trust me, at least some, right? Please?"

She sounded like she was asking for no more than a piece of cake. "It won't help you."

"Please?" She reached for my shoulder again, patted it twice, and let her hand drop.

I kept walking, pretending to examine the ground I couldn't see in the dark. She was right—she had saved my life, and I'd saved hers. Dixon sure as cow-flop didn't seem to have taught her much. If I helped a little bit now, she might not make some bad sorcery mistake later on and die an agonizing death. Or at least not as soon. "Fine. The book did three things. It put an unending column of brilliant light over my head."

"That doesn't sound helpful, but all right. What else?"

"Another time it gave me the power to wither and kill things I stepped on."

"Now that is a power!"

Halla hissed. Pil caught her breath and lowered her voice back to a whisper. "What did you do with it?"

"I killed grass and bugs."

"Oh. Well, I guess I shouldn't judge. It seems a little . . . unambitious. But what else?"

I took a couple of deep breaths as I walked. The book's third effect had been one of the more appalling experiences of my life. As fast as I could, I said, "It brought the ghosts of people I've killed."

"Really? That's amazing. What did they do? Could you talk to them? Which one did you call first?"

"There was no first. They all came at once. There, that's what the book did. I'm not going to talk about this anymore."

"Everybody you've killed. Fantastic." She sounded as if I'd done some great sleight of hand for her. I wouldn't have been surprised if she had applauded.

A sudden thought flung my stomach into my feet, and I halted with such a jerk that I stumbled and almost fell on my face.

"Bib?" I heard Pil whisper.

I couldn't make a sound and didn't think I was breathing. It felt like I might have been hit by a door, or walked into a wall, but I hadn't.

I had killed Manon. I could use Harik's book to call her back. I could talk to her. The idea terrified me. I knew I should never do it. Part of me yearned to do it.

Pil had walked on ahead for a few seconds. Now she came back and grabbed my arm. "What's wrong, did you see something out there? I can't see anything."

Before I could speak, I heard Vang sprinting away, a little awkward with his hands tied. He didn't trip on a single damn rock or hole, though.

Pil ran after him.

"Stop!" I shouted as I sprang toward the sound of her footsteps. I grabbed her around the waist and hauled her to the ground. She struggled until I whispered, "There might be a thousand seven-foot-tall barbarians out in that darkness. You wouldn't know it until they cut you into strips."

By that time, Halla stood over us. "How did he get away?"

I jumped to my feet. I preferred to stand in a dignified way while I admitted I was stupid as hell. "I let Whistler hold the rope. Whistler?"

Whistler grunted. "He was nearly choking himself to death every time he tripped. I got tired of listening to him cuss and bitch. I only loosened the rope a little. He was such a clumsy fart I didn't think he could slip away. Or run away in the dark, neither. I'm sorry."

"What happened?" whispered Bea, who trotted up holding Affie's rope.

Halla said in a flat voice, "Bib and Whistler were outwitted by an uneducated soldier with food in his beard."

Someplace ahead of us, Vang started shouting. "It's me! It's me! Don't kill me!"

Pil snorted. "There's not much point in being quiet now."

I drew my sword. "All right, let's creep up there and kill them. Maybe we can do it before they ride off to warn Leddie." I stepped off toward the sound of Vang's voice, moving at a decent clip but not so fast that I'd run myself onto somebody's sword in the darkness.

From behind me, Pil huffed, "What about the thousand barbarians?"

"Screw the thousand goddamn barbarians! I hope there are two thousand of the greasy bastards for me to kill!" Of course, that was ridiculous boasting, but I wouldn't have objected to a dozen barbarians if I could string them out and fight them three at a time. That was ridiculous too, and it might kill me, but I'd never pay off Harik's debt by being timid.

There was not much chance of barbarians out there, but there were soldiers in the darkness who didn't like us much.

I couldn't see any sort of campfire on the plains, but soon I spotted something big blocking out a load of stars. Ten more seconds at a gliding walk revealed a huge, well-spread tree. I said over my shoulder, "This way, toward that big tree."

"What stinking tree? I don't see it," Affie complained.

I heard shouting from at least three men out near the tree. That stopped me, but I couldn't make out any words. Running footsteps sounded from ahead, and more came from the left. I turned my head from side to side to fix the locations.

"Watch out!" Halla yelled.

Something slammed into me from the right, hurling me into Pil and then onto the grass. I responded by noting I should remember to tell Halla that her warning was the least helpful thing she had ever said to me. I stayed on my back for a moment in case somebody was about to swing weapons around above me. Nothing like that happened, so I scrambled toward the place I thought Pil might be.

Before I could find the girl, I bumped into a big man on his hands and knees. He bulked a lot more than Whistler, so I figured he was the one who had crashed into me.

"Krak's pits!" Whistler yelled from someplace ahead of me. Steel weapons clanged.

The man at my feet was pushing up to stand. I still held my sword, but it wasn't well-suited for close-in fighting. I grabbed the knife that I'd scavenged from the bandits, and my numb hand almost dropped it. I reached around to cut the man's throat. The night was as dark as Harik's bowels, but throat-cutting didn't require too much precision.

I functioned well without sight. Ten months in a slimy, lightless underground cell had taught me that trick. However, all I could discern now was that between ten and twenty people were shouting, groaning, stomping, and fighting all around me. It was an awful performance on my part.

Somebody fell right past me and flopped onto the ground. I couldn't tell whether it was an enemy or a friend. A moment later, somebody else stumbled past in front of me, right after the first one. I couldn't identify them worth a damn, either. I thought about killing them both, but I settled for knocking the second one to the ground, kneeling, and holding my knife to his throat.

"Get off me!" Whistler yelled.

"Hell, I should have killed you both." I let him up and spun toward where I thought the first one had landed. It seemed that person had run, because I couldn't tell that anybody lay or stood close by. In fact, the fighting sounds seemed to be drifting apart.

Bea screamed off in the darkness, unmistakable. Whistler hobbled fast in that direction, and I kept looking for the person he'd been chasing. I took three steps after Whistler before the sound of approaching hoofbeats stopped me. Odds were good that was one of Leddie's men riding to warn her.

"Stop that rider!" I bellowed.

Somebody scuffed the grass behind me. I turned to find a woman jumping at me, starlight touching the knife she had pointed at my chest. I stabbed her in the throat before realizing she might be Pil attacking what she thought was an enemy. I panicked for a moment and shouted, "Pil!" I held her upright, as if that could keep her alive.

I eased the dying woman to the ground and peered hard at her face from a foot away. It wasn't Pil. Some person had set Affie free, and I guess she had decided to murder me. Although, in the darkness, she probably didn't know it was me in particular.

The hoofbeats drew close, so I ran toward them. The huge outline of a horse surged to cover the stars, and I jumped toward it. I went for the rider's leg to drag him down, but I was only able to slap his boot as he galloped past. The hoofbeats receded, and I heard more yelling and fighting, some in the distance. I paused to wonder how many of these blood-spitting assholes we were fighting. While I was at it, I wondered who they were.

I started trotting back to where I'd first been knocked over. The fighting had become more distant and sporadic. A skinny man appeared in front of me with a knife in his hand. Bits of starlight glinted off his wide-open eyes. He thrust faster than me, since I was struggling with my hand. I dodged, and his blade scratched my cheek and ear. Then he paused as if he were waiting to see how his thrust had turned out. I stabbed him in the chest and didn't pause until I'd stabbed him three more times.

As the skinny man's body collapsed, I heard somebody crying out in pain not far away. The moaning and whimpering sounded almost like a suffering dog. I crept toward the sound, in case it was a trap of some sort, but I found a woman writhing on the soft grass. She panted for a few seconds before bellowing in pain. Then she panted some more.

Bea lay on the ground, wounded, and I chose not to remind her that I had predicted this very thing would happen. I grabbed one of her hands while I felt for her wound. I found a ragged slice in her belly, both agonizing and most likely fatal.

Bea started to scream, and her whole body clenched as she bit it back.

"Don't worry that you have to keep quiet, Bea. Anybody who comes to kill us will be surprised when they find me waiting."

Bea sat halfway up, screamed like it might be her last, and flopped back down flat. "Save him! Bring him home! You promised."

"Most of my promises aren't worth a bucket of sand, but I'll honor this one. Don't worry." I patted her shoulder.

Bea stopped breathing. Then she shouted, "Don't worry? Don't goddamn worry? I'm dying, you toad!" She turned her face away from me and started crying. "I'm scared."

After saving Whistler, I had just a tiny amount of power left. I might keep Bea from dying right away, but her open wound would fester and kill her before long. If we tried to carry her someplace, she would die for sure.

"I know you're scared, darling. But I've seen a lot of death, and you're braver than most." That was a damn lie, but it might have been the only good lie I'd told in a month.

"Why do I have to die?" Bea cried harder.

I couldn't say anything to that.

She grabbed my arm hard. "When Harik takes me, you stab him in the ass as he leaves!" She let out a short scream and went back to panting.

I sat back on my heels, although I kept hold of Bea's hand. If those were her last words, I approved. I almost laughed, but it would have come off as impolite.

Of course, she wouldn't have been lying there like a gutted mackerel except for my carelessness. I let those young people in Bindle get slaughtered and stolen, including her baby. Maybe I owed her a life.

But hell, if I saved her now, likely something else would kill her tomorrow. She was like a baby bunny in a dog fight. It would be a waste.

On the other hand, I had been prepared to bargain with Harik to save Whistler's life.

I admitted that I was scrambling for a reason to save her too. I guessed I just wanted to keep people I knew alive, which didn't really sound like me.

Saving Bea would cost me something. If I did everything just right and the universe cheered me on, whatever the price was, it would be painful. Most likely, Harik would make me lose something I could never get back or do something I could never get over. I could only find out by calling on him.

I squeezed Bea's hand once. "Don't go anywhere just yet, darling. Hold on."

I called for Harik and lifted myself toward the place where gods offer power to sorcerers if they agree to eat dirt and pay too much. A moment later, every star was smudged out of the sky, along with the useless hint of light drifting from them. Every sound and touch suffered instant death, as abrupt as chopping off a chicken's head mid-cluck. I felt my heartbeat stop and I couldn't draw a breath.

Harik's curt, cultured voice rolled over me, the only thing I could perceive. I'm sure that fact satisfied his ego as much as sweaty frolics with supernatural beauties ever could. "Murderer, at last you have come. I am here to save you."

After so many years of insults, threats, and diatribes, I thought that nothing Harik could say would terrify me anymore, but he had just shown me I was wrong.

EIGHTEEN

When I was sixteen, my teachers told me that I had learned all I could from them. It wasn't that I was exceptionally smart. They knew thousands of things I still didn't understand, knowledge they passed on to my fellow students. But they said I was too willful to learn anything more from another human being. They told me to go away, do some good things, and try not to get myself killed right off.

Since then, I have saved dozens of people from death, at least temporarily. I've healed their bodies on the cusp of expiring, and I did the same for myself on occasion.

One winter when I had become a mature, settled man, I preserved two important assholes from dying. I don't remember who they were or why I did it, but I thought it vital at the time. Afterward, a tavern keeper I knew well slapped me on the back and shouted congratulations. He bought me a drink and proposed that we open a healing shop. We'd be rich in a month. He would handle the business details. All I'd need to do was relax, heal whoever wandered in, and enjoy a few drinks between customers. It would be like an eternal holiday.

I didn't kill the tavern keeper. Instead, I explained how much it would hurt if I decided to turn his liver to the consistency of porridge. I slit open the skin of his forehead so that a cascade of blood gushed over his face. I pressed my knife against his neck until I had him rolling his gigantic, twitching eyes and gurgling out of his slack mouth. I convinced him that merrily prancing around in the grim affairs of sorcerers was self-destroying behavior. Then I hauled him off the floor and set him trembling in a chair before stomping out of the tavern, which was full of silent people who had watched me terrorize him for no reason.

I can attest that this is how people get a poor reputation.

However, my behavior toward the man was abrupt at worst. The healing that impressed him so much was accomplished with power I had bargained from Gorlana, the Goddess of Mercy. In exchange, she required that I give my little girl, Bett, a puppy that was destined to die within a month. I couldn't explain or warn her of what would happen. But once the little creature died, I then had to tell my daughter what had happened and what I had done so she'd know how I decided to hurt her.

That's a horrible thing to do to a six-year-old girl, and I am a cast-iron piece of shit for doing it. But with two men dying in front of me, I couldn't quite convince myself that their lives were less important than my daughter's happiness and mine.

Sometimes I recall that self-sacrifice and can scarcely believe I engaged in it. It sure as hell doesn't sound like me now. Urges toward selflessness tend to perplex me. My little girl forgave me, but afterward she never looked at me the same way. She didn't fully trust me, and she was right not to.

In the Gods' Realm, with Bea busy dying in the world of man, Harik said to me, "Murderer, why have you waited? Have you been counting blades of grass? Attempting to recall how it felt to bathe? That woman's remaining breaths number less than twenty."

"How much less than twenty?" I tried to say it sarcastically, but it shocked me that he even recognized Bea's existence.

Harik sniffed. "That is unimportant."

"Which means it's critical." I tried to push down my fear so I could be ruthless and clever, or at least less foolish. Harik didn't answer me, so I said, "Otherwise, you wouldn't have mentioned the number of breaths, you reeking nest of armpit hair."

Harik still didn't answer. I tried to picture confusion on his relentlessly ideal face, but he had said he was here to save me, and I couldn't imagine what that meant.

I envisioned drawing my sword, which allowed me to see in the Gods' Realm. Harik perched forward on the top bench of the marble gazebo above me, but he didn't appear confused. He smiled at me like I was already salted and on a plate.

Before I could come up with a sharp comment about Harik's attitude, the entire sky convulsed with lightning, sheets of yellow, orange, and blue flame, and what appeared to be geysers of lava. None of the shattering violence made a sound, though, unless it sounded like the breeze and some cheerful birds.

Although no clouds floated amid all that carnage, little hailstones started falling. I caught a couple and saw they were diamonds the size of my pinky nail. I stared up at the firestorm. "What in the ass-knackering hell . . . ?"

Harik glanced up. "It is Krak's birthday."

I dropped the diamonds. "The Father of the Gods, the Master of Creation—hell, the Creator of Creation—has a birthday? I thought he was supposed to be eternal. How can he have a birthday?"

"He can have whatever he wants." Harik grimaced. "If someone possesses a thing that seems amusing, Krak will have one tomorrow. And it will be a nicer one, by far."

I drove that knowledge into my memory. Someday it might be the perfect thing to save me when death was climbing up my spine. I turned my thoughts back to trading for the power to save Bea. "Mighty Harik, since you know everything, and have done everything, and have screwed up many of those things I'm sure, I extend to you the opportunity to make me the first offer."

"Very well. I will save you, Murderer. I'll do you a kindness that you do not in any sense deserve. I offer one square of power."

Magical power was measured in squares. With one square, most sorcerers could produce one impressive, unnecessary, and wasteful effect. Or they could create several modest but useful effects. Theoretically, a sorcerer could accomplish a lot of small, critical tasks using that one square, but not many of us were smart enough and disciplined enough to manage it. I wasn't.

I knew I would want far more than Harik's pissant offer of one square, but he was simply bargaining hard. I needed to better understand what was in his termite hive of a mind. "What would Your Magnificence expect in exchange for this foundation-shaking amount of power?"

Harik pressed his lips tight. "You may refuse this by reflex, Murderer, but that is because you have no greater scope of vision than does an ant in a bowl. Thus, I command you to think hard before you respond. Think hard."

Harik seemed to be waiting for me to answer, so I nodded. "Think hard. Think long. Think deep. Think high. I can keep going."

"I want your memories of the Tooth, the sorcerer girl you killed. Stop!" Harik held out his hand as if he were commanding his hound to sit.

I had opened my mouth to shout no. Well, first I would have told Harik he could strangle himself with his own bile-dripping tongue. But when a god yells to stop, few people can keep going.

I found I was hunched forward, like a bull about to charge, so I stood tall and breathed deep. "Harik, let me be certain I understand this ridiculous impossibility. You want me to let you take my memories of Manon—my second daughter—as if she never existed for me. She would disappear from my life and my memory. That is what I gather from that reeling waterfall of ass-drool you called an offer." No matter what I said, I wasn't considering his proposal.

After a few seconds of silence, Harik leaned back and crossed his legs. "Your feeble awareness cannot understand how damaged you are."

"Horseshit!" I paused and realized that was a sickly answer. "A wagon full of horseshit! Fifty wagons of horseshit pulled by a herd of horses shitting as they go!"

"You have been here two minutes and have not yet insulted me in a truly repellent manner. Armpit hair? Fah! Your thoughts dwell elsewhere. Agree to trade, or I doubt you shall survive."

I laughed at the God of Death. I suspect it didn't sound convincing, but it was a laugh.

Harik didn't seem to notice. "Consider your recent greater-than-usual incompetence. You allowed Memweck to outwit you and pile guilt upon you. He has forced you to chase these stolen children as if you were some absurd cat chasing string. Pathetic."

"I don't believe that! You don't believe that, do you? Are you playing a trick for Krak's birthday? Is this a riddle?" I knew I was sounding silly, but it didn't matter. I realized his offer to take Manon away was a ploy. He was just aggravating me until the real bargaining started.

Harik said, "Murderer."

I waited a few seconds. "What?"

"Murderer."

I slipped and lost my temper a little. "Harik, you ripe bucket of fluid mashed out of a dead cow!"

Harik didn't answer or even move. I knew he was exaggerating this business about my thoughts being someplace else. He was an overdramatic, prissy old stump of a god. I admitted I'd been distracted at times. Well, going forward, I'd just concentrate harder on putting Manon out of my thoughts each day. I could remember her in the evenings at leisure.

But there was no way in the world of man, the Gods' Realm, or the Void that I would let Harik take my memories of Manon. It would be as if I killed her again.

I made a couple of absent cuts in the air with my sword so I'd appear disdainful when I said, "No, I won't give up Manon. But I will give up my memories of ever saying something nice about you."

"Why suffer through guilt and grief? They will destroy you. Let them go."

I paused. I had been telling myself these past days to let Manon go, just not so thoroughly as Harik was suggesting. The idea seemed less desirable when it came out of his mouth. "I reject that offer. I have a counteroffer. You give me five squares, and I'll convince Bea that Whistler abandoned her and let those soldiers cut her up."

"How terribly weak." Harik walked to the bottom bench, spread his Void-black robe, and sat with ten times the grace I will ever possess. "Your memories of the Tooth are my only offer. I will trade three squares for them, however."

"I had forgotten how amusing you are, Harik. You are the funniest self-obsessed, inbred, pie-faced eternal being I know. For three squares, I'll be tickled to tie up Whistler and abandon him under that big tree."

Harik shook his head. "Four squares for the Tooth."

"Leave off this shit about the Tooth!" I snapped at Harik, but that was for effect. I had my temper shackled now. I opened my mouth to say something crazy to show Harik how infuriated and out of control I was, but I noticed my hand instead.

I had entirely forgotten about my numb hand. All pain and harm fall away when a sorcerer enters the Gods' Realm, and that had distracted me. The numbness had spread halfway to my elbow, so I'd better deal with it right away. "Mighty Harik, I was wondering if you'd take a look at my hand."

The god squinted one eye and regarded me.

"It's been numb for a few days." I held up the hand. "I can't tell what the heck is wrong with it."

Harik kept squinting for a few more seconds and then leaned forward. "Come, let me see it."

I walked toward him as far as I could without stepping off the big patch of dirt, and then I stuck out my hand, palm up.

Harik leaned farther forward and scratched his mighty chin with his thumb. "Does it hurt?"

"No."

"Turn it over. Did it go numb all at once?"

I shook my head. "It started with my thumb, and it's way up past my wrist now."

"So it's spreading, then. Hmm. Hold it up over your head. Shake it a little."

I suddenly felt stupid. "Wait, are you screwing with me?"

"Do you want it to rot and fall off? Then shake it."

I shook my hand over my head.

"Ah. Did you drop anything on it recently? Slam it in something?" Harik's eyebrows pulled together as he examined me.

"No and no. Nothing like that."

"Flex your fingers. Have you touched a poisonous creature lately? Or a supernatural one?"

"No! Oh, wait. Sort of. A possessed, talking dog slobbered on it. On my . . . well, on my thumb." I closed my eyes so I could pretend I was alone while I felt as stupid as a dead rat.

"Ah, Memweck's spittle. That is your problem, most certainly." When I opened my eyes, Harik had leaned back again. "I regret to say there is nothing you can do about it." He shooed me with one hand.

As I backed up to the center of the dirt patch, I said, "Do you mean it's going to stay numb?"

"Oh, no. Not after the numbness spreads to your heart and kills you."

"That is amusing, Mighty Harik. I'm sure I'll think about it and laugh someday. Maybe I can't fix it, but somebody sure as hell can. Would you be interested in telling me who?"

"I could help if I choose. I'd need a reason to do so." Harik showed a little smile.

"Fine, we'll roll it into our bargain today!"

Harik shook his head. "Let us not taint our current bargain with minor issues."

"Damn it! All right, but I won't forget." I considered things I might do—or do without—that Harik might like. "How about this? Five squares in exchange for a month of impotence."

Harik snorted and gazed at the forest. "Ridiculous! It is the Tooth or nothing, for five squares."

"That's as tempting as an acid-soaked thorn under the tongue. Six months of impotence for four squares."

Harik jumped up and bellowed, "Listen, sorcerer! That woman down there in your world will lose her life! However, the Tooth is already lost. She is a memory. She is the memory of a girl who was not really your daughter. A girl you knew little more than a month. A person's life is worth far more than some memories. Pay attention! I am the damned God of Death! I know about these things!"

Listening to Harik boom was like taking a beating under a waterfall. I gazed at the brown, grainy dirt under my feet. Sorcerers were required to stand on it while the gods consented to trade with them and ruin their lives.

Everything Harik said about Bea and Manon was true. If I didn't take the deal, Bea would die. And if I lost Manon, what had I really lost except for pain and grief?

Harik sat down and leaned on one arm as he pushed back his night-black hair. "Well, Murderer?"

I tried to obliterate Harik with my stare, but it didn't work any better than the past hundred times I had tried. Harik's deal made sense. I needed to agree before I thought too much about it. I opened my mouth to say yes, but instead I coughed and said, "I won't take your deal, Harik. I'll never take that deal."

I dropped out of the Gods' Realm. I didn't want to hear any arguments from Harik, since he might convince me. Smacking back into my body, I found myself holding Bea's hand.

With the power I still had, I could save Bea from dying right away. Maybe Halla still had some more silk to bandage her with. I bellowed, "Halla!" I didn't care if Leddie's whole army came. I'd have loved for a few to show up just then.

Nobody answered except Bea. "I think I saw here there . . ." She flopped her hand over with one finger pointing straight at my knee.

I pressed my palm against Bea's belly, and she screamed.

"Yell all you want, young woman. You'll feel a damn sight better in a couple of minutes." I didn't say that I could only give her less than a day of pain lying on that grassy spot. If we moved her, she'd die within a few hundred feet. I also didn't tell her that I'd given her life away for some memories.

I levered my other hand out of Bea's grasp so I could use it to mend her guts the best I could. I flexed the hand and realized it was still numb. Staring at my still-numb hand, I said, "Son of a bitch!"

NINETEEN

During the deepest part of the night, the half-moon dragged itself up from behind the worn-out civilized mountains. Those peaks stood between us and the Empire proper. I had already murdered one bumbling man who walked up and nearly stepped on Bea in the darkness. Now in the good moonlight, I felt confident I'd spot any visitors before they saw us, and I dared to converse with Bea in whispers.

I carried the conversation, but she nodded along and even asked a question now and then. I described the wonders and horrors of the Empire, the fine things a clever person could accomplish, and the damn fool things I myself had done. We discussed how the capital had more taverns than Bindle had houses, which ones were my favorites and why. I described the marvels that her son would experience after I saved him and found a prosperous, loving home for him in the Empire.

Bea demanded that I go save him right then and leave her to die, and she cursed me as salty as a sailor when I didn't walk away that minute. She had no strength for a prolonged argument, however.

Well before dawn, Pil stalked past us, not far off, and I called her back when I saw she wasn't being followed. She held Bea's hand and tried to get her to laugh at a couple of jokes. When that proved a disaster, Pil turned away and cried for a bit, but she came back around to smile her broken smile at Bea until sunrise.

Halla arrived when the sun nipped over the mountains, walking straight toward us the whole time. I didn't know how Halla managed such accuracy, but she often could not be explained.

Daylight showed us a couple of bodies close at hand. I had killed those men. I spotted seven more lying within a quarter mile of us. Neither Halla nor I could figure out what the hell had happened.

A little after sunrise, Whistler appeared, limping toward us from the west. When he saw Bea, he staggered like he'd been hit with a club. He pulled Halla and me aside and scratched some dirt out of his hair. "I found one of those soldiers dying and convinced him to talk. Later I captured a bandit who was squatting down like a bunny rabbit behind a bush. I convinced the hell out of him too."

I said, "Fine work. Now if you can hold off burying every dead thing on the plains until you've enlightened us, that would be a kindness."

Whistler glanced at Bea. "The soldiers were moving to a new camp when Vang showed up yelling not to kill him. Another pack of bandits were headed into the bog to find out why they hadn't heard from their friends. When they heard the soldiers shouting, they ran away from it—right into us."

"Ah, then the soldiers investigated the noise." Halla scratched her chin. "They walked into the fight."

I patted Whistler's shoulder. "It almost makes a man believe in fate, or religion, or something like that, eh?"

Whistler chuckled. Then he looked at Bea again, and his face aged five years.

Halla glanced at the sky. "Since we did not stop the rider, I think Leddie's men will be here before noon. Maybe midmorning, if we can trust what Vang told us."

"Which we can't." I scanned the area around us, but it was open, rolling land.

Behind me, I heard Whistler say, "Pil, trot over to that tree and bring me a limb for another crutch, please."

I pointed at Whistler. "You can't order her around. Besides, she's on watch."

"It will take me an hour to hobble over there and back, but Pil can do it in ten minutes. We need to be gone before those fake soldiers arrive."

At that moment, I decided to stay with Bea until she died. I hadn't saved her, but I wouldn't traipse off and let her die alone. "I'm staying."

"What?" Halla said.

"As long as Bea stays here, I stay too."

"But she may hang on for—" Pil's face reddened, and she looked away.

Whistler sneezed twice, hard enough to knock his hat askew. "Beg pardon. I'm staying too."

Bea groaned. "Go. It's suicide. Halla, tell them it's suicide."

"It is not suicide." Halla examined the horizon. "It is a very stupid thing to do, but it is not suicide."

"If it's stupid, do something else instead!" Bea yelled and then groaned.

Halla shook her head. "If Bib fights, I will not leave him."

"He's not worth dying for," Bea said more quietly. She was breathing heavier.

Halla nodded. "He is a vain, reckless, murderous person. You are a much better person than him." She turned her back on Bea.

Pil gazed at the ground. "Bib, is this one of those times we should run, even if we're sorcerers?"

I laughed. "This is absolutely the time to run! I'm not asking you to stay. You'd be crazy to stay."

"Why are you staying?" she asked.

"Pride and arrogance."

"I see."

I grinned. "Also, if we flee, they'll run us down by midafternoon."

Pil nodded and started jogging toward the tree.

Halla motioned for me to follow her thirty feet away from Bea and Whistler. "Bib, since Bea cannot move, we will make a stand around her."

"A fine battle plan, General."

She ignored that. "I can prepare the ground. But that will be all. It is my last power, and there will be no more."

I examined the terrain around us. "We might beat ten or twelve horsemen, if Krak himself manifests and kills a couple for us. My sense is that Leddie will bring more than that. Do what you can, darling."

I'm glad Halla offered to spend the last of her power. We staked out a perimeter fifty feet across. Then she used sorcery to create a ditch, twenty-five feet wide and eight feet deep all the way around us.

Few horses could jump such a ditch, nor could they run down into it and back up, or scoot through it on their butts. If we stayed put, the soldiers would need to dismount, drop down into the ditch, and climb back up the other side to fight us. Halla followed that work by building up a short earthen berm just around Bea.

I hungered to ask Halla what she had traded for that power, and why there wouldn't be any more. But sorcerers are jealous of our secrets, like whispering, squabbling teenagers who can burn things down with lightning.

Since Whistler couldn't move well, he'd stay put at one spot on the circular ditch, the point closest to the enemy. Halla and I would hustle around to wherever soldiers came across the ditch. Pil would stay in the middle with her insane bow and try to kill fewer of us than of them.

When we finished preparing, we waited. Nobody had much to say, although after Whistler examined his sword, he sat with Bea.

I saw the horsemen coming well before midday. We watched them for ten minutes as they trotted in and out of sight crossing the grassy rolls. By the time they'd closed to shouting distance, I saw that Leddie was leading the column.

I bellowed, "We only have that one big tree for me to drop on you, General. If you wouldn't mind, ride over there and wait under it. If that's too much trouble, I can just stab you in the liver."

Leddie laughed. In the harsh daylight, I saw that her face was mottled with horrible scars. "My master wants to talk to you, Bib. I don't know why, because you're as boring as dog shit. But I have his permission to cut your face off your skull so he can talk to that, which would probably be a hell of a lot more interesting."

"Just come on over here and get killed, you long-winded sow!"

Leddie pointed at me. "That is what I am talking about! I predicted you'd say that. Sergeant! Give me that paper."

The sergeant leaned over and handed Leddie a slip of parchment.

"I wrote it down right here!" Leddie yelled, waving the paper. "It says, 'Come get killed.' Bib, you're not just boring—you're predictable!"

I nodded at Pil. "This is useless. Go on."

Pil drew her bow and fired. The arrow struck Leddie under her left eye and bounced off.

Leddie wiped her cheek and examined her fingers. "I apologize!" she shouted. "I wouldn't have predicted that if I'd had until the end of the world. What the hell was that? Am I poisoned now? Am I so pretty you can't stand to know I'm in the world?"

Pil fired again. The arrow zipped over Leddie's head and then angled down, ramming through the column of soldiers like a wild boar. Three soldiers flew through the air, one of them cut in half and trailing guts. Two horses fell to the ground, and one of them didn't move.

Everybody in Leddie's force started screaming or yelling orders, and horses bucked or bolted, carrying half a dozen soldiers away on their wild mounts. Leddie was riding in a circle, bellowing and whacking people with the flat of her sword.

Whistler turned to me and shouted, "Maybe we should charge them. We'd kill half and never see the rest again."

"No, that is foolish," Halla said. "We would only kill one in three."

Leddie and her sergeant were snappier than I expected in

getting their men's attention. A dozen dismounted. Pil's next arrow whizzed over their heads, sounding like a thousand hornets, and three soldiers jumped out ahead of their mates to charge us on foot. Leddie yelled and gestured for them to come back, but they kept running toward us.

"Should I try again to kill her?" Pil asked. "This thing has to hit what I aim at eventually."

"Go ahead," Halla said.

Pil drew and fired. The arrow shot up in an arc and kept going. It probably landed on the other side of Leddie's force.

The three charging soldiers reached the ditch and scrambled down into it. Halla and I killed the first two as they helped each other climb out, and I knocked Whistler aside to get the third.

Dismounted soldiers were shouting, stomping around, and drawing weapons, but no more of them charged.

"Are they going to try to starve us out?" Whistler said.

I shook my head, although I don't know whether he saw me.

All at once, the soldiers became much quieter. There was less running around and banging into each other. Leddie bellowed, "Now!"

A wall of two dozen soldiers charged toward us.

I shouted, "Pil! Now!"

Pil fired twice. The first arrow struck a soldier in the chest, split him in two, and kept going, not hitting anybody else. The second plowed into the ground and left a furrow thirty feet long and two feet deep. She fired again as the first soldiers reached the ditch. The arrow slammed into the far side of the ditch and collapsed it, forming a handy ramp for the soldiers to run down.

"Shit!" Pil shouted. "Shit, shit, shit!"

Whistler, Halla, and I ran to meet the soldiers as they crawled out of the ditch. We killed the first three, but by then, four more had climbed out. I lost track of Whistler as I stepped back, facing three men. I gave one a deep cut on the wrist, dodged two cuts from a second man, and stabbed a third in the chest, not quite in the heart. I retreated again because four men had climbed up, and now I faced five soldiers, which was a ridiculous number of foes.

The five men fought awkwardly, being so tight together, but they sported an awful lot of sharp blades. I forced two together and tripped one, and I killed the one on the ground before retreating. Halla appeared behind them, near beheaded one with her spear, and disappeared off to my left.

A young man surprised me on my right and sliced me deep across the thigh. I blocked his second stroke and slashed his throat, then parried an attack from a tall, fat soldier. I thrust into his heart, felt something wet on my side, and glanced at it. At some point, I'd taken a deep, ragged cut at the left wrist, but numbness had kept me from feeling it.

I had just glanced at my wrist for an instant, but when I focused on my opponents again, somehow five soldiers faced me. I was breathing harder than I should have. I roared just to deny that I was tired and older than twenty-five. Two of the soldiers froze for a moment, but that's all I needed to stab one in the belly and cut the other on the shoulder. The remaining three jumped toward me at once.

Over the next ten seconds, I dodged, parried, and took two healthy cuts on my left arm. At last, I slashed one across the face and disengaged when the other two hesitated. A man tripped right in front of me, so I kicked him in the head. Then I blocked a thrust from a fellow who immediately turned and ran away.

No more soldiers stood near me. I saw Halla fighting a man with her spear one-handed. Her right arm appeared broken or dislocated. She thrust the spear into the man's chest so hard he flew backward, trailing blood. On the other side of me, Pil knocked a man to the ground and knelt to stab him in the chest. Whistler stood over Bea, his sword dangling in his hand. None of the soldiers on our side of the ditch was standing, although a number were wounded and moaning. I killed a man writhing on the ground with a fatal belly wound, and then I went from one wounded man to the next, killing them as I went.

Pil panted, "I hope everybody thought that was fun because we get to do it all over again." She pointed at Leddie's force where twenty more soldiers had lined up.

Leddie shouted, and her soldiers ran toward us. They didn't charge with as much vigor as their fallen comrades, most of whom had died. That fact might have blunted the second wave's zeal, but that didn't matter. We were so torn up that twenty fighters could destroy us even if they were morose and weeping.

I hadn't prayed since I was a boy, or even recently sworn by Krak and all his sparkly whores. Just then, I was witless enough to wonder whether prayer or swearing might help us, but of course they wouldn't. I had only one stratagem left, and I dreaded it. But now that I was forced to use it, I admitted I'd been hoping to be forced.

I reached for the pouch under my shirt and pulled out a small book, bound in black leather, cool to the touch and too heavy for its size. The mark of Harik, God of Death, was set in white on the cover. I held the book in both hands as I opened it to page three. The page showed only a black rectangle, and no ink could possibly be that black.

As I stared at the page, I turned toward the oncoming soldiers. I held my sword high, slid down to run across the ditch, and ran out the other side using the ramp Pil's arrow had created.

Leddie's twenty soldiers stopped and stared, some banging into others. I charged them, limping a little but howling like the damned. After another few seconds, the soldiers bolted away from me, throwing curses and shouts behind them. One of them tripped, and I stabbed him as I ran past. A few dropped their weapons. Those who looked back screamed and ran faster.

When all of them, including Leddie, were fleeing, I stopped and turned around.

Almost five hundred men, women, and children stood facing me, slightly transparent and glowing bright enough to show at midday. Most were armed, and they stood fanned out in front of me. They made no sound, and most stood motionless. Then they began shifting places to form up in a huge wedge behind me. They were all the people I had killed in my life. In death, they were harmless, but they would scare the hell out of somebody who didn't know that.

A small, skinny girl with long red hair stood closest to me. She was Manon, my daughter who I had murdered this past winter, and she was not motionless. She gestured at me like her hands were clubs. She mouthed a lot of bad words, and she glared at me with hatred.

TWENTY

I ached when I saw the loathing in Manon's eyes, but it didn't surprise me. I forced myself to nod at her and turn away, but not because of her anger. She wouldn't get any more dead, but other people might soon. I limped away from her like she was a horse I'd once owned and sold for something better.

I needed power to treat people, unless I wanted to spit, make mud, and pack that into the wounds. I breathed deep, looked around, and kicked Halla's earthen wall hard to distract myself into thinking about survival.

Before I could lift myself to call for Harik, he yanked me out of my body with a surge of nausea.

"Murderer!" Harik shouted like thunder inside my head. "I did not give you leave to read my book again! I should refuse to trade with you for a month. For a year! I should manifest there before you and extract your bones one by one through the closest convenient orifice!"

I called up my most businesslike voice. "May I point out, Mighty Harik, that you never said I couldn't take a peek at the book again."

Harik's voice dropped and sounded like he was dragging it across a wasteland of petrified trees. "Do not attempt to engage in sophistry with me. You are nothing to me—no more than a bad smell that will blow away in a moment."

I put on a huge smile. "Ouch. That hurts like holy hell, Your Magnificence. I thought you liked me at least a little."

"I care no more for you than I would a fruit tree growing in a convenient spot. You are filth in my sight."

I drew my sword, revealing the place of trading in the Gods' Realm. Harik stood on the bottom level of the marble gazebo, the sinews bulging on his crossed arms and his teeth gritted. Wind appeared to swirl his black robe, even though the air lay still and damp.

Harik's crashing tirade had come close to unnerving me, but I pushed ahead. "I have come to trade with you, oh great, whiny nose-goiter. My memories of Manon are off the table, though."

Harik wrinkled his forehead and frowned, allowing himself to appear less than ideally handsome. "Yes, fine, you made certain of that by poking through my book as if you were a jittery magpie. Now that you have called the Tooth, removing your memories of her would cost far too much."

I couldn't keep myself from perking up like a dog that saw a rabbit. "Cost too much? Why? Do you mean it would cost you something?"

Harik paused. His robe stopped swirling and fell straight with a soft whoosh. "No."

"No, as in it would cost more than the right amount?"

Harik shook his head. "No. No, nothing."

The gods had always acted as if they could just burp or wave their little finger to make things happen. For more complicated things, they may need to wave two or three fingers, but that was an annoyance to them, not an effort. Yet Harik had just implied that it cost a god something to make things happen, which I had never heard a god say before. "So, if it's nothing, how could it cost far too much? 'Too much' doesn't apply to nothing."

Harik sighed. "Do you want to trade or not?"

I held up a hand. "Just a minute. I want to go back to where you said that removing my memories of Manon would cost too much."

"I never said anything like that."

"But—"

"Not at all."

I stared at the God of Death, hoping he'd give away a little more.

Harik raised his voice. "And you can't prove I did! I would be overjoyed to let you and all your pathetic friends die if you don't want to trade."

I figured that was as far as I could push him, but I intended to chat about it another day. "I do want to trade, Mighty Ball-Dangling God of Death. I ask that you extend an offer."

Harik sat, leaned back, and crossed his legs at the ankles. "Finally. This will be severe, but you have earned it. For one square, you will kill ninety-nine people in the next seven days."

"I congratulate you on making an offer that's like a boot to the face. For six squares, I will steal Pil's bow and burn it."

The corners of Harik's lips twitched up. "You will kill seventy people in the next seven days. Killing an innocent counts as two deaths. For one square."

It was a ridiculous offer, but I couldn't help asking the obvious question. "What do you mean by 'innocent'?"

"A person not trying to harm you or your allies."

"Bullshit! I don't plan to kill innocent people for no reason at all. There are plenty of wicked bastards to kill for damn good reasons. For six squares, I won't use a sword in my next two fights. Just a knife."

"Murderer, are you approaching these negotiations seriously? That offer was ludicrous. I offer two squares if you kill seventy people in seven days, innocents count double. Before you answer, I assure you that either you will leave this negotiation obliged to kill more people, or you will leave with nothing. This is your punishment."

That was a hell of a disappointment. Without power, Bea would die for sure. The rest of us would need awhile to heal, maybe weeks. Any hope of saving Bindle's children would fade to nothing.

I didn't know whether I could find seventy assholes deserving death in the next week, even if I applied myself with exceptional diligence. In my experience, about one in fifty people is a brute or villain, and that's generous. If I traveled through populous lands, I might meet a few hundred people while chasing Memweck over the next week. Hell, maybe I'd catch the horrible horse's ass himself before then and could make him part of the count.

"All right, Harik, you goat-faced son of your own whore sister, I'll kill ten people in the next week, and to hell with killing innocent folks."

"Grief has made you so much less interesting, Murderer. I will bend this much: kill fifty in the next week."

"Fifteen!"

"Forty-nine." Harik raised an eyebrow.

I sensed that the negotiation might be near disaster, at least for me. I decided to throw all my bait into the water at once to see what would bite. "Harik, I offer this: I will kill one person every day for the next week in exchange for five squares. I also want my numb hand fixed. Plus, I want you to tell me all about Memweck."

Harik laughed, which put me on edge. "If you want to bargain with gusto, Murderer, I can oblige. Kill three people a day, innocents counting twice. I shall tell you three things about Memweck. I may as well, since you persist in hunting him, a self-destructive act if ever one existed. As for your hand—I prefer that curse remain as it is for now."

I didn't like the offer, but at least I was an expert on flushing out thieves and murderers. I had done it for weeks in Bindle. "Two people a day for two weeks in exchange for four squares and answers about Memweck."

Harik sat forward, smiling. "Innocents count twice, and you must kill two people by sunset each day."

I dropped the point of my sword and sighed. "Sunset and killing innocents? Do you want to add a girl in a magical coma and a singing fish to make this a little more mystically theatrical?"

Harik acted as if he hadn't heard me. "Not two weeks. Your task shall continue until I say it has ended."

"Damn you, Harik, and all nine of the babies you ate for breakfast! That's too much."

"Did you overlook the part where I said you are being punished?"

I was already killing people until he told me I could stop, so I supposed this deal wasn't that much worse.

Harik crossed his arms again. "And the murders will not count toward those you already owe me."

I realized that every objection I threw in would make things worse. No good deals were to be had, not a surprise since that was always the case when bargaining with gods. "All right, Harik, I accept, if I can read your book whenever I want."

Harik's mouth fell open, and he stared at me for several seconds. "You may read it thrice more. I shouldn't allow you that much, but Memweck is going to kill you anyway."

"Done!"

"Very well, you mewling wretch. I shall tell you about Memweck."

I held up a hand. "Wait! Since you're telling me three things about him, let me ask three questions."

Harik grinned. "Is that truly what you want?"

I closed my eyes and imagined Harik answering every question with evasions and double meanings. Or he might leave out one or two facts to change the whole intention of his answer. "I guess not. Go ahead and tell me what you think I should know."

"Good. You are not bright, Murderer, but you can occasionally learn from your many embarrassing failures. I could speak regarding who, what, why, or where. Any three of those four. Let us begin with who. Memweck is the son of Lutigan."

I waited for more, or to hear him say it was a joke. Then like a drooling moron, I said, "The God of War?"

Harik went on, "There is only one Lutigan, thank the Void. Memweck is one of his many sons. The voracious bastard has despoiled a nearly incomprehensible number of human women. Memweck was favored, one of his father's fourteen demigod shield men. Do you understand?"

I nodded. A demigod was now stomping around in the world of man, staining everything with its inexplicable magic, divine hubris, and bad taste.

Harik held up two fingers. "Second, what is Memweck doing here? The jovial twit misbehaved at Lutigan's birthday celebration. He portrayed his father in a comic, indeed prurient, manner during an homage to Lutigan's recent victory."

Harik scooted forward to the edge of his bench and lowered his voice. "Lutigan was incensed, and I believe he would have destroyed Memweck utterly. However, Krak found the whole thing hilarious. He congratulated Lutigan and actually smiled at Memweck. Lutigan couldn't very well obliterate Memweck after that, so he banished his son to the world of man. Memweck's person must remain within the environs that Lutigan selected for him, an area which must feel quite cramped."

I said, "What does he . . ."

Harik lifted his eyebrows, waiting for me finish the question.

"Never mind. Go on."

Harik raised his head, literally looking down his perfect nose at me. "That brings us to the question of either why or where. I think I'll choose . . . why." He waggled a finger. "Why does Memweck do things? He wishes to go home. He wants his father's forgiveness so he can go home. That, and no more."

I turned my back on the gloating toad and examined the papery, golden leaves in the forest. I'd never seen those particular leaves on any of my visits to trade. Maybe they only sprouted on certain occasions, such as a sorcerer finding out that a divine being wants to destroy him. "All right, Harik. I can't tell you the where, or even the when, but I can take a good stab at the how. Lutigan despises me, so Memweck figures that killing me would make his father happy enough to forgive him. Shit! A demigod, eh?"

"Oh, yes, a demigod, although inhabiting an unfamiliar realm."

I whipped around to face Harik, hopeful. "Is that a weakness?"

"An inconvenience, perhaps. I wouldn't speak of it as a weakness."

I nodded and scratched my forehead, trying to imitate those

scholarly fellows I'd gone to school with. "That's just damn fascinating. Memweck must be like a shark among tadpoles here, but he's not a god. What kinds of things would he bumble around trying to do, Mighty Harik? Things that you could do a thousand times better, right?"

Harik waved away my question, or maybe he was waving away my visit, or even my whole existence. "Do not be obvious. I will say one thing more to you, Murderer. Since you have thus far survived Memweck's toadies, he now believes he must kill you with his own hands, otherwise his father will not think he exerted himself. Also, Memweck cannot leave his sad domain. That means . . ." He looked at me like I was the student with the most snot on his face.

"I should bring a gift?"

Harik hissed and stared at the ceiling of the gazebo. "Go to the northern kingdoms, deliver the book as I instruct, and then ride away, Murderer. Just ride away. Let Memweck alone."

Harik flung me back into my body without his normal ferocity, and it didn't even drive me to my knees. I scrambled over to Bea inside the short earthen walls. She was still breathing, but Whistler lay on his side next to her covered in so much blood I thought he must be dead. He wasn't quite gone, but any one of his three stab wounds could already have killed him.

I needed a healing strategy. If I started with some horrible wound and got crippled by the pain, I'd be useless to the others. I helped Bea and Whistler just enough to prevent them from dying right away, hoping all the time that I wasn't creating connections with them. If they both connected with me, that would be awkward as hell. I healed Halla's arm and sent her to catch stray horses with Pil, who wasn't badly wounded. Then I dealt with my own wounds before going back to Whistler and Bea. By the time I finished with them, I felt as stabbed and beaten as everybody else put together, just with shorter blades and lighter clubs.

I lay on my back and hoped I might pass out, but that didn't happen. After a minute, I realized that Manon was standing six feet away, glaring at me with her arms crossed. After struggling to sit up, I managed to draw my sword and point it at her.

Manon walked toward me until the sword's point touched her chest. "You killed me, you butthole!"

"I'm sorry, darling."

"I'm not your darling! You stabbed me in the brain!"

I tried to sigh, but the pains in my chest and belly twisted so hard that tears came to my eyes. "I know. I shouldn't have done it."

"Then why did you? Oh, are you going to cry about it like a little baby?"

There wasn't a good answer to any of that. I said, "I'm happy to see that you're free of your mother." In life, Manon had given most of herself over to the goddess Sakaj, who was a cruel and subtle being.

"Setting me free? Is that your excuse? Whe—" Manon had been waving her arms but now stomped away, which cut her off mid-word. She shook herself and ran back to the point of my sword. "So, she took me—so what? That wasn't the end of the world, was it, you bastard? So what if she was killing people? She and I didn't kill hardly as many people as you have! You're not one to criticize, are you?"

I realized that everybody around us was watching and listening, but I couldn't much care. I smacked away the urge to tell the girl to calm down. If she didn't have a right to be pissed off, who did? "Manon, what I did wasn't right."

"Oh, no?" she shouted. "Are you sure? Do you want to think about that for a while?" I didn't know if ghosts could get winded, but Manon was huffing and her voice hit a screeching tone I remembered. I might have cried a couple of tears that I couldn't blame on the pain.

Manon caught her insubstantial breath. "You were supposed to protect me. Not kill me!" She slapped me with the words like they were her open hand. "You know what, Father? Do you want to hear something funny? At the end, my mother wanted to kill you, but I wouldn't let her. I protected you!"

"Manon, I'm truly sorry." I couldn't think of a single thing to say besides that.

My daughter crossed her arms and scowled at me, something I

had seen at least twice a day when she was alive. "Do you want to say you're sorry another million times? I know you're sorry, and you want me to forgive you. Well, I don't forgive you!" She pointed her finger at me. "I don't forgive you at all!"

She turned and walked away toward the four hundred and ninety-seven other people I had killed. For the next hour, she stood with her back to me, unmoving.

TWENTY-ONE

The pain a sorcerer experiences from healing somebody usually lasts a few hours. Mine lasted nine hours after Manon finished bitching me out from beyond the grave. We assumed Leddie had regrouped and would be chasing us, so I could only rest for one of those hours, then we would need to mount and ride on.

Before we departed, I told everybody what I'd learned about Memweck. Halla didn't look happy, but she never looked happy about anything. Bea acted like she didn't care whether Memweck was a god or a yappy little dog. Pil appeared to be terrified, which was the proper reaction, but she tried to cover it up.

When Bea proclaimed how much demigods didn't scare her, Whistler stared at the ground, rubbed his forehead, and grumbled, but then he nodded and trudged off to check the horses' saddles and tack. He hadn't shown any inclination to bury the two dozen dead soldiers scattered around. Those dead men had once ridden horses, though, and seven of the abandoned beasts allowed Halla and Pil to round them up.

I didn't tell anybody about the people I'd be needing to kill every day. I feared they might get distracted wondering whether I'd kill them next to make quota.

Before we rode away, as I lay on the dirt like a clubbed mackerel, Pil walked up to stand over me. "Can I ask something that's none of my business?"

"Ask ahead, I'm bored. Let's see what you think is none of your business."

She sat beside me and whispered, "Why don't you take a horse and ride away from this craziness instead of struggling to get someplace where a demigod wants to tear you apart? And pick his teeth with your bones, or whatever demigods do?"

I cleared my throat and then wished I hadn't when my entire torso throbbed. "That's a damned incisive question, worthy of any sorcerer. I don't leave because I'm stupid as hell."

She frowned at me as if I were trying to sell her a blind horse.

"All right," I said, "I'll give you a well-considered answer. "I'm going because it would be a fine exploit. I could sneak into Memweck's home and move all his furniture around to aggravate him. Then I could drink all his wine and steal his magical livestock."

Pil raised a hand to hit me but stopped when I flinched. "Tell me! You didn't cause all this trouble. From what I hear, Memweck tricked you into bargaining with him."

"Sorcerers can't let gods get away with tricking them, Pil. Demigods, either. It's bad practice."

Pil leaned toward me and whispered, "You don't owe the people of that little town anything!"

"They don't know that. I wouldn't want to disillusion them."

"If you can't tell me why we should keep going to what sounds like an awful death, I'm going to go somewhere else, and you can go without me!"

I patted her arm. "That would make you a genius among fools."

This time, she did hit me and called me a couple of names. Then Pil jumped up and stomped away, carrying her insane bow. I hoped she'd climb up on a horse right then and ride some direction that wasn't north. I didn't want to get her killed too.

Less than a minute later, a crow flew straight over us, laughing like a man. It returned and flew a circle around us, and then another, still laughing.

I possessed little breath for shouting, or even laughing, but I managed to speak out a bit. "Hello, Memweck, you pompous wad of slime. Is life boring here in the world of man? Nobody to play with? That's about the saddest thing I ever heard."

Crow-Memweck laughed again. "Stop lying on the grass like a dribble of filth, mighty Murderer! It's unsightly and boring too. The worst offense a man can commit is to be boring!"

"I promise to be more interesting if you give back all the people you stole." I raised my voice as loudly as I could stand. "You give them up first. Then I'll tell a joke or two."

The crow laughed again.

"Show some courage, Floppy-Ass! Maybe Lutigan will be impressed and add a mile or two to your prison." I was starting to pant, which hurt worse than talking.

Instead of laughing, Memweck bobbed in flight, dropped a bit, and said, "Who in the name of Krak's best suit are all the dead people?"

"I like to travel with a few of my victims," I said. "My enemies can see what their existence will be like soon. It's polite, don't you think?"

Crow-Memweck cackled and flew faster. "Do you mean that to be an understatement? Or does the cracking great number of ghosts count as hyperbole? Come visit me, Murderer. We can drink wine and argue semantics before I yank off your head."

The crow flew higher, still circling us. Something began falling from the sky, and I thought it was rain. It wasn't wet, though, so I decided it was hail. Then I realized it wasn't hard.

I picked up something that bounced on the grass next to me and examined it.

Bea screamed.

I was holding a human finger. In fact, it was a child's finger. They were still falling. Hundreds of them must have fallen already.

Bea was clinging to Halla and hiding her face. Pil had nocked an arrow and was aiming at the crow. She fired, the arrow missed by one hundred feet, and the crow laughed louder. Whistler stood hunched in the shower of fingers with his face tight and pale.

At last, Memweck flew away, and the shower of fingers stopped. We met each other's eyes, but none of us spoke. I can't imagine what we would have said.

Whistler walked up beside me. "Didn't the thing try to peck off your face or something?"

I snorted. "I would say not to give Memweck any ideas, but apparently he wants to slay me with his own holy little hands. I don't guess beaks, or claws, or tentacles count."

Everybody mounted, with Halla boosting me up behind Pil. I then spent eight hours on the back of Pil's horse, hanging onto her waist and wishing I would hurry up and die. A couple of times she laughed about how just a few days ago she had been forced to ride behind me, but now I was the one who had to bounce and hang on. Her fun-poking seemed forced, though.

We traveled at the head of the great, glowing herd of dead people, and we didn't halt to camp. Leddie wouldn't interrupt her pursuit to build fires and roast rabbits, so to stay ahead, we pushed hard toward Fat Shallows. We paused to rest twice, and both times Manon stood with her back to me.

During a pause late in the night, Halla touched my shoulder. "You should repair Pil's face."

Everybody turned to look at us.

I said, "It's not a crippling or fatal wound, so I prefer to husband the power for other needs. I'm sorry, Pil."

Pil held up both hands. "I agree. I won't be able to enjoy a nice face if the rest of me is bled out, or crushed, or burned up. And if I'm disintegrated, it won't matter anyway." She grinned around at us. "That part was a joke. People can't get disintegrated by sorcery."

Halla narrowed her eyes. "Who has traveled to the northern kingdoms before?"

"I stopped in a few nasty, sinful port towns, but that's all," I said.

"Pil, you have never been there?" Halla asked.

"Never."

Most of my pain had eased away by that hour, so I clapped

Halla on the arm. "Woman, I recognize your words, but your meaning is too subtle for me. Stop wasting our damn time and speak plainly."

"Most men in the northern kingdoms—"

"They're dogs!" Whistler laughed. "You're right—they're randy-ass dogs. They'd chew granite and drink lava to impress a woman. It's how their fathers have done things forever."

Halla nodded. "But they are dangerous. They can be brutal if they do not get what they want." Halla turned to Pil. "A beautiful woman can help us in many ways. We will protect you. But you could still be hurt."

Pil said, "No."

Nobody spoke.

"I'm joking!" She smiled, showing the gaps in her teeth. "I'll do it. Those boys will be so in love with me they'll be ruined for any other women."

"If we can get some answers when we need them, that's all the love we'll ever need," I said. "You don't have to leave broken hearts all the way north to the ice."

I glanced back toward the ghosts before I mounted, thinking maybe I'd see Manon's face. But she was gone, along with all my other victims. I had thought they might remain longer, and that I could speak to her again, even if she wouldn't forgive me. Nine hours must have been their limit. People kept talking until it was time to ride again, but I didn't hear any of it.

We rode on toward Fat Shallows, a nasty smuggling town with no dock at all. All cargo was rowed between ships and the beach. The place boasted one warehouse, an inn for sailors, and a dozen haphazardly painted shacks. Storms would blow the whole place down every five years or so, but it was so primitive that the residents rebuilt everything in a couple of weeks.

Fat Shallows was named for its broad, shallow harbor, which was just deep enough for small vessels at low tide and not much deeper at high tide. The harbor entrance was enormously wide, over three miles. The wind blew out to sea most all the time, so only small, handy vessels could sail close enough to the wind to enter the harbor. Those same vessels could shoot out of the harbor past blockading ships any place they wanted.

The town sat at the bottom of a sixty-foot cliff, and a crazy collection of ramps, ladders, and walkways connected the town to the cliff top. Anybody who wanted to attack Fat Shallows from the cliffside would find it a harrowing proposition, since three men at the bottom with mallets could collapse the whole structure in one minute. For raising and lowering cargo along the cliff, the townsfolk had constructed a winch.

Fat Shallows was not impregnable, not by a long sight. But wiping it out would be arduous, and its activities were more annoying than destructive. Year after year, rumor said the Empire would bring Fat Shallows to justice soon, but the Empress always found better and less bothersome things to do with her ships and soldiers.

No person could bring horses or livestock down the cliff unless they were herding courageous goats. Some foresighted individual had built a large stable atop the cliff. As we rode close, an older boy with long brown hair bounded out into the yard. He examined us from behind the rail fence, smiling and rubbing horse shit off his cheek. "Hallo, you look as if you might be hurrying. I'm Sammit. You boarding or selling?"

"We should sell. We might return another way," Halla said to me.

"Hell, we might not return at all." I dismounted. "Let's deal, young man, and I warn you I've traded horses for over twenty years. I have seen every twitch and swindle you might possibly know."

"I'm honest, sir. Straight as a thorn. I can afford to be, sir, since you don't see nobody else along this cliff buying horses, do you?"

"I grant that," I said. "Make me an offer."

"Wait," Halla said. "You help the girl. I will do this."

I didn't want to start a three-hour argument with Halla over who the best trader was, so Pil and I strode a hundred paces from the stable, where I repaired her face. It was delicate work, and I took my time. Then Pil, my aching face, and I marched back to see how well Halla had served us in the trade.

We found Sammit holding back tears. Halla had bargained him to ninety-three silver coins, an amethyst ring, two good knives, an ivory carving of a horse, four bottles of wine, a new belt for Whistler, and a box of warm pies.

Halla pointed at the boy. "Remember, do not sell these horses for a month. We might want to buy them back."

Sammit nodded, his eyes damp and glazed.

"Damn it!" I shouted at Halla. "It's not like you're trading with Krak to knock down a city! Don't pauperize the boy!" I gave Sammit back half the coins, the wine, and the carving. Halla showed no contrition.

I made Whistler carry the box of pies down the cliff.

Three ships lay anchored in the harbor, smallish and handy. Although the Empire wouldn't so much as lean over to squash Fat Shallows, it hated to lose even a scrap of customs money. Empire captains loved to run down smugglers, behead them right there at sea, and bring nice presents home to their wives, sweethearts, and favorite whores. Any smuggler who survived long would be a competent individual.

As far as nautical supplies were concerned, the lanes of Fat Shallows were tidy. The residents had stowed cordage, spars, nets, and bundles of sailcloth around town in a fine and tight fashion. Everything else lay more or less where somebody had dropped it. A couple of dogs dug through piles of trash on the street. The grimy scent of pitch mingled with the reek of rotting fish. A few men wandered with no evident tasks, and four fellows appeared to be halfway done building a long boat. I saw no women at all.

The day had turned gray and blustery, but no rain had fallen. I found a barrel standing on end against the long, weathered warehouse right in the middle of town, and I hopped up onto it. "Halla, you handle our passage since you're so goddamn much better at trading than me."

She watched me, as if I might say something else. Instead, I drew my sword and lay it across my legs before pulling out the gold lump to carve off some bits. I gathered two onlookers before I'd even scraped off a sliver.

Halla stared at the ground and sighed before trudging off toward the inn. Bea and Pil trotted behind her. Whistler leaned against a weathered shack not far from me.

More than a dozen toughs and sailing men had gathered by the time I finished and stowed all the gold back in my pouch. "I think I'll take a quiet, meditative walk down the beach before supper," I announced, as if the men were an audience I should entertain. I sheathed my sword and ambled down a scarred, wooden ramp to the black sand beach.

I strolled a quarter mile down the shore, ready to kill however many men decided to murder and rob me. But not one of those thugs and smugglers followed me onto the beach. They did watch me as earnestly as if gold might start pouring out of my ears, though.

I walked back to town and ignored those gawking men of unexpected virtue. When I stepped between two shacks, four of their friends jumped out to steal my gold and probably kill me.

They lacked any real fighting skills and must have expected to overwhelm me. I killed two, knocked down another, and bashed the fourth on the back of the skull. Then I jumped back several steps lest the temptation to kill the survivors prove too enticing. The two still alive lay motionless anyway, eyes on my sword and mouths slack.

I smiled at them. "You surely are enterprising fellows." I scrutinized them and cocked my head. "Are you twins?"

The one wearing a torn shirt nodded. They both were young with nice features, curly brown hair, and a solid layer of filth on every part of them I could see. "I'm Dab. Brother's Wentl. You gonna kill us?"

"Maybe. Were you planning to kill me?"

Both shook their heads hard and began swearing about how much they hadn't planned to kill me.

"That's heartening, boys. I'd like to hire you as bodyguards then. We're crossing the sea as soon as may be, and I'll pay you four bits a day—each. You have to promise to protect me, though."

"We promise!" Dab said.

Wentl raised a hand. "I swear we won't lift a hand in anger or threat, or even curse you, sir."

I smiled at the lying bastards. "You're hired. Collect your belongings and be on the beach in an hour."

My new bodyguards scrambled to their feet and trotted toward the beach. Evidently, they didn't own a thing apart from what they carried on their nasty bodies.

I could see that fulfilling my new debt to Harik would require significant planning. I had just murdered two men for today, hours before sunset. The passage to the northern kingdoms required three days. Who would I kill on the journey? Well, tomorrow I'd be killing Dab and Wentl, criminals who would be pleased to put a blade in my back at the first chance.

After tomorrow, I'd have to come up with something more creative.

When I returned to the middle of town, I saw Halla standing next to the inn facing two men in faded cotton working clothes. One was near my age, tall and blocky, with a yellow beard like a curtain down to his chest. The other was young and skinny with shaggy brown hair and a patchy beard. Both examined me as I walked up to them.

Halla nodded at me. "Bib, this is Captain Garett and Skip. They will sail us to the northern kingdoms for a fair price. They will leave right now for double that price."

I smiled at the yellow-bearded man. "Captain, if we pay four times that price, will you crack on as if Harik were chasing you and pissing fire in your wake all the way?"

The big man raised an eyebrow at his young, skinny friend, who frowned at me. "I am Captain Garett. If you pay us six times the price, and if you pay for ruined spars and cordage, then yes, we will."

I rubbed my chin. "I don't claim that six times the price is robbery, but my dear, honest mother wouldn't dare charge that much."

Captain Garett sniffed. "Was she much of a seaman?"

"Circumnavigated the islands of Ir before she was fifteen." I pointed at the harbor. "Maybe we ought to discuss it with the masters of those other two ships."

"Wouldn't help." Garett spit on the wooden planks. "I own all three of those ships."

"I admire your industry." I spit to match him. "I suppose we could just ride the long way around."

"On horses you've already sold?" The captain smiled, showing brilliant teeth.

Before I could propose my next objection to wear the man down, Halla snapped, "Enough! We will pay. Where should we go, Captain?"

On the beach, I introduced my new bodyguards to my companions. Pil, Bea, and Whistler stared at me as if snakes were flowing from my mouth like drool, but they didn't say anything. Halla ignored my new retainers.

Two sailors ferried us out to Garett's ship, *Steffi's Thumb*, a sixty-foot caravel with two masts and triangular sails. The vessel was open to the weather except for a stern deck covering the rear third of the ship. We'd all be sleeping wet from the spray and any rain that found us.

We'd be sleeping close together too, since Garett crewed his ship with twenty men. That was six more than I'd have expected. I wondered whether he engaged in a little piracy when tempted.

Once the crew had set sail and the deck was less hectic, I caught Garett at the stern deck. "Your beautiful ship has an unusual name, Captain. Is there a story behind it?"

Garett rubbed his mangy beard. "Not anymore." He turned his back to me and swung up onto the stern deck like an ape.

I picked my way forward between lashed-down cargo and grumbling sailors until I reached Halla. "I don't think the captain will be serving us beer or singing us shanties tonight. Doesn't it seem crowded on this ship to you?"

Halla gazed around and nodded. "Let us stay in the bow. Out of the way. And not annoy them."

TWENTY-TWO

The seagulls started shitting on us right after sunrise.

All the clouds had blown away late yesterday afternoon, and we had been sailing north all night on a sweet following wind. Fat Shallows stood below the horizon behind us. The ship's timbers creaked as it lifted on the swells and settled back down. Water shushed against the hull, and wind hummed through the lines, popping the sails now and then.

My traveling companions and I had gathered into the ship's bow to be less underfoot and less easily surrounded. As I gazed at the sunrise over the starboard bow, three birds flew past and voided themselves on me at almost the same moment. By the time I had shaken my head and assessed my state of filth, all my companions had been treated the same by at least one bird each. The sailors laughed at us, since none of them were getting a dung shower. With no hiding place, Bea broke loose, scrambled aft to the stern deck, and ducked under it.

The sailors' laughter quieted when they saw that not a one of them was receiving the birds' attention. Only we were growing whiter and nastier. Then a gull swooped down into the ship, turned at the stern deck, and launched a wad of filth sideways, striking Bea on the forehead.

The sailors all stopped laughing then. They began muttering, spitting between their fingers, and giving us raw looks. Halla fetched Bea and brought her back to the bow. I pulled a yellow band of power and whipped it around a gull, hoping to send it someplace else, but the band dissolved when it touched the feathers. Memweck was behind this prank then, although I had already suspected it.

The birds stopped painting us within a few minutes. We must have emptied every gull within a mile.

The captain, backed by most of his fidgeting crew, edged forward from the waist of the ship until they had us well trapped in the bow. With his hand on his knife, Garett said, "That's a peculiar way for birds to behave. Odd. Unlikely."

I decided that acting timid was a good way to get thrown overboard with a slit throat. "Sure as hell was! In the islands of Ir, it's a sign of remarkable good fortune." I dabbed my finger in some of the bird shit and drew a nonsense symbol on the gunwale. "There, I shared some of that luck with you."

Garett crossed his arms, tapping one finger against his shoulder. "Never heard of anything like that. Nothing like it at all. Not a single thing."

I laughed. "It's poorly understood on the mainland. You should regret that they didn't crap all over you too." Behind me, I heard Halla sigh.

Garett gave a slow nod. "I understand enough. You're cursed. Demon-struck. I planned to rob you tonight and throw you over the side, but . . ." He glanced back over his shoulder. "I guess we should do it—"

The man stopped talking when I thrust my sword into his chest. I withdrew, and the sailors behind Garett yammered as he fell to his knees and then flopped onto the deck.

I craned my head to examine the clustered sailors. "Who is captain now?"

Several men stared at Skip, who snarled at me through his blond beard as he reached for his knife. Before he pulled it, I killed him too. "Who's next in line?"

The two sailors closest to me glanced at each other and scooted backward. Three other men edged forward, shouting uncertain insults. When one of them holding a club ran at me, I killed him too. Halla rushed up and swept another man's legs with her spear. He scrambled backward on his butt, begging not to be killed, and she let him go.

Weapons could be heard hitting the deck all the way back to the stern.

I bellowed in a fine, seagoing voice, "I don't feel bound to kill every one of you. Let's make terms."

The remaining sailors were backing away past midships. Then five men moved forward through the group, all armed with swords that they seemed comfortable handling. I lay my sword over my shoulder and grinned at them. "So, you must be the bunch of murderers Garett hired to deal with us. You're clever to wait until he got killed before you presented yourselves. Now you can take everything, if you live."

None of them seemed jolly, but the one in the center looked as grim as a boot to the head. He was a big, clean-shaven man with black hair, and he balanced himself without a bobble as the ship rode the swells. "Here are the terms for you," he said. "Give us the gold, and we won't cut your throats. You can take the boat and go wherever the dick-dropping hell you want." He and his friends all stood ready to attack or defend.

Before I could say something sarcastic, Halla made a standing, six-foot leap forward. At the same time, she thrust one-handed with her seven-foot spear. In that one movement, she drove the broad spearhead through the man's throat and out the back of his neck. She withdrew while the corpse was still spurting blood, and the man's four companions watched him collapse.

I pointed my sword at the closest one. "Let's talk about that boat."

Before sunset had dissolved into pure dark, the four surviving killers lay in the boat that *Steffi's Thumb* had been towing, all bound hand and foot.

"Why keep them prisoner?" Halla muttered to me. "Kill them, or let them row away."

Of course, I wanted them alive so that I could kill them tomorrow and the day after, and so keep my bargain with Harik. However, I feared that Halla might find fault with that reasoning. "I may wish to question them later."

"About what?"

"About the state of piracy and thuggery here on the Bending Sea."

Halla's brow furrowed. "Why?"

"Hell, I may want to be a pirate someday! I wanted it when I was a boy, and it's not too damn late to give up on it." I strode back toward the bow before she could ask me about my childhood or what kind of pirate ship I wanted.

Twelve sailors remained out of Garett's crew, which left us a bit short-handed. I assigned Dab and Wentl to help work the ship, although they lacked even a speck of seamanship between them. The crew could sail the ship with twelve if they stepped fast, even burdened by my bodyguards.

Steffi's Thumb needed a captain. I understood why the surviving sailors might hesitate to volunteer. I insisted that they choose one of their number as captain, though, and a bald old man named Coog, as brown and weathered as one of the masts, agreed to give orders. He knew Garett's intended destination, a busy little town called Paikett in one of the dumpier northern kingdoms.

I told the new captain to proceed with our journey. He was to tell me if he had any trouble. He himself was not to cause me any trouble. Then I took my stained, stinking person to the bow where we had made informal camp, and I slept while Whistler stood watch. From that point on, one of us would always stand watch. We didn't trust Coog and the crew not to beat us to death in our sleep.

The next morning, we enjoyed sweet, clear weather and a breeze on our quarter. I took Pil aside, although it was impossible to locate a quiet spot on a sixty-foot ship carrying nineteen people. I settled for a place that wasn't well traveled. We headed as far aft as possible, to the end of the stern deck. I scared away a loafing sailor.

"Are you satisfied with the work I did on your face, Pil?"

"Yes. Thank you," she muttered.

"You don't have to sound so grudging about it. I could have given you three nostrils, but I didn't."

She didn't smile a bit. "Bib, I need you to teach me about sorcery before you lead everybody off and get killed for no good reason, or nearly no reason, and certainly no reason for me to go off and do it. You go without me. Once you teach me what I need, then you can go whatever way you want when we dock. I'll go the other way."

I crossed my arms and leaned back. "That was an elegant request. I feel flattered all to hell. Why should I spend a second helping you now?"

"I'll owe you a favor, sorcerer to sorcerer."

"Well . . . I have often found it useful for other sorcerers to owe me favors. All right, let's begin." I didn't anticipate a difficult lesson, because Pil's sorcery problem was a lack of confidence. I didn't know how Dixon had trained her, but she had ended up uncertain, even hesitant. "Pil, what did Dixon tell you sorcery is all about?"

The young woman opened her mouth and then paused. "I don't think he ever said a thing about it. At all. Isn't that strange? I just assumed it's all about magic."

"Well, it's not!" I frowned. "Not all of it, anyway. Any sorcerer worth a damn can get by without magic most of the time. Sorcery's not about learning, either. Some sorcerers are as stupid as baby birds. You wouldn't be far wrong to say it's about arrogance, but that's not exactly it, either."

"What is it, then?" I could hardly hear her over the water rushing against the hull.

I took a deep breath. "You can do just about anything as a sorcerer if you're willing to give up enough of yourself in trade. And that's a cost nobody can question but you."

Pil nodded and then gazed out at the ocean. "That's a lot."

"Hell, that's not even the big part. Listen now. Since you can do anything, you're responsible for everything. Everything in your life, at least."

She leaned away from me and stared. "No. That's foolish, and you can't tell me it's not. What if somebody holds a knife to my throat and forces me to do something? Or what if they trick me?"

"That doesn't matter a damn. Even if they make you fall in love with them, it still doesn't matter. Nobody else is on the hook for making things happen to you—not gods, not men, not a broke-leg jackrabbit. If you don't like something, figure out a way to change it. Do you understand what I'm saying?"

"No." She shook her head, squinting.

"When you were tickling my privates with a sharp knife, whose fault was that? Don't bother to answer. It was my fault for letting a pretty girl distract me."

"You're trying to trick me about something," she said slowly.

"If I succeeded, whose fault would it be?" I leaned against the deck rail and patted her arm. "Sorcerer, you are the willing author of all the good and all the bad in your existence. That's what sorcery is about. You don't need to look so terrified. Since all sorcerers are people, and since people are flimsy, unreliable pains in the ass, we often fall short of the standard."

Pil leaned on the railing beside me and watched the ship's wake. I kept quiet and let her stare until she said, "I guess it's too late to say I don't want to be a sorcerer."

"Not even a little bit. You could decide to never again use magic and to ignore the gods like they were a rash on somebody else's butt. Stick to that the rest of your life, and your existence as a sorcerer would be over. But it's a nearly impossible vow to keep."

Pil gave me a faint smile. "I can see that. The first time something horrible happened, something I could make better with magic, I'd be calling Fingit's name like a lover."

"Yes, you probably would."

"All right, then!" Pil stood straight. I could imagine her clapping her hands together to dust them off. "A favor for you." She said it like it was a chore such as brushing her teeth. "I owe you one favor. Or is there anything you need now?"

"No, nothing I can think of."

"Fine." She gave what might have been her idea of a wise, inscrutable sorcerer nod, and I managed not to smile. "Bib, thank you for telling me all that. I might have died ignorant, and that would have been a shame."

I gave her my idea of a wise sorcerer nod in return. People have told me that when I nod in this way, I look like my dog has just bitten my best friend. It seems to confuse people, so I've seen no call to alter it.

Pil led the way back to the bow. Whistler was guarding us against the crew. Halla and Bea stood staring over the gunwale at the swells. I saw Bea reach over and squeeze Halla's arm before leaning on tiptoe to murmur something to the much taller woman. I stopped dead. Bea would have surprised me less if she'd pulled a tiger's ears and sung to it in baby talk.

The two women kept conversing. I wanted to know everything about their unexpected conversation, but I couldn't think of a subtle way to ask. Finally, I walked over to stand on the other side of Bea and said, "So, what are we talking about?"

Both women glared at me as if I were a mouse in their soup. Neither one spoke.

I said, "The ocean sure is pretty. It's full of secrets, which is why so many ships are at the bottom of it. It's a fine thing that we don't have any secrets on this ship, isn't it?"

"Oh?" Bea raised her eyebrows. "Like the secrets you and Pil have been sharing?"

I waved that away. "That was a mystical discussion, not a bunch of secrets."

Bea lifted her jaw. "Our conversation is for people who have lost their children. Not for people who've murdered their children."

Halla grabbed Bea's arm, but the small woman didn't take her eyes off me.

I nodded for a few seconds, wondering why I wasn't cutting Bea's throat. When I accepted that she wasn't dead, I tried to think of something that would make her jump overboard, but before I was done, the wind swung around to blow hard from due north. The ship heeled over as the sails cracked like thunder, and everybody who wasn't a sailor tumbled to the deck.

Coog shouted only two orders, but the crew was already taking in sail. Within a few minutes, we had recovered and were sailing close to the wind, not quite northwest. Even though we were gaining some northward distance, the wind was blowing the ship itself back south. I estimated that one mile of northward travel would require us to sail five or six miles back and forth into the hard breeze.

If the wind didn't swing back around, our three-day crossing had just become a two-week journey. That would delay us awfully, but my real concern was that I'd be forced to kill every person aboard before we made land.

Bea grabbed my wrist hard. "Did you do this?"

"Not me. It was coincidence, and it saved you from my harsh retort." I pulled her hand away, not too rough. The swells had grown, and the ship was pitching. I shouted at Halla, "We're going to lose a fair amount of time if this persists."

Halla shrugged. "Can you change it?"

I had been assessing the possibility. Altering the wind for two days would require a lot more power than I had. "I fear I can't."

Halla shrugged again.

Kneeling on the deck, Whistler bent over and vomited. I hauled him up to the gunwale so he could puke over it. He threw up with a sound like being hit in the stomach with a haunch of meat. Then, Halla flung herself at the ship's side and vomited over it.

I turned and found Pil sitting on her butt on the wet deck, looking as green as a dead frog. I gave her a hand up, and she joined Halla and Whistler. All three of them hurled over the side as if that's what they'd been born to do.

Bea glared at me, unsteady on her feet but composed.

The wind suddenly shifted five points so that we were headed straight into it. It jarred every timber in the ship, but I felt glad about it, since we'd be able to sail near northward again. The captain ordered the ship to come about on the new heading, and the fresh wind sent us bounding right along.

Two minutes later, the wind shifted straight into our faces once again. The captain came about, searching for the best heading he could make. No more had he settled onto the new course than the wind swung again so that we faced right into its eye.

"I do not know why you might be doing this," Halla yelled into my ear, "but if you are, then I will throw you into the ocean." She bent over the gunwale again.

"I'm not." I reached out and pulled four white bands, one after the other. I flung them out and twisted for a minute. Then point by point, I swung the breeze back to the southeast. The captain and crew came about to head due north.

Five minutes later, the wind freshened to a gale and whirled all the way back to the north. It slammed the ship to a stop, shivering as if it had run onto a sand bar. The sails all popped and went slack for a moment before billowing backward.

"You!" a man's deep voice roared from the waves off to starboard. "You, sorcerer! Cease. Stop farting around with the wind. It's aggravating and stinks like a shark's bowels!"

Before I could scan the water, a woman's voice shouted from off to port. "It's not merely aggravating. It's arrogant, petulant, and, even worse, it's useless! Desist, or you'll regret it."

I peered over the portside. One hundred feet away, the head and naked upper body of a stunning, pale woman stood up from the water. I wouldn't say she floated. The waves surged around her, but she stood as motionless as a rock.

From the other side of the ship, the man yelled, "You! Be polite! You'd better not be staring at my wife's bosom! Just come over here and look at me and pretend she's a beautiful voice with no bosom at all."

Both Whistler and Pil answered that by vomiting. I heard the sailors shuffling around and exclaiming in the most profane terms from behind me. It sounded as if they'd all crowded themselves under the stern deck. I stepped forward to the prow so I could stare out both sides of the ship without scurrying back and forth like a squirrel saving for winter.

A hundred feet to starboard, the head of an elephant seal floated up and down on the waves. In a man's voice, it shouted, "Good, just keep looking over here. And stop this five-times-damned-to-Krak screwing around with the wind! It's exhausting."

TWENTY-THREE

Back when sorcery flourished, the second greatest threat to new sorcerers was bumbling around with mystical spirits. The greatest danger to sorcerers was trading away all their humanity, wandering off, and dying of exposure. But spirits wiped out a lot of sorcerers in their first year.

Most spirits appear perfect and beautiful, and even the homely ones are exotic. Just by standing there and existing, spirits beguile new sorcerers the way shiny, jagged things beguile toddlers. The teachers of sorcery explained how to deal with spirits and other supernatural creatures. They taught that lesson last of all, just before sending sorcerers into the world.

The main lesson was simple. Whenever a spirit comes into sight, a sorcerer should make an immense detour and, if possible, hide behind some hills or thick forests while circling around. Those who possess exceptional powers of concentration should convince themselves that the spirit doesn't exist, that they're just riding in a circle because they saw some pretty flowers. It sounds foolish, but it helps.

If that all fails and the spirit notices the skulking sorcerer, the only hope is to be polite. A smidge of fawning is fine, but not too much. If the spirit suspects insincerity, it may tear the sorcerer into a thousand bits before he takes a breath and then make a belt out of the sorcerer's tendons and ears.

Only a desperate or foolhardy sorcerer would try to bind a spirit into servitude. I had done it twice, but in both cases, I was damned polite about it. I had never known Halla to behave so foolishly, and when the elephant seal chastised us, Halla did not behave recklessly. She took care to stay quiet and stare at me until I spoke and took all the risks.

I resisted, but at last my discomfort and her moral superiority forced me to speak.

"Wise and persistent spirits!" I shouted. "We apologize for dragging this nasty ship across your fine ocean. Please let us continue our voyage. When we dock, I promise to burn this horrid vessel to the waterline!"

The woman's voice sang out from off the portside. "You are a sorcerer. Falsehoods spill from your lips like wine."

I turned toward the voice.

"Wait right there!" the seal bellowed, loud enough to echo off the sail behind me. "Look over here, right here at me. I know what your kind thinks about."

The woman called out, "We shall hold you here. We will becalm you until you eat one another rather than starve."

I didn't think either of these spirits could be Memweck in disguise. Neither of them spoke as if they thought they were the most amusing creature ever to draw breath. Also, we had conversed for over a minute, and neither of them had threatened to destroy any cities, tear anybody apart, or throw bits of dead children down on us.

I decided to say something stupid, on purpose. They might feel forced to correct my stupidity and so accidentally tell me something that was true. I waved at the elephant seal. "Memweck, it's kind of you to wait out here to welcome me, especially since I'm coming to pull out your heart. I'd like to feed it to my dogs, but they're at home. I guess I'll feed it to Whistler here."

The seal swam backward twenty paces before shouting, "Damn you! Break all your teeth! I'm not Memweck. You don't really think

I'm him, do you? Really? He's a horrible little squat. Just nasty. His lineage is exceptional, true, but for a superior entity, he bounces around and blathers a hell of a lot. I assure you that I am not Memweck, and my wife isn't either!"

"We merely do Memweck's bidding," the woman said in a flat, carrying voice. "Before you ask, we're not proud of it." I glanced over in time to see her shrug before I averted my eyes.

"Ah," I said in what I hoped was a wise tone. "You are spirits, then. Water-woses."

"We are." She flipped her pale hair, and I glanced.

"Eyes over here!" the seal bellowed.

The woman went on: "So, you are within our power. We can destroy you or make you suffer as easily as swallowing."

"That would be a sad thing," I called out. "Is there some way to avoid it? Riddles? Or a contest? If we win, you—"

"Quiet! Hold your face shut!" the seal shouted. "Do we look like the one Spirit of the Bending Sea, entitled to bargain with you?"

"We were allowed to bargain last week," the woman said with a certain coldness. "Somebody thought a poetry contest would be fun and so got our riddling privileges revoked . . ."

The seal grumbled, shook its head, and dove with a slippery wiggle.

I had assumed they were water spirits of the Bending Sea—the sea across which we were sailing. They weren't the one Spirit of the Bending Sea. That being would be a tremendous, mighty spirit. But it could allow any number of water-woses to live in its sea.

These spirits had said some awful things about Memweck, who seemed to have bound them in some way. Of course, Memweck was a nasty bit of business.

I shouted, "All right, forget the riddles. So, you're forced to do Memweck's bidding? Well, that's some goddamn injustice for you!" I tried to sound as outraged as a loving, over-protective mother. "How can a babbling, half-assed foreigner with pretentions of divinity come to your world and compel fine spirits like yourselves? It shouldn't be allowed!"

The woman turned her perfect face down, gazed at the water in front of her, and didn't answer.

A man popped up where the seal had been, the water at his waist. He was as pale as his wife, almost glowing, hairless except for wild green hair. He, too, was as beautiful as only a magical creature can be. He didn't shout this time, but I could hear him just fine. "The gods never loved us. But they never despised us until now."

The woman murmured, but I could hear her over the splashing ocean. "I felt myself die, you know. Our existence ended. It did. But then we existed again, right between breaths. I cannot make myself understand it."

I assumed they were describing the moment years ago when all magic ceased in the world of man, and then the moment that the way for the gods reopened. All kinds of magic and mystical creatures returned. That would have included spirits.

The man said, "The Spirit of the Blue River saw Krak curse you to be the Way-Opener. You made us exist again."

"You're welcome."

"We're not thanking you." The man frowned, and his ideal forehead wrinkled.

The woman spirit plunged underwater and a moment later appeared beside her husband, rising out of the sea like a porpoise. "You did this, so tell us. If our existence comes and goes like rain, does it have meaning?"

"Hundreds of spirits are asking this question." The man surged halfway to the ship. "Do you know the answer?"

I hadn't known exactly what to expect when I began conversing with the water-woses. I had intended to talk a little, listen a lot, and hope for inspiration. I had not expected them to engage in such heartfelt philosophy with me. I wished I could tell them something that wasn't a lie, or at least wasn't a guess.

"Noble spirits, I regret that I can't answer that question for you. I admit I can't answer it for myself, either. Krak cursed me with a task and a sword, not with knowledge."

The woman spirit rushed to the ship, spraying water half as high as the masts. She gripped the gunwale and stared at me with unblinking amber eyes, her webbed hands almost touching mine. "The gods can give sorcerers knowledge in trade. It's told that the gods will do this."

I resisted a powerful urge to lean back. "The gods only give the knowledge they want to give, and it's usually something you wish you didn't know."

The man roared, "You're not much use then, are you?" The wind rose to a gale, made the rigging whistle, and heeled the ship over so that everything not stowed tightly tumbled against the inside of the hull.

Pil's watery voice called out from behind me. "I know the answer to their question."

The wind died as if somebody had shut a window. The woman spirit shouted at me from four feet away, "Make her tell you, sorcerer!"

I gaped at Pil and raised my eyebrows.

She pretended not to notice. "I don't belong to him, not a bit, because I don't belong to anybody. I really don't. But I can answer if I decide to."

I did not open my mouth and say that the spirits would get a better answer from any random bug they pulled out of a dead stump. It wasn't a polite thing to say, and it might convince the spirits to pop us open and repaint the ship with our blood.

The man spirit boomed, "Tell us now! Or somebody torture her and make her tell. Or let me do it! You'd be amazed how much better torture is using an octopus or two!" The spirit had grown two-inch fangs, and I had never seen any spirit do that before.

Pil raised her chin and pulled back her shoulders as if she were going into battle. Then she threw herself against the side to vomit some more. Her spew sounded like a clump of mud falling down a rainy hillside. I damned myself for convincing her that she controlled everything in her life.

The woman spirit swam backward thirty feet. "This is a joke. You are joking, aren't you?"

The man raised out of the water with no strain, standing naked on the ocean surface. "I damn well hope they are joking. I've wanted to kill them ever since I first smelled them."

"I can answer!" Pil panted. "But you have to promise not to kill us!"

The woman spirit jumped over the gunwale, as graceful as an otter, to stand on the deck beside me. "In one minute, I will kill everyone on this vessel! Almost everyone on this vessel. Nearly everyone on this vessel will be killed, except for one person, whom I might decide to . . ." The spirit glared at the deck and shook her head. "In fifty seconds, I will kill most of you!"

"And I will laugh as you die," the man spirit roared from out in the water.

"Wait!" I bellowed, both hands up as if that would help anything. "What if Pil tells you the truth, but you don't like it?"

The woman frowned at Pil. "That is possible. Maybe likely. The truth is rarely pleasant."

I stepped between Pil and the woman spirit. "So, we offer this: Pil will answer with the truth, and you won't kill us even if you don't like the answer."

"You're just trying to cheat us!" the man yelled. "If you do a bad job, you should all be killed. If I could still tell riddles, I'd have torn you all into bits the size of snowflakes ten minutes ago!"

I glanced toward Halla but saw only her back as she dangled over the side. "Noble spirit, think about this. Your wife, whose bosom I am not staring at, by the way, acknowledged that a true answer is likely to be disagreeable. If you threaten to kill us for an answer you dislike, why would we tell the truth? We'd be smarter to lie and tell you something you'll like."

"Shark shit!" the man bellowed.

"No," the woman said. "It makes sense. Tell us the truth, then, and we promise not to kill you for it."

"Wonderful!" I said. "Nobody will be killing anybody, then. Right?"

Both water-woses nodded.

Pil hurled over the side again. It sounded like whatever she threw up came all the way from her feet. Whistler was draped limp over the side. Halla stood tall now, her black skin the color of ash, and she swallowed three times.

I patted Pil on the back and pulled her upright. "Sorcerer, we stand ready to hear your wisdom. I hope it sounds good."

Pil cleared her throat. "Our existence has no meaning."

The woman leaned over Pil. "And?"

"I think that 'no meaning' implies pretty strongly that you shouldn't expect an 'and' to come next."

Halla cleared her throat. "Does any logic stand behind this answer?"

Pil nodded and then swayed.

"Open your mouth and let it roll out then, you miserable cow-eater!" the male water-wose boomed from out in the water.

Pil took a breath and put on a grave expression. "You asked for an answer, not an explanation, which I am not giving you, because if I did, then you'd kill us as sure as hell is full of priests."

After a few seconds, the man spirit leaned forward and said, "Is that all?"

Pil nodded. Then she stumbled to the side and vomited over it again.

"Treachery!" the woman spirit shrieked, but she didn't shift from where she stood on deck. "I'll destroy this leaky box that you ride in!"

"We'll die if you do that!" I said, edging over between her and my puking companions, a futile act at if one ever existed. "You promised. We gave you the truth, and you said the truth can be disappointing. It disappoints us too."

The man spirit surged up to the side of the ship and leaped aboard as light as a moth. He touched his wife's shoulder. "We'll find a way around this damn bargain. Come on."

She closed her eyes.

Something hurled me to the deck and across it to slam into the side of the ship. I thought I was dying, but after I took my next breath, I sat up.

The spirits had gone. None of us seemed to be dead, but we were definitely all naked. All the lines on the ship, from the shortest rope to the longest, were woven into a massive, tangled nest between the two masts, fifty feet above us. I assumed that the spirits had tossed in all the cloth on the ship too for the sake of thoroughness.

The experience shocked my companions out of their seasickness.

The water spirits hated Pil's answer so much that they refused to let us sail on. The sailors sent men shinnying up the masts to begin untangling everything and gradually rerigging the ship. Meanwhile, the spirits swam the waters around the ship, sometimes surfacing to curse us and sing the disturbing songs of the undersea creatures they said would be devouring us soon.

The rope towing our boat had also been sucked into the spirits' nightmare of hemp and cloth. However, we were becalmed, and the boat didn't drift far. Without much delay, I swam to the boat, knife in my teeth, and I killed two of the prisoners with neat thrusts before rolling them over into the water. I had hoped to accomplish that unobserved, since the crew was consumed by this freakish disaster. That had been mere dribbling optimism. By the time I pulled my unclothed self back aboard, all the sailors knew what I had done. None of the crew spoke to me or even looked at me.

The next morning, the water-woses disappeared, but we spent another day becalmed, drifting on the current with the ship sluggishly spinning to all points of the compass. All the rubbish and filth we threw overboard floated beside us in the water. No pleas, compliments, or bribes convinced the spirits to offer a breeze.

I reattached the rope to the boat and took that opportunity to murder the remaining two prisoners, who would have murdered me with a cheery grin if they could. Afterward, the crew kept as far away from me as possible, which wasn't far on a deck sixty feet by eighteen feet. By that evening, the ship was rerigged and everyone wore cloths. No garment had as much as a rip or a hole torn in it. That didn't surprise me, since spirits are known for their refined touch.

The spirits allowed the wind to return. Before they departed, the woman told me, "Sorcerer, you cheated us."

"I regret you feel that way. How did I cheat?"

She swam in an agitated circle. "I cannot say precisely. By some sorcerer trickery, without doubt."

I smiled and tried not to seem nervous. "Good spirit, I can't promise I will ever find out anything more about your question, but I will try."

"Liar. I cannot understand why Krak chose a liar to be the Way-Opener."

After a pause, I said, "This isn't an answer, but I will tell you a real thing if you want to hear it."

The woman spirit halted and glared at me. "Fine. Why not?"

"I can't say where meaning comes from, whether it's from you, or other people, or the gods, although I doubt the hell out of that last one. Meaning has nothing to do with time, though. Great things can happen in a month or a minute. They may be remembered for a thousand years or forgotten in a week. It's all the same."

The spirit opened her mouth, but I interrupted. "Just because you stop existing for a while, that doesn't wipe out what you mean. That is, if you had meaning in the first place. I can't speak to that."

"That is a lie. Or a guess."

"Nope." I rapped on the gunwale three times. "It's something my little girl taught me."

The spirit didn't look too impressed by that. "Sorcerer, you must know why Memweck wanted us to delay you."

"Sure. He wanted to send his flunkies across the sea to be waiting for us when we dock in Paikett."

"You will therefore sail elsewhere."

I nodded. I had already agreed with Halla that we would sail for Sububb instead of Paikett.

"That is what Memweck wants. His . . . flunkies await you at Sububb." The spirit examined my face.

"That sneaky son of a dickless dog!" Then I cocked my head and peered at the spirit. "How do I know that your intelligence on this is good?"

"How do I know that your philosophy on time and meaning is good?" She dropped beneath the swells and didn't return.

TWENTY-FOUR

On any particular day, only so many parts of a ship need to be cleaned, mended, or polished. Sailors spend long periods of time doing not much on the same small deck with the same few fairly ripe people. Occasionally, a horrifying catastrophe will threaten to kill them all, and then they are given more boredom, which in truth is their greatest enemy.

The crew of *Steffi's Thumb* did not thank us for making this passage so interesting. We had killed several of them, which of course put us in a bad light. I had murdered helpless men. They had also seen us talk to evil spirits that commanded the wind and didn't wear clothes, so we must be evil spirits too. It stood to reason. They fell to speculating about why we weren't naked, especially the women.

I didn't care what they thought or did, so long as they took us to Paikett and went away. We ruled out sailing to Sububb, and a ferocious, hour-long argument between Halla, Bea, Whistler, and me had led to that decision. Physical violence was only employed once to emphasize a point. Pil stood back and giggled at us once in a while. After we decided our destination and then huffed away from each other, Whistler spent several minutes glaring and muttering. At least the argument had been something interesting to do for an hour instead of sitting around bored.

During the evening, after the spirits released us, we caught up on sleep and rested the cuts, bruises, and strains we had endured in the past week. Conversations tended to deal in practicalities or superficialities. Unless one chased three or four people to another part of the ship, privacy was as scarce as a tortoise.

The next morning, springtime handed us another beautiful day for our journey. I sharpened my knife early and tried not to stare at Dab and Wentl, who I would be murdering before sunset. During the crossing, they had been inept sailors but had caused no one grief. I felt a tithe of misgiving about executing them, but they had tried to kill me in Fat Shallows. I preferred not to murder two other members of the crew just so that Dab and Wentl could live.

As the sun passed midday, I sat with my back against the damp timbers of the ship's side, my eyes closed under the warm sun and my hand on my sword. Somebody walked up, putting me in their shadow. I opened my eyes just as Pil threw down a slim dagger, embedding its point in the deck a foot from me.

I didn't twitch. "If you want me to kill somebody for you, don't make me reach for the weapon. I'm tired. Put it in my hand for me." I closed my eyes.

Pil squatted and slapped my leg. "Get up and move around some, or you're going to get fat—but not on this food, I guess. I wouldn't feed it to a rat on a pile of crap, or even to my brother. Get up anyway—it's the polite thing to do when a lady comes to visit you."

I sighed and stood up.

"Krak and Fingit, bring the dagger with you!" Pil stepped back, almost trampling Whistler's hand. "I can't believe I have to tell you that. If I wanted to be the one holding it, I never would have thrown it down there next to you, would I?"

I bent over.

"With your left hand!"

I shook my head at her upside down, pulled the dagger out with my numb left hand, and stood facing her. "I can't wait to see what you have me do next. This is better than a village dance." I yawned.

"Be nice—this is a present."

Whistler grunted. "That's not much of a present. It looks just like the daggers those paid killers carried."

"Be quiet!" Pil narrowed her eyes at Whistler. "It can be a present and be stolen from a dead person too, and don't argue about it—that's how a lot of presents throughout history happened." She turned back to me. "Swing it around, really, really fast."

I grinned. "It'll slip out, and I'll throw your present right into the ocean. Or into the back of Halla's skull."

"I stole two more exactly like it, so if you lose this one, you can have one of those. And Halla can take care of herself."

I shook my head and started to tell her how foolish this all was, but she cut me off.

"Swing that weapon!"

Facing out toward the ocean, I cut at the air as hard and fast as I could. I swung three more times. The dagger stayed in my numb hand, and my grip seemed snug. I examined the knife and saw that the once-rounded wooden grip had been carved down to a shaft with seven sides.

"It won't come out of your hand unless you want it to," Pil said, smiling a little. "I mean, it probably won't. I haven't tested it under all possible conditions, but it should stay unless you do something crazy with it."

"Thank you, Pil, an enchanted weapon is always a handy thing. What kinds of crazy things should I avoid doing with it?"

She bit her lip for a second. "I don't know, really. At the very least, don't stab any stone walls or let anyone try to pull it out of your hand." She reached to give me a blood-stained sheath for it.

Pil had spent some of her power to create that enchantment for me, and I couldn't guess what that power had cost her. She seemed a little brisker to me than she had yesterday, or maybe even harsher. "Pil, thank you, thank you sincerely. This is a kind gesture and may help me at a difficult time." I smiled with as much gratitude as I felt, which was a lot. I had been taught the importance of a sorcerer acting stern and aloof lest he show an enemy some weakness. I had thrown that rule into the ditch as I was walking out the temple gate, along with a number of other boring lessons.

She patted my numb arm, almost as if I were a dog. "I know you may be killed, and you probably will be, but we don't have to make it easy for whomever does it. I'm sorry, but it's the truth. Bib, thank you for helping me."

I nodded in acknowledgment. "I try to be nice to other sorcerers. Most of them. Well, hell, I kill them as often as not, but I admit being partial to you."

Pil bit her lip again. "I don't intend to go off and die with you. When we dock, I'll buy a horse and ride to someplace you're not going."

I approved of her plan, although she sure as hell didn't need my approval. I had grown accustomed to her presence and expected I'd miss her a little, but it surprised me when sadness closed my throat, as if I had thrown away something important and couldn't get it back. I coughed and said, "I think you're wise to go."

Pil nodded. "Good. That's good."

"Do you know where you'll go?"

Pil shrugged, turned, and walked five paces to the other side of the ship, steady on her new sea legs despite the swells. She lay down on the wet planks and went to sleep.

A perfect landfall is a ticklish thing to achieve. That afternoon, when land came into view with no sign of a port, it did not reflect poorly on Captain Coog's seamanship. We sailed west along the coast of the Kingdom of Five Falls, appreciating the pale beaches that rose up to a clotted mass of dark-green tropical trees.

I said to nobody in particular, "I've never had the pleasure of visiting this kingdom, but everything I hear about it is bad."

Whistler chuckled. "I lived here for a bit after I deserted the Empire. It was so charming I almost sailed back and begged them to hang me."

"What's so bad about it?" Bea asked. "It's pretty. The weather's nice. There are beaches. Do they have a lot of plagues or bad water?"

Whistler grinned at the coastline. "It's the name."

"Don't try to be clever," Bea said.

"I'm not joking. Used to be the Kingdom of Beringslack, but a new king slaughtered all the Beringslacks, so the kingdom needed a new name. He thought naming it after waterfalls would be cute."

Halla nodded. "He had to change the name to something."

"Sure," Whistler said. "But he had only three waterfalls, and he didn't think Three Falls sounded poetic. So, he invaded the next kingdom over, took their waterfall, and made all their people slaves."

"What an awful piece of scum," Bea said. "Why is it Five Falls, then?"

"He didn't like the sound of Four Falls, either, so he had his slaves dig a channel to make the fifth waterfall. They say it killed half of them. The whole awful mess took twenty years."

Pil hissed and turned away.

Whistler went on: "The next winter, the king's son assassinated him. That's justice you don't see too often."

Bea said, "My merciful gods, that's horrible. "

Whistler waved his hand. "No, that's not even the horrible part. The people of Five Falls are boastful about all this history. They tell stories about it. Sing long-ass poems. They hold a festival in the spring and build little waterfalls of wine, and they make prisoners dig ditches all day. My wife hauled me to it."

All of us stared at Whistler. Pil's mouth fell open.

Whistler shrugged. "Why can't I have a wife?"

We went back to watching the beach glide past. I glanced at Dab and Wentl now and then. I'd need to hunt more victims tomorrow, and I found it heartening that the people of Five Falls were such a nasty lot.

An hour before dusk, the port town of Paikett came into sight. It was far bigger than Fat Shallows, and tidier too, with a real dock. Coog guided us into the harbor and dropped anchor, then he shouted for a boat to come row his passengers ashore. That was partly for our convenience, but I figured he mainly wanted to get rid of us as soon as he could.

I beckoned to Dab and Wentl. "Boys, come guard me while we row to the dock. Then I'll pay you off and release you from my service."

They laughed, slapped each other's backs, and thanked me three times.

Halla watched me and those boys with a mighty sour face. I hadn't told any of my companions about my need to kill two people a day for Harik. They must all have suspected that some curious thing was happening, but nobody asked about it. However, it wouldn't have shocked me if Halla had figured it out down to the details. I had never met anybody so adept at starting with a feather's worth of knowledge and figuring out the whole damn bird.

After a short row from the ship, we climbed out of the boat onto the orderly dock. I tossed a coin to an oarsman and scanned the huge open area next to the dock.

Whistler leaned in and tapped my shoulder. "That fat one looks familiar," he whispered, nodding at the oarsman I'd just paid.

I peered and recognized him as one of Leddie's men.

He had already pushed off from the dock, and he grinned at me.

Halla was watching, and she gripped her spear with both hands. "Be ready."

I drew my sword and turned back toward the town proper. Beyond the open area stood six or seven blue-painted wooden buildings roofed with brown clay tiles, each big enough to be a home or small shop. A long white building lay to our left, probably a warehouse. I did not see a single sailor, craftsman, or townsperson. That fact depressed me.

I raised my voice. "If you haven't prepared yourselves, do it now." I didn't try to lift everybody's morale for the coming fight. They had already proven they'd fight if they had to, and frankly, my own morale was dragging.

Two dozen of Leddie's false soldiers came charging toward us from between buildings, shouting as they ran. I recognized the sergeant right away. I had few options. I couldn't bring storms or lightning out of the bare blue sky. I would need minutes to call together any vicious insects or animals, and none lay right at hand, unless I wanted to command some fish to fling themselves onto the dock, flop over, trip the men, and bite them to death. I had seen less likely things happen, but I didn't care to stake my chances on it now.

Our tactical position could only have been worse if we'd been trapped in a pit and tied to stakes. Leddie's men were rushing us from three sides, and the water lay right behind us. Lutigan himself could not have prevailed in our situation.

So, I changed the situation. I shouted, "Follow me!" and sprinted down the edge of the dock to my right without looking back. In just a few seconds, I reached one end of the semicircle of charging soldiers, and two were close enough to attack me. I saw they carried clubs rather than swords, so I supposed Memweck really did want to slay me with his own hand.

I blocked the first man's swing, slammed into him with my shoulder, and knocked him into his friend. They both staggered and blocked the men behind them. That opened a gap between me and the dock's edge, and Halla raced through it behind me, her spear ready. Bea followed right behind her.

The mass of soldiers shifted in my direction to follow us. I glimpsed Leddie standing in the back, motionless. Before the two staggering soldiers untangled themselves, I hamstrung one and thrust my sword deep into the other's chest. They fell, and I roared at the men behind them as I attacked. Pil, Dab, and Wentl ran through the gap behind me while I fought two and then three men swinging their clubs hard. I killed one, but two more arrived, threatening to surround me.

Whistler reached the gap, tripped on nothing I could see, and fell on his face. He squirmed on the ground and seemed stunned.

"Whistler, come on!" I bellowed. "Hurry up, you slug!"

One of the soldiers whacked my left arm, and it went wobbly. Another grazed my left knee, which hurt like ants in the eyes. I stabbed a man in the throat, and he grabbed the man next to him to keep from falling. I cut that one's arm deep as he struggled, and they both went down. More were running around behind them to cut me off, though.

Whistler was up on his hands and knees, but a soldier kicked him in the ribs and knocked him over. For three seconds, I attacked like a wild man with nothing to live for, and I cut two men, one badly. When the soldiers eased their attack for a moment, I glanced at Whistler, who was lying facedown and surrounded by four men. I broke away to follow Halla and the others.

The soldiers didn't remain bemused for as long as I would have liked. They chased just a step or two behind me, and more raced along on the inland side trying to flank me. I reached the end of the dock and ran up onto the dirt road just as Halla jumped up from kneeling behind a stack of crates. She swung her spear twice, near decapitating one man and knocking another down. While soldiers gaped at her, I spun and gave two of them fatal wounds. Both those men staggered and fell.

Halla and I fled, the time-honored battle tactic. We led the soldiers by at least three steps, and I started to believe we might escape. Pil and the others led us by forty feet, running along the edge of the water. Then Bea stumbled and fell. When Pil helped her, Bea came up hobbling.

"Fingit's fat fingers and ass!" I shouted. We had killed or disabled close to half of them, but they showed no sign of running away. Pil and Wentl were half carrying Bea, but at her speed, the soldiers would run us down in seconds. "Over there!" I pointed to two white houses with a ten-foot gap between them. I didn't see anywhere else to make a stand that was within a ten-second run.

Halla planted herself twenty feet from the gap in the houses, facing the soldiers. Then she made a ferocious face and howled. The soldiers' pace faltered just a bit.

"Pil!" I shouted. When she turned, I pointed at the other side of Halla. She ran to cover that side and pulled her knife. I jumped to Halla's other side. "Bea, if they come from behind, yell!" I didn't glance back to see whether she understood. I shoved Dab to stand on my left, and Wentl followed him.

As the soldiers reached us, I lunged out to meet the first two, and in the next thirty seconds, I killed two men and wounded a third while almost getting my shoulder crushed. The club scraped down the side of my face instead, just missing my eye. I stabbed that man in his eye and laughed.

My fight lulled for a few seconds, and I glanced left. Dab lay on the ground. Wentl had picked up a club someplace, and a soldier was driving him back with furious swings. On the other side, four bodies lay on the ground around Halla, but Pil was one of them. Halla stood over Pil, fighting off attacks from three sides. I took one step that direction, but two soldiers jumped in my way, having decided it was important for me to kill them without delay.

When I had murdered those two men, one of whom grabbed at my shoulders and apologized as he fell, I turned to help Halla. She faced three soldiers and still stood over Pil, who lay shaking her head. I attacked from the side, but before I'd even made a good cut, one of the men let out a short scream and stiffened. A second man, the foulmouthed sergeant, retreated toward his screaming friend, who swayed and fell forward. Leddie stepped out from behind the falling man to thrust her sword into the sergeant's back.

A third soldier stared at Leddie. I did too, since she carried a bloody sword and wore nothing but boots. Blood had sprayed or splashed over a good amount of her pale skin.

Leddie swung and cut into the third man's neck. Then she dropped her sword and backed up fast, her hands in the air. She stopped thirty feet away, raised her chin, and struck a pose. Her face and chest were badly scarred. She mumbled something.

I answered with as much wit as any shit-stained cowherd. "What?"

Leddie raised her voice. Although she still mumbled, I could make out her words. "I had to do something to make you hesitate before killing me."

"All right, we've hesitated." I pointed my sword at her.

Pil had gotten to her knees and was swaying as she pushed herself upright. She took one step toward Leddie, swayed again, and would have fallen if Halla hadn't grabbed her arm. I had been about to shove Pil aside anyway so she couldn't cheat me out of killing Leddie.

I walked toward the naked woman. "I don't accept your surrender."

"I didn't surrender," Leddie mumbled, backing away. "Did anyone hear me say, 'I quit—please tie me up and let children throw shit at me'? I want to make an alliance."

Laughing, I kept walking toward her. "I've been telling everybody you're crazy, and that removed any doubt."

"I can take you to Memweck," Leddie said. She snagged her heel on something as she backed away and almost fell, but she caught herself. "I can get you there . . ." Her words trailed off into mumbling.

Pointing my bloody sword at her eye, I said, "What is wrong with you, woman? Did you bite off part of your tongue?"

Leddie shook her head and mumbled louder. "I have a lock of Memweck's hair in my mouth."

Everybody must have heard her, because we all paused and went silent. I said, "You should have said that instead of pulling off all your clothes. I don't think I can kill you until I find out why you're sucking on Memweck's hair."

TWENTY-FIVE

Two of Leddie's men escaped into the countryside. We could have trailed them, but they were probably hurt and didn't seem a threat by themselves. Four more men had taken wounds that weren't deadly. I stabbed two of them to death before Halla grabbed me and threw me fifteen feet, spinning like a water wheel.

I stood up and brushed at a grass stain on my knee. "You're right, I should save some for tomorrow."

Halla grunted. "So that you can kill two per day. For Harik. By midnight."

"Wrong! By sunset."

Halla grunted again and stood in my way like a grumpy mule, so I decided to treat her like one. "You cannot tell me, you great, pounding stump, that you give a single good goddamn about these men or how they get killed! I won't believe it, so save your words and shift aside so I can take them prisoner! For later." I shooed her with my left hand.

Halla didn't shift. Her jaw worked for a few seconds, and then she croaked like she was lifting something heavy. "You are right. I do not care. But you still may not bind and kill them. We will release them."

Bea had been tending Whistler's cuts. The soldiers had battered him hard before Leddie called them off and saved him. Now Bea ran to stand at Halla's shoulder. She frowned at me but didn't say anything.

I rested the point of my sword on the grass and squinted up at Halla. "So, you intend to thwart me . . . because you don't care."

Halla clenched her teeth and then relaxed, letting out a calm breath. "Yes. That is correct."

I glanced from Halla, whose face was impassive, to Bea, who was biting her lip and wiping her palms on her trousers. "What is the noise between the two of you? Are you lovers? Does one of you owe the other money? I don't really feel much concern about it, but you're interfering with my murders."

Bea said, "No. No, it's nothing like that. I don't think a killer like you could understand it."

"I expect that's true." I sighed and gazed around. "If we're setting these two fellows free, I guess I'll go hunt down those two cowards."

Bea didn't give me a mean look or say anything nasty. Instead, she trotted back to Whistler.

I called out, "Whistler, you can get nursed anytime. Would you and Pil please hunt for supplies? We need a blanket to cover up Leddie's nudity." I glanced at Leddie and raised my voice even more. "We also need some rope and hot coals and an assortment of blacksmith's tools in case she goes shy about talking. Although I admit that shyness seems as unlikely for her as a goat singing love songs."

Pil and Whistler trudged off toward the middle of town.

"Bring some cloth too!" I shouted after them. "For bandages and blindfolds and gags. I hate listening to a woman scream." I glanced at Leddie again. She didn't appear worried.

I had believed the marks on Leddie's face and chest to be scars, maybe from hurts I had caused by dropping that tree on her. But they were long, open wounds like claw marks. None bled, but some were deep, raw, and appalling. Bea had worried over them for a few seconds, caught herself, and called Leddie a nasty, baby-stealing slut before walking away.

I didn't comment on the wounds. "Leddie, I lack the skill to torture you properly, for which I apologize, but don't worry. Halla is a champion at cracking bones and pulling off skin."

Leddie smiled, but her face faded to a paler shade than normal.

Halla stalked over to face the woman from half an arm's length away. Her dark bulk overwhelmed Leddie, who edged away. Halla breathed, "For days, I have imagined torturing you. I may fill your mouth with boiling mud. I may cut a small hole in you and see what I can pull out through it." Halla glanced over Leddie's head at Bea and gave a tiny headshake.

Ten minutes later, we had covered Leddie with a blanket, pushed her down to sit against a tree, tied her to it, and bound her hands and feet tight enough to bruise. Her eyes had stretched wide, like a frightened horse's, but she otherwise seemed calm.

I told Leddie, "General, if I like what you say, I may let you live with only a leg or two sliced off. So, speak."

Leddie pointed at her open mouth and mumbled, "I stole this lock of Memweck's hair. It isn't big, but after you hold the damn thing in your mouth for a while, it feels like a coil of dirty rope. Understand this: When Memweck's hair is inside you, he can't see you. Unless you're right in front of him, then of course he can see you—he's not an infant. I mean he can't see you from far away."

I grimaced. "The hell you say."

Leddie nodded. "The hell I do say, you son of a farting toad." She choked a little. "Don't worry, I didn't quite swallow it."

"We cannot hold hair on our tongues until we reach our enemy." Halla gestured around us. "Unless he is in one of these houses here."

Leddie shook her head.

Halla picked up a heavy smith's hammer. "Where is he?"

"Wait!" Leddie said. "You don't have to hold the hair in your mouth. I wouldn't recommend such a thing anyway. Although his hair does taste like blueberries."

Whistler coughed as if he were choking. "Not in my mouth? I'm not poking any holy hair up my butt. It sounds blasphemous."

"And temporary," Bea added.

"No, no, no! You're not a single damn bit of help!" Leddie glared at me. "You! You're such a smart, tree-throwing son of a bitch! You stick it under the skin!"

I stared down to think. Her proposition sounded idiotic. But when dealing with gods, crazy things were more likely to be true than normal things. I had heard that Effla's tears were an aphrodisiac so powerful people would screw until they died of thirst. And whoever carried Chira's fingernail clippings could call any kind of bird and make it do tricks until predators came and ate it. In general, using bits of the gods' divine selves brought curses and blessings both.

While I was thinking, Halla squatted in front of Leddie. "Your hair trick means nothing. We cannot trust you. You tried to kill us."

Leddie laughed with care. "Is that all? Who hasn't tried to kill somebody here? Bib, this hillside of a woman once tried to kill you, right?"

I thought back to Halla slamming me against those crates when we were young.

"And you left that oaf to die." Leddie nodded at Whistler. "Oh, Bib, this girl almost killed you and nearly gelded you." Leddie pointed at Pil, who turned red. "I tried to kill you too. Damn it, Bib, every woman you've ever met probably wanted to kill you." She squinted at Bea. "Do you want to kill him? No? What's wrong with you?"

I held up a hand. "Just wait—"

"We even kill our wives and children, don't we, Bib?" She raised her eyebrows at me. "Memweck told me all about every one of you."

Part of me wanted to cut her throat, but that part of me felt beat up and tired. "Now, wait. You have a semidivine ally."

"You mean I have a cruel master."

"Maybe. Why do you want to jump out of his godly ship and crawl into our leaky rowboat?"

"I only want one little thing, and he made it clear he'll never give it to me." Leddie dropped her voice. "I want his sword. No one can capture me if I have it. I mean, no one can defeat me if I have it."

"And why do you want that so much?" I said slowly.

"That's my business."

"Fine. Halla, break her knees."

"Shit! All right." Leddie glowered at me. "Have you ever been powerless while people hurt you?"

"You're powerless now."

"I didn't ask about me, you whirling raccoon's ass!"

I frowned but answered her. "All right, yes, I've been as meek as a newborn piglet."

"For how long?"

"Um, nearly a year, not that it matters."

"Nowhere close to me, then." Leddie shrugged as much as she could while tied to a tree. "Nothing like me at all. What did they do to you?"

"They cut off my hands." I admit to smirking a little, but she didn't flinch or even glance at my hands.

"Oh? That's not so bad. But it's something, so shut up and let's help each other."

"I do not care about Bib and his hands," Halla grated, "and your whimpering means nothing."

Leddie thrashed against the ropes for a few seconds and fell quiet. Then she started laughing hard, but her chin was trembling and her eyes were still too wide. I was surprised she didn't choke on the near-divine hair. She may not have been insane all the time, but at that moment, she looked crazy as hell.

"Why don't we toss all that crap in the corner for now and come back to it?" I said briskly. "Where is Memweck?"

Leddie's face grew calm, as if somebody had wiped calmness onto it with a rag. "I would be an idiot to tell you that, wouldn't I? I mean, why would you even need me? It hurts me that you think I'm so stupid."

"You don't need to come at me teeth-first," I said. "I don't expect you to tell me precisely where he lays his big, holy head at night. I mean what direction do we go?"

She gestured with her chin. "West."

"Along the coast?" Whistler asked.

Leddie nodded.

Halla raised the hammer. "You're lying. The oracle said go north."

Leddie snorted. "Oh, the oracle said it? I guess she was right then, because you came north to get here, and now you'll go west if you want to find Memweck."

"The oracle was a man," Whistler muttered.

"That's nice. Did you fall in love?" Leddie gazed around at us. "Say, why don't we do a bold thing and return to the problem of Memweck watching everything you do? I'm not a military expert like everybody else here seems to think they are, but it's hard to surprise somebody who can look at you whenever he wants!"

"Certainly." I nodded at Leddie. "I'll scratch you, put one strand of Memweck's hair under your skin, and heal it. If you don't strangle, or burst, or start telling us about your childhood, I guess it will be safe enough for the rest of us."

"I approve," Leddie said.

"I do not!" Halla stepped between Leddie and me.

But I had already made up my mind. When I saw all that laughing, crying, and terror on Leddie's torn-up face, as if three people were using it at once, I decided that somebody had wrecked her mind too much for her to connive and plot with any skill. She was dangerous. We'd have to watch her. But I couldn't see her as part of some deep strategy to destroy us.

I gave myself a seven-in-ten chance of being right about all that.

Patting Halla on the shoulder, I said, "It's all right if you don't want to do it. You can board that ship and go straight back to Bindle."

"She is lying!" Flecks of spit flew from Halla's mouth.

"No, she's not. Probably not. She knows where Memweck is. You may recall that I am a liar. I therefore possess a fine sense of what the truth sounds like. Leddie, who did all that to your face?"

The woman didn't move. Her face froze as if it had been caught doing something bad. "Memweck."

"She's not lying about that," I said.

That set off several minutes of arguing, name-calling, and dirt-kicking. At the end, we had established that I would travel west with Leddie, protected by Memweck's hairs, and everybody else could either come along or go to hell, as they pleased. But if they came with me, they'd be carrying Memweck's hair under their skin.

Bea stepped up first to receive a semidivine hair into her arm. Whistler came after her. Halla grumbled and cursed throughout the brief, near-painless process.

Pil declined.

Halla and Bea escorted Leddie to fetch her clothes.

I took Pil aside. "You shouldn't be leery of carrying Memweck around inside you. He tastes like blueberries, after all."

Pil's words tumbled out. "I told you I'd be leaving—maybe not exactly now, but you knew it would be soon, and soon is now. So don't act surprised and don't act sad, either. Just give me some of that silver so I can buy a horse."

"When did you try to kill me?"

"It was . . . I'm sorry!" She turned red. "I wish I hadn't done it. It was a foolish thing to try, and I'm sorry, really. I won't do it again."

"Oh, don't say that. You may find someday that you badly need to kill me. Sorcery is an unpredictable endeavor."

Pil's forehead was drawn with worry, but she nodded. "I need a horse."

I plucked seven silver coins from my pouch. "There, buy one with good wind." I pulled out two more coins for her. "And get a warm cloak. It looks rainy."

Pil lay her hand on my arm and squeezed once. Then she walked away fast and rounded a corner in a few seconds.

Whistler had been leaning against a tree, watching everything. "I'm sorry she left. She wasn't too tough, but she was smart. Do you think she'll come back?"

I shrugged. Fighting, thinking, and arguing had exhausted me.

"I'm taking a walk." Whistler muttered something, but I didn't listen.

The nighttime sea breeze should have made for a pleasant little jaunt, but I cursed and kicked bushes for about a mile. I had known Pil was leaving, so I shouldn't have been in such a foul mood about it. I just wanted to bitch and kick things.

I finally flopped down under a juniper tree, drew forth Harik's book, and stared at the third page.

Ten seconds later, all 518 of my victims appeared in front of me, glowing and translucent. The ones I had killed that afternoon must have been somewhere in the herd. Manon stood in front of me and glared as if her eyes could shrivel my heart from beyond death.

I stood and pointed my sword at her. She walked toward me until the sword touched her chest.

"Manon, I have already said I'm sorry a number of times. Saying it again won't make me any sorrier."

"Why did you call me if you don't want to whine and cry about how pathetic you are?" Her words were as sharp as granite, like an angry twelve-year-old's.

"You need to hear that you're not blameless in all this." I stayed calm, as if I were explaining how she'd burned dinner. "You ignored just about everything I told you to do, things that would keep you safe. You wanted power, and you used it foolishly. I did wrong, but you have to understand how you did wrong too."

"Why?" Manon sounded puzzled.

"So that you won't suffer like that anymore!" The moment I said the words, I realized they were stupid.

"Father, I don't have any 'anymore.' I'm dead. There's nothing else for me."

Embarrassed, I muttered, "Nothing?"

"Nothing I can remember. I guess there could be things I don't remember, but we won't ever find out." Manon sneered. "Maybe you damned me to be nothing forever. You don't know."

"I shouldn't have called for you," I said.

"Wait!" Manon dropped her voice as if she was about to tell me a secret. "If you really love me, you'll bring me back."

"I don't know how. And anyway, I shouldn't."

She pointed at my face. "You and the God of Death chat and whisper secrets all the time. Ask him! Are you scared?"

"I'm scared of this. I can't imagine how it would be done." But I admitted to myself that Harik must know how to bring somebody back. It was his damn book that had just brought back Manon's ghost.

"You can figure it out." Manon grinned. "I know you love me, or you wouldn't be torturing yourself like this. You wouldn't be so sad. You'll do it."

"No, I won't. I won't mention it to Harik."

"You are such a liar, Father! I love you anyway."

"You're saying that to manipulate me."

"Yes, I am. That doesn't mean I'm lying about loving you, though. You always knew when I was lying. Am I lying now?"

"Shit!" I realized that I was hoping my daughter had lied when she said she loved me. "Yes, I love you too. I'll find out what I can."

Manon's ghost jumped up and down. I couldn't hear her because she bounced away from the sword, but she had a big smile. I hadn't often seen her that happy when she was alive. After a bit, she calmed down. "Father, I know something that will help you. When you fight Memweck, don't try to be smart about it. Go straight in, right straight in, and walk up to him."

I chuckled. "Are you sure you don't want me dead like you?"

"I'm telling the truth. I am." Manon rolled her eyes. "Don't be stupid! He wants to stab you with his own sword. Why would he send somebody to stop you before you reach him? Trust me."

"Then, thank you, darling. I'll include that in my tactical considerations." I intended to forget all about it when I walked away. It sounded too obvious.

"Father, will you sit and talk with me?"

Manon and I sat on the long grass in the dark and remembered things we had done when she was alive, laughed about the foolish things I'd been doing since, and planned what she could do when she returned to life. We hadn't had such leisure for talking when she was still alive, since destruction was always running in our tracks.

A couple of people came and spoke to me in the darkness, but I ignored them. Manon and I talked most of the night, lit by the glow of her skin. Two hours before sunrise, she was recalling how much her boots had pinched when we fled up the cliff from the city of Parhold. She disappeared in the middle of a word, along with all the others I had killed.

TWENTY-SIX

None of my teachers ever warned us not to bring people back from the dead. They did name a few other sorcerous acts that would produce catastrophe, a term they did not need to explain further. Sorcerers deal with gods and vast power, so when one says the word *catastrophe*, it's understood that everybody within miles will be destroyed.

Resurrection was never said to be catastrophic. It wasn't discussed at all. If a student mentioned the subject, the teacher pretended she didn't hear it and started talking about woolen trousers, or frogs, or similarly dull topics.

I considered how I might bring up the idea to Harik without looking like a bouncing fool. I already owed him an unknown number of murders, and he expected me to kill two more people every day. I hadn't yet delivered his book, either. Could I stand to pile another obligation on top of all that?

Hell, he probably already knew what I wanted. I might spend all day calling him a razor-faced, cross-eyed, jackal's frisky dream, but he was still the God of Death.

I glanced at Halla as she rode beside me scanning the countryside. The horse trader in Paikett had warned us of bandits on the western road, which pleased me.

"Halla, those trees up on the left look suspicious. Oh, and have you ever raised somebody from the dead?"

She peered at the lush trees, swaying in the cool, wet sea wind. "No, and I have been waiting for you to ask."

"You have not!"

Halla stared at me with no expression. "I have. I understand why you are asking. It would be unwise to try it."

She was right, of course.

"You're full of shit! You may be afraid to pull somebody back from wherever they go, but I'm not." I hadn't even decided to try resurrection, and I realized I was talking myself into it. I drew a huge breath. "All right, tell me this. If we find that your nephews have been killed, mightn't you consider bringing them back?"

Halla's eyelid twitched. "No."

"What if their parents came to you weeping, in pain that can't be measured, and asked you to help? That they might as well be dead themselves?"

Halla closed her eyes and clenched her teeth a few times. "I don't know." She glanced up. "Yes. I might. No." She shrugged.

A dozen snips of her behavior made sense all at once. "Wait, wait, wait!" I said. "You don't know, do you? You're trying to figure out the answer you ought to give, right? I've been wondering why you're so dedicated to this rescue. It sure doesn't sound like you. But you don't really care, do you?"

"I do!" she growled. "I should. And I do. You, you go raise your people from the dead—raise your wife and children." Her face closed as tight as a door. "Raise all the pigs you have eaten and flowers you have stepped on too if it will keep you quiet for an hour." She said it with what sounded like anger, but her face was almost blank.

Halla watched the road with an empty gaze for most of a minute before she kicked her horse into a gallop. The path wound through thick stands of swaying trees less than two hundred paces up from the beach. She rode out of sight in a hurry.

I now felt sure that Halla didn't care about those boys or their lives one bit. Maybe she was fulfilling a debt to some god. Or maybe it bothered her that she didn't care.

In the next moment, I felt the stretching, nauseating yank of a god pulling me up to trade. I hadn't yet settled on how to open the subject of resurrection with Harik, or even whether I wanted to try. As with so many of my dealings with the gods, I would just have to pay close attention, be aggressive, and say no a lot.

"Mighty Harik, I wish I could say I've missed your cataclysmic stench, but I hesitate to lie to the God of Death." I imagined drawing my sword. The place of trading appeared, and it was a clear, dewy morning in the Gods' Realm. The sun hadn't yet topped the nearby forest. I smiled up at the marble gazebo, but my smile fell like ice off a calving glacier.

A coarse, cutting voice said, "Don't talk about smells, Murderer. You're as foul as a hairy buffalo's groin. Have you taken a bath in the past month? Even scraped out your mouth? Don't answer. Anything you say isn't worth a speck of snot."

I conjured back a few bits of my smile. "Hello, Mighty Lutigan. It's been awhile since we chatted."

No god despised me more than Lutigan, and really it was all due to a misunderstanding. I once helped Fingit, Blacksmith of the Gods, play a minor prank on Lutigan, but by accident, it became more of booby trap combined with an assault. While I didn't plan for all that calamity to happen, I thought it was awfully damn funny. Lutigan felt my apology was insincere.

Lutigan didn't have the appearance of a being who forgave easily. Most male gods wore robes, but he wore armor made from the hides of the fourteen most horrible creatures he had killed. He wore sharp, crushing boots instead of sandals. The tiger's head on his red helm sported a crown of needle-sharp spikes. He carried a plain red shield on his back, and fourteen hilts stuck out from underneath it, the hilts of his fourteen swords, each fourteen palms long.

Most gods chose to wear a physical form of perfect beauty, but not Lutigan. His body was designed to kill the greatest number of beings in the shortest amount of time. His red, bristly body hair served as a second armor. His jutting eyebrows were both a challenge and an insult. He could drive his long, ridiculous nose into somebody's brain and slay them instantly.

Over the centuries, sorcerers had argued with great fervor about Lutigan's obsession with the number fourteen. The debates often involved drinking, physical threats, and broken marriages. Assaults and murders weren't unknown, since quick tempers always accompanied any discussion of Lutigan. No consensus had ever been reached. Dozens of explanations seemed possible. The most popular held that the number fourteen was the key to conquering the universe by force. The second most popular was that Lutigan just liked fourteen and that was that.

It would not avail me to be nice to this god. Nothing I could do would make him hate me less or hate me more. The only reason he hadn't destroyed me years ago was that I belonged to Harik, who was known to get pissy about his things.

Lutigan growled. "When I think about crushing your throat, Murderer, my entire, mighty being feels tingly. This interview won't take long. You have treated my servant with disrespect."

"I treat everybody with disrespect. They shouldn't feel I'm singling them out."

"Quiet!" Lutigan's voice echoed inside my head, which was a nice trick.

I stayed quiet and waited.

"Well?" Lutigan shouted.

"Ah, which of Your Magnificence's servants have I treated like shit?"

"That woman down there. The one with the face."

"Leddie?"

"Right, that one. You threatened her and dropped things on her." Lutigan held up a fist and squeezed. Cracking sounds echoed off the forest. I didn't know what he was crushing, but it was impressive as hell.

"How can she be your servant, Mighty Lutigan? She's not even a sorcerer."

"I didn't say she was a good servant."

"Can she even know that she's serving you?"

"She's not a smart servant, either. You're boring me, Murderer."

"But . . . she tried to kill me."

"I'm fine with that."

Pleas and explanations wouldn't avail me with the God of War. I stepped forward and threw back my shoulders. "I have to disrespect her a certain amount! We've been in deadly combat until now. And if she tricks me, I may have—"

"Quiet!" Lutigan boomed loud enough for my teeth to hurt. "I don't care about your trials and your journey, you little snip. Can't think of anything more boring. If I wasn't immortal, you would already have bored me to death."

Lutigan wasn't the smartest of the gods. Maybe I could tease something useful out of him. I scratched my beard for effect. "Mighty Lutigan, Leddie is just riding along with me to kill your son, Memweck."

"Who cares? The boy's a giggling, insolent tower of butter." Lutigan slapped the marble bench hard enough to show he did care even a little.

"A disappointment, huh?"

"The little dangler thinks he's funny." Lutigan stared at me. "Shut up about it."

I shut up and waited.

"By Krak's flaming, all-destroying testes!" Lutigan roared. Dust drifted down from the ceiling of the gazebo. "Aren't you even going to say you're sorry?"

I bowed. "I'm sorry, Your Magnificence. Really. Sincerely."

"I hope you eat a thousand bugs in hell. Fine, regardless, here's how you'll make it up to me. I want the Knife. You will deliver her to me."

I blinked twice while my brain adjusted. The Knife was the gods' name for Pil. I cleared my throat. "I believe she's associated with Fingit, who I know is just as sorry as I am about everything that happened in the past. I have no pull with Fingit, though."

Lutigan laughed. "I can deal with that wobbly blossom. Except for one thing. He won't give her to me unless she asks." The god leaned forward, perched on the bench like a tiger watching a chubby, stupid calf. "Make her ask."

I blurted, "I don't even know where she is."

"Piffle."

I silently asked myself whether the God of War had really just said "piffle."

Lutigan went on, "You'll see the Knife again. And she owes you a favor. Make her ask."

"Well, maybe we can formalize things," I said, angling for some clever way to escape this. "Mighty Lutigan, I offer you the honor of making the first offer."

I saw only a blur as Lutigan jumped forward while drawing a sword, and he swung a savage cut into the dirt of the arena. I found myself lying on my back, buried up to my waist in a pile of grainy brown earth.

Lutigan pointed the pure white sword at me. "This isn't a damned trade. Sorcerers think everything is about bargaining. You're no cleverer than ducks! Gods don't have to bargain—we can just take what we want. I want the Knife. Make her ask! Do it before sunset on the thirteenth day from now, or I'll destroy you."

"Sunset? Why does everybody love sunset? Isn't it a little trite?" I said. "How about when the birds stop singing for the night? When the campfire dies out? Nine hours?"

"Sunset!" Lutigan bellowed.

The god returned me to the world of man with such grim power that I fell off my horse.

Leddie laughed and pointed at me.

"Are you drunk?" Whistler stared at me, his chin up in disapproval.

"No, but I wish I was." I stood and mounted. From the saddle, I examined the trail back down the slope toward Paikett, but I didn't spot Pil. She had been gone all night and part of a day.

I could ride back to town and track Pil. A hard, two-hour ride would take me to the spot where I'd last seen her. I almost turned back and said to hell with our chase, at least for now. Then I realized that since Lutigan was trying to work through me, Pil was better off if she never saw me again.

I kicked my horse and rode on up the slope.

Leddie laughed again. "What, no smart remarks about drinking, or not drinking, or wishing you could watch somebody drink? Are you sick? Broken heart? Blisters on your asshole from the saddle?"

I ignored her.

That's a lie. I pretended to ignore her while she didn't shut up for the next ten minutes.

TWENTY-SEVEN

On the second day traveling west from Paikett, the road swung inland. We climbed several hundred feet through hills thick with rich, swaying trees. Cool rain soaked us most of the day. Fog sifted in whenever the rain stopped. We passed a dozen villages and one sizable town, full of people who seemed to prefer that strangers stay quiet and ride through fast.

About midday, five skinny bandits carrying clubs jumped out at us when we topped a rise. I killed two while the others were still shouting for us to throw down our weapons. After that affair, we pushed hard and made a cold, wet camp for the night.

The next day was sunny, still, and steamy, and we climbed through higher, sparser hills. By midday, I figured us to be ten miles inland. Three mountains had emerged from the fuzzy distance ahead of us. We saw plenty of villages, none of which seemed friendly or even interested enough to throw rocks at us.

Midafternoon arrived, and I hadn't found anybody to kill yet. "I think I'll ride ahead for a bit and contemplate our situation," I announced. "Stay back here and don't distract me."

Leddie said something, but I ignored her as I kicked my horse into a gallop.

I outpaced the others by a mile, slowed to a trot, loosened my sword in the scabbard, and started singing like a drunkard. My wife had once said my singing voice sounded like a seal slammed between two boats, but I could be heard far off. I called up a memory and sang "The Whore Song," written by a morose soldier named Ralt, who had died a thousand miles away from this steamy road.

I was hoping that a loud, drunk old man would attract a couple of bandits, or even a couple of greedy farmers with a mean streak. I was still waiting on such people to arrive when fast hoofbeats sounded from the trail behind me. Halla and the others were riding to overtake me, so I drew rein to wait.

Bea shouted at me before her horse had even halted. "You horrible liar! Killer! I'm sick just looking at you!"

"It seems bad, Bib," Whistler said. "You've got to admit it does. Two people every day? If you can't find two, are you going to kill us?"

Leddie frowned. "I don't care how many you kill. Kill a thousand a day—I don't care one bit. But you can't hide this kind of crap from us."

I raised my eyebrows at Halla.

"They deserved to know, so I told them," Halla said.

I yelled, "Damn it, isn't anybody even going to ask whether this is true? Am I just assumed guilty because Halla says so?"

After a pause, Whistler said, "Is it true?"

"Hell yes, it's true! Not that it concerns any of you."

Leddie, Bea, and Whistler started talking on top of each other.

"Hush!" I shouted. "How about if I promise not to kill any of you?"

Leddie snorted. "Speaking as an expert on dishonesty, your promise is worth less than a loose toenail."

"It is not just our lives," Halla said. "What if we need you, but you are away finding people to kill? What if we had been ambushed today while you were up here singing badly?"

I could have told them that I was obliged to do these killings because I chose to save Bea and Whistler from death. But that knowledge might not have swayed their feelings, and I preferred not to share details about my deals with the gods.

I met each of their eyes in turn. "So, you say I'm a bad dog and can't be trusted. How do you suggest dealing with me? Not that I'm agreeing to anything. I'm just asking."

Bea curled her lip. "We don't need you anymore. Leddie knows where the children are, and she's a soldier."

Leddie beamed. "You sweet thing! I might lead you away into the bushes if the chance pops up. Don't be stupid, though—we need all the swords we can get."

Halla raised a hand. "Bib, swear that you will kill no one unless I agree."

I pointed at her and laughed. "I'll think about consulting you, if I have time. Unless somebody is already trying to poke us full of holes. In that case, I'll kill them and worry later whether I hurt your feelings."

Halla gritted her teeth. "Very well. Also, do not go away by yourself. Stay with the rest of us."

"That sounds perfectly fair," I said. "I wouldn't argue against that."

"Will you do it?"

"Maybe. Let's find out." I winked at her.

Halla gazed down at the dirt trail as she turned her horse to trot on uphill.

"Is that all?" Bea whipped her horse with the reins and caught up to Halla. "That's nothing! That's all you can make him do?"

"No," Halla said. "I can prevent him from following us if I break his legs. It will only delay him for twenty minutes, though."

I felt pretty frisky about Halla recognizing that she couldn't force me to be her version of good. I smiled about it for a while and even thought about singing some more just to aggravate everybody. But by late in the day, no bandits had run out to rob and kill me, and no mean farmers had, either.

The village I spotted threw long, end-of-day shadows. It smelled like soup cooking, with a hint of dung to fertilize whatever food they grew to put in soup. A few people carried out domestic tasks among the two dozen plastered daub and wattle buildings. Most residents were probably still in the fields planting, which was a shame. I had less than an hour to find two of them who ought to be dead.

I turned off the road and cantered toward the village. Bea and Leddie shouted at me, but I felt sure they'd follow. At the edge of town, I dismounted and shouted, "Does this nasty, rat-dick place have a name?"

A few people, mostly women wearing plain, undyed clothes, ran out to gape at me. Nobody answered.

"Does it have a name? Or do people call it That Place You Throw Turds at as You Ride By?"

Several women, children, and older men appeared but kept far back from me.

That discouraged me. I had hoped to attract a couple of cruel bastards such as you'd find in any human habitation in the world. I handed my sword to Halla so I'd appear less fearsome. "Well?" I shouted.

A black-haired young woman with a strong chin and a straight nose mumbled, "Segg."

"What? Segg?" I bellowed. "What a horrible name. I wouldn't name a dead slug Segg. Who gives the orders in the undoubtedly diseased village of Segg?"

Everybody stared at a clean-shaven old man who was hanging back. He blushed and stared at the ground.

I walked around a little, stomping my feet. "Damn! Is there anybody here who might be able to speak words that sound kind of like orders?"

A few more women and children crept around the corners of the closer buildings. Nobody answered me. The sun was falling like it was a stone I had pitched into a lake.

My insults hadn't called out any of the nasty sorts. I lowered my voice to a more reasonable tone. "Look here, I want to talk to the men of this place, particularly the ones who everybody hates. The ones who steal from their neighbors, or hurt their children, or molest women. You know who I mean. I want to talk to them. Bring them here." I pulled out the gold lump. "Tell them about this gold."

The black-haired young woman crossed her arms as if she was cold. "I'm sorry. Our men are gone to war. We'll try to help—just don't hurt anybody."

I have killed men and women who were wicked but probably didn't deserve death. I must have killed fine people in combat—honest, generous folks who loved their families. I have killed innocents who should not have died, who were certainly better people than me.

I could kill a couple of these poor Segg folk to honor my debt to Harik. It wouldn't have been the worst thing I had done, or even close. I had to kill, and these people had to die sometime. But on that day, I didn't think I could make myself walk up to that young woman and cut her throat. I told myself it was because killing her was exactly the kind of thing Harik hoped I would do. So, I wouldn't do it. It would be like poking him in the eye.

When I reached up to take my sword from Halla, the villagers scurried back, and several ran away. I lifted myself to call on Harik, who didn't dawdle about answering me.

"Just select two and kill them, Murderer," Harik said. "Don't complicate it. Your intellect is too feeble for deliberations."

I imagined drawing my sword. Harik sat halfway up the gazebo, leaning back. He might have been twiddling his thumbs, but he stopped an instant after my sight cleared.

"Mighty Harik, those puny specimens are unworthy of a debt to your noble self. Instead of staining my sword with their pathetic blood, how about I kill four right deadly bastards in your name tomorrow?"

"That was not our bargain."

"Yes, I understand that's true, but I don't want to waste effort killing sad people whose deaths could only offend you."

"Offend me? Pray, did you say, 'Offend me'? As if the virtual athenaeum of abuse and slander you have offered me over the years was not intended to offend? If you have no spine for killing today and wish to kill tomorrow, I shall allow that. You may kill four tomorrow, but I shall select which four people you kill."

"Mighty Harik, you waddling turd, I can't accept that. But I will slay eight people tomorrow, if I choose the people."

"Eight? Inadequate in every respect. Unless we also say that if you fall short, you shall make up the deficit by killing people I select for a week." Harik stood. "Further, let us say that this is my only offer. Take it, or go home and slaughter some squalid peasants right now."

I wavered, changing my mind five times in as many seconds. "I accept, you runny ass-biscuit."

Harik hurled me back into my body.

I staggered, turned away from Segg, and mounted my horse. "Somebody ride in some direction so I can follow you."

Bea glowered at me. "Aren't you going to kill them?"

I didn't look at her. "I cast a spell on the village. As soon as we ride over the hill, everybody will fall down dead and swell up like a sausage."

"You're a monster. Filth and a monster," Bea said.

"He did not do that," Halla said. "There is no spell like that."

"Hell, I wish there were." Leddie smiled. "It's just what I've needed a couple of times in my travels. Now, if we're all done whining about doing right or wrong, Memweck may think I'm dead, and he may think he's lost sight of you, but that won't last forever. We need to move now, move fast, and not stop."

"How far off is he?" I asked.

She stared into my eyes. "Nope, can't tell you. Your only choice is to trust me."

"I don't trust you any farther than I can sling an anvil with my dick."

Leddie laughed until her eyes watered, and she was still chuckling when she took the lead and trotted her horse up the road.

We didn't stop to camp. Even though we slowed once an hour to walk the horses, by sunrise, we had traveled far. The road had continued to run inland and climb. The trees and bushes had grown smaller but still were full and healthy. We could occasionally appreciate the far-off valleys and lowlands to our left.

I began thinking about who to kill. This debt to Harik was insidious in its regularity.

Breakfast went unheeded. We rode past two villages during the morning and approached a third before midday. Halla drew rein. "We will stop here and rest the horses while we eat."

The village was sure to have water for the horses and food for us. I began prowling for nasty people I could kill. The villagers weren't nice or even tolerable company, but none seemed vicious enough to murder.

The horses weren't fully restored by an hour's rest, but they weren't quite as worn down. We rode on, pushing as hard as our mounts could bear. The road had stopped climbing and now wound inland through a mass of gentle, green hills. The three mountains ahead of us had become distinct and jagged. Snow capped all three.

I felt myself yanked out of my body in a sickening swoop, and a moment later, I existed in the near-complete nothingness of the gods' trading arena.

"A city stands ahead of you, Murderer," Harik said.

Since I wasn't asking for a favor, there might never have been a better time to talk about resurrection. "Mighty Harik, I—"

"Find the man who rules this city," Harik interrupted me. "Give him the book."

Harik flung me back into the world of man before I could squeak.

I lifted myself and called for Harik, but he was either ignoring me or had hurried away to some divinely jaded birthday party or naked concert. At least, that's what I imagined.

I drew rein and gathered everybody. "There's a city up ahead there."

Leddie peered at me. "Yes, there is. We're going around it."

"Not me!" I smiled as if I were going to that naked concert. "I'm riding into it, right through the main gate."

"No!" Halla slapped her thigh.

Leddie sat back in her saddle. "You damned moron. It doesn't have a gate, and you'll be captured in a minute. Memweck will have his servants searching for you under every barrel and in every woman's bed. You might as well stab yourself in the throat. Let me do it. At least somebody will have some fun."

"If you're scared, you don't have to go," I said. "I'll meet you back here when I'm finished."

"How many people do you need to kill today?" Halla asked.

I silently damned her ability to figure things out. "Never mind. I won't ask you to help."

I trotted up the road and realized I had forgotten to ask Leddie the city's name. I glanced back and saw that she sat her horse without stirring to follow me. That didn't surprise me, but it startled me to see Whistler and Bea back there.

As Halla pulled even with me, I said, "They're going to get bored as shit out here. Counting knotholes, bad storytelling, bug races. I'll make up some terrifying, fun adventures we can brag about later to make them feel bad."

"Do not go into the city." She didn't sound upset about it, but she wouldn't meet my eyes.

"I'm on an errand for Harik. I don't have a choice."

Halla smiled a little, which surprised me. "You have defied him many times. Tell him to swallow his elbow and flap like a goose. Bypass the city and return when we have dealt with Memweck."

"I will definitely tell him to flap next time I see him. But I've already defied him on this, so I'm shy of doing it again."

"You mean the book?" Halla sat taller.

I tossed my hands up. "Damn it! That's a fine guess."

"How do you know . . ." Halla started, then trailed off. "Will you need the book to resurrect someone? If you give up the book, you may give away your only chance. Do not risk it."

I felt a little ashamed that Halla had thought of that and I hadn't. "Did somebody tell you that? Maybe your mother? Or are you just guessing?"

"I am speculating."

"Ah. Well, I speculate that I'll have hell to pay from Harik if I dawdle over this. Come on if you're coming."

I trotted my horse on toward the city, whatever the hell its name was. I turned around to ask Halla whether she knew, but she had ridden back and was gesturing to the others, urging them to follow me. Leddie laughed, and Bea started arguing.

Halla shouted, "Do you think you can succeed without him?" She dropped her voice, but I could still hear. "That's stupid. You are stupid for thinking that. But you are more stupid if you think you can succeed without him and without me." She wheeled her horse and rode up to join me.

The others followed her in a ragged line. I led our whole stupid procession up the road toward this unnamed city.

TWENTY-EIGHT

In ages past, the people of the western kingdoms gave their countries and towns mundane names, almost literal. Their descendants rarely changed those names, even though the words aged poorly. The city of Bellmeet was where the People of the Bells once gathered. Bellhalt was their landholding that they defended against their cruel neighbors from Grimhalt. The port of Deephold was the deepest harbor in the west. Regensmeet was where the western kings met every five years to marry off their children and write treaties they intended to break.

Not every name showed such a piddling amount of creativity. Nobody knew why my home islands were named Ir. My people enjoyed speculating about it, often punched and kicked each other about it, and regarded the most fanciful theories with favor.

When I was a young sorcerer, always walking the rim of destruction, I traveled outside the western kingdoms for a time. The variety of nonsensical names stunned me. I visited the depraved port towns of Lilligat and Roolipp in the northern kingdoms. The island realm of Hep lay northeast beyond the isthmus of Cliffthrot. I once traveled east with Halla to visit her homeland, Mamalan, which means "Deep Places" in her language.

The Hill People have two names for everything: a work name and a love name. The work name for their empire is Arisapop, which just means the Hill Lands. Its love name is Liss-Queripai-Ma. To my knowledge, they have never translated that name for anybody outside their people.

Frontier folks name their villages Nob, Kek, Sandypool, and so forth. Frontier life breeds unpretentious people.

Harik had commanded me to deliver his book in the city ahead of us. When I finally asked, Leddie informed us it was the city of Caislin. Four hours before sunset, we topped a long hill and rode onto a green flatland so rich it looked like you could eat it. Half a mile away stood a sizable, neat city built of gray stone and reddish wood. No wall protected the place, and it appeared we could ride in from any quarter we wished.

"Stop! Stop, damn your shrunken narbs!" Leddie yelled from behind me. "You can't be this stupid after all you've lived through!"

"Halla?" I said, staring straight ahead.

"He is that stupid. Do not underestimate his stupidity."

"Thank you, darling." I kicked my horse and pushed on toward the city. I heard Leddie following, throwing out a rope of curses.

I soon saw that the velvety, green fields were smeared and peppered with herds of fat, white goats. I hesitated to guess their number, but there must have been thousands. I spotted no farms growing crops. Maybe the goats had overwhelmed them and eaten every shoot of barley and wheat that pushed out of the ground.

I angled to make our entrance at what seemed to be a side street. It wasn't deserted, though. A soldier stood in the middle of the road, and another leaned against a stone wall. Both wore leather armor and carried scabbarded swords. Two helmets lay on a barrel beside them. I saw one of them drink from a skin as I rode closer.

The drinker appeared to be a powerful man in his prime. His long hair was black and his skin pale. The one leaning against the wall was tall, thin, and gray, probably older than me. They watched us, but neither called out as I rode closer.

With no plan in mind, I halted. "Hello, boys. We're strangers here."

"Yep." The older man nodded, still leaning. "I can tell that." He yawned. "I hope that all strangers might eat rocks and shit cactus in hell. Not a personal comment."

The younger man held up the skin. "Have a drink?"

I reached out with my numb left hand, careful not to drop the skin. The numbness had crept past my elbow and was headed toward my shoulder. I grasped the skin, sniffed it, and squirted a polite amount of decent wine into my mouth. I reached out to return it, but he waved me off. "Pass it 'round. Keep it. I got more." He shrugged as if he didn't care what I did.

"Thanks." I handed the skin to Halla. "I'm Desh the goat merchant, here to buy a shipload of goats. Who has goats to sell?"

"Guess that would be the goat farmers," the older man said, standing and stretching his back. "Look around. If you spit hard, you'll hit one. Can't buy any goats, though." He yawned again.

I waited. After ten seconds, the younger man added, "Lord Babardi's got to say if you can."

I smiled. I had seen lazy soldiers before, but these were exceptional examples. "So I'll ask him. Where is he?"

"You won't ask him." The younger one scowled for a moment, and then his face drooped again. "He doesn't see anybody."

"Anymore," the older man said. "Desh, you turn around and head home. That's just advice, nothing more. I won't try to make you or anything."

Halla was watching me. Leddie was staring down, hiding her face from these men. Whistler and Bea sat their horses in the rear.

I said, "Gentlemen, I think I'll try anyway. Where does this lord live?"

"Don't," the young one said. The older one was shaking his head.

"I have no choice. I've got people who'll starve without goats to eat."

The soldiers glanced at each other. Then the older one said, "All right, Desh. I'm Aran. Let me show you something." He turned and ambled up the street. I followed on my horse at a slow walk.

Aran led us down a stone-paved lane, made a jog to the right, and turned onto a wider street. Fifteen minutes and two more turns later, we reached a big square. Aran nodded toward a rough, wooden structure in the middle. It stood ten feet by ten feet and was guarded by at least four dark-haired, well-armed men.

"What in Krak's back teeth is that?" I said.

Aran put his finger to his lips and cupped his ear with the other hand.

I held my breath and listened. Somebody was crying in there. In fact, more than one person was crying.

Aran rubbed his eyes. "Babardi says we must ignore that. He won't even look at it or listen. Sorry, I mean to say His Lordship the Mighty Lord Babardi won't look. I can't be disrespectful." He farted, an echoing, five-second event, and then he walked back down the street toward his post.

"I think fate is commanding us to do something foolish." I dismounted.

"It's not fate!" Leddie snapped as she dismounted too. "You're doing this just because you goddamn want to!"

"Well, come on and make sure I do it right." I didn't even glance at her as I said it. I didn't mind helping some people who were weeping, but I mostly wanted to kill the bastards guarding them.

Leddie paused, hissing. "I'll stay in the back."

Whistler stamped his foot. "Oh, shut up! Stop complaining. You caused your own damn problems, so stop whimpering about it."

Leddie reached for her sword, and Whistler jumped back.

"Stop!" I shouted. One of the men guarding the structure turned toward us. "Shit!"

Halla had stepped between Whistler and Leddie. "I do not care if you kill each other, but go somewhere else to do it."

"Harik's flopping tits! You're worse than my sisters fighting over a new shawl!" I strode out into the square, not much caring who was following. The guards saw me coming and swung around to face me. I saw six of them now.

"Stop there!" said a heavily scarred man.

"Yes, sir, I'm stopping," I said without slowing down. "I'm bringing supplies. You can inspect them."

"No, stop there!" The man raised his sword, and his friends did too.

I held up my empty hands and kept walking. "Yes, I am stopping. You can't inspect the supplies from that far off, though. Here, let me show you." By then, I was thirty feet away from him.

"Don't take another step!" The man shouted, but he didn't close with me. He was waiting until I was near enough to kill with no strain, which was perfect.

A pale fellow to the man's right pointed with his sword. "Hey! That's Leddie!"

All the men gaped at Leddie.

"Damn it to Krak's dick!" Leddie shouted. She drew her sword and charged the man who'd spoken. At the same time, I drew my sword, bounded forward, and slashed the scarred man's throat while he was still squinting at Leddie.

The scarred man fell right away, but the fellow next to him was a skilled fighter. He almost cut me on the first pass. I riposted, he blocked, and I disengaged. I hoped he would think I was overmatched and in retreat. He fulfilled that hope by rushing me hard. I drew him off balance and stabbed him in the chest.

Whistler was overpowering a swordsman with a furious string of cuts. I knocked Whistler aside and killed that man two seconds later. He died looking confused.

Then the fighting was done. To my left, Leddie had disabled a man, and to my right, Halla had killed the last two with brutal, bloody cuts from her spear. Whistler ran to the structure and started unlatching the door. Leddie killed the disabled man before I could reach him.

"Those will be Memweck's warriors in there," Leddie said.

"What does that mean?" Bea scowled.

"Memweck is training his soldiers and shield men. He likes to start them young."

I peered in as Bea pushed past me. Nine children sat on the

ground inside, most of them wailing. None seemed to be over ten years old. "Leddie, how many of these warriors has he stolen?"

"About two hundred, I guess."

Whistler swore an oath so repugnant that when my father heard me say it, he punched me in the eye.

Halla murmured something and shook her head.

From inside the cage, Bea said, "I'll kill him. I'll kill him."

Leddie shrugged. "The last I knew, about a hundred and fifty were still alive. That training's worse than disembowelment from what I hear."

Bea charged out of the cage toward Leddie, screaming, "Is he alive?" She grabbed at Leddie, who sidestepped and threw her to the ground.

Leddie held one arm up and shook it. "Gah! I think you got snot from one of those little rodents on my wrist. All the infants were alive last time I was there. You can't exactly make babies have a knife fight, can you? Think about it!"

"Watch out!" Whistler shouted.

That was as non-specific as warnings get, but it might have saved my life. I leaped toward the cage. I figured if somebody thought the kids were valuable, then they wouldn't drop a boulder on top of them or shoot a volley of arrows at them.

A phenomenal boom shook the wooden cage behind me as I came to my feet. Whistler had thrown himself backward and was sitting on the ground against the cage wall, his head down.

Ten armed men stood across the square, about sixty feet away. A wide trench had opened in front of the cage, just a few feet away from me. A sheet of flame erupted out of it and then disappeared. Whistler flinched away. Halla had been teetering on the edge, and the fire set her left leg and arm ablaze.

Leddie stood on the other side of the trench from me, using one hand to pull Bea away from the trench by her hair. Then Leddie dropped Bea and charged the ten men straightaway.

I expected Halla to fall down and roll, but she didn't do that at all. Instead, she ran four steps toward our attackers and hurled her spear. Once it left her hand, she threw herself onto the paving stones, rolling to put out the flames.

At least two sorcerers were attempting to kill us, but they had begun shabbily, so none of us was dead yet. One of them was a Breaker, who could make things not exist. He had made the trench. The other was a Burner, who could set nonliving things afire. He had set the air in the trench alight in a brief but furiously hot blaze. He probably would have enjoyed burning all our clothes and weapons, but the chance of accidentally burning the children was high.

As I sprinted around the trench, Halla's spear bore down on one of the men. She had aimed for the Burner, who was our most dangerous enemy. The two sorcerers reacted, but I suppose they were young for sorcerers. Their inexperience hindered them. The Breaker should have disintegrated the spear, but instead he created a pit in front of Leddie, who was charging and howling like a mad wolf. Leddie darted around it, proving that she was more agile than me.

The Burner had not yet learned one of the fundamental rules of sorcery: Do not set something afire when it is flying toward you. He tried to destroy the spear in the air, failed, and was spectacularly impaled by a flaming spear.

Leddie had raced almost to the line of men, and I was rushing not far behind her. She ran straight toward the Breaker, ducked one man's sword, and shoved another man aside. She threw a cut at the Breaker, who disintegrated her sword mid-swing.

Leddie spun and nearly fell. She caught herself and hurtled straight through the remaining men and on past, away from their swords.

When I reached the line, four of the men were either chasing Leddie or watching her run. The others had formed a half-assed defense around the Breaker. I darted in and killed one, retreated, and sidestepped to another angle of attack. They must have expected an easy victory and now were shocked at their setback. They outnumbered me five to one but hesitated to rush me.

The Breaker slipped on some bloody cobblestones, squawked,

and almost fell. Two swordsmen glanced toward his squeal. Five seconds later, I had wounded them both, one fatally.

"Filth-licking bastard!" the Breaker yelled. He threw a knife and nearly hit me in the throat. I leaned at the last moment, and the knife scraped the side of my neck.

I fenced the two men in front of me for several seconds before realizing that Leddie had rejoined the fight carrying somebody's sword. I bashed a man with my shoulder, and he cursed. From the corner of my eye, I saw Leddie spin and stab a man, who collapsed.

The man I had bashed stumbled and fell. His friend held his sword with a lazy grip, and I pointed that out by mangling his wrist. He staggered aside, crying, and I turned to the Breaker. The man backed away, gave a grim smile, and stared at my sword. I'm sure he was trying to disintegrate it. Being a divinely forged weapon, it was not destroyed. The Breaker's eyes and mouth popped open, and a moment later, I thrust my blade into his throat.

I turned to deal with the man who had stumbled, but I found Whistler knocking him unconscious using his sword's hilt. Whistler appeared to be a bit singed but not seriously burned. I spun back around to see the last two of our enemies go down, one killed by Leddie, and the other disabled by Halla using a sword she must have picked up during the fight. Halla scanned the square and then limped toward me. Her face didn't show pain, but I could smell her burned flesh.

The man whose wrist I had wrecked was trotting away. I caught him in two seconds and stabbed him in the heart from behind. Then I ran back to the man Whistler had whacked on the head, and I killed him as he lay there. Whistler stared at me like I had dirtied his clean kitchen.

At least I had killed enough men to pay today's debt to Harik.

I ran back to the trench and found Bea sitting beside it, shaking her head, just as charred as Whistler but not badly burned. I ducked into the cage, and a few of the whimpering children screamed when they saw me. The sharp smell of pee told me they were about as terrified as they could stand.

I stepped back out of the cage. "Bea, you look less like a horrible murderer than the rest of us. Try to calm those kids down." She nodded and scrambled into the cage.

Out in the square, Leddie, Halla, and Whistler made a slow retreat toward the trench, watching the streets and buildings around us.

"Halla, come here!" I called.

She shook her head. "The fight may not be done."

"Damn right. If we're attacked again, I want you healthy and as ferocious as Lutigan's shaft, not hobbling around like Lutigan's sense of humor."

"Here come their friends!" Whistler shouted.

I glanced over and saw a few people edging into the square. Several more walked in from another direction, and within seconds, over a dozen stood around the edge of the square staring at us.

"They're nothing but city rats!" Leddie shouted back to us. "We don't have to worry about them, unless their hearts burst from terror and they fall on us all at once. I bet they don't even thank us." She spun toward me with her mouth open. "Fingit's weaselly face! You haven't thanked me for saving your shitty little life! Bib, have you fallen out of love with me?"

I almost laughed but turned to Halla instead. "Sit down, darling. I don't care to reach up over my head to work on your arm."

"That is foolish. You are not that tiny and frail." She sat on the ground anyway.

For the next five minutes, I healed the burns on her arm and leg. Pain grew in my leg as I worked, but thanks to Memweck's curse, I felt nothing but numbness in my arm.

When we finished the healing, I gazed around. More than a hundred city dwellers had entered in the square, many of them gathered around the cage and the trench. Aran and two other soldiers were shouting at Leddie, their weapons drawn. Whistler stood in front of Leddie, shouting back at the citizens. Several folks had brought the children out of the cage. I saw some families weeping and laughing at the same time.

A squat soldier strolled into the square, surveyed the situation, and nodded at Halla before approaching us. A purple scar ran along the side of his face, slanted down his neck, and disappeared under the collar of his shirt. He carried his helmet in the crook of his left arm.

The man stopped twenty feet away, and his face unfolded in a brilliant smile. "Thanks, and more than thanks for all this, friends. My name's Tapp, and I wish to high, holy horse knobs I could have done it myself. Thank you, and everybody in Caislin thanks you even more than me. Especially those kids." He nodded at Halla, Whistler, Bea, and me. Then he stared at Leddie, and his smile wilted. "Not her. She can die of a disease that makes her guts squirm like snakes."

"I hate her too," I said. "We're just using her, and then we'll throw her off a cliff. Don't tell." I made no effort to lower my voice as I said it.

"Huh. You help us, which we do like, but you travel with our enemy, which makes you evil or stupid."

Halla sniffed. "Bib, are you done here? Can we leave?"

"Hell no, I'm not done! Tapp, I need to talk to Lord Babardi. I have a gift for him. Or if you can't swing that, tell your superior officer."

Tapp shifted his helmet to the other arm. "I wouldn't say I'm the most superior soldier in His Lordship's army. In some ways, I'm average, really average, or maybe not that good. But Lord Babardi put me in charge, so I have to do what he says, and not what anybody else says." Tapp gazed away as he explained that but then smiled at us again.

"Does that mean you're the general or whatever?" Whistler said. "Where are your men?"

"To be honest, really honest with you folks, you've been out here killing sorcerers and throwing spears that burn and who knows what else." Tapp stopped smiling. "Maybe you'd like to kill a few dozen soldiers next—not that I'm accusing you, but it had to cross my mind. If you just have to kill some soldiers today, maybe you could kill me and leave my men alone."

Halla said, "We killed all of Leddie's soldiers. We are satisfied with killing soldiers for now." She jerked her thumb at me. "My idiot friend wants to meet your lord. Then we will ride away."

Tapp said, "I'm sad—and you can ask my wife, I don't get sad so easily, so this is unusual for me—very sad to say that Lord Babardi hesitates . . . well, *hesitates* isn't the right word . . . as he *contemplates* our welfare—that's 'our' as in 'his people,' not as in 'you and me'—he judges that a further show of goodwill is required before granting an audience since you travel with that poison-spewing whore who has caused us so much pain."

Whistler said, "Screw this. Beg pardon. What's so important about meeting this turtle-face bastard in person? Does he puke up gold coins or something?"

"I don't know why we're still here!" Bea stepped up and punched me on the arm, the one that wasn't numb. "You saw those children. We should leave this minute!"

I held up my hand. "Tapp, what show of goodwill are you talking about?"

The solider stepped closer for easier conversation. "Things have been poor in the city for months now. That's when these child-stealers showed up, may they stab their own mothers in the tits. His Lordship, who is the wisest man in the city, and probably in all of the northern kingdoms, and undoubtedly the handsomest too, has determined that these bad things are happening because the hereditary city signet ring has been lost. He requests that you find it for him so that . . ." He reached into a pouch, fetched a slip of vellum, and read aloud. "'So that beautiful peace and great, astounding happiness may be restored to the city and all the lands around it.'"

Without a pause, Bea asked, "Where did you last see this ring?"

"Ah, I haven't ever personally seen it. I'm pretty sure His Lordship hasn't, either," Tapp said.

"How do you even know the damn thing exists?" I crossed my arms. "Maybe it's a fairy story!"

"Oh, I have a drawing of it!" Tapp pulled a piece of parchment from his pouch. It had been folded several times and was heavily creased. He handed it to Halla.

The ring appeared to be unexceptional, although the huge "C" on it was ornate. The edge of the parchment was stained.

Halla waved the parchment. "Blood?"

Tapp raised his eyebrows and nodded. "Don't worry, though! We have an excellent idea of where to start looking, and it's right here in the city. In a cellar on His Lordship's grounds."

"That shouldn't be hard to search. What kind of cellar?" I said.

"Big. Quite sizable, really."

We stared at Tapp.

"More than a cellar, if you want to split hairs. Maybe a basement."

"Or a cavern?" Halla asked.

Tapp lowered his eyebrows and shook his head.

"A vault?" Halla said. If possible, her voice had gotten flatter.

Tapp rubbed his nose. "From a certain point of view, an open-minded person might say that."

I slapped my leg. "Is it a damn dungeon?"

"Definitely not!" Tapp said. "No prisoners have ever been held there. It's more of a, oh, I'd say more of a crypt. Ancestors and that sort of thing."

I took a step toward the soldier and growled, "Haunted?"

Tapp grimaced and shrugged.

Halla said, "Has anyone else searched for the ring?"

"Oh, a few people. Nobody important."

"Can we talk to them?" I asked.

"Not so much." Tapp smiled. "But this place is full of valuable things, according to lore and documentation. Really, and you can keep anything you find apart from the ring."

"We have no interest in this," Halla said.

"Wait! Just wait!" Tapp was digging in his pouch again, and he came out with a cracking sheet of parchment that he unfolded. "Just listen! 'Gold and silver pots, platters, symbols, and jewelry buried with thirty-three dead ancestors. At least six nice swords, a few rare books, a golden swan with emerald eyes—or maybe that's golden spawn with emerald eyes, it's hard to read. And listen to this list of possibly enchanted objects! The Tongue of Saint Vigitiss, the Iron-bent Bow, the Infinite Regression Ruby, the Bloom of Unheeding Prowess, and Cofter's Fine Trousers.' How about that, eh?" Tapp held the parchment poised as if waving it would make us say yes.

I noticed Tapp's pudgy enthusiasm without really paying attention. I heard Whistler, Bea, and Leddie arguing about something. None of that meant anything. Halla and I stared at each other, not talking but relying on years of friendship to know what the other was thinking.

Halla turned to Tapp. "We will go."

TWENTY-NINE

The sun had set by the time our conversation with Tapp ended. He called for a lantern and led us to his house, which lay three shadowy streets away.

"Goat fat makes for a horrid, nauseating candle," he said. "Tallow from other places costs dear—you might as well set your own finger afire—and oil's worth more than molten silver. Not many people choose to light the outside of their houses, under those circumstances."

The captain had demanded we sup with his family and then stay the night with them. We could then search for the ring with proper vigor tomorrow. I didn't argue. Everybody appeared tired, and they were all younger than me.

We arrived at a long building and walked to one of many doors leading onto the street. Tapp turned and pointed past Leddie. "You can sleep in that barn across the way, although I won't be sad if you fling yourself down a well, you grinding whore. Go eat a rat."

Leddie laughed and swaggered away as if a palace had been aired out and waxed for her.

Tapp and his children called his wife Mama, and she told us to do the same. She was short, energetic, and pretty, with a crooked smile. At least five children ran through the house, wrestled, asked us questions, sang loudly, sat and ate occasionally, and showed us a kitten. We monopolized four of their seven stools, but the kids didn't hesitate to sit in somebody's lap to eat, and our laps weren't off-limits.

I found it pleasant to visit with happy people. The children weren't strictly well-washed, and they fought quite a bit until their ma would grab one by the ear. They reminded me of my childhood. Halfway through supper, I realized that Bea was watching the children and weeping like the world was done. Mama gathered her up and took her outside.

Tapp passed a pitcher of beer to Halla. "I don't want to discourage you in any way at all from setting off to find this ring, but I am curious. You seemed to be damning the idea, and then quick as spit, you grabbed onto it. I'd appreciate understanding why."

I swallowed a mouthful of boiled goat. "You described those golden bowls and whatnot so beautifully that we have to go see them ourselves."

"Sure." Tapp nodded. "I thought you might have interest in magic too, considering the way you killed those sorcerers all to hell. Although I doubt that you're pining for Cofter's Fine Trousers."

"The Bloom of Unheeding Prowess," Halla said.

I threw a chunk of bread at her.

"I won't say anything." Tapp shrugged. "I don't know what I'd say. I don't know what the heck this Bloom thing is, anyway."

"We do not, either." Halla filled her mug again.

I paused to think and then smacked Tapp on the arm. "Since you're a wonderful host and have a beautiful family, we will confide in you, Captain. Nobody knows what the Bloom of Unheeding Prowess is. Few people even know that such a peculiar thing exists."

Halla said, "It is probably a weapon. The evidence is not good, but it exists."

"Although it might be a crown or a hat," I added.

"It could be a shoe," Halla said. "Some people have thought that. It would surprise me, though."

"No living person can tell us, but it's said to be potent as far as magical doodads go," I said. "Such a thing will be helpful to us soon, or so I predict."

Halla grunted. "Bib cannot predict the future. But he is right about this."

"I hope you find this Bloom thing then." Tapp belched and rapped the table. "It sounds to be a fair shot more interesting than training recruits and disciplining drunk soldiers. I can't go into the crypt with you, though. It would be irresponsible. And Mama might stab me in my sleep for taking risks."

We all slept on the children's three big pallets, and the children draped themselves on us to sleep. I have passed more restful evenings.

Before dawn, Tapp led us back to the square, up a shallow hill, and around behind a three-story stone house. Chilly mist sucked in around us. Bea had remained with Mama, so Halla, Leddie, and Whistler tramped along behind me. Leddie and I carried lanterns, and I had paid Tapp lavishly for the oil we'd burn.

Two dozen white stone monuments of varying sizes stood behind the house, and a slab of pink granite, bigger than a wagon bed, lay flat on the grass near the center. A tall but puny mahogany tree stood thirty feet away. Two iron doors had been set into the granite, each with an iron handle. Somebody had wound a thick chain through the handles to fasten the doors together. Three iron locks held the chain in place.

I nodded toward the doors. "Open them up."

Tapp raised his eyebrows but pulled a big key off his belt. Two minutes later, Halla and I hauled both doors open. They moved with a greasy whisper, as if the hinges had just been oiled.

Halla peered in. "Do you know if there are traps?"

Tapp said, "Well, when people go in . . . I'll just say that from all the screaming, I would assume you'll find some traps."

I joined Halla and peeked too. Stone steps plunged into the ground, disappearing into darkness. "Whistler, go with Halla."

Whistler took a breath and drew his sword. Halla grabbed his sword arm and pulled him away with her as she walked back toward the street.

Tapp squinted at me but didn't ask a question.

Leddie blew a kiss at Tapp. "You're so ugly you're fetching. Would you consider having an affair with me? I bet we have ten minutes."

Tapp grimaced and spit on one of Leddie's boots. She laughed, leaned against a stone statue of a sleeping lion, and closed her eyes.

We did not converse again until Halla and Whistler returned half an hour later, each of them toting two buckets filled with bent horseshoes, rusty brackets, nails, broken knife blades, and various pieces of scrap iron.

"Back away, friends." I handed Halla my lantern and hoisted a bucket. I heaved the iron pieces down the steps, and then I ran. A rolling hell of clanking echoed up through the doors, followed by ten seconds of distinct clicks, swishes, and scraping stones. The opening went silent. I walked back to the doors and listened. "To hell with disarming traps by hand."

I tossed another bucketful through the doors just to be scrupulous. Soon, the clashing and jangling died away. Halla nodded at me, so I eased down onto the first step with my sword drawn. I stopped and spoke over my shoulder. "Tapp, will you guard the top so that somebody doesn't come along and lock us in here forever?"

"Well, that means I have to miss inspecting eighty lockers and beds, but for you, I'll make the sacrifice."

The steps dropped down through a shaft wide enough for one person. It was hardly tall enough for my head to clear. I smelled dry earth, mold, and faint rotting, which I did not welcome. Twenty-four steps took me to the bottom, and I didn't welcome that, either. It's an especially ill-omened number. An open doorway stood in the wall opposite the stairs.

"Leddie, guard that door," I said.

I hadn't expected the chamber at the bottom to be quite so large, about eight paces square, with a stone floor, brick walls, and a vaulted brick ceiling. Dust hung thick in the air, doubtlessly raised by all the iron scraps I had tossed in. The iron lay scattered everyplace, along with a dozen crossbow bolts, two deep pits, and a long, thin blade sticking out of a wall at waist height. Four skeletons in dusty clothes lay about, and two mostly dried-up corpses slumped in a corner, one of them cut in two.

We examined the room and its contents, but we kept quiet. Nothing seemed to merit comments.

I peeked around the edge of the open door while Halla held out her lantern. The next room was similar to the first but about half as big. Most of the bricks had fallen off the walls and ceiling, and they lay in piles. The soil behind the walls had crumbled, leaving several long heaps of brown dirt that came to my waist. I examined the dirt ceiling from a distance, and it appeared to be intact.

"Whistler, bring up that bucket," I said.

Halla, who was a considerably more powerful individual than me, selected a horseshoe. Standing outside the room, she hurled it at the ceiling. A bit of dirt fell off, but nothing more. She flung ten more iron pieces at different parts of the ceiling, to no effect.

I could see a wooden door in the middle of the far wall, partly blocked by fallen bricks. Easing into the room, I crept across it toward the door, and the others followed. When I had walked most of the way there, something heavy smashed my shoulders and head, driving me to my knees and then flat onto the ground. I tried to yell at the others to go back, but I couldn't get any air. I realized that enough dirt to cover me up had dropped onto me, and it sounded like the dirt was still falling up above.

If the women I have lived with taught me anything, it's that I possess flaws in abundance. If I were a squash patch, I'd have a lot of bug-filled squash, maybe more than the squash that you might ever want to eat. One of my most inconvenient flaws is a mindless fear of getting trapped underground and eaten by something nasty. That flaw nearly killed all of us there in Caislin.

I thrashed, cried, and tried to shout for a hundred years or so, and I at last forced myself to lay still. I wiggled three fingers side to side, pulled a white band, and sent it whirring out into the world. Within seconds, it showed me a few hundred tons of dirt that hadn't fallen on me yet, thousands of earthworms, snakes, beetles, and other bugs, ten terrified groundhogs, and a great cluster of roots from the mahogany tree, some of which stretched lower than the chamber.

I can make a tree grow fast. By that I mean I can make it grow a season's worth in a couple of days. I wish I could make a tree root grow fifty feet in ten seconds. That would be handy at times, but the magic doesn't work that way.

However, I can make a tree root move fast enough to shock most people. It doesn't have to grow longer. It just has to stretch on one side while it squeezes down on the other. Once a Caller gets the knack of making a root or limb corkscrew, some nice feats become possible.

I pulled four bands and sent them to the closest four roots. I admit to getting frustrated with how slowly they moved at first, but it took time for them to loosen the earth that was in their way. Less than three minutes after the ceiling fell, a root started thrusting through the dirt above me, spreading and shifting it. Soon, all four roots were working around me, and dirt began sloughing away. Once I could breathe again, I sent the roots off to unearth the others.

Still trapped, I pulled a green band and ran it across everybody. Halla was dazed, Whistler was unconscious, and Leddie wasn't breathing. I examined Leddie and found she wasn't hurt too much yet, so I got her breathing again. Since I couldn't touch her, it cost more power than I liked, but she would have died if I'd waited.

The roots dug us all out, and we assessed our sad situation. First, it was dark as hell. Both lanterns had gone out. We searched by feel and found one, and it seemed serviceable. After a bit more searching, I concluded that the other lantern lay buried someplace that we'd never find.

Halla took ten minutes to relight the lantern in the dark with flint and tinder. I could have worked on it an hour and probably accomplished nothing.

Whistler nodded at the wooden door. "I wonder what's waiting behind that."

"Sweet girls and sour beer," I said. "And neither will wait around for a hesitant man. Help me with these bricks."

Leddie laughed and pinched Whistler on the butt.

The four of us cleared the bricks out of the way, plus a few hundred pounds of dirt. Then I stood to the side of the closed door and held my hand close to the latch. I didn't expect to feel a damn thing, but it seemed like something a clever person would do.

"Wait," Whistler said. "Why is Bib going first every time?"

"Would you like to go first?" Halla said.

Whistler took a step back and bumped into Leddie. "No, I wouldn't. I just don't understand. Is he especially skilled at this kind of thing?"

Halla pursed her lips. "No. I am more skilled than him at many things. Maybe most things."

"I love you too." I patted her arm.

"He takes these risks because he is lucky. Bib is the luckiest person I know."

Whistler nodded slowly. "I guess that's good."

Halla went on, "He is so lucky, he must have worked very hard to ruin his life the way he has."

Leddie growled, "Can we go through the damn door now? Do you think you talked loud enough for the ghouls to know we're here? They probably don't give a shit about your personal trials—they just want to know if our marrow tastes good!"

I swung the door open and peered around the edge as Halla held out the lantern. It was another square room, halfway between the first two in size. The walls and ceiling hadn't fallen all to hell, at least not yet. An open doorway stood in the middle of the far wall. Stone shelves were set into the right-hand and left-hand walls, and the objects lying on those shelves glinted gold. I stepped into the room, and Halla followed. Her lantern showed that the shelves were crowded with bowls, urns, candlesticks, plates, boxes, and a big set of scales. All of them appeared to be gold or silver.

A powerful, energetic voice yelled from deeper in the crypt, "If I still had bricks on the ceiling, you'd all be pulverized, damn you, mashed right flat into the ground, chunks of brains flying around like sparrows!"

I walked two more steps into the chamber. "I can't say we're sorry, but I can wish you better fortune with your next visitors."

A figure entered through the door on the far wall, more gliding than walking. I could see through the thing and make out the doorway behind it with no trouble. It appeared to be a bearded, round-headed man, although the face lay in shadow. Its clothing looked expensive but archaic, and it wore a peaked hat with four red feathers so stylish it was almost foppish. I made note of these things, because who the hell knew what detail might mean my survival, but I focused mainly on the extra-long broadsword in its hand. It was a weapon well-suited to battering an armored man to death, but if necessary, it could disembowel me just fine.

"Everyone gets yanked into shreds now!" the figure proclaimed. "Who wants to go first?" It pointed at Leddie. "What about it, you grabby, dripping, jumped-up tart?"

Leddie's eyes glinted huge in the lantern light, but her voice was steady. "Let me go last. I want to write a ballad celebrating our heroic deaths. I especially expect Bib there to make some interesting noises when you rip him asunder." Leddie edged closer to the being, her sword held low.

I held up my free hand. "I apologize, good ghost, for interrupting your rest."

"Ghost?" the thing boomed. "Don't call me a frippy, whining, no-balls, insubstantial ghostly entity, you toad fart!"

"I apologize twice, then." I wondered what in the name of Weldt's shaggy chest this thing was, if not a ghost.

Halla stepped up beside me. "What kind of thing are you, then?"

"Please!" I smiled. "She meant to say *please*."

"I wasn't made into a damned unliving thing! No god or sorcerer has rubbed his loathsome fingers all over my spirit." The figure surged forward and grabbed Halla's throat. I heard her choking, but she stood unmoving as a boulder. "I made myself! I said no, I am not done." It pushed Halla away and turned toward me. I heard Halla coughing.

"The God of Death must like you a lot," I said. "I know for a fact that he doesn't let many people engage in such pranks."

The creature floated back from us a few feet. "Don't try to impress me, you floppy little daffodil of a sorcerer. I don't care if you pounded all thirteen gods to death with just your member—it means nothing to me!"

I didn't feel too cozy about us killing this thing, or if it was already dead, then subduing it. I didn't want to give up on diplomacy. "Sir, I understand that you're not dazzled by me, and that's quite proper. My name is Bib, and we've come on behalf of the city's lord. We're not common looters here to carry off the best bits and smash everything else."

"Babardi!" The creature might have been saying, "Diarrhea," because he said it with so much revulsion. "Worthless, mindless, feckless, dick-less, limp-tongued slice of clotted snot! I hoped he would come here himself, but he's too busy being a pale, wheezing coward."

Leddie spoke up: "We don't give a good crap who runs the city. Is there somebody you like better? We'll slit Babardi's throat and toss the new man or woman on the throne. Or behind the desk, or whatever you people have here."

The being whispered, "That is enough. You are rude and you bore me."

Halla tossed a pebble at the figure. Instead of passing through, it bounced off the thing's chest.

The being pointed at Leddie. In a conversational way, it said, "Think of what was done to you."

Leddie gave a short scream and fell to one knee, dropping her weapon and hiding her head under her arms.

It pointed at Whistler. "Think of what you did."

Whistler closed his eyes and began shaking.

It pointed at Halla. "Think of what you're keeping."

She staggered back two steps and stared at me.

The thing pointed at me. "Think of what you're giving away."

I saw myself handing Harik's book to somebody and losing my little girl forever. The image was like a battering ram. I may have staggered, or wheezed, or played the nose-whistle for all I know, but I think I was dazed for no more than a moment. Losing Manon forever was not a new thought for me.

The figure stood less than two steps in front of me. "That should do it! Now—"

The lantern snuffed out, leaving us in darkness that was just about as pure as could exist.

Without thinking, I aimed a thrust straight in front of me. I hit something. My long experience living in darkness may have helped. I followed up with three ferocious cuts. My first and third connected. Something big fell on the floor near me, and I dropped onto it with my knees. It was a writhing body that made a crackling noise. I held it down.

"Is everybody standing?" I shouted.

Halla, Leddie, and Whistler all agreed that they were. I pulled my knife and stabbed whoever I was kneeling on. I stabbed again to be sure. I stabbed it eleven more times to be really sure, and because both eleven and thirteen are strong numbers. Then I felt safe to conclude that I was kneeling on an unmoving body that might not start moving again.

I remained on my knees with my knife point pressed against the body while Halla took forty damn minutes to light the lantern. Had it been somebody else, I'd have thought they were flustered.

The lantern light showed I was kneeling on what remained of the insulting, unliving entity, although it wasn't transparent anymore. It was so emaciated that all the water might have been drained out of it, and it crackled like dry leaves when I stood up. The entire face was sunken, as if it had been smashed with a face-size stone.

I pulled the city ring off its left hand, shoved the feathered hat inside my jerkin, and handed the broadsword to Leddie, who looked at it like a lover. "I found the ring."

Halla and Whistler were already peering into the next chamber. Halla said, "Is it the right ring?"

I opened my mouth and then closed it.

Halla reached for the lantern and led Whistler into the next room. I knelt over the body just in case.

Several minutes later, Halla stepped back into the room. "Thirty-three ancestors. The ring is not there."

I held up my hand. "This must be it then. I found it on the unliving guardian, or whatever the hell you want to call it."

"Let us forget that creature instead of naming it," she said. "We found a medallion, two swords, a big hammer, and a pair of boots that look new. No bow, and all the trousers are rotten."

Whistler had followed her in, and he grinned with his arms full of weapons. "We'll be rich!"

"Son, you're already rich," I said.

"I'm not the richest yet!"

I sighed, hoping I wouldn't have to kill Whistler when he went crazy with greed. "Let's leave. If there's anything else down here, I don't want to look at it."

"What about all the gold?" Whistler almost whined it.

Halla asked, "Are you a dead ancestor?"

Whistler shook his head.

"Then it doesn't belong to you, does it?"

THIRTY

I turned the left boot over in my hands so that the morning light shone inside it, and I nodded as if that would help me understand a single thing about it. I had already examined the right boot and learned not a damn thing from it, either. Holding the boot out to Tapp, I said, "Would you care for a look?"

He shook his head and waved me off, then he glanced at the iron doors leading back into the crypt. "There's something I need. I'll hop right back over here in a couple of minutes. Don't stir." Tapp hustled off around the corner of the stone house toward the street.

Halla said, "If Pil were here, she could tell us about all these things. Bib, what did you do to make her leave?"

"Nothing. It was time. She was like a baby bird leaving the nest." I tossed the feathered hat to Leddie. "Put that on."

Leddie held the hat far away from her body and frowned at it.

"Give it to me," Whistler snapped. He grabbed the hat, dropped his own hat on the grass, and eased the feathered hat onto his head. Then he pulled it down to a stylish angle and used one finger to primp the feathers.

"Do you feel smarter?" I asked. "What's thirty-one plus two hundred and twelve divided by nine?"

Whistler's eyes got big. "I couldn't say."

Halla said, "If you had to kill all of us in thirty seconds, what would your plan be?"

"I'd hire a hundred crossbowmen."

I smiled. "I admit it would be effective, but we're looking for something a little more creative. Take off the hat, unless you want every little old lady in town to fall in love with you."

Whistler put his own hat back on.

Halla put on the medallion, but she couldn't read my mind, and when I slapped her, it still hurt. She tried to fly to the top of the house, but she only made it three feet off the ground.

I couldn't run faster or jump higher when I put on the boots, but they fit well, so I kept them.

Tapp returned carrying a butchered goat carcass over his shoulder. "For testing the swords."

"Me first!" Leddie yelled. She swung her new extra-long broadsword at the dead goat four times, but the weapon never produced more carnage than one would expect. She flung the sword down and damned the private parts of Effla and Weldt. "Give me another one!"

I handed her one of the other two swords. It performed no better than the broadsword. She grabbed the last sword and whirled a prodigious cut, struck a bone, and broke the blade. Leddie ran to the hammer, a rusty, unwieldy thing with a broad head and a four-foot long handle. She lifted it with both hands, tried to find the balance, and finally threw it toward the house where it rolled across the grass.

Leddie sat straight down on the ground and pouted.

I nodded at the hammer. "You try it, Halla. I'd rupture myself."

Halla lifted the hammer, tried three different grips, and swung at the air twice.

"Don't be shy!" I said. "Smash that goat to bits, and Mama will boil it tonight."

"I will not hold back." Halla aimed at the goat carcass but then spun the other direction, bringing an overhand blow down on the life-size stone lion monument. The front half of the lion was pulverized. Each of us bled from stone chips and flakes hurled into our faces.

"That's probably the Bloom thing, huh?" Tapp smirked, wiping his face with a faded blue handkerchief.

"Unless I can walk over and kick down that house with these boots, I'd say yes. Halla, that monstrosity may not prove decisive, but it's a damn good thing to have with us, don't you think?"

Halla was rubbing at the rusty head of the hammer with her thumb, and she didn't answer me.

"This isn't fair at all!" Leddie smacked the ground with her fist before she stood. "You must promise me that I will get Memweck's sword. Me! Promise!"

"Sure, I promise." I nodded.

Leddie threw up her hands and walked away from me. "You're such a liar! I hate you!" She pointed around. "Everybody! All of you swear that you'll make Bib give me Memweck's sword. Swear, or we're going to stay here and eat goat until we die!"

Whistler and Halla promised.

Tapp cleared his throat and held up the city ring we had recovered. "Thanks for this, and I really do mean thanks. Thanks from Lord Babardi too. I'm sure he'll want to show his gratitude in person after all this. Follow me. I'll report and then introduce you."

The guardian's nasty opinion of Babardi had been stomping through my head. Maybe it was nothing but bile. But when a murderous, otherworldly creature hates somebody that much, it shouldn't be ignored. Also, I had long experience with how grateful people were once sorcerers had saved them. It ranged from a little bit grateful all the way to embarrassed loathing.

I slapped the captain on the shoulder. "You go ahead, and we'll catch up. I know Bea wouldn't want to miss meeting Lord Babardi."

"That's fine and good." Tapp walked off toward the street, waving over his shoulder.

I sent Whistler to fetch Bea. The rest of us walked to the spacious, blue-painted upper-city stable where we'd left our horses.

Halla and I agreed that although Babardi might put on a feast for us, it seemed unlikely. He might even find a reason to dislike us. Kings and lords got embarrassed and did that sometimes. We decided not to laze about once he finished lauding us.

We saddled our horses and rode back to Babardi's home, the three-story stone house beside the crypt. I gave a boy two copper bits to hold our horses and promised him two more when we claimed the beasts. I also told him what a pleasure it was to find an honest man such as himself, since I had hated to kill those last two boys who tried to run off with my horses.

Tapp waved at us from the top of the broad stone steps. "His Lordship is waiting for you. Expecting you. He couldn't be more excited if you were arriving in a golden coach and bringing him a diamond chamber pot." Tapp didn't sound excited about it, though.

We followed Tapp inside through an open double doorway set with thick, scarred wooden doors. Half a dozen soldiers saluted when we walked into the clean, chilly stone entryway. Two marble busts had been set into alcoves. Maybe those were some of Babardi's forebears, or his patron gods, or the drunks who owed him money.

"Follow that servant girl," Tapp said, walking beside me. The young girl smiled and waved us along as she skipped ahead, her pale, yellow skirt swirling.

The thick-timbered doors thumped shut behind us, dimming the hallway just as I entered it. I stopped, and Leddie almost ran into me.

Tapp lowered his voice. "I'm sorry for the doors, but don't concern yourself over it. His Lordship almost always keeps them closed in case of assassins or invasions." It seemed as if he might say more, but he shrugged instead and followed the girl. I glanced at Halla, who looked about as displeased as I felt.

Thousands of goats trotted, ate, slept, and fornicated in the fields around Caislin. That meant hundreds of dogs stood out there guarding them. As I walked beside Tapp, I pulled four yellow bands and sent one off in each direction.

Two hundred and fifty-four fuzzy dog ears went up.

The servant girl led us to a darkly waxed wooden door, guarded by two soldiers. A third solider opened the door, and I walked through just behind Tapp.

We trooped into a sparse audience room big enough for fifty people to spread out in. Oil lamps lit bright, rich tapestries covering the walls, and faded rugs lay thick on the floor, but I didn't see a stick of furniture. The smell of burning oil hung flat in the room, as if lamps had smoked steadily there for a hundred years.

A trim, middle-aged man in plain, well-made clothes stood at one end of the room with a soldier off to each side of him. I assumed he was Lord Babardi. I marked two other doors in the two corners behind him. Eight more soldiers lined the walls.

"Who is the one who leads you?" Babardi said, hardly loud enough to hear.

I smiled. "We fight about that every day, my lord. Sometimes both before and after breakfast."

Babardi stared at the ceiling. "Crap. Great crap, monkey crap, Cassarak's flying crap. He's not just a hero." The lord raised his voice. "He's got to be a jovial goddamn hero who thinks he's witty. Krak, destroy me now!"

Krak did not destroy him at that time. However, Tapp spoke up and dipped his head to Babardi. "My lord, these people, being such fierce and devastating fighters, don't have just one leader. They retrieved the ring for us and had a mighty perilous time doing it, I think."

I cleared my throat. "I do apologize, my lord. I don't mean to poke fun or anything. I sure don't mean to interfere with us offering our respects or receiving any thanks Your Lordship feels fitting, as long as they don't require much of your valuable time."

"Oh, your reward. I thought hard about it, I did. I considered gold, or maybe titles. Would you like to be Door Guardian of the Third Ward? No? Provisions for your journey, then?" Babardi raised his left hand and showed the ring. "I count on this to set everything right in our city. It should. I read about it. Since you retrieved it for me, I shall honor you by allowing you to ride away from this city alive."

"What does that mean?" Whistler said.

"So, you're in charge now?" Babardi asked Whistler. "Did I miss breakfast? No? Shut up then." He glared at me and then at Halla. "You must have had some sort of good intentions in all this, but you screwed everything up to the Void! And to the Void's dark woman-parts! You killed a few of Memweck's men and freed a few children. Great bouncing bull balls for you—congratulations!"

Tapp and three of the soldiers fidgeted when the lord mentioned children. Tapp said, "My lord—"

Babardi cut him off. "What happens when Memweck's thugs don't come home to him? Does he send fifty men next week? Or a thousand? Those men won't care that some fools full of heroism and tight sphincters galloped in here, killed everybody left and right, and then disappeared like farts in a storm. Will they?" The man glared at me, his chin raised and a violent frown just about bouncing off his face. "Will they?"

"I guarantee they won't," I said. "We apologize for freeing your city and saving a bunch of children. I see now it was the worst turn we could have done you. A right kick in the nuts. We're sorry. We'll take this reward, which we don't deserve, and go."

Everybody in the room relaxed just a breath.

Babardi stamped the floor with his shiny boot and then nodded past me at a soldier waiting beside the door. The man pulled the door open wide. Babardi said, "Leave. May you have a pox on your assholes so that they swell like melons."

I almost couldn't make myself raise my hand, but I managed it. "I beg your pardon, my lord, but I have something for you. Something the God of Death commanded me to give you."

Babardi frowned. "Well, that cannot be good in any way."

I reached with glacial care into my shirt and pulled out the pouch. I held up Harik's hand-size black leather book.

Babardi's eyes brightened. "A book! I love books. It's from Harik? Maybe he's sending us some sort of assistance. Does it call monsters, or turn men into bushes?"

"I've never seen it do that, my lord." I stopped. Maybe I didn't need the book to bring back Manon. Hell, I didn't even know if I dared to bring her back. I didn't know anything except that when I gave the book over, it would belong to this man.

I struggled to step toward Babardi like I was walking across the bottom of a lake. I shifted the book to my numb hand and held it out.

Babardi grasped the book, but I didn't let it go. He flinched, as if the thing had given him a shock. "Let me," he said, pulling against me.

I let him take it out of my hand.

Babardi held the book up, examining Harik's mark on the front. "Oh, it's heavy. Have you read it?" The lord smiled at me.

"Just a little." So, I had delivered the book. It was over.

I whipped out my knife and plunged it into Babardi's heart. His eyes and mouth all popped open in perfect circles. I stabbed him again in the chest. As he wobbled, I snatched the book with my left hand and almost dropped it, but I held on.

Everybody behind me in the audience chamber was shouting. I felt sure that not a single one of them was cheering me on.

THIRTY-ONE

Babardi flopped down dying, and the soldier to his left gawked as if I should have asked permission before I murdered the man. I stabbed him in the chest too, then spun toward the soldier on Babardi's other side. I kicked that man's knee so hard he called his mother a whore, and then I shoved him toward the real craziness in the middle of the room.

I stuffed the book into my shirt and scanned the fight. Halla, Whistler, and the others who used to be my friends were cursing me with rank gusto as they defended themselves from the eight soldiers surrounding them and two more that charged in from the hallway. Those soldiers didn't concern me overmuch. I worried about the dozens or hundreds of their allies waiting for us out in the city.

I backed away from the fight as I sheathed my knife and drew my sword. Then I pulled yellow bands, one after another, and whipped them out in all directions. It brought my reserve of power low.

Tapp charged me from the middle of the room, knocking down one of his own men on the way. He was cursing, with his teeth bared and his sword held too high. I waited for him, prepared to cripple one of his legs and then slice his throat. When I killed

Babardi, I had done just about the worst thing that anybody could do to Tapp, and if I let him live, then I'd just have to kill him another day. I could swear off murdering him of course, but I knew he wouldn't stop trying to kill me. Mercy would be like driving a knife through my own neck.

I made a deep slice through Tapp's upper leg. He screamed, stumbled, and then limped backward one step. I pressed him, and then I saw Leddie step out of the fight and aim her sword at Tapp's back.

I shouted, "Stay away!" Tapp's life was mine, and I'd be damned if I let her steal it.

Leddie laughed as she kept coming.

I grabbed Tapp's collar and pushed his unbalanced self to the floor just as Leddie swung at his head. Then I knocked Leddie's sword aside with a ridiculously furious block. She cocked her head, shrugged at me, and turned back to the main fight. I looked around for Tapp, and somebody shoved a white-hot spiny viper with barbs into my belly.

Tapp lay on the bloody rug, holding the hilt of his sword while jiggling the other end around in my guts. He withdrew for another thrust, maybe hoping for my testicles this time. I jumped up beside his head, screamed while my intestines rearranged themselves, and kicked Tapp in the face with my boot heel. That surprised me. I should have killed him, and I told myself to kill him. Right away. But when I turned, he wasn't dead. He only lay passed out on the floor with a broken nose.

Four soldiers still blocked our escape toward the main doorway. I limped in and cut one down from the side. Leddie crippled a man, Whistler charged the door, and Bea tried to knee me in the crotch.

As I slipped aside, Bea shouted, "You . . . why, you crazy . . ."

Of course, she was ignorant of all my reasoning, so I nodded and said, "Wait," before I hobbled on toward the door. Halla had hefted a puny soldier with one hand and had just slammed him against the ground when I arrived. I almost dropped my sword when she seized me with that same hand, hauled my face up to hers, and roared like a bear. She didn't hold back on the flying slobber, either.

My spirit was hauled out of my body like a scrawny fish jerked out of the ocean. I hardly felt any nausea before nothingness wrapped me and dissolved all my pain.

"Murderer!" Harik bellowed.

I imagined drawing my sword, and the trading place appeared in bright afternoon sunlight.

"Murderer!" Harik shouted again, and my head rang all the way to my lower teeth. "Did you intend to accomplish anything more in your life? Experience anything else? Your answer should be no, because this is the end of you!"

My eyeballs seemed to be vibrating. Harik stood on the top step of the gazebo with his hair and black robe whipping in a hard breeze that I couldn't feel. The god appeared even more well-muscled than usual.

"Greetings, Mighty Harik." I tried to keep a casual tone, as if we were laughing over some foolish thing we'd done drinking yesterday. "It's a shame you're in poor spirits. I delivered the book like you asked."

"I wanted that man to have the book!"

"You mean Lord Babardi?" I pointed at the ground with my sword, although the Gods' Realm wasn't physically above the world of man.

"I mean that fatuous lump of sinew and goose fat that you killed! Him! Not you!" Harik's robe flapped wild, as if the wind had become a gale. "I did not intend for you to keep that book, you mewling speck!"

I winced and shook my head. "Damn, I'm sorry about that. I wish I had known. But I couldn't have known if you didn't say it, Your Magnificence. You always say I'm not too bright."

"Do not try to be clever." Harik spit each word like a nail.

"All right, I won't. To make a good start on that, how do I keep this numbness from crawling up my arm and killing me?"

Harik's nostrils flared twice, and then the wind died to a nice breeze. "You dare seek a favor from me? Now?"

"You did say not to be clever."

Harik descended the gazebo benches with inhuman grace. He took one long, slow step onto the patch of dirt. I had never seen a god set foot on the dirt of the trading place. I didn't move. The dirt patch was small, and I had nowhere to go. Also, my mind got stuck at asking whether this was really happening. I sure as hell didn't raise my sword or try to kill the God of Death.

Harik placed the tip of his left thumb against my chest. I stopped breathing, my heart stopped beating, and I collapsed like a barrel of severed arms poured onto the coarse ground. All sensation disappeared as my sword dropped out of my hand. A moment later, it all came back when Harik wrapped my fingers around the hilt.

Harik was leaning over me. He squeezed my fingers tighter on the hilt, and pain rushed out of his thumb and into my chest. "I want you to feel this, Murderer."

I couldn't move even a fingertip, but I started shivering. Then my body began twitching as pieces of it died. An entire sun of pain flowed through my chest from Harik's thumb.

Harik said, "The degree to which I deprecate your thoughts cannot be overestimated, but my unfathomable sense of courtesy demands that I ask whether you have any."

Shockingly, my lips worked. "If you don't want to fix my arm, how about helping me raise the dead?"

Harik paused and then pursed his lips. "You cannot bring back the Tooth."

"It's impossible?" I creaked through the agony.

"You cannot bring back the Tooth."

"I heard . . . I heard . . ." I hoped he'd be curious enough about what I had heard that he'd take his damn thumb off my chest.

"What did you hear?" Harik lifted his thumb, and the searing pain faded. I could breathe again and even wiggle a finger or two.

"I heard it's been done."

The thumb connected with my chest again.

I squeaked, "Lutigan did it behind your back!" It was the stupidest form of a lie, based on guesswork and gall. Any detail would be as likely to shatter it as support it.

The thumb lifted again. "Who did he supposedly raise?"

"That's all I know! Sakaj told me!" Harik's sister, Sakaj, despised him and would lie to him about anything. He couldn't believe her—or disbelieve her—no matter what she said.

Harik stood and stepped back up into the gazebo where he sat on the bottom bench and clasped his fingers. "You are almost certainly lying to me, but I have in the past discovered . . . never mind. I must not act precipitously simply because you are an infuriating, yammering smear of filth. You can still serve me."

"I'd rather lick warm shrimp off the beach, Mighty Harik." It wouldn't do to act like I was afraid of him.

Harik ignored my comment. "You must, however, put the Tooth out of your thoughts. Even better, make yourself of use and trade your memories of the Tooth to me. On any other day, you would be correct not to trust me, but I am not attempting to deceive you now. Give her up, or your grief will kill you. Observe how you unwisely allowed that man who stabbed you to live."

I sat up and clambered to my feet with the grace of a newborn rhino. "Your Magnificence, where should I start? You admit I shouldn't trust you, and then you tell me to trust you. Should I give up the idea of bringing her back, or the memory of her, or my grief over her, or the memory of the grief, or the idea of the memory? Shit . . . I got lost. Just assume I want her back. Since you didn't deny that you could make that happen, how would we do it?"

"I will not assist you," Harik said, unmoving.

"Aha! Then it's a thing I can do if I have assistance!"

"No!" Harik surged to his feet. "You cannot do it. I am the God of Death, and I forbid it."

I stared at Harik for two breaths. "I see. We can talk about this again later, I guess. She's not getting any deader. I'll hang on to the book. It might be handy."

The God of Death issued a growl that might have been part fury and part indigestion. "Keep it, for now. Preserve it from harm. Accept your punishment for being such a disobedient, niggling toad!"

"What punishment?"

Harik grinned. "Goodbye, Murderer."

"Wait! Mighty Harik, I believe I could kill a lot more people on my journey to visit Memweck if I had more magical power. Allow me to extend to you the great honor of starting negotiations."

Harik stared at me and remained silent.

After an uncomfortable length of time, I said, "Allow me to extend to you the great honor of—"

"Yes, I heard you!" Harik snapped. "Tell me, Murderer, why should I offer you power when you have behaved so abominably?"

"You know that I will kill people and create seventeen kinds of hell with it. And as a plum to set atop that, I will use it to aggravate the spawn of Lutigan's crusty loins."

Harik grunted. "I offer half a square if you sail straight back across the ocean and forget Memweck."

I rested the point of my sword on the dirt and clenched my jaw. "I cannot do that, Harik. I allowed Memweck to fool me, destroy people, and steal innocents. I'm obliged to bring them back."

"I should just kill you now and deny Memweck the pleasure." For a moment, Harik looked like a mopey child. "You care little about innocents, Murderer, but you care a great deal about looking foolish. Very well. I offer half a square if you remain alone for the next year—a hermit."

"I wouldn't have to kill every person I meet, would I? In order to remain alone?"

"You could if you wished. I would encourage it, but it wouldn't be required."

"Here's a counteroffer, you carbuncle that walks like a god. Or floats, or whatever. In exchange for four squares, I will remain alone whenever I camp for the next month."

"Fatuous. Both you and the offer." Harik wrinkled his nose. "For one square, no one will ever stay by your side to help you or come to your aid again."

"I won't laugh, but only because I'm the politest one around here. For three squares, the next time I call for help, people won't come." It could be awkward in practice, but I felt confident I could slip out of most situations on my own.

Harik nodded. "If you agree that it will happen three times, I offer two squares."

I didn't feel quite that confident. "No. How about the next two times I call for help, nobody will come? Three squares."

"Oh, no," Harik said. "Nothing so simple. They will not come to your aid, nor will they stay to aid you. And it shall not be the next two times. I shall choose which two times you will be abandoned. It could be the first and the fiftieth. You will not be abandoned until I say so."

Of course, I didn't want Harik choosing when people would ignore my call for help, but he was still pissed at me. If I acted too hardheaded, he might just throw me out and not trade at all. Also, I didn't feel tingly about fighting Memweck with just a sword and my lousy singing voice. "Four squares instead of three?"

"Done."

Harik flung me back into my body, which convulsed. It convulsed again when my guts spasmed. I might have fallen, but Halla was holding me up like an awkward sack of turnips. Halla unleashed another juicy roar at me.

I smiled at her and tasted blood. "You can drown me later, darling, once we're away from this awful place. Set me down, and I'll lead us out of here."

Halla set me on my feet with a disgusted frown. "Lead, then."

Whistler and Leddie had cleared out the doorway. I held my belly with one hand and limped past them toward the sounds of barking. "Don't stop for anything!"

I reached the building's main door and found pandemonium in the street. I did not find true violence, however. Thirty or forty soldiers struggled to remain upright and effective, and more came running from within the city.

Also, seventy or so healthy goat-herding dogs bounded about, ears and tails up, convinced that the soldiers were the most vigorous playmates in creation. Chests were jumped upon and the insides of mouths were licked. Crotches were well sniffed. Jaws clamped sleeves with unending grips and plenty of fake snarling. I saw a furry black-and-white mountain bowl down two men and then stand on one of them, licking his face.

The soldiers appeared stunned. I imagined most of them had played with dogs before and wouldn't see this behavior as threatening. That couldn't last, though. At some point, a solider would fight, so I hustled around the side of Babardi's home at a fast stagger. The boy was still holding our horses. I grabbed the last silver coin from my pouch and flipped it to him as we mounted. I followed Leddie northwest at a gallop, with razors in my gut and tears running down my face.

Once we cleared the city, I let the dogs pause their play and follow me. They loped after us, anticipating the fun they'd have frolicking with the horses of any pursuing soldiers.

THIRTY-TWO

I thought I knew every way a man might go from horseback to the ground, on purpose or otherwise. That included flying over the horse's head, as well as getting smacked off the saddle sideways by an angry woman leaping off a rock. I thought I knew every way, but I did not.

We had slowed to a trot, and Babardi's men had left off chasing us to go home. Their pursuit had been shattered by seventy ecstatic dogs barking, nipping at their horses' hooves, and clamping onto the soldiers' ankles with the intention of dragging the men down to play.

Also, the soldiers may not have been chasing us with much diligence. Babardi had not seemed like a man who inspired loyalty or love.

I must have passed out as we trotted along. I awoke sliding off the saddle to my right. I pushed against the stirrup, but it was slippery from all my blood that had been running down the saddle and beyond, so my foot slipped out. Then I grabbed the pommel with both hands and held myself up, screaming about Harik's private parts and all their deficiencies.

I pulled my left foot free of the stirrup, hiked the leg, and pulled with it to bring myself up. That leg slipped. I strained, lying along the side of my mount, clinging to the pommel while I tried to run backward up the side of the horse, both feet slipping on the saddle. I finally let go of the damn creature, but too late realized my wrists were tangled in the reins. The horse dragged me for a few strides until I got my feet under me and bounced alongside it.

That annoyed my horse, which decided to rear. The last thing I remembered was dangling by my wrists from my horse's head like a seed pod ready to blow away.

Sometime later, I opened my eyes.

"He's awake," Halla said.

Leddie started applauding, and Whistler joined in.

Halla glanced at my belly. "I hope you can heal yourself. This looks bad."

"Why are we waiting for him?" Bea said from someplace I couldn't see.

Fifteen minutes later, I had repaired the damage to my gut. It still hurt as if a weasel were chewing in there, but that was an improvement. Earlier, it had hurt as if a lion were chewing, or six weasels. Or two weasels and an angry wolf. I sighed and admitted I was thinking ridiculous thoughts so I wouldn't have to ask Bea what she meant by not waiting for me.

I rolled to my feet and glanced around. "I guess you have questions."

Leddie said, "Questions? I have one. Why do you go around doing stupid things almost sure to get you killed? My gods, I feel like killing you right now, and I'm not the only one." Leddie pointed at Bea. "She wants to bite your throat out! I had to hold her back. Look, we all have reasons for killing Memweck. Your reason must not be too damn important, since instead of slaying him, you want to kill random people every day and murder the head of a city while we're right in the big middle of it! The rest of us don't want to be slaughtered for whatever your inane reason is. We're better off without you!"

I squinted one eye at her. "What was your question?"

"Smartass. Here it is: Why don't we just murder you and take your body to Memweck? Maybe he'll trade."

I didn't think they'd try to kill me, but I edged back so I could see them all.

Bea hadn't stopped glowering at me since I stood up. "No, we shouldn't kill Bib. We should tie him up and take him with us. That way, Memweck can do whatever he wants with him."

I put my hand on my sword. Leddie and Whistler stiffened. Halla relaxed, her breath slowed, and her eyes seemed brighter. I said, "If Memweck decides not to be a nice host, you may wish my sword and I were along to help out."

Whistler coughed and grinned for a second. "Well, now that Halla has this Bloom That . . . this Bloom thing, we're fine. That is, she can knock anything to pieces, and she says that should include demigods."

I raised an eyebrow at Halla. "She said that?"

"I did," Halla said in a softer voice than normal. "That's not the important thing, though. The important thing is that Memweck searches for you. If he finds you, he will find us too. We should leave you before that happens."

It almost made sense, but not if you scrutinized it. Halla would be the last one to accept logic so shallow. It was Harik, then, driving them away so they wouldn't help me. Well, I had agreed to this bargain. I'd find a way to murder my enemies in spite of it.

I smiled around at them. "All right, then. I can see you don't trust me. Well, don't think you're special. I don't trust you, either, so go on, I won't follow you. Well, maybe I will if we're all hunting Memweck, but it will be coincidence."

Halla glanced at Leddie.

"Oh, all right, fine!" Leddie scowled. "Memweck is about two-thirds of the way up that mountain there. There's a back trail through the hills and up the other side of the mountain. We're going that way, so stay off it. It's ours!"

"Where's the front trail?" I said.

Leddie opened and closed her fist a few times. "Just keep going up this path. But he'll see you coming from forever away, even with that hair in your arm."

I stared back down the road toward Caislin. "Maybe I'll go home, then. You've made your plans and have your Memweck-slaying weapon. I'd just be in the way."

Bea sneered. "Good! When you get to Bindle, keep going."

"I'll hold a war council with my horse and then decide." I stepped over to my mare, pulled a spare shirt from a saddlebag, and wiped as much of the blood from my saddle and stirrups as I could. I heard the others mount and trot away. When I looked up two minutes later, they were already lost to sight.

Midday had passed just a little while before. I had already done my murders for Harik today. By Krak and the Black Drifting Whores, I wasn't going home. I didn't even have one. This trail would take me to Memweck's front door, unless Halla had allowed Leddie to lie about it.

I pulled out Harik's book, opened it to the third page, and stared at the black square. Soon, I became aware of glowing, transparent Manon waving and jumping up and down in front of me. I drew my sword, and she touched her chest to the point.

"Father! Are you going to bring me back?"

"It's proven to be a complex endeavor, sweetie. I will press the issue the next time I talk to Harik, though."

Manon fell still and stood blinking at me. "That's all right. I'm not crying."

I tried to joke a little. "Is there much crying among the dead?"

"I don't think so. I think maybe I can't cry."

I started to reach out to her, but I caught myself. "Manon, you told me to walk straight into Memweck's home and then right up to him. Do you remember?"

She scowled at me as if I had asked whether she had a tongue. "Of course I remember!"

"I want to be sure I understand that correctly. So . . . is it still correct?"

"Yes. Wait. Is that the only reason you called me?" Her lips formed a hard line. "To get stupid fighting tips?"

"No, darling. But I don't want to do a foolish thing and get killed. If I was on that side with you, I couldn't bring you back here."

"I don't want you on this side!" She sounded a little panicked.

"I wouldn't fit in?" I winked at her. "I might embarrass you?"

"I think . . . I think it would be different. People aren't the same."

"What do you mean?" It wasn't often one could learn about the afterlife from somebody who had been there.

"Nobody . . . people don't pay much attention. Even if they loved each other when they were alive, now they just walk past each other. Like they never met. I think it's like that. Or maybe I dreamed it! Do you think dead people can dream? Just don't you die! You won't love me anymore."

That was like a knife in the chest. "All right, I won't die. I'm headed to kill Memweck now, and then I'll talk to Harik. I love you."

Manon hadn't been one to show happiness. She had been more inclined to show how dim and oblivious she thought I was, which I guess is common among teenage girls. Now she showed me a beautiful smile, although not quite happy.

I mounted and trotted my horse on up the trail. The path soon curved through modest pine trees, with a layer of needles piled on dry dirt. The afternoon grew cold and cloudy, but the air felt as dry as sand. Sometimes the trail ran right along a cliff's edge, and other times it swung a hundred paces back toward the hillside.

More people than I would have expected traveled that path in the high hills, both up and down. I paused to gently interrogate a couple of them and found that a fine hunting ground lay in those hills. Although I could scarcely believe it, the people of Caislin sometimes tired of eating goat. They always welcomed hunters bringing game.

A few silver miners traveled that path too. Little groups of them marched uphill with their tools and empty sacks. Some strode back downhill laughing, or else trudged down the trail as glum as if they missed supper.

The sun set, but I kept riding. I walked my mare every so often to rest her. Manon and the dead disappeared sometime between sunset and midnight. I didn't notice them leaving. At midnight, I led my horse far off the path and slept until daylight.

I passed fewer hunters and more miners the next day. I had ridden onto the mountainside proper, and scary cliffs became more frequent. Throughout the day, I remained watchful, since I owed Harik two deaths before sunset. However, the only people I passed were miners, guilty of no more than vile gossip, taking small things left unattended, and sleeping with other people's spouses. If they deserved killing, then ninety-nine people in a hundred deserved it too.

The sunlight was growing dim, and I still hadn't murdered anybody. I started to sweat in spite of the cold. If I failed to deliver two lives to Harik, he would demand that I follow his orders in deciding who to kill from then on.

I heard shouting off the trail, along the cliff, and I galloped my mare in that direction. A rough, well-armed man had just shoved a miner to the ground. Another such man threatened a second miner with a long knife. It was precisely what I needed. I almost thanked Harik under my breath.

The men turned toward my horse's hoofbeats and backed away from me as I halted and jumped out of the saddle. I preferred not to charge my horse straight off the cliff. I ran toward them and half beheaded one before he could shift out of the way. I spun toward the other, who was shuffling one direction and then the other, as if he couldn't decide whether to run or fight. Then an arrow sprouted from the side of his head, and he crumpled.

A hundred feet back down the path, Pil stood holding a bow and smiling at me. I stared at her for a moment and then examined the miners—a huge-eyed, chubby man and what appeared to be his teenage son. With my mouth open, I blinked at each of them in turn—Pil, then the man, and then the boy.

I wondered which one of them I was going to kill in the next two minutes.

THIRTY-THREE

Pil loped toward me, holding her bow. The miner babbled his thanks, maybe in two languages, while his son cried and laughed at the same time.

I sure wasn't going to murder Pil. As for the boy, I had killed three children in my life, and I hoped I'd never kill another one. That left the bug-eyed miner, and I hated to kill him. He hadn't done anything especially bad that I knew of. Killing him seemed harsh since I had saved his life sixty seconds ago.

I didn't have a choice, though. If I failed, Harik would be telling me which people to kill, and he'd certainly point me to the ones who deserved it least.

The grinning miner shut up when I raised my hand. I met his eyes. "Would you like to say goodbye to your boy? You have a few seconds." I lifted my knife with my other hand. The man squeaked and nearly fell over backward, but I grabbed the front of his shirt.

"What are you doing?" Pil screeched as she arrived beside me.

"It's a debt. I have to kill one of you. I don't have a choice."

Pil punched me on my numb arm. "You are stupider than . . . a really damn stupid thing . . . what did you tell me, huh? Try to think back. I know it was days and days ago, but a powerful sorcerer like you can remember little things, right? Or are things only important when you can make yourself sound wise saying them?"

"Don't play around. I only have a minute. Maybe less." I glanced toward the dim clouds in the west.

"You shut up and come with me!" Pil seized my spirit as she lifted her own out of her body. It shocked me too much for me to think about struggling. Disembodied Pil called, "Harik! Harik, receive us!"

All sensation except hearing ceased when we reached the trading place.

"You've made a singular entrance, Knife." Harik's voice rolled out like layers of silk. "Perhaps I should send the Murderer away so that we may converse in private."

I imagined drawing my sword. The Gods' Realm appeared under a nighttime sky. I looked again. The sky was unmarred blackness, even though I had seen stars there in the past. I stared straight up and fell to one knee when I became convinced that we were spinning inside something. Harik sat in the middle of the gazebo, and the only light came from a lantern hanging over his head.

Pil stood staring at nothing. "Please don't send him away, Mighty Harik. I have come to shame Bib into showing some courage."

"That sounds promising. Continue."

"Wait!" I sounded a little whinier than I liked, so I cleared my throat. "Pil, I know what I need to do, and I don't have too damn much time left to do it in. Unless you have some unexpected, stupefying way in mind to change things."

"Of course I do, or I wouldn't have brought us here. Keep up!" Pil seemed a bit harsher to me, and I wondered what she had been trading away.

Pil went on: "Harik, I want Bib's debt of two killings a day to be ended. I mean I want you to declare it paid. As of now. Paid off."

Harik grinned. "I do not find that enticing in the least."

"There's more," Pil said. "Bib will get five squares of power, and you'll tell him about Memweck's greatest weakness. No, not weakness—that's not right. His weakness could be collecting spoons or craving dumplings. I mean his greatest vulnerability to physical harm."

Harik stopped smiling. "Anything else? A winged horse? Krak's best coat? My wife to be used as a plaything for your holidays? No?" Then he shouted, "Be silent, you puerile girl! Murderer, do you propose to waste my time as well?"

Pil raised her voice. "Your Magnificence, just one more moment. I did come all this way, you know. You . . ." She closed her eyes. "You rotten mule's tongue."

"Good effort," I said.

Neither Pil nor Harik showed that they heard me.

"In exchange for all this," Pil said, "I'll ask Fingit, through you, to give me to Lutigan."

"You sure as hell will not!" I yelled. "How do you even know about that?"

She ignored that question. "Bib, I think maybe I should belong to the God of War. It might be better. After all, they named me the Knife."

"Those names don't mean piddle on the porch!" I pointed at her even though I knew she couldn't see me. "The most horrible sorcerer I ever met was named the Farmer."

Harik cleared his throat. "I am still here. In case you've forgotten."

"That's my offer, Mighty Harik," Pil said.

"Knife, are you not concerned that you should instead be making this offer to Fingit, who owns you? He might be angry."

"Are you concerned?" Pil said it like a challenge.

"Not even the tiniest bit. Pretend I said nothing about Fingit."

"Who?" Pil smiled, although she wasn't aware of it. "So, Mighty Harik, I say it again. That's my offer."

"And a pathetic one it is," Harik said, almost without interest. "Listen to me, Knife. There will be no power for the Murderer, nor will I discuss Memweck's vulnerabilities. I will end the Murderer's obligation to murder each day, but once you offer yourself to Lutigan, you shall dedicate your next one hundred kills to me. I can already hear him raging about that. And you will give up all your memories of the recent ocean voyage you made to the northern kingdoms."

Pil paused for two seconds. "Maybe . . . maybe you needn't provide Bib any power. He's tricky and mean, so he can get by without it. But he needs to know how to kill Memweck. That's not negotiable. I'll dedicate thirty kills to you instead of a hundred. That way, I won't have to listen to Lutigan complain as much. About the memories—"

"You stop right there!" I stood in front of Pil's unseeing face. "You're too young to be dedicating murders and losing memories! That sort of shit kills new sorcerers." It was a ridiculous statement on my part. Thousands of sorcerers younger than Pil had lived through more ignorant and self-destructive things. "Besides, you have no idea what you're offering. Fingit is a kindly uncle with candy and ponies compared to Lutigan."

"No, Bib. It's just exactly like you told me." Pil said it with patience, as if she were teaching me to tie my shoes. "I'm responsible for everything in my life. Well, I don't like what's happening now, so I'm doing something about it."

I didn't enjoy Pil reminding me that I was a bumbling hypocrite. I hated even more that she was pointing out that I always had choices, just maybe not good ones. I stepped toward Harik and pointed my sword at him. "Ignore this young woman. She doesn't know you perverted, ass-tucking barnyard rats the way I do. This deal benefits me, so I should pay my side."

"This is my negotiation!" Pil shouted, her face set in hard lines.

"Hush!" I boomed.

Pil flinched and shook her head. I felt the force of my own voice bouncing between my ears.

Harik stretched like a giant cat with the ego of a god, which was about the same as the ego of a cat. "You know what I want most, Murderer."

I had no conception of what he wanted most, so I nodded. Then I stood tall like one of those ignorant heroes on the battlefield.

Harik said, "Trade me all your memories of the Tooth. Do yourself a good turn. Trade them to me."

I crossed my arms. "God of Death, I know that you gods understand all about existence. But now I see that existence must be far simpler than I was led to think. You understand it, but you can't comprehend that I will never give up my memories of her. Your ignorance is sort of sad."

Harik sniffed and turned back to Pil. "The Murderer has proven as disappointing as ever, Knife. Shall we continue negotiations?"

"No!" I snapped. "How about something else? Something simple."

Harik grumped, "Simple. How boring."

I made myself laugh. "I think simple is good for us right now. If you'd rather have a five-cornered deal with secret obligations, unilateral options, and somebody humping a gargoyle on the temple roof, I will oblige and give a fine accounting of myself. But that sounds arduous, and I am not suited to great effort at this time."

Harik shook his head. "No. That was too sarcastic to bear, even for me. Knife, let us continue."

Without thinking, I shouted, "I know what you want next! What you want if you can't dig out my memories."

Harik raised an eyebrow. "Of course you do. Say it."

I had yelled by reflex, not knowing what I'd say next. Then the answer slammed me like a barn door. I didn't want to say it. It was the last damn thing I wanted to say. I stared at Harik for a time that seemed awfully long.

"You can say it, Murderer." Harik spoke in a bright tone. I felt like his dog.

I whispered, "You want the book."

"Good! Yes! Give it to me, and I shall lift your obligation for two murders each day. You may have none of the other things the Knife was mumbling about."

I clutched the book in its pouch under my shirt, squeezed it hard, and stared at Harik some more.

Pil whispered, "Don't, Bib. Let me do this."

Harik laughed. "She cannot help you. The book will not help you. Trust me."

I shouted, "Trust you? I wouldn't trust you to save me from

drowning if all you had to do was flap your ass cheeks from a mile away!"

"Do not test me, Murderer. I shall allow you time to decide. You have ten seconds."

I threw myself out of the Gods' Realm toward home, but Harik dragged me back. I searched my mind for a better offer, but my creativity failed. I must have made a mistake of some kind, but I couldn't grasp it. If I lost the book, I couldn't bring Manon back, or even talk to her anymore.

Then I saw it, and it wasn't even complicated. A child would have known it. Manon was gone, but I had said no, I

could get her back if I was clever enough and willing to suffer. I had tried to do the same damn thing when Bett, my first little girl, was dying, but it had helped nobody.

I wanted it to be different with Manon. The book had let me think it could be.

I felt something warm inside me tear loose and drop into the earth. I muttered, "Yes. I agree."

"Fine," Harik said. "You have certainly been an aggravation over this book business."

I still clenched the book tight in its pouch. "Where should I take it?"

"Oh, just drop it anywhere." Harik gazed up at the lantern. "Someone will come along."

"Harik . . . can I use the book one more time to say goodbye?"

"If you wish." Harik flicked something off the sleeve of his robe. "That is, if you can do it in nineteen seconds."

I bit my lip and tasted blood. I'd need more than nineteen seconds of staring at that damned black square before Manon appeared.

Harik dropped me back into my body with such ease that I didn't even stagger. I let go of the miner's shirt, and he fell on his butt, begging not to die. I sprinted across the road, pulling the book out of its pouch as I went.

A tall stone stood beside the cliff's edge, and I leaned against it while I weighed the book in my hand. I traced the mark on the cover with my finger and lowered it to my knee. Then I opened my hand, and the book fell out. It dropped, bounced over the cliff's edge, and was gone.

I sat on the stone for a time, pretending to think wise sorcerer thoughts, or at least pretending to remember Manon. I didn't think about anything, really, apart from occasional images so out of place they might have gotten separated from their herd.

Pil came and sat on the ground at my feet. She was wise enough not to say a damn word, but she leaned her head against my knee once in a while.

THIRTY-FOUR

People generally aggravate me. They cling to foolish, whimsical notions, and they get offended if others don't cling to them just as hard. They pick out their neighbors' bad behavior with an unerring eye while doing the same damn thing at the same time. They treat useful strangers politely and are mean to the people they love. They are far less brave than they believe, and no matter what they tell themselves, just about everything they do is for their own safety and comfort. Damn them all three times.

Of course, I possess every one of these same traits. I rarely admit it, because disliking other people who share your failings is easier and more enjoyable.

I wondered which of my reckless and stupid actions Pil was condemning in her head as we rode up the mountain path. I also wondered how she'd feel when she did those same things one day, if she lived.

I had dropped Harik's book at sunset. After a time, Pil and I made camp. We didn't converse while building the fire, eating, or switching guard duty. We were at a high elevation, and a cold rain came in the night. We both put on every garment we owned.

The next day, weather shifted back and forth from drizzle to pelting drops that hurt, but the rain never lifted entirely. The dark, ragged clouds seemed to hang just fifty feet above our heads. The trees had given up on such rocky soil, and only bent, wobbly bushes remained. The path grew narrower all day until it wasn't much more than a game track.

The nasty weather discouraged talk, and neither of us made the effort. But during a spot of afternoon drizzle, when we stopped to rest the horses, I glanced at her and then back at the saddle I was checking. "Why did you come back? I'm happy you did, but at the docks, you seemed awfully determined not to let me get you killed."

"I'm still determined, you can believe me about that. It's just that I received some new knowledge about this whole set of crazy events, and it seems that I'm equally likely to get killed these next few days no matter what I do. If that's true, and I think it must be, then I might as well help you with this dumb thing you're doing. At least saving kids is nice, assuming we can do it." She raised her voice. "And where the hell is everybody else?"

"Harik ran them off." I waved my hand. "It's a long story. Why do you think you're about to die?"

She pursed her lips. "Maybe I shouldn't say. It might change the course of events. Of history, even."

"So, Fingit told you."

Pil glared at me. "Yes. You pig's butt. Don't think you're too smart, though."

I examined the clouds and even reached up as if I could touch one. "Let's see. Memweck's hooligans are stealing kids all around the kingdom and are murdering anybody who shows some spine. That would be you. No ships are sailing south through the spring storms. Memweck might even start searching for sorcerers to either serve him or get ripped to bits. I doubt you want that. How am I doing?"

"Harik told you all this."

I started to say it was all logic and pure living, but instead I said, "He can be helpful once a year or so. Why two bows?"

Pil had shown up with two bows. She carried the hexed one on her back. The new one was pale, not as long, and tapered instead of square. She had used the new one to poke an arrow into that bandit's head. Now she held up the new bow and waggled it. "I enchanted this before I started up the mountain. It's a lot more reliable than the one I got from Peck."

"I'd throw that hexed one in a ditch. It might kill you. Or me."

"I don't know why, but I feel as though I ought to keep it." Pil reached over her shoulder and touched the big weapon. "Maybe it's strong enough to kill Floppy-Ass." She winked at me and then looked grim. "How do you plan to kill him?"

I had been thinking about that problem for days and still didn't have a solution that I liked. "If you don't shoot him in the eye, I'll assault him with the forces of nature. From far away. I don't think we should close with him. Although he might not enjoy getting stabbed with my stupid god-named sword."

"That's your plan?"

"Yes, although I expect we'll improvise a bit."

Pil worked her jaw from side to side. "Will it hurt your feelings if I ride back down the mountain and leave you to die?"

I grinned. "Yes, I think it would."

"I'd better not do that, then. I'm tired of talking to you, though. You're depressing me. Let's keep going."

An hour later, the scant trail widened into a broad dirt path. Shortly after that, it became a road paved with smooth stones. We halted.

"Do you think we're here?" Pil put a load of sarcasm into that.

I chuckled as I examined the twenty-five-foot-tall marble statue of Lutigan standing before us. I dismounted and peered over the edge of the road, which ran straight for at least three hundred paces and was wide enough for five wagons. I saw that we were on a bridge that bypassed the winding edge of the mountain. Memweck had created a magnificent, elevated thoroughfare into his domain.

"I admit I'm impressed," I said.

Pil nodded. "You could offer to join up with his side if he didn't want to expunge you from the world."

"Yep, that's too bad. Let's prepare." I pulled several white bands and whirled them into the sky. Within five minutes, dark, raging storm clouds had begun to gather ahead of us.

We rode down the stone bridge at a smart trot. Two hundred paces along, I spotted a figure walking toward us. By the time we'd drawn near, I could see it was a powerful bald man wearing deerskin.

The man grinned and lifted a hand, and we all stopped. "Welcome, Bib. We've been awfully anxious for you to arrive. You wouldn't believe the tension. I'm Smif, Lord Memweck's majordomo. What questions do you have before I escort you to Lord Memweck?"

"What's the best way to kill the son of a bitch?" I said.

Smif nodded like a chicken pecking corn. "That's a phenomenal question. I don't think he can be killed, at least not by anyone in this realm. I doubt he can even be hurt much."

I sat tall. "But he can be hurt? You've seen it?"

"Yes, a bit. I've seen him shake his head after some titanic blow. He's never bled or bruised, though."

"Thank you, Smif," I said. "That's all I need. Pil?"

"Does he like music? Or poetry?"

Smif's forehead wrinkled. "Yes, of course he does. He's civilized. I mean, he's divine, for the sake of Krak and his knickers. Semidivine."

Pil clapped her hands. "That's wonderful! He'll probably allow us to recite our death poems before he kills us. He will, right?"

Smif shrugged. "It's getting late. Anything else?"

There was nothing else. Smif led us across the bridge, whistling a song I'd never heard. I pulled another band along the way to freshen the storm clouds, and I made a few more preparations. We reached the other end of the bridge, which I estimated to be a full thousand paces long. A thirty-foot-tall marble statue of Krak stood at that end.

I had expected a massive gate or entryway, but the bridge spilled out onto an enormous clearing full of flourishing trees and flowers. Stone and wooden benches, tables, and statues dotted the area. A natural stone wall fifty feet high stood on one side of the area, and the marble façade of an eight-story building stretched the length of another side.

"You have put me out! Put me out in the worst way!" I couldn't tell where Memweck's voice came from. "I promised Gondix I'd be home three days ago. We planned a hunting trip. And then a party! Well, an orgy with maidens. A welcome home orgy for me, and you ruined the whole dog-rotting thing! Do you have an explanation?"

"Maidens, you say?" I dismounted and scanned the area, smiling. "What a fine subject of face-to-face conversation! I am always eager to talk about girls, wherever you are. My first love was Anni, a tenderhearted young thing. Her father and mine despised one another, being rivals for the rich halibut fishing waters."

"I don't care!" Memweck stepped out from behind a twelve-foot-tall statue that was sixty feet away from us. "Be quiet! I can see why my father hates you so much!"

Memweck stood about seven feet tall and wore his white hair long. Most of his skin was a rich copper color. I knew that because I could see most of his skin. He wore short, tight trousers that came up almost to his belly button, and that was all. The muscles of his arms and torso stood out hard and broad. I glanced next to him and realized he was standing beside a statue of himself, identical in every detail, including his stance.

"Oh, shut up and come over here!" Memweck yelled. "I'll pop off your head like a bushy little apple stem. It will hardly hurt. But if you make me come over there . . ." He pointed at the natural stone wall to my right, and a white curtain fell.

Two chains hung from a rough scaffold. Whistler's right arm was manacled to one of the chains, and a weight hung from his left ankle, pulling him into a body-breaking position. Leddie hung from the other chain by her ankles. A leather collar was fixed around her neck, and a weight hung from the collar, pulling it down against her head. Neither of them was moving. I didn't see Halla or Bea anywhere.

I pulled two more bands and spun them into the sky. With no warning, the sky flung down a deluge, and I focused it on Memweck. He collapsed under the water's power and tried to crawl behind his statue. Pil fired the hexed bow, and the arrow shattered the statue, two stone benches, and a palm tree. It landed in a pond, launching ornamental fish in all directions.

I pulled another white band, and another, and five more. A bolt of lightning struck directly on top of Memweck's form, followed by six more lightning bolts in ten seconds. The furious storm had spent most of its water, so the cascade soon stopped pounding Memweck.

Memweck stood up. His trousers had been burned off, and I saw that he would have been welcome at his orgy, but I did not see a single burn or mark on him.

It didn't really surprise me. If anyone could resist natural phenomena like water and lightning, it would be a god, or a demigod. I pulled the last of ten yellow bands I had thrown since the bridge, and an appalling roar sounded from behind me.

Two great brown bears loped off the bridge and charged Memweck. He cocked his head at them.

Memweck peered at the bears as if I'd broken some rule. "Wait . . ."

The two bears smashed into the demigod at almost the same time, and all three creatures tumbled forty feet across the grass. I hung back with my sword drawn. I couldn't add a thing to the fury of that attack.

One bear rolled away from the tussle and clambered back to its feet, shaking its head. The other was crushing Memweck's head in its jaws. Lying on his back, Memweck punched the bear over and over on both sides. The bear let go and roared. Memweck scrambled to his knees, and when the bear leaped at him, he punched it in the forehead. The bear collapsed and didn't move.

Pil fired again, striking Memweck in the throat, but the arrow ricocheted off, nearly impaled Smif, and hurtled over the bridge out of sight.

"My lord!" Smif shouted from a hundred feet away as he threw a sword at Memweck. While the other bear ran at him, Memweck grabbed the sword out of the air, swung, and sliced off the bear's head.

"Nicely done, Murderer!" Memweck called out as he threw the sword back to Smif. "I thought this would be boring!"

Pil fired again. Memweck snatched the arrow out of the air. He bounded to a small stone bench and hurled it over a hundred feet. It smashed Pil straight across the chest and her crossed arms. She bounced twice, rolled three times, and came to rest, not moving.

Memweck laughed and walked toward me in no hurry. He had almost reached another statue when I spotted Halla crouched down behind it where he couldn't see her. She was holding the Bloom thing hammer close to her chest. I didn't know how she had gotten there. Maybe she had run out to that hiding place while the lightning bolts fell.

Halla popped out and swung a horrific blow at Memweck's belly. The demigod cried out in pain and bent over. I sprinted toward Halla to help her. She followed with a massive overhead smash to Memweck's skull, but his hand shot up with unbelievable speed and grabbed the weapon's handle to stop the blow. Halla struggled, but Memweck pulled the hammer out of her hands. Then he shoved the tall, marble statue. It toppled over onto Halla, and she didn't move.

Memweck lifted the hammer. "Oh, this is pretty." He held it by the head with one hand and the end of the handle with the other. Then he smiled at me like a happy dog, flexed, and broke the handle in half.

I had almost reached Memweck, moving at a dead run. He laughed. "You don't plan to hit me with that sword, do you?" He aimed a punch at my right shoulder. I dropped my shoulder enough so that the blow just grazed me, but it knocked my sword out of my hand and left my arm tingling. Memweck bent to pick up my sword, and he threw it toward the building, at least three hundred feet away.

As Memweck turned back to me, I used my numb hand to draw the knife Pil had enchanted for me. I twisted and drove it into Memweck's right eye with all my strength. It bounced off. The last two inches of the knife blade were bent.

I ran like hell. I didn't expect it would help anything, but I figured nothing would help at that point.

"Where do you think you're going, sorcerer boy? Although I admit that this is a lot of fun."

I reached the spot where the bench had crashed into Pil, and I grabbed the hexed bow. Then I scrambled around searching for an arrow, but I couldn't find a single damn one.

Memweck grabbed me by the left shoulder, turned me to face him, and squeezed. I heard bones and tendons split, and I felt grateful that my shoulder was numb.

"I know I shouldn't play with you, but it will make a better story to tell my father." Memweck yelled, "Are you writing all this down, Smif?"

"Yes, my lord. It will make a blasting great song."

Memweck kicked my left thigh. It snapped in two with a bang, bending in the middle to almost ninety degrees. I fell to my right knee and threw back my head. My mouth was open, and I realized I was screaming.

I was face-to-face with the demigod's belly button. It was stupid, since I was about to die, but I wondered what a divine being was doing with a belly button. Then I saw a dab of blood in it. The hexed bow was still in my right hand. I jammed the end of the bow into Memweck's belly button, twisted, groaned, and shoved half the length of the weapon up into Memweck's torso.

Memweck staggered back twenty feet. "Krak hump it with your father's willy! Damn it! Damn, that hurts! Shit!"

I waited for him to fall over, or explode, or anything that was like death.

Memweck scowled. "You must think you did something awfully special here, stabbing me and everything. Well, you didn't! I've been hurt worse than this by unicorn ponies." He looked back at Smif. "We're not going to put this part in the song, right?"

I pulled two blue bands and whipped them over to the bow. I twisted, spent an obscene amount of power, and slammed pressure down on the enchanted, hexed wood. It exploded into hundreds of big splinters.

Memweck made a sound like a seal gagging on a boot, fell on his face, and didn't move.

I rolled onto my back, closed my eyes, and thought I might pass out. Then a shadow fell across my face.

Smif was staring down at me, Memweck's sword in his hand.

I panted, "Unless you want to hold still for an hour while I chew through your throat, go ahead and kill me."

"Huh. Damned Memweck and his gods-be-damned songs," Smif said. "If I had to write another song about his courage and might, I would've eaten glass."

THIRTY-FIVE

I decided that I'd heal myself first so I could then heal everybody else who was still alive. It was an easy decision, since my leg hurt like a cactus shoved in a bad place. I pulled a green band to investigate the damage, but I couldn't sense a thing wrong. My leg was lying there bent in a way legs ought not to bend, so I felt mighty sure something was wrong.

My crushed, numb shoulder also seemed fine when I explored it with magic, but with my hand I could feel it was deformed. Well, when I had first examined the numbness crawling up my arm, it had also seemed healthy.

Smif squatted beside me. "Don't bother ganking around with sorcery on those wounds. 'That which is harmed by Memweck's hand shall not mend.' I know, because he made me write that down. It's true of any part of him, though, not just his hand. Foot, elbow, tongue, anything. I'm sorry to see that the curse remains, even when Memweck doesn't."

"That's a hell of a note. Shit!" I lifted my spirit and called for Harik, but he chose not to answer. He was probably punishing me for doing some niggling thing he didn't like, never mind that I'd been ignorant of it.

"Smif, I can't leave my leg like this. Will you help me?"

The man patted my good shoulder. "You freed me. I'll buy you three drinks and two whores."

I lay back, cursed Memweck with fine creativity, and had Smif pull my leg straight. I sweated, screamed, and called him a flat-assed, slat-tongued whale chaser, but I didn't pass out. Smif then helped me up on my good leg and supported me as I hobbled toward Pil. That lasted ten seconds before I couldn't stand it when the toes on my broken leg banged on the ground. Smif, a tall and broad man, just picked me up and carried me over to her.

The bench had broken Pil's arms and done her chest no good at all, but she wasn't as grievously hurt as I had expected. She had benefited from the hardiness of sorcerers. I repaired her enough to wake her and get her upright with working arms. Then I sent her off to bring down Whistler and Leddie, or their bodies.

Smif carried me, my newly throbbing arm, and my aching chest to Halla, but she was already hobbling toward us. When Memweck had pushed the statue onto her, he had cracked one knee and broken her jaw, knocking out most of her teeth. Blood lay thick on the left side of her head and her left shoulder, and she had a flat spot on her skull that would kill her soon. I felt obliged to heal most of her hurts just to help her move around and be of use.

Leddie and Whistler lived, but they had been beaten, torn up, and dehydrated. For both of them, the weights had pulled some joints out of socket. I healed them just enough to prevent death in the next day or so, and then I blacked out.

I woke up lying on a couch or bed in a room lit by lanterns. The only detail I noticed was the ceiling, which was covered with a single painting of a distant valley seen from a height. My leg throbbed, but all the other pains had faded to whispery aches. Pil sat next to me, holding my hand.

I said, "By Gorlana's shapely ass, I hope we're not connected again."

She shook her head. "Sleep."

"Sleep? One word? Did you sprain your tongue? Where are Whistler and Leddie?" I sat up and shook her hand off.

Pil chuckled. "They're all right. Rest a little, and we'll bring them." She pushed me back down, and I only pretended to resist.

I scanned what I could see of the room. Two couches lined the other walls, along with three tables. Each table held a vase with a single flower. Something moved around them, and when I peered, I saw several butterflies flapping in the vicinity. "So, we're in Memweck's palace, or castle. Maze. Smokehouse."

"Yes. Smif says there are a hundred and eighty-seven rooms. That doesn't include the barracks, training rooms, and nurseries."

I sat up again. "Did you find the children?"

"We found them, or most of them, I suppose, which is good but also a shame, if you know what I mean. One hundred and sixty-one children live in the barracks and twenty in the nurseries. Yes, Bea's son is here, and he's healthy. I don't think she's stopped singing to him. Memweck had forty slaves too, people to keep this edifice clean and fetch him puppies to eat. I just made up that last part."

"What about Halla's boys?"

Halla spoke from the doorway: "They are alive."

"I'm glad. How do you feel about it?"

"Glad. You should sleep."

She didn't sound glad to me. Maybe when Halla was glad, she looked the same as bored, or worried, or constipated. "I'll go to sleep if you sing to me," I said.

"That is foolish." Halla sighed. "I am sorry we abandoned you. It puzzles me."

"Don't kick yourself in the ass too hard. It was Harik. The grunting little weasel made you decide to leave."

Halla's eyebrows flew up. "That makes more sense. I would not want it said that we left you to die. I think your death might make me sad."

I guffawed. "Hell, that may be the closest you've come in years to saying you could tolerate me! I'd have been happy if you promised me that when I died you wouldn't let your dogs eat my corpse."

"I do not have dogs." She left the room before I could say anything else.

"Pil, I'm off to see Harik. Do you want to come?"

She slapped my good shoulder. "No, I'll wait here until you get back. I want to laugh at whatever bad deals you made."

I lifted myself and called for Harik, who answered without delay. All of my pains slipped away from by body.

"What do you want, Murderer? I have little patience for frivolities today. That is a warning."

I imagined drawing my sword, and the Gods' Realm at dawn appeared. The field of pale-blue flowers seemed to slope away forever. A scent drifted up from them on a puff of breeze, and it smelled like Bett's newly washed hair.

I smiled at Harik, who stood at the bottom of the gazebo regarding me with a blank face. "I won't drag this out then, Mighty Harik. Memweck touched me three times before I killed the flaming hell out of him, and the wounds won't heal. I'm here to explore how we may deal with that problem, since I know that not a single problem exists that Your Magnificence can't solve."

Harik pointed at me. "Murderer, I advised you in the most vigorous terms to leave Memweck alone. Well, you have slain him. Oh, joyous day for you! Now you must embrace the repercussions of your act. Survive them if you can."

I had expected Harik to bargain tough and act like a puffed-up, snotty blowhard, but I hadn't expected a dull refusal. "Harik, I continue to slaughter people by the wagon load on your behalf, and I intend to keep doing that for a good long while. But I fear I won't kill nearly so many if I'm working with one leg and one arm. Or if this numbness makes my heart explode."

"That's a sterling bit of logic, Murderer. You have persuaded me. I shall relieve you of one malady."

Harak hurled me down like a plummeting anvil. When I arrived, I thrashed on the bed but didn't fall off. Then my body refused to breathe. I gagged while spears of pain flew from my crushed shoulder down my arm and my back. Harik, that wriggling, rank, craven blemish on all that is pure and joyous had chosen to heal my numbness.

I took some time to adjust to that enthralling development. Pil didn't laugh at me out loud, but I could see in her eyes she thought I was an idiot for merrily trotting off to Harik and expecting him to be nice to me.

Before dawn, I told Pil, "Bring Whistler and Leddie. There's no call for them to sit around and suffer."

Whistler seemed stunned as well as physically thrashed. He sat silent while I healed him, and he walked out without speaking when I told him we were done.

When Leddie tramped into the room, she said, "Fix me, you fine man. Then I'll be ready to kill anybody who farts loudly at me. Not that I will. But I could!" She held Memweck's sword in her hand. It was a short, bronze, broad-bladed weapon, and she didn't put it down during the whole time I helped her. I investigated the awful cuts on her face and chest, but they were as much a mystery as my leg.

I said, "Memweck really did give you that face, then?"

Leddie grinned. "He did, but he won't do it again! Thank you, Bib. If I can grant you a favor sometime, just say it."

Now that I had taken on the wounds from healing Leddie and Whistler, I tried to lay still. I dozed a bit through sunrise and on until midday. A big window filled most of one wall, and in daylight, I could see that the other walls had been painted the color of pomegranates.

I called on Gorlana, Fingit, Chira, and every other god I knew except Harik, Lutigan, and Krak. Harik had already denied me. I didn't expect a cozy welcome from Lutigan since I had just killed his son. I didn't call Krak because nobody called the Father of the Gods unless no other choice existed. Calling Krak for some persistent wounds was like trying to cook soup over a volcano.

Giving up on the gods at last, I asked Pil to fetch Halla for me. When she arrived, I said, "I suppose it's time."

"You should not wait," Halla said with no emotion.

"All right. Will you do it?"

Halla was already unwrapping a cloth that held a nice selection of knives and a saw.

"You don't have to be so goddamn eager!"

Halla smiled for an instant and then handed me a piece of leather.

I had spent most of my power fighting Memweck and healing us afterward. The wise course was to save what remained for any deadly situations. So Halla cut off my leg using plain, uncomplicated steel, severing it above the catastrophic break. I used a tithe of power to stop the bleeding, and Halla bandaged it with yellow silk.

Unhealed, the leg would have poisoned my blood and killed me within a couple of days. I could have used magic to pull out the poison, but it would need to be done every day. My power would be depleted before too long.

I hoped that I would be able to restore that leg sometime. In the past, I had brought severed hands back into existence. But a leg would require far more power than I had now.

Everybody else had been making plans without me. Most of the slaves and children had been stolen from various parts of the northern kingdoms, and many of those parts lay close by. Smif volunteered to see that those people found their way back home. He felt it would begin to make up for the wickedness he had done as Memweck's servant.

Halla would return her nephews to their home in the farthest east. That meant she would cross the Bending Sea with the rest of us before heading east through the Empire.

Memweck had stolen the rest of the children from Bindle, twenty in all. Whistler and Bea would travel south to bring those children home. Pil had decided to escort me back to Bindle too. When I found out about it, I argued and bitched at her—not because it was a bad plan, but because I wanted to act contrary. However, after making two mean comments and throwing a bowl at her, I found I was too tired to sustain a rebellion.

We left the next day. Whistler, who was much recovered, had found a cart and a donkey to pull it. Halla loaded me in, and despite being the conqueror, I departed Memweck's home in as little glory as one could imagine.

The weather had turned to true springtime, and we traveled down the mountain for three bright, cool days. We reached the open land above Caislin, and the new grass had erupted with a legion of red and blue wildflowers. Since we wanted to make a big, big circle around Caislin, Smif left us for the city to begin finding the homes of the slaves and children. Captivity had dazed many of them, so finding their homes would prove a prodigious task.

Two more days of travel brought us to Paikett in the afternoon. The cart had banged and jounced me all the way down, but Pil had developed the knack of binding my arm and shoulder to cushion it against the worst jarring. My leg still pained me, and my missing foot hurt, but I was healing well.

We rode toward the Paikett docks, hoping to find a ship to take us across the sea next week, after the threat of spring storms had passed.

"Watch your ass," Leddie said. "This is a fancy place for an ambush. I ambushed you here, didn't I?"

"Yes," Halla said, sitting tall and squinting toward the harbor. "We killed most of your men."

"But I helped!" Leddie cackled like a crow.

When we were a hundred feet from the dock, a tall man stepped out from behind the warehouse. He wore a shaggy fur coat and a cowl made from what looked like a bear's head, although the fur shone like silver.

Another man, so short as to be almost square, ambled onto the dock from the other direction. His blond hair hung in a long braid. He wore a full, clover-green coat over a yellow shirt, with orange trousers and shiny black shoes.

A third man climbed straight up onto the dock from the harbor side. He was average height with long, loose arms and huge hands. Two vicious scars cut across his face, and he wore scuffed armor made of some oddly pink leather, along with tall, crimson boots. He also wore a feathered hat similar to the one we had found in the crypt.

None of the men smiled, waved, or even moved once they took a stance. All of them carried swords in their hands.

After a silence I found uncomfortable, the short one in the green coat called out in a ringing voice, "Murderer, we are Gondix, Paal, and Zagurith. Memweck was our brother."

THIRTY-SIX

Three gaudy people had blocked our way to the Paikett docks. Still sitting on my butt in the cart, I peeked out between Leddie and the donkey to examine Memweck's brothers.

I considered the possibility that they might all have the same human mother as Memweck and also a human father, or fathers. That would make them regular people, although flamboyant. But that was a foolish hope, and I knew it. These sons of Lutigan had been sired on human mothers, likely different mothers, since Lutigan was known to be as randy as a dozen sailors. That made them demigods like Memweck. They were probably some of Lutigan's personal shield men. If they wanted to hurt me, my best move was not to squirm and moan while they did it to avoid upsetting them.

The short one said, "Make yourself ready to die, for we are the hands of divine vengeance."

I called out from the cart, "Divine vengeance has three hands, eh? That must be convenient. Human vengeance only has two hands, and there's never any place to hold a beer."

The short one paused. "Are you being sarcastic?" He turned to the one in pink armor. "Is he being sarcastic?"

The one in pink grinned for a second. "Yes, he's being sarcastic. He's probably voiding his bowels in terror, but he's not timid. He wouldn't be if he killed Memweck."

The one in silver fur shrugged. "Yep."

The short one squared off with us and lifted his bare chin. "When we tear off your arm and make you eat it, you will not concern yourself with counting hands, will you?"

I yelled, "Just hold on a second! Before you start tearing, let me get a better look at you. Halla, help me down from here."

Halla lifted me out of the cart, and I hopped one-legged toward the demigods using a heavy stick for balance. I employed those seconds to make plans. By the time I stopped sixty feet from them, my best plan so far was keeping my eyes closed when they killed me so I wouldn't see how horrible my death was.

"So, let me consider this," I said, looking from one to the other. I nodded at the short one. "You're Gondix. You over there, in the manly pink armor, are Zagurith. And you, with fur the color of a queen's chamber pot, are Paal. Am I right?"

The one in silver fur nodded. "Mm-hmm."

Gondix stepped forward and thrust his sword toward me. "How did you know that?"

"Well, I am a sorcerer." I scratched my beard in a scholarly way with my good hand while trying not to drop my stick or fall over. "I knew how to kill Memweck. Knowing your names isn't much of a feat."

Gondix and Zagurith glanced at each other, and then Zagurith smirked at me. "Is that a challenge? I hear your balls clanking, but I see only one arm and one leg."

I smirked back. "I had only this arm and this leg when I destroyed your brother. I sent him wherever wiseass demigods go when they die."

Their eyes got big, but none of them snarled, or glared, or cursed me for murdering their brother.

I leaned forward as well as I was able. "Be frank with me. You never really liked the vainglorious shithead, did you?"

They all glanced away in different directions, which answered my question. Then Paal straightened his furry shoulders. "Doesn't matter. He's family."

Zagurith said, "Bear in mind that you simply killed him, Murderer. It's not as if you betrayed him."

Paal charged Leddie, the silver fur on his coat bouncing with every step. Leddie held her ground and thrust with Memweck's sword at the last moment. I thought she had impaled the demigod, but somehow, he twisted aside and grabbed her wrist. I heard the bones crack from fifty feet away, and Paal plucked Memweck's sword out of Leddie's hand.

Leddie screamed. "Stop it! I'll annihilate you! I'll pull out your guts, you twisting bastard!" She kept cursing Paal, her voice getting louder and higher.

Gondix laughed. "Traitors are not afforded an easy death. Not until they beg for it."

Zagurith added, "She may not literally beg for death before we kill her. We'll probably weary of her before that."

Paal scribed a big arc in the air using Memweck's sword, and a mountain valley appeared inside the arc as if it were a window. He shoved Leddie hard, and she fell through the hole, still cursing. Paal jumped through after her, and the hole closed behind him.

"That was a tactical error." I spit on the bare ground. "You just reduced the size of your force by one-third. Pil, write that down. That stupid decision should be in the song you make up about their destruction."

Gondix glanced at Zagurith. "Is he being sarcastic?"

Zagurith squinted at me with one eye. "I'm not sure."

"Well, let's just kill everybody and go home."

I lifted myself out of my body and called for Harik. After two seconds of paralyzing nausea, every one of my senses fell away, except for sound.

I heard Halla speaking. "Yes, I am ready."

The rich, motherly voice of Sakaj, Goddess of the Unknowable, answered. "Finally, dear. I'm so impressed that you waited this long. You're such a good girl."

"I agreed to trade," Halla said. "I did not agree to listen to your mockery of love, oh vile and ass-ripping goddess."

I imagined drawing my blade, and the Gods' Realm appeared. I jerked and turned my face to the ground, squeezing my eyes shut against the painful light. The sunlight there was normally comforting, even sweet, but when I forced myself to squint around this time, the daylight and harsh reflections hurt my eyes.

I stood on the usual expanse of dirt with Halla to my left, stiff and awkward. Sakaj stood on the lowest level of the marble gazebo, flipping back her black hair as she silently laughed at Halla. She wore a pale gown that glittered and refracted in the sunlight, and she was so perfect that I almost couldn't breathe because I desired her so much. I jerked my eyes away from her to Harik, who was leaning back on a bench near her with his legs crossed at the ankles.

"You!" Harik pointed at me. "You be quiet!"

"Who must be quiet?" Halla said, turning her head from side to side.

Sakaj glared at her brother. "Did you have to let her hear you?" she whispered. "Sloppy. You're sloppy."

Harik hunched but didn't answer her. Instead, he shook his finger at me like he was my mother. "Nobody must be quiet! Continue with your trade."

Sakaj said, "Pay no attention, dear. Harik has lost his mind again. Soon he will swallow his tongue and engage in intimacies with a tree. Now, darling, I offer you two squares in exchange for these memories."

"That is a wonderful joke, Sakaj. I am sure all my friends will laugh when I tell them," Halla said. "I want an open-ended debt. I know you gave one to Desh. I mean, to the Nub."

For a moment, nobody spoke. An open-ended debt created an obligation but didn't reveal how large it was. My deal with Harik was open-ended. I had to perform a certain number of killings for him, but only he knew what that number was.

I tried to imagine my friend, the sorcerer Desh, receiving power every month—or maybe every week or day—without having to trade for it. The enormity of it stunned me. I shouted, "She gave Desh an open-ended debt?"

"Bib?" Halla turned her head.

"Murderer!" Harik bellowed, coming to his feet.

"Harik!" Sakaj growled, grabbing the arm of his robe and shaking it.

"Wait! Just wait!" I waved one arm. "The gods are taking on open-ended debts? Halla, what are you offering? What the hell is going on? Harik, are you taking on open-ended debts too?"

"No one is doing that!" Harik glanced sideways at Sakaj. "Almost no one."

Halla jumped in. "So, I would like one, Sakaj. I want three squares every day until the debt is fulfilled."

Sakaj snorted, an odd sound to come out of such a staggeringly lovely creature. "No. I will grant you three squares once and one time only in exchange for all your memories of him."

"Him? Who?" I said.

"You, frumpy little boy," Sakaj chuckled. "Her memories of you."

I opened my mouth, but it just hung there.

Sakaj went on: "She has refused to let me have them for years now. It's been so precious. She says it's the last thing of value she can give up. If only she knew how untrue that is!"

Halla said, "Two squares every day, and I will not tell anyone how sentimental and weak you sound."

In the distance, somebody shouted, "Krak damn me! Thrash it all!"

Sakaj, Harik, and I turned to look.

The voice came closer. "Pound it in the ass with a spiked club! Never a convenient time! I should crush her skull with two fingers!" It sounded like Lutigan. The voice seemed nearer now but was suddenly muffled. "Stay there! This will just take a minute! No, I said by Harik's flat, dripping maw that I'll return in a damned minute!"

Lutigan trotted into the gazebo with a red shirt over his head, struggling to pull it on, although his head was pushed against a sleeve hole. "Damn it! Damn and red-hot damnation! Oh, there it is." The God of War shrugged into his shirt and plopped down on a bench.

Pil materialized to my right.

Lutigan growled, "Now, what do you want?"

"Mighty Lutigan, I've come here to trade, and I know what I want, but would you please see your way to making the first offer? For the sake of form?"

Lutigan held up a hand to Harik and Sakaj. They sat back and watched him, laughing silently. Lutigan said, "Certainly not. I won't make you an offer, you little snip! Knife, tell me what you want and what you'll give. Be fast about it too—I'm otherwise engaged."

Pil stared down for a moment. "I want you to send your sons away and let us live. In exchange . . . I am ready to belong to you. Your Magnificence."

I called out, "Pil, please wait!"

"Bib?"

"I am here too," Halla said.

Pil turned her head until she was staring directly away from me. "Is anybody else here? Is there a practical limit to how many sorcerers can be here at the same time? Really, what's the largest number of sorcerers you've ever been here with at once?"

Lutigan roared, "I did not come here to listen to this shit!"

Sakaj started giggling, and Harik joined in.

"Everybody, wait!" I bellowed. The volume of my voice hurt my head.

The gods all leaned forward and examined me. After a moment, Harik raised an eyebrow at Lutigan.

I pushed on. "Since I killed Memweck, I claim the right to clean up this unholy mess. That way, Pil doesn't have to enslave herself under duress, and Halla can keep her memories of me. Except for that time I dropped her sword overboard, she can forget about that."

"Do not try to be humorous, Murderer," Harik said. "You are a twitch away from losing your existence."

"I'm not as afraid of losing things as I used to be. Besides, do you want me to cry about it when I can laugh?" I turned to Lutigan. "I want to pursue Pil's line of bargaining, Mighty Lutigan. Send away your sons and let us live. Also, heal me of Memweck's wounds. And relieve me of your command to make the Knife offer herself to you."

"What?" Pil squeaked in the least sorcerer-like way possible.

I pushed on. "Oh, and I want ten squares to go along with that."

"Hah!" Lutigan made a rude gesture at me. "Would you also like me to give you my privates so you can use them to have carnal relations with some diseased harlot? Memweck must have stabbed you in the brain."

Sakaj smirked. "Maybe getting stabbed in the brain runs in the family."

Lutigan didn't comment on that. Instead, he turned to Harik and raised his eyebrows.

Harik shrugged and whispered, "Go ahead. If you destroy the Murderer, you shall owe me his worth."

"You shall owe me his worth . . ." Lutigan mimicked his brother in a whisper. "You're such a floppy feather."

Sakaj flicked two fingers. Halla and Pil disappeared.

Lutigan stood and regarded me. That unnerved me more than if he had bellowed. At last, he sighed with a smile. "Murderer, you iota of filth, the Knife sounds ready to join me of her own choice, so I will relieve you of that. You'd probably just screw it up. I might send my sons away and provide you a square. Maybe, if you debase yourself and promise to do something incomprehensibly dangerous in the next week. Something that will almost certainly lead to your death. And you get no healing. But everything depends on what you offer me."

"There must be something specific you want." I made myself smile back at him instead of calling him a cross-eyed, wart-tongued, bony crocodile incapable of mastering basic clothing.

Lutigan looked over his shoulder. "There are much more interesting things to do than this. You have five seconds to make an offer."

The obvious slammed me. "I'll start a war!"

"Weak." Lutigan curled his lip but sat back down. "And certainly not worth ten squares."

"A big war! At least a thousand fighters on each side." I was not much more than babbling, trusting to long experience and luck. Mostly luck.

"Ten thousand on each side."

"Fifteen-hundred?" I nodded, trying to look cooperative.

Lutigan gazed at the ceiling of the gazebo. "Hmm. Five thousand, or I'll kill the Knife. Two daughters have already died on you, and she'll make it three. I might even kill all the children traveling with you and let you live with the guilt for a while before I annihilate you."

I lowered my voice and put as much gravity into it as I could. "I don't have any children, Lutigan. You can threaten Pil if you want. To me, it's the same as threatening anybody else. The same with those kids. Two thousand on a side, your sons let everybody live, and I want ten squares."

"If everybody lives, then you'll get one square and like it. Two thousand warriors in each force—fine. But once you start this war, you will fight in the front line of every battle. In the middle. Right in the front, fifty feet ahead of the rest of the army. By Krak's back teeth, that way somebody will kill you! Or maybe the Murderer is too clever to get killed that way? Do you think so? Eh? Do we have a deal?"

I pointed my sword at Lutigan. "No, I want more than one square."

I wanted more power for excellent reasons, or they seemed excellent to me. I wanted to restore my leg. I feared we'd have a nasty reunion with bitter, angry water spirits when we recrossed the sea. But mainly, whenever I escaped a truly awful situation, Harik ignored me for weeks or even months. I didn't want to be caught short while Harik disregarded me.

Lutigan shrugged. "Two squares."

Harik stood. "Murderer, I will offer you three squares for all your memories of the Tooth. She is gone for once and all. Ease your grief."

"My grief and I get along fine," I said. "No deal."

Harik tapped his fingers against his leg. "Then since you intend to start a war, you shall bring the war to a king you consider a friend. Engage the King of Glass in this war."

The king in question was a young man I had come to know well when I saved him from an extremely comfortable imprisonment. I could start the war and then help him win, probably, if he never knew what I had done. "I want five squares from you."

"No, three," Harik said.

I walked toward the gazebo. "Four squares and heal my wounds from Memweck."

"I can offer four squares if you ensure that your friend loses the war."

Sighing, I leaned on my sword. "Forget I said anything about four squares."

Harik chuckled. "I can't forget it now. You said it. Deal with the consequences. To receive four squares, you must bring war to your friend and lose the war. I will not heal your—"

Before Harik had finished, Sakaj said, "I feel I should join this fun. Murderer, I will heal your wounds if you ask me for knowledge. You must accept this bit of knowledge gratefully, even graciously."

"Hell no!" Whatever Sakaj decided to tell me would be something I wished I didn't know. It was the most dangerous kind of bargain a sorcerer could make. Despite my intentions, I glanced at Sakaj's face. It was like being hit with a hundred-pound sack of weakness and lust. I almost staggered over to kiss her foot. I hauled my gaze to Lutigan, who was as ugly as a bunion.

"Murderer, you sweet boy," Sakaj crooned, as tender as the most loving mother in existence. "You dear, lovely creature. Think of the obligations you've already assumed. How can you do battle in your war if you possess just one leg and one arm? You'll be beheaded in the first minute. Or you will default on your deal with Lutigan instead. I can't imagine how he'll punish you for that, but I doubt even Harik could protect you."

Sakaj stood and crossed the gazebo with a gait that was part slink, part saunter, and part promise of ecstasy. She lay one hand on Harik's shoulder, and he shrugged her off.

The hell of it was that she was right. Unless I was healed, I'd never survive my other deals. "Mighty Harik or equally Mighty Lutigan, would you extend your offer to include healing?"

Harik shook his head. Lutigan grinned and made a filthy gesture.

"Sakaj, will you provide six squares in addition to healing me?" I asked.

"I'll offer four squares. Which brings you to the ten that you wanted. Isn't that accommodating of me?"

I ran through the deals once in my mind. I didn't dare run through them twice. "I agree to all three bargains."

The gods started laughing. Lutigan slapped Harik on the back.

"Done!" Sakaj was smiling as she yelled it. I could only tell because of the sound, since I was still staring away from her toward Lutigan.

If I could have blotted them all from existence, I would have. Without thinking much about it, I said, "Hey, how much are these ten squares costing you boys and girls?"

"What are you babbling about, rodent? I mean, Murderer?" Lutigan said, still chuckling.

I lay my sword across my shoulders. "I've been led to understand that gods don't just produce power like it was a fruity belch. You've got to pay something. Or gather it maybe."

Sakaj eased herself down on the bench. Lutigan's mouth opened as he squinted at me. Then he stared at Harik, who was examining the ceiling of the gazebo.

"You misunderstand," Sakaj said in a much less motherly tone. "Your limited faculties cannot encompass the subtle mysteries of the cosmos. So, shut up about it. Here is your knowledge, Murderer. Your greatest friend caused your most enduring suffering."

"What? That makes no sense. It's hardly even good grammar." I shook my head.

Sakaj went on: "The Freak, your greatest friend, is responsible for your open-ended debt with Harik. Without her doing, you would not be bound to murder people for him."

"Bullshit! How do you think this supposedly happened?"

"Oh, I know it happened," Harik said. "As for how, ask the Freak."

I felt like I'd been dropped into the ocean and was swimming for the surface. "You mean she knows?" I shouted. "It wasn't some incidental bargain that she never even knew about?"

"She knows." Sakaj giggled. "Goodbye."

I was catapulted back into my body, where I collapsed and skidded across the dirt, my stick flying off someplace behind me. When I sat up, I felt something wet on my neck. Blood was running from a gash on my chin.

Zagurith guffawed. "Is that an assault? Are we supposed to laugh ourselves to death now?"

A big hole in the air whisked open, showing the mountain valley inside. Paal poked his head out and said, "Hey."

"You wait there!" Gondix pointed at me. "Don't even get up."

Gondix and Zagurith strode over to the hole, and the brothers conferred. Demigod conferences seemed to involve a lot of gesturing, angry whispers, and Paal slapping Gondix on the face. Gondix lowered his eyebrows and pointed at me. Then all three of them leaped through the hole, which disappeared a moment later.

Relieved babbling and a fair bit of crying broke out behind me. I felt like babbling and crying a little myself. I wiggled my bound shoulder and worked it around, and it caused me no pain. I felt the power that the gods had promised me, and I scanned the area for a private place to restore my leg. It would be a lengthy, arduous endeavor.

Before I could struggle up to stand on one leg, Halla lifted me and set me upright. She whispered, "Thank you. Without you, I do not know who I would be."

I wanted to stab her first, then break her neck, and then interrogate her about how she had ruined my life. I wasn't in shape to do any of those things, though. Rather than let on that I knew about her betrayal, I said, "Whoever you'd be, I know you'd annoy the hell out of me."

She smiled, grabbed me, and kissed the top of my head.

THIRTY-SEVEN

I had never restored anything bigger than a hand and a forearm. Bringing back my leg taxed me more than I would have expected, but Pil sat with me through the entire five-hour ordeal.

Halla would have been much more helpful to me than Pil. Her experience was greater by far, but I couldn't bring myself to trust her. When I told Halla I wouldn't need her for the effort, she looked surprised and maybe a little hurt. She didn't object, though. She went back to helping Bea, who had proven skilled at organizing both children and adults for the passage south.

After the healing ended, Pil said it was the most rewarding thing she had done the entire trip, since she was there to mock me when I took a step on my new leg and tumbled like a baby bird.

I thought the problem was that I was wearing only one boot. After all, my newly restored leg had arrived barefoot. But when I pulled off my old boot, I still couldn't walk worth a damn. It turned out I had made the new left leg an inch shorter than the right. An hour's work resolved that problem. However, I fell down twice more before I figured out that the knee was half an inch higher than it should have been.

I relaxed enough to let my body decide for itself where all the parts should be. Twenty minutes after that, I eased myself outside and experimented with walking, marching, and skipping. When I sprinted to the dockside and back, I felt fully restored.

Pil handed me my right boot. I glanced around for the other one but then realized it was probably still on my severed leg back in Memweck's guest quarters.

"Bib!"

I turned in time to catch my missing left boot as Pil tossed it to me.

She said, "There's your sticky boot."

My eyebrows raised. "What was that?"

"Sticky boots. They stick to things, so I would call them sticky boots, which I guess whoever created them might have another name for them, but if he wanted to fight over names, he should have shown up."

I stared at the boots, holding one in each hand.

Pil walked over to me. "I thought you knew. You should have suspected. Do you think I'm going to pull that boot off your nasty, bleeding leg if it's just a regular cowhide boot? And then carry the smelly thing over a hundred miles for you? Are you a crafty old sorcerer, or are you not?"

I answered that by furrowing my brow like the worst student in class. "What do you mean by 'sticky'?"

Once I had pulled on the boots, Pil made me try walking up the side of the warehouse. The boots did stick and hold my weight, but when I tried to walk as if I was standing on the ground, I collapsed and fell off.

"You should creep like a lizard," Halla suggested.

I tried, but I couldn't hold on with my hands. I fell off again.

"This is perplexing," I said. "Are you sure they don't give these out at parties to keep the kids busy?"

Halla got on her hands and knees to examine the boots. "You may need a rope. Or something to dig handles in the wall."

"I'll think on the problem." I shrugged. "At least they fit well."

Four ships lay in the harbor, all of them unknown to me. The captains planned to depart in a week when the spring storms would have passed. I engaged two of them to carry the twenty-seven of us across the sea to Dunhold, a far more reputable port than Fat Shallows. However, when I opened my pouch, I found no gold lump. Instead, the pouch contained a large hole in the bottom that the gold had worn through. The gold might have escaped any place between Paikett and Memweck's domain.

I have never had much yearning for wealth, so I didn't feel sad to lose the gold. The loss presented a challenge, though, since we couldn't pay for passage south. I turned to Whistler, who wasn't as rich as he believed, but who possessed infinitely more money than me now.

Whistler scratched his eyelid for a couple of seconds. "Well, I had plans. But plans don't mean much when you're stranded in the goddamn northern kingdoms. I beg pardon." He shrugged out of his pack and pulled from it one of the golden plates from the crypt.

"Grave robber, eh?" I said.

Whistler grinned and handed me the plate. "Belongs to the dead ancestors, my ass."

We took rooms at the landside inn, and with twenty-two children, we filled up the place. Whistler helped Bea care for the children. He cursed about it and taught the kids a lot of new words, but Bea showed no doubt that it was Whistler's job to help her.

I tried to avoid Halla without appearing to avoid her. She spent some time attending to her nephews at first, but by the second day, she lost interest. After that, she only spoke to them when they crossed her path.

Bea hinted to Pil that extra help would be useful. She may have thought Pil would be inclined to care for children since she was a woman. Pil told her flat-out to go away and wipe noses. Bea was a stern woman and pressed the point. Pil smiled and said that as a sorcerer, she could kill Bea for her arrogance, and nobody would speak a harsh word about it.

Bea let Pil alone and didn't walk close to any of us sorcerers for the rest of the evening. I sat and talked with Pil for a while, and she showed no sign of an unexpected, sudden ferocity. She seemed the same as always—smart, friendly, brisk, and sometimes introspective. Of course, she had developed an ocean of confidence over the past weeks.

The next morning, Bea came to me as I stood outside the inn enjoying the morning breeze. The days were getting warmer in a hurry.

I smiled at her. "Hell no! You and Whistler can wipe those children's asses yourselves."

Bea gave me a lopsided smile in return. "I should have thanked you days ago for saving everybody, especially since you lost your leg, but I just didn't know what to say."

"That was perfect. I heard thanks in there someplace, so that's good enough."

"But it's wrong that I didn't thank you." She shook her head.

"I didn't do it for thanks."

"You did it for duty?" She glared at me and then looked down. "You were sort of responsible for all this."

"Nope, not for duty, either." I took a step toward the tavern to buy a drink before I remembered I didn't drink anymore, which was fine since I was broke.

"Why did you do it then?"

"I have no idea in the world." I shrugged. "I just did it."

"Maybe you wanted to get killed," Bea said, still staring at the ground.

"I doubt that! Why would you say something like that?"

Bea glared at me again. "If I murdered my baby, I'd want someone to kill me."

The idea hit hard, but not as hard as I expected. "You might have a thought there, Bea, but I won't say it's true."

Bea turned and walked off without saying anything more. I didn't point out that she still hadn't thanked me.

Six days later, we set sail. Bea took eleven children in one ship, and Whistler took eleven in the other. I sailed with Bea, who seemed more comfortable not sharing a sixty-foot living space with Pil.

Halla sailed on my ship too, and I felt damn well torn about it. On one hand, I just wanted her to keep some distance from me. If she had stayed in the northern kingdoms, that would have been a good distance. On the other hand, I thought I might surprise her sometime, bind her tight, and interrogate her.

I kept a nervous watch for the water-woses during the three-day passage, but they never appeared. Halla and I chatted for most of the first day, and on the second day, we argued about every meaningless thing we could think of.

Most of the time, I ignored Halla or turned away when she tried to speak to me. Midafternoon on the second day, after her seasickness had passed, she trapped me in the bow. "Damn it to Krak and his iron dog!" she said. "What is wrong with you?"

I shrugged.

"No! You will not shrug and walk away this time. If you do not talk, I will cut off your leg again."

I couldn't help smiling for an instant, but then I said, "Give me all your weapons. Come on, give them."

With a wrinkled forehead, Halla passed me her spear along with five knives she carried in concealed spots. "This is strange. Do you want my boots now?"

I pulled my dagger and held it at my side. Halla raised an eyebrow. I said, "Sakaj told me you were responsible for my open-ended debt with Harik. Is that true?"

Halla let out a breath fast and leaned back against the inside of the hull. "Yes." Her face was blank as she glanced at the dagger in my hand.

"Why did you do such a goddamn stupid thing?"

She swallowed. "I . . ."

"Are you going to make me ask a separate question for every single word you say?" I kept my voice low, but Bea was staring at us from the waist of the ship.

"No, I will tell you. I did not mean for it to happen."

I stepped in so I was looking at her face from a foot away. "That doesn't make a hell of a lot of difference, does it, sorcerer?"

Halla shook her head. "I needed power to—"

"I don't care why you needed it! Keep going!"

"Sakaj offered it if I agreed that Lin would be hard of hearing for a week."

I backed up and almost dropped the dagger. "You bargained for my wife to go deaf?"

"Not deaf! But she would not hear well for a week." Halla's eyes were wide, as if she hoped that would help me see better. "I thought it would aggravate you when she kept asking you to repeat yourself. That's what I thought the gods wanted."

I tried to work up some more rage but couldn't. Deals like that weren't common, but they happened. "I don't see what . . . hell, keep going."

Halla looked down and then at my face. She licked her lips and looked past the gunwale at the low clouds and gray swells. "Lin did not hear Bett leave the house. She would have heard. But she did not."

I blinked a few times, because it didn't make sense at first. Then it did. Lin didn't stop our daughter from leaving that night to go play by the river. Wild dogs mauled her nearly to death. Harik traded me the power to save her, and I agreed to kill people for him until he said I could stop.

Halla shook her head again. "It is not what I wanted. I did not imagine it would happen."

I examined Halla's face. It could have happened to any sorcerer. It could have happened to me. It wasn't her fault.

I thrust my dagger forward with all my strength. I buried the blade four inches deep in the wooden hull next to Halla's ribs. "If you're smart, which I doubt, you'll stay the hell away from me. I don't care if you have yourself towed on a rope to do it." I left my dagger in the hull and stomped aft. I must have put on a mean face, because nobody dared talk to me.

Later in the afternoon, I saw Halla sitting on the deck in the bow with Bea kneeling beside her. Bea was arranging and rearranging her arms around Halla and patting her hand, but Halla sat so stiff that it must have been like trying to comfort an old tree trunk.

When we docked in Dunhold, Halla bought horses, gathered

her nephews, and waved to me. "Buy a belt buckle. I do not want you to die."

I ground my teeth and kicked the dirt for a few seconds. Then I called out, "Don't monopolize the conversation with those boys. I know you can talk about any subject forever."

They rode east and were out of sight in a minute.

Whistler purchased us horses as well as four wagons and mules to pull them. He argued hard and loud that we should buy just two wagons, since ten children could fit well, if cozy, in each. Bea shouted and berated him until at last he gave in. He cursed the unnecessary expense the rest of the day and part of the next.

We made poor time pulling four wagons, but we had no urgent tasks. Seven days of travel were sunny and pleasant, much cooler than the northern kingdoms. Then three days of heavy rain and violent storms brought us to the Eastern Crossroads, where the fair had been held. Pil had named that event the Slaughter of the Breakfast Animals. Whistler found that amusing enough to regain most of his good humor.

The crossroads was peppered with white stone mounds about two feet high. I assumed that each stood where a family had found a dead relation after that murderous festival day.

I pointed to a mound and said to Pil, "The crossroads seems a poor place to stack rocks, even memorial rocks."

She smiled at me. "People could stack the rocks someplace else, I guess, but these places are where the people died. They didn't die over there in the grass, or beside their front door."

"Still, the rocks will all be scattered before long."

"Bib!" She ginned at me as if she were telling her younger brother a secret. "It doesn't matter whether one is there for a minute or forever."

The weather had turned fair again on the day we reached Bindle. Word spread fast, and families snatched up their missing children within thirty minutes. Citizens crowded us, smiling, shouting thanks, and pushing drinks into our hands. I decided not to insult them by refusing their drinks.

The accolades that people heaped upon me were just a piddly

nod compared to the adulation Bea received. She explained everybody's role in the rescue. She described it all several times with listeners exclaiming at all the exciting parts. No matter what she said, she was their hero. When the celebration moved to the town square, a carpenter knocked together a dais for her, and she told the story twice more, holding Tobi in her arms. She soon pulled Whistler up to stand beside her, and a few merrymakers called out suggestions that had them both blushing.

Pil and I had found a quiet corner of the town square and were leaning against the whitewashed wall of the bakery when Paul walked past. He stopped and stared back at me. "Bib, it's proper that you made things right by bringing these children back. That's good." He looked thoughtful. "Of course, you wouldn't have had to rescue anybody if you hadn't made such a turd pie out of everything. You sure wouldn't." He gazed around and then walked off into the crowd.

"Time to leave," I said.

"Why?"

I walked around the bakery and down the street toward the stable, with Pil following. "If we don't leave now, we'll have to kill a dozen of these people to get away."

"But they're happy." She ran to catch up and walk beside me. "They thanked us. They're giving us drinks! They're grateful."

I laughed hard. "Pil, they're never grateful. At least not for long. If you want gratitude, become a blacksmith. Everybody appreciates a good horseshoe."

We walked along in silence for a minute. "Where are we going?" she asked.

"To the stables." I waved my hand. "You can go wherever you want from there."

"Can I go with you?"

I laughed again. "Think twice about it. I'm off to start a war and break my friend's heart."

CONTINUE BIB'S ADVENTURES IN THE NEXT BOOK:

DEATH'S COLLECTOR: VOID-WALKER

It's just a little bit of treason.

The petty, vicious gods demand that Bib the sorcerer lure his friend, the young king, into a losing war. Bib thinks he's clever enough to arrange things so that the king is defeated yet keeps his throne - and his head.

But the king won't listen until Bib crushes some traitors for him. Faced with rebellious nobles, mystical killers, and allies he can't control, Bib finds that cleverness needs a sword and some vicious magic to back it up. Because if he fails, the gods have torture, death, and even destruction beyond death waiting for him.

Struggling across a landscape of brutal armies, immortal vengeance, and a highly aggravated ex-lover, Bib does what he does best: mock the pretentious, take no crap, and murder people who almost certainly deserve it.

Purchase at: https://tinyurl.com/billmccurrybooks

ABOUT THE AUTHOR

Bill McCurry blends action, humor, and vivid characters in his dark fantasy novels. They are largely about the ridiculousness of being human, but with swords because swords are cool. Before being published, he wrote three novels that sucked like black holes, and he suggests that anyone who wants to write novels should write and finish some bad novels first. You learn a lot.

Bill was born in Fort Worth, Texas, where the West begins, the stockyards stink, and the old money families run everything. He later moved to Dallas, where Democrats can get elected, Tom Landry is still loved, and the fourth leading cause of death is starvation while sitting on LBJ Freeway.

Although Dallas is a city that smells like credit cards and despair, Bill and his wife still live there with their five cats. He maintains that the maximum number of cats should actually be three, because if you have four, then one of them can always get behind you.

CONNECT WITH THE AUTHOR

Bill-McCurry.com
Facebook.com/Bill.McCurry3
Twitter.com/BillMcCurry
Instagram.com/bfmccurry

Sign Up for Bill's Newsletter!

Keep up to date on new books and on exclusive offers. No spam!

https://bill-mccurry.com/index.php/newslettersignup/

PURCHASE OTHER BOOKS IN THIS SERIES

Book 1 - *Death's Collector*
Book 2 - *Death's Baby Sister*
Book 3 - *Death's Collector: Sorcerers Dark and Light*
Book 4 - *Death's Collector: Void Walker*
Book 5 - *Death's Collector: Sword Hand*

Companion Book - *Wee Piggies of Radiant Might*

Shop at: https://tinyurl.com/billmccurrybooks

LEAVE A REVIEW

Please leave a review on the platform of your choice!

https://linktr.ee/reviewsorcerersdark

Made in the USA
Monee, IL
25 September 2022